The

ENEMIES

of

VERSAILLES

The

ENEMIES

of

VERSAILLES

A NOVEL

SALLY CHRISTIE

ATRIA PAPERBACK

New York   London   Toronto   Sydney   New Delhi

ATRIA PACKBACK

An Imprint of Simon & Schuster, Inc.
1230 Avenue of the Americas
New York, NY 10020

First Atria Paperback edition March 2017

ATRIA PAPERBACK and colophon are trademarks of Simon & Schuster, Inc.

For information about special discounts for bulk purchases, please contact Simon & Schuster Special Sales at 1-866-506-1949 or business@simonandschuster.com.

The Simon & Schuster Speakers Bureau can bring authors to your live event. For more information or to book an event, contact the Simon & Schuster Speakers Bureau at 1-866-248-3049 or visit our website at http://www.simonspeakers.com.

Manufactured in the United States of America

10 9 8 7 6 5 4 3 2 1

Library of Congress Cataloging-in-Publication Data

Names: Christie, Sally, date.
Title: The enemies of Versailles : a novel / Sally Christie.
Description: First Atria Paperback edition. | New York : Atria Paperback, 2017. |
Series: The mistresses of versailles trilogy ; [3].
Identifiers: LCCN 2016032052 (print) | LCCN 2016038629 (ebook) | ISBN 9781501103025 (paperback) | ISBN 9781501103049 (ebook).
Subjects: LCSH: France—History—Louis XV, 1715–1774—Fiction. | France—Kings and rulers—Paramours—Fiction. | France—Court and courtiers—Fiction. | BISAC: FICTION / Historical. | FICTION / Literary. |FICTION / General. | GSAFD: Biographical fiction. | Historical fiction.
Classification: LCC PR9199.4.C4883 E54 2017 (print) | LCC PR9199.4.C4883 (ebook) | DDC 813/.6—dc23.
LC record available at https://lccn.loc.gov/2016032052.

ISBN 978-1-5011-0302-5
ISBN 978-1-5011-0304-9 (ebook)

To Joe, my lion and my rock
RIP

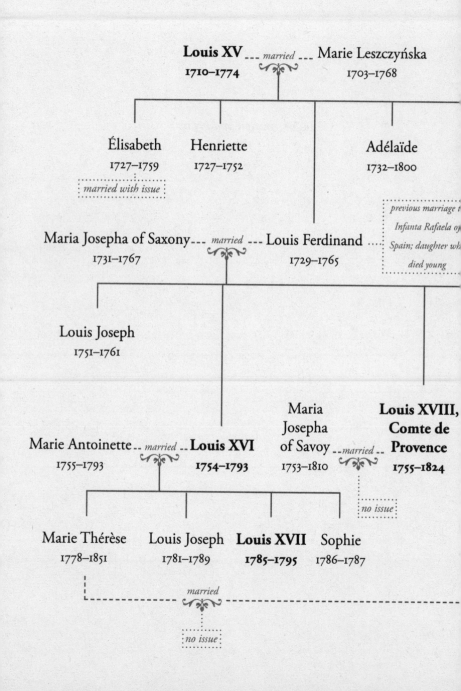

Louis XV --- *married* --- Marie Leszczyńska
1710–1774   1703–1768

Élisabeth   Henriette   Adélaïde
1727–1759   1727–1752   1732–1800

married with issue

Maria Josepha of Saxony --- *married* --- Louis Ferdinand
1731–1767   1729–1765

previous marriage t[...]
Infanta Rafaela o[...]
Spain; daughter wh[...]
died young

Louis Joseph
1751–1761

Marie Antoinette --- *married* --- **Louis XVI**   Maria Josepha of Savoy --- *married* --- **Louis XVIII, Comte de Provence**
1755–1793   **1754–1793**   1753–1810   **1755–1824**

no issue

Marie Thérèse   Louis Joseph   **Louis XVII**   Sophie
1778–1851   1781–1789   **1785–1795**   1786–1787

married

no issue

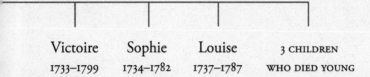

Victoire	Sophie	Louise	3 CHILDREN
1733–1799	1734–1782	1737–1787	WHO DIED YOUNG

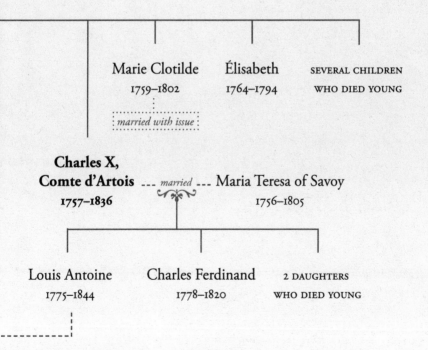

Marie Clotilde	Élisabeth	SEVERAL CHILDREN
1759–1802	1764–1794	WHO DIED YOUNG

married with issue

Charles X,
Comte d'Artois --- *married* --- Maria Teresa of Savoy
1757–1836 1756–1805

Louis Antoine	Charles Ferdinand	2 DAUGHTERS
1775–1844	1778–1820	WHO DIED YOUNG

The
ENEMIES
of
VERSAILLES

Part I

Convergence

1750–1769

Chapter One

In which little Jeanne Bécu is exposed to life

I slip away from the warmth of the kitchen and out into the deserted hall. Behind me, my mother is elbow-deep in a giant bowl of flour and spices, gossiping to a neighbor, while four chickens roast over the fire. Out here, life is colder and grander. I creep up the marble staircase that rises before me like a giant ladder to Heaven, the banister smooth under my hand. I reach the landing and crouch in silence, but I heard Frederica leave earlier. She left behind a trace of her scent when she wafted down the elegant staircase, her special blend of roses and grace.

I creep along the passageway and peek into Frederica's boudoir. If she were here, I might get a kiss and a bonbon, or a slap depending on her mood, but now the room is deserted. I enter and the plush carpet softens my steps. A painting of Monsieur Dumonceaux, who owns the house and Frederica and everything in it, looks down on me. Monsieur Dumonceaux is an old lover of my mother's, and he brought us to Paris and gave us our lodgings. He's not a lover anymore—Frederica is now his lover—but he is always kind to us, and Ma says he is a good man.

His portrait watches over Frederica, but when she has a new guest, she asks the footman to cover it. The rest of her room is cozy and sumptuous: a fire still licking lazily in the hearth; a wardrobe so big I once slept in there, hidden for hours; crimson curtains hanging over the tall, airy windows; a marble table set with a decanter of a wonderful-smelling potion called brandy, which always makes me think of men and candy. I sniff at the little array of perfume bottles on her table then head to my destination: her bed with its layers of green silk sheets and heavy white furs, lace and velvet trimming the pillows. A mattress as soft as a dream welcomes me down in its embrace, so different from my pallet in the kitchen. I burrow under the heavy blankets and nestle in. Ma always says I am lazy, but I'm not lazy, I think as I drift off to sleep, just . . . happy.

"And what have we here?" says Frederica in her bright, charmed voice, the one she uses with Monsieur Dumonceaux and her other gentlemen. Frederica has dark, curling hair, and laughing blue eyes that can turn as cold and hard as gems. The man with her this evening is not Monsieur Dumonceaux but an older gentleman with watery eyes, wearing an orange coat that reminds me of the skin of a cat.

I am sleepy and dreaming under the pile of furs. I smile up at Frederica, then at the man as well; Frederica's moods are always changing, but men are generally pleasant.

"Little scamp," says Frederica fondly, and tousles my hair. "Now go on back to your mother, and tell her that Monsieur de Braque here will want a juicy chicken later."

"Such a charming child!" declares the man, who must be the Monsieur de Braque who wants a juicy chicken. "And what harm would there be, were she to stay?" he asks, raising his brows at Frederica, as though making a joke, though I know he isn't.

"Oh, quiet, Jérôme," says Frederica, laughing and picking me up roughly. I avert my eyes from the man's gaze and struggle to pull down my dress that is now tangled around my waist. "She's only a child."

"Ten?" asks the man eagerly. "How lovely she is!"

Seven, I want to protest, but I don't say anything, for suddenly I want to get out of the room and away from the man's watered green eyes. The color of scum on a pond, I think with a shudder, and squirm against Frederica to let me down. I hear the soft tinkle of her laughter, raindrops on smooth glass, and she pushes me out. "Get back to the kitchens," she hisses before closing the door. "Now, la, monsieur, to be so interrupted . . ." I hear her say as she turns back to her evening entertainment.

I lean against the door but the thick oak muffles the scene behind. I imagine what they will be doing, dogs rutting in the street that stay together, joined and panting, even after slops are thrown on them.

Joined and panting, I think, traipsing languidly down the corridor now that Frederica is safe with her guest. I stand at the top of the staircase and imagine, for one moment, that the house is mine, and that Frederica is my mother and instead of sleeping in the kitchen that reeks of raw chicken and mold, I have a room next to Frederica's, and my own bed is as soft and glorious as hers.

A few days later, another push, but this time out onto the streets. We hear Frederica shouting at Dumonceaux that I am a little tramp, tempting her clients, and claiming she has no more use for us. Ma loses her position as cook and now we have to leave the comfortable house and all her clients in the neighborhood who buy her chickens.

"Snozzle-faced bitch," complains my mother. We gather our belongings off the street and prepare for the long walk to my stepfather's house. My feet are bare, though it is cold out; I can't ruin my only pair of shoes in this mud.

"What sort of a woman is threatened by a seven-year-old *child*?" Ma continues, spitting and glaring up at the impassive windows of the little house.

A porter from next door watches us without curiosity. "An angel in the making," he says, gesturing to me. "She'll be trouble all her life."

"Come on, dears, let's get going." Ma's lover, the monk Guimard, stands beside us in our distress. He leans over and hoists a sheet filled with heavy iron pots, my mother's treasure and trade. "I never liked her, but at least Dumonceaux still does right by us."

"But how does he do right by us if we cannot live in his house anymore?" I ask, but no one answers. I am dragging a basket filled with our clothes, vainly trying to avoid puddles and the deep mud as we start our journey. It will take us two hours at least to cross the city and already the October night is cold and the streets grim.

"Well, aren't we a raggedy bunch!" says the monk Guimard in his jolly way, always ready with a kind word or funny story. I wish he were my father, but whenever I say that my mother tells me to be quiet, or he will be arrested for indecency. "Joseph and Mary without an inn," he continues, "and with a little babe in arms. That's you, Jeanne. But time will be our friend; chickens are always in demand and your skills are beyond compare," he adds kindly to my mother, wobbling slightly under his burden as he steps over a dead dog.

"Rançon will take us in," says Ma, carrying her enormous copper kettle and a heavy gridiron, referring to her husband and the man she says I must call father. "And at least we don't have to worry about Jeanne."

"Why don't you have to worry about me?" I ask, jumping quickly out of the way as a magnificent six-horsed carriage roars by.

"Monsieur Dumonceaux has agreed to take on your education," my mother says.

I stop. "What do you mean, Ma?" I ask, thinking, I don't know why, of the man's green watery eyes and the hungry way they devoured me.

"He has agreed to send you to a convent, where you'll be educated and even learn your letters. Imagine that!"

"A convent! Oh no!" I cry, thinking of the convent on the corner of our street and the grim black-clad nuns that circle in the courtyard. Nothing goes in or out: What do they even eat?

"Ah, now don't cry," says the monk Guimard kindly. "Nuns can be dear ladies, I remember one particularly fine young novice when I was young—"

"Shhh," hisses Ma. "You talk too much. It'll be the Bastille for you, one of these days. Careful—I know that pig—took a chunk of Madame Fargé's ankle last week." She pulls me away from a snortling boar that has started following us.

I trundle on, crying now, because I don't want to disappear into a convent and leave Ma and the monk Guimard. And I may never see Frederica's room again, never burrow in her soft sheets, never be treated to butter bonbons and little drops of her scent. My fate has been decided, I think, sobbing openly now as we walk wearily through the dark streets. I am to go to a convent, and I'm quite sure they won't have any satin sheets for me there.

Chapter Two

In which Madame Adélaïde contemplates
sisters and all things sororal

"Do tell us about the convent, dears," says Henriette, smiling kindly at my two youngest sisters.

Sophie and Louise are seated opposite us on the sofa, looking like two frightened rose-clad hares. Well, Sophie at least; Louise appears quite calm. They returned last week from the convent at Fontrevraud, where they were sent for their education twelve years ago. I too had been destined to go with them, but with my wiles and charm managed to escape that fate.

I incline my head, to show that they may answer, then sit up straighter, hopeful that Victoire, slouching beside me, will copy my example. Victoire returned a year ago, ahead of her two younger sisters, but she has been woefully slow in learning the way of our manners here at Versailles. She still eats with her mouth open and last week even addressed one of her ladies as Madame Comtesse, not Madame *la* Comtesse!

To be a daughter of France is an enormous burden; a sacrifice of the self on the altar of obligation and duty. Our conduct—and here I talk of my sisters, as well as, of course, my brother the dauphin, and Josepha, his wife—must be exemplary; no stain must touch us, of either the amoral, indulgent sort, or of the more practical kind, like ink.

In all we do, we must strive to be better than others, for indeed, we *are* better than others. But Victoire ignores my rigid spine and just takes another cream pastry from the plate and slouches back happily.

"Eleven years away." Henriette sighs. "And now the six of us, here together. How wonderful!" My elder sister looks around in contentment, her eyes resting on each of us in turn. In addition to my three younger sisters, our eldest sister Élisabeth, known as Madame Infanta and Henriette's twin, is also with us. Little Félicité—my only memory is of a pink-faced baby who cried too much—remains behind in the graveyard at Fontrevraud.

"Well? What did you learn?" asks Élisabeth lazily. Élisabeth is very plump and has tiny black eyes, similar to the Malaga raisins she constantly eats.

Sophie blushes. I can't imagine what there is to blush about at a convent, but her timidity pleases me. Victoire has already proved herself agreeably tractable, though a little scattered.

"Oh, we won't bore you, sisters," says Louise, speaking out of turn—Sophie is the elder and should have answered the question. "I'm sure Victoire has already tired you quite silly with her tales. There just isn't much to tell, really."

Victoire startles then nods, her mouth full of cream pastry.

"Nonsense," says Henriette softly. "You must tell us about the nuns and—"

"Well, Victoire did tell us quite a bit," I cut in, deciding that Louise has talked quite enough. "And I can't imagine it much changed. A convent is the very definition of timelessness."

"Rather like Versailles," says Élisabeth, raising an eyebrow at me. She returned last year from Spain, where she was sent eleven years ago to marry a Spanish prince. Now she is en route to her husband's new kingdom of Parma, bringing her high-and-mighty manners with her, and never failing to remind us how little we have changed, and how infantile she considers us.

Though we welcomed her back with duty and love in our hearts, in truth she irks me. She feels superior simply because she has been to Spain and married. *Knows the pleasures of the marriage bed*, as she likes to point out, an expression that has already caused Victoire much mortification. I shudder that Sophie's and Louise's purity may also be compromised by her crass words.

No matter; Élisabeth is set to leave next month. November 18.

"Yes, Versailles is rather constant," says Victoire happily, wiping her mouth with the back of her sleeve. Heavens! I fear I shall choke on my (small and modestly sized) bite of the pastry. "Always the same routines and such. But I like it here, and I am sure you will too."

"Did you at least learn to ride?" asks Élisabeth, before I can. Just because she is married to a Spaniard, she believes she has the monopoly on inquisitions, I think sourly. Élisabeth has very bad skin—the Spaniards are notorious for their filth—and wears her hair in a curiously oiled style.

"Yes, we did," answers Louise. "Though Sophie doesn't like horses—she's rather scared of them."

Sophie blushes again.

"Oh, so am I!" exclaims Victoire. Victoire has a rather unusual dislike of all animals, except for cooked ones.

"Victoire could barely ride at all when she came back last year, but now with enough practice she is passable," I concede. In truth, her failing was our pleasure: under the pretext of lessons, all summer we rode out with Papa, and those mornings were truly the happiest of times. I smile at my thought: if Sophie and Louise are similarly lacking, perhaps we might continue the tradition next spring.

"Well, I'm sure Sophie will learn soon enough," adds Henriette, smiling at all of us. Henriette is very soft and kind—a little too kind, I believe.

A commotion outside—the Duchesse de Beauvilliers, our *dame d'honneur*, enters and alerts us that the king is back early from the hunt and is coming here for his *débottée*, the ceremony to take off his boots. Here! To Élisabeth's apartments! And heavens—an hour before we expected him!

Versailles is certainly *not* unchanging!

"Oh my, and we haven't even finished our pastries!" cries Victoire in distress.

"How lovely to see Papa, and we only saw him yesterday!" says

Henriette happily, as she says every day. "He does like to see us all together—six sisters."

"Sisters," whispers Sophie, grinning like the simpleton I am beginning to suspect she is.

"And coming to see us before going up to see the fish woman!" I announce, referring to my father's detested mistress, the Marquise de Pompadour. An excellent sign. "But straighten your sleeves!" I snap at Victoire, who always manages to look perfectly untidy. Has Beauvilliers told the women to bring the refreshments in early? And the lights—are they sufficient? The late-afternoon sun is still strong enough, though perhaps more candles—

"Indeed the king is coming," says Louise, looking around as though in amusement. I resolve to talk to her about her tone of voice—she sounds almost *sarcastic*, though I am sure that is not her intent. A little lecture will no doubt have a reforming effect.

"Get my daughter!" hisses Élisabeth to Beauvilliers, "and quickly." Little Isabelle, Élisabeth's child and our only niece—though married for four years, our sister-in-law the dauphine has only managed two stillborn sons—is Papa's only grandchild. Élisabeth seeks to endear the child to the king, but as Papa can't abide dribbles or snivels, thus far she has not been very successful.

The doors fly open and my father enters, bringing with him his attendants and the men in their blue hunting garb with high yellow boots, now stained with mud and blood. Their dogs scamper in eagerly, tumbling over themselves and barking away. Of course, if one wishes to see Papa, one must endure the presence of men, but their masculine energy positively smothers Élisabeth's delicate salon.

Papa settles into an armchair and a valet removes his hat and wig while another attendant tousles a cloth through his sweat-streaked hair. He looks so handsome, flushed and hearty from his afternoon in the forests. He is almost forty and in the prime of his life: a more resplendent man France, or the world, has never known. My heart swells with love and pride—dear Papa.

His hair mopped, Papa looks around and all fall silent as the great moment approaches. The Duc de Villars stops hitting the bust of Venus with his crop, and the Marquis de Meuse inches closer, breathing heavily and almost falling over the Prince de Soubise in the process. "Vill—no Meu—no, Richelieu, you may have the honor," Papa says, his eyes finally coming to rest on the Duc de Richelieu. "That was an excellent kill of that stag."

Richelieu—a man I positively despise—smirks and settles on one rather shaky knee to do the honor of taking off the king's boots. As each one is taken off, it is replaced by a brocaded slipper, respectfully handed by the Duc d'Aumont, respectfully taken from a gilt-crusted box held by two valets.

"Three times since September," whispers Henriette dubiously. Henriette loves everyone, but even she finds fault with Richelieu, a man the priests call the devil's footman. "Papa certainly honors him."

"Four times," I correct her—Richelieu took over last week when Papa thought to honor the old Maréchal de Saxe, who fell while attempting to kneel down. Though I cannot criticize him, Papa really should spread his favors to more virtuous men. I look around at the assembled company, but come up short in terms of someone more suitable.

"Ah, wonderful," Papa says as the trays of refreshments arrive, followed by the rest of our ladies. There is a small wait as a glass of ale is passed down through the lines of respective attendants until it reaches the Duc d'Aumont, who proudly hands it to the king. Papa takes a sip and waves his hand, indicating his courtiers are off ceremony. Richelieu makes a beeline for the Marquise de l'Hôpital, the Comte de Leddie feeds two of the hunting dogs some cake, and I see with horror that the Duc de Chartres is about to slip over toward Henriette. Heavens, no! The duke had once asked for my sister's hand in marriage, but was suitably refused. Just in time Papa motions us all over to him.

The six of us advance in unison to ring his chair. He looks up at us in pleasure, his delight genuine. "All six of you here, together. What a delight. And how are you settling in, my dears?" he says to Sophie and Louise.

"Very well, Papa," Louise says as Sophie blushes. "It is most agreeable to be home." They chat awhile and I watch them, alert to where I might jump in and stop her prattling, for I fear she is boring Papa. Louise has a certain confidence that I find rather unnerving in one so young. And intelligence too, though surely she is not as intelligent as I—I don't think she knows any Greek, or even Latin, for that matter.

Papa turns to Élisabeth. "My dear, you will leave us soon," he says. "How we shall miss you." Élisabeth curtsies and rises with a look of pained sorrow.

"We are devastated, Papa, all of us," I say, inching closer, wondering if he will notice and comment on the book of Confucius I hold in my hand.

"Mmmm," acknowledges Papa, still smiling at Élisabeth.

"Dearest Father"—Élisabeth always calls him Father, an affectation at once annoying and provoking—"what sorrow as each day brings us closer to our departure! And little Isabelle: she cannot sleep for crying, such is her sorrow over leaving her grandpapa." Élisabeth darts her eyes to the door, but Beauvilliers has not yet returned with the girl.

"Can't sleep for crying? Indeed?" says Papa, and I see he is delighted at this lie.

"Nonsense, Élisabeth," I cut in. "Her nursemaid tells me she sleeps like a sheep. But *I* can scarcely sleep, for—"

"Alas," says Papa, draining his glass and handing it to Victoire, who turns pink at the honor, "such is the fate of kings, to have their daughters depart for far lands." He looks us over fondly again, then his eyes seek out the ladies standing or sitting behind us. "Élisabeth, you are not the only one who must depart. Where is our dear friend the Comtesse de Narbonne, who is to accompany you? Her mother is sorely troubled, for her delightful daughter is only fifteen."

"Indisposed," says Élisabeth shortly. Narbonne is pregnant

and was retching all morning; she has been banished until she can learn to control her emotions better. Suddenly Élisabeth kneels on the floor in front of Papa and takes his hands in hers. What is she doing?

"It is the sad fate of princesses to be separated from their beloved parents," says Élisabeth, staring up at Papa in perfect filial piety. I burn with anger that I did not think of such a pose, then burn more at her next words: "You must let me know what we can do from Italy to help my dear sisters get married—there is, of course, the King of Sardinia, who would be most suitable, and have we quite given up on Prince Charles?"

Betrayal, I think, glaring at Élisabeth, who is looking ever so smug in her pious pose on the floor. That she would wish her own tarnished fate upon the rest of us! The threat of marriage and all its horrors—the terrors of a foreign land and the bestial side of men—hangs in constant heaviness over our heads. Papa is the only man we need to love. Victoire turns bright red and I can feel Sophie start to tremble beside me. Louise's composure has left her and now she has the darting, hunted look of a mouse. One of her shoulders inches higher.

"Indeed," says my father, oblivious to the distress Élisabeth's words have caused. He rises and instantly the room falls silent. The Marquis de Meuse rushes over to fit Papa's wig back on his head. "I forgot to mention—there have been Sardinian inquiries for Sophie. Now I would bathe, then stop by the Marquise's before the evening."

He leaves with his retinue, a great clattering of men and dogs and smells, and the salon is once again restored to feminine harmony.

Sophie moans and covers her face with her hands.

"Oh no!" cries Victoire. "Not Sophie! Oh, terrible, terrible news!" She stops an attendant gathering the refreshments and takes a violent swig from one of the men's ale glasses. Victoire is menaced by Ferdinand of Spain, but his queen is not dying as expected. Victoire prays nightly for her continued good health.

"Why did you say that, Élisabeth?" chides Henriette gently. "You know how talk of marriages distresses us, and now look at poor Sophie." Thank goodness the Stuart prince wasn't able to reclaim his throne, or Henriette would be in England now. England, for goodness' sake, where they pour their tea themselves and can't even bathe properly. Recently there was another scare with the Elector of Bavaria, but at twenty-two, Henriette now feels the safety of her years.

I myself am only seventeen, and though I can see the journey's end and sense the sweet reward, I still consider myself in danger. That I am the most attractive of my sisters is without a doubt, and my beauty has even caused romantic indiscretions: when I was fifteen, a lace merchant, at the palace to show his wares, declared himself impossibly in love with me. He was taken to the Bastille, of course, but I was secretly pleased, for that dalliance has made me more worldly than my sisters.

Louise is the most vulnerable—she is twelve, the perfect age for a princess to marry—but she stuffs the left shoulder of her gowns with rags to raise it higher than the other, to pretend she is a cripple. She started this conceit before leaving the convent and I feel a small prick of jealousy, for it is rather a clever move.

Sophie looks around wildly, a lamb about to be shorn.

"Never fear, dear sisters, we will not let this happen! Never," I say firmly, glaring at Élisabeth. I pat Sophie's trembling arm. She knows I will protect her. "Sardinia! And Sophie has told us how much she hates fish!"

"She'll never survive the childdeath," says Victoire, hiccuping dolefully into her glass of ale. "I mean the childbirth. Beauvilliers' cousin died last week; she was only fifteen, and as small as Sophie." Victoire collects the names of women who have died in childbirth, a rather morbid hobby in one usually so placid and happy.

Beauvilliers enters with the little Princess Isabelle.

"You quite missed him!" snaps Élisabeth as the child is deposited on her lap. She starts to tidy her daughter's hair and looks around at us complacently, unmoved by our distress. "I only want what is best for Papa and for France. And for yourselves— you must know the pleasure that comes from being a mother." She kisses Isabelle's head and the child twists around and yanks on her mother's pearled choker. Dribbling little hoyden, I think in disgust.

"Oh, but, sister, to leave Versailles and Papa and go far away— we are not as strong as you are," says Henriette in genuine affliction.

"We are as strong," I snap, "but Hen is entirely right—who would want to leave Versailles? And go somewhere dreadful, like *Parma*?"

"Do you have no wish for a natural life?" Élisabeth cuts back. "And is that not woman's fate as prescribed by the Bible? Quite frankly, I am glad Papa is considering marriages for you. Perhaps he is coming to his senses."

"Treason," I hiss as Sophie continues to moan and Victoire starts sobbing, "to talk of our father that way! As though he were not of his senses!"

"I only speak the truth," says Élisabeth mildly. "Father has been sadly remiss in his duty of finding you husbands. Lazy, even."

"Only from his love for us!" I shout, my heart beginning to palpitate madly. What insubordination! I realize I am gripping Sophie's arm rather tightly. Little Isabelle starts wailing for no reason, and I have a sudden image of tops, hundreds of them, spinning out of control over a vast parquet floor. "You must never talk of our father in that way again," I say, struggling to modulate my voice. It is my duty to control this chaos; I must not snap under the pressure. November 18, I think grimly, November 18, and then order will be restored.

"There, there." I pat Sophie again, her little arm reminding me of a bird's wing. "We will never let this happen, never! I will do all in my power—and my influence with Papa is great—to avoid this calamity."

When I was six—it is my most treasured memory—I ran and beseeched my father not to send me to the convent with my younger sisters. Since that time I know he can refuse me nothing and I will not hesitate to use my charms on him again. I sit down and enjoy a quiet moment with my image of the scene: myself with tears in my eyes, humbly beseeching Papa—perhaps I might strike that pose on the floor that Élisabeth just used to such effect—as he looks down fondly at me, perhaps with tears in his eyes too!

Little Isabelle slips off her mother's lap, pursued by a hapless nursemaid.

"I don wan go! *No quiero*—" *Whump!* The little girl trips over the edge of the carpet and goes flying, hitting her head on the corner of one of the gilt sofas.

November 18, I think again as the tops finally stop spinning and make one last turn before coming to rest in silence on the floor.

Chapter Three

In which Jeanne develops a fear of falling

The bed is far too narrow for two, and the mattress is just a hard wisp of an idea, a rough straw pallet barely a finger thick. The bells start tolling at five, even before the sun starts to rise. The door flies open, and at the end of the vast dormitory a ragged crow in black calls out to us to rise and consecrate our day to God.

We tumble out of bed in sleepy silence and start to dress over our shifts. Even though it is a hot July morning, we must never be naked, for nakedness is a sin. There are many, many sins, and the threat of their constant presence keeps the nuns very busy.

Outside, the day is brightening, but inside, the long attic room is still dark. I climb into my white wool dress and then comb my friend Charlotte's hair with my fingers and secure it under her bunting. She is about to do mine when Hermine pushes her away. "You don't know how," she hisses, pulling my locks. "You always make a mess of hers."

"Oh, I don't care who does my hair," I say. "Really. But do hurry, or Sister George will be back again." A lie; I want Hermine to do my hair, but don't want Charlotte to feel bad.

Hermine produces a small comb from under her mattress, a hidden luxury, and starts to untangle my hair. For a precious moment I am back with Frederica combing my hair and calling me her little angel, perched on her lap at the toilette table, bathed in the scent of rose powder. I hate wearing the bunting and the veil; I want my hair loose and free over my shoulders. Once a month we bathe and wash our hair and that is my happiest day; when I am older, I will wash my hair *every day.*

"You're so pretty,' whispers Charlotte. I smile, for I like being told I am pretty. I wish I had a mirror, that I could see for myself, but they are not allowed. I love my thick, blond hair—love is another sin, though I am not sure why—and the other girls love it too. After Hermine has combed it out, everyone touches it and we all agree it must feel as soft as satin. I'm the only one who has ever felt real satin, and I confirm it does. Sister George reenters, and deft as the thief her mother is reputed to be, Hermine slips the forbidden comb into her sleeve.

"What is happening here?" says Sister George harshly, coming toward our little cluster. She softens as she sees me in the center. "Ah, Jeanne, and how are you this morning, my angel?"

I murmur something and look at the floor. Sister George takes the cloth from Hermine and proceeds to wind it around my head, stroking me and soothing my hair into it. Sister George makes me uneasy; she is always looking at me as though she is hungry and I am a cake she wants to eat. Once she even took me on her lap, and I was shocked because I never thought nuns could hug like mothers.

"Now! Off to the chapel with you all," she says, giving my head one last caress. I take off with the other girls, running and tumbling out the door. The only time we are allowed to run is when we are on the way to God. I remember at Frederica's how I used to run up and down the staircase, and sometimes even up and down the street in those happy days before I was sent to this convent. Punished, and all because of that man with the dirty green eyes.

Now mornings, afternoons, and days pass long and dreary inside the thick stone walls of the convent. When I first came I cried, a lot, but soon I learned to be happy—even in this grim prison there are things to smile about. I have so many friends, and some of the nuns adore me—some perhaps too much—and lessons are never taxing. We learn the Bible, of course, but in addition to our catechism we are taught reading and writing, and how to keep account books. I hate numbers. There is also lots of sewing: we sew for the poor children and for the fallen women, endless lengths of scratchy cream linen we make into rough skirts and capes. It seems that once a woman has fallen, she can no longer sew for herself.

The nuns watch over us like hawks, afraid that we too will fall. Bastards and girls with no fathers, like most of the little girls here, are in the most danger of falling. Though what we might fall into is less clear.

"Perhaps they don't want us to fall down?" says Hermine dubiously.

"It's because bad women don't have shoes," says little Annette solemnly. "And then they trip and fall down." We only have yellowed calf slippers that are too thin and in the winter our feet feel like lumps of ice. Annette has a bad cough and what the sisters call the devil's lungs; I hope she doesn't die like her sister Marie last year.

"They don't want us to fall into wells, or out of windows," says Charlotte. We nod, for Charlotte is older and more knowledgeable. The well in the courtyard is covered, tightly, and only the porteress, a beefy woman who smells of sweat and something darker, is strong enough to uncover it. The windows don't open properly, and they are too small to fall out of in any case.

"But we *fall* asleep every night," wails little Agnes, a shivering slip of a girl who, according to the rumors that seep around the convent, is the daughter of a hanged man.

"But falling has nothing to do with sleeping," I add, though I am not entirely sure. Frederica was a fallen woman, I think, but her bed was so soft I gladly fell into it!

All we know is that fallen women are sent to Louisiana, where bears will eat them, or to the prison at La Salpêtrière, where they shave your head. From the narrow windows of our garret we can see onto the rue des Vignes, and once we saw a whole cartful of fallen women on their way to that dreaded prison. The women were calm, and some were even smiling, and none seemed to care too much.

&

My friend Charlotte is leaving next year to be apprenticed to a lace maker, far away in Passy. She doesn't want to go and cries every night. I don't know what Ma's plans are for me; she comes once a month to visit but doesn't bring the monk Guimard, whom I miss terribly. The nuns would not approve of a man of God in the company of a married lady, but I am not surprised: they do not approve of anything.

When it is warm enough, we crawl onto the roofs of the convent and watch the world in the streets below and marvel at the city that spread around us, hiding so many people and lives unknown to us. Sometimes I long to be out there in the squalor and energy of the streets, but other times, when the January cold bites us in half and pigeons freeze in the gutters, the thin blankets and thinner gruel of the convent seem like the greatest sanctuary in the world. The nuns have taught us that the outside world is a dangerous place, with many dangerous situations to fall into.

"Look," says Charlotte, pointing into an uncurtained window across the street that we can see into from our perch on the roof. The room is small but seems like a beautiful gem box, draped in red and orange sheets.

"Oh, how lovely!" We watch as a woman pulls on a bright pink gown over her gray chemise. We both sigh—imagine wearing pink, not this horrid white that turns so fast to gray. The woman disappears from view and then we see her again in the street below.

"I wonder where she is going?" I say, following her movements toward the Palais du Luxembourg. She looks very small from up here, a forlorn pink dot. Would I like to be her, outside and all alone? I don't know, but regardless, soon I must leave; no girl can stay here past her sixteenth birthday, and I am already fifteen.

&

The day when I must leave comes far too soon, and not soon enough. I am not as sad as I could be, for Charlotte has already left, apprenticed to the lace maker, and little Annette went home to die of her lungs. I'm not sure what awaits me on the outside, but I am sure something good will happen.

Mother Superior gives me a final lecture and Sister George cries and makes me promise to write. I promise, but only to make her happy. Lying is a sin, but here I cannot see the harm.

Then I am out of the convent gates, for the first time in nearly a decade. The street, so long familiar from our perch in the attic rooms, is now mine in all its glory. But it looks different from here below, narrower and meaner. The street—where everything happens.

I tear off my head covering and my hair falls glorious and loose down my back. I'm about to throw my hated wimple into the gutter, but instead I drape it over my shoulders like a cape and turn my face to the sun, and feel as though it is shining just for me.

"Mademoiselle! You are lost, I shall help you to your destination!" declares a man carrying a stack of books, stopping with a smile.

"No, thank you, I am not," I say, smiling at him and thinking how kind his face is. "I am waiting here for my parents."

"Then I will wait here with—"

The grate of the convent door flies open and Mother Superior's voice cries out for the man to be gone.

"Ah! Such beauty," a priest exclaims softly as he walks by, and puts a black-gloved hand around my waist and murmurs a blessing on me.

A carriage drives by and halts a little way past. A fine-wigged older gentleman leans out of the window and smiles at me. He reminds me a little, in my faded memory, of Monsieur Dumonceaux. The coachman jumps down and comes toward me with an important face.

"Mademoiselle, my master, a fine connoisseur—"

"Darling!" It is my mother and the monk Guimard. The carriage takes off reluctantly, the coachman running to catch up with it. We embrace and hug and start the long walk to my mother's new lodgings. Greedily I drink in the sights and sounds so long forbidden me: the squalor and energy and life, the splashes of beauty and elegance overwhelming after the austerity of the convent.

My mother and the monk Guimard live on the fourth floor of a narrow house near Les Halles. It's humble, but cozy and clean, and I run through the apartment and marvel at my own room—small but still mine!—and twirl into the salon. And then I see it, hanging above the mantel. A mirror. Finally. I drag a chair over and step up on it, and there I am.

A girl with mountains of golden curls, dark eyebrows and dark blue eyes, large and hooded in a perfect cherub face with pretty pink cheeks, looks back at me. I giggle in delight: I *am* pretty!

Maybe even beautiful!

Chapter Four

In which Madame Adélaïde catches a fish

The river flows glassy and cold before me, a warped mirror reflecting back an odd, rippling Adélaïde. I stand erect as I stare into the depths; never for a moment shall I bend or falter. I am known throughout the palace—perhaps throughout the country—as a paragon of virtue and discipline. Once one of my ladies dared to grumble about the heaviness and general discomfort of the court gowns they must wear during their week of attendance on me. I quickly reminded her that I am on attendance upon myself every day of the year, and have no relief, and therefore neither should she.

This week we are at the palace of Choisy, where less formal wear is permitted. Only with reluctance do I follow this fashion, for I believe that slackness in dress produces slackness in mind; stays are the harness that keeps us on the right path. But even if my dress is comfortable, I shall never sacrifice my erect posture.

"Madame, why not give the rod to the man, for a while?" suggests Françoise, the Duchesse de Brancas, and one of our ladies in attendance. Frannie—as some of the more informal ladies call her—impulsively puts a soft, white hand on my sleeved arm and I flinch; at least at Court the wide panniers generally prohibit such intimacy.

"No, I shall continue until my labors bear more fruit," I say, moving my arm away. "The Bible tells us that is the way to happiness." We are on a wooden pier by the Seine; behind us, a vast expanse of lawn leads up to the terraces of the château. Beside me, my sister Victoire has already abandoned her fishing rod and is vigorously fanning herself and complaining of the heat. Earlier, Sophie caught a fish, then promptly fainted and had to be carried away. Louise is on my other side, and she has already caught two.

I hear her chatting away with the Duchesse de Broglie, one of her ladies who is distressingly pregnant again—the woman is like a rabbit, I think in disgust. Occasionally they laugh and I strain to hear what they are saying. Then Louise pulls another fish from the river, to great clapping from her ladies—and from mine, I note acidly. The Marquise de Belsunze proudly brings me the fish.

"Look, Madame, it's almost two feet long!"

I glance at the floppy, glassy mess in the iced basket. "Nearer a foot," I sniff—humility is a virtue that Louise cannot claim to have mastered. My little fish—the four-inch fruit of two hours' labor—lies in a basket beside me, ignored and uncomplimented. I am determined not to relinquish my hold on the rod until I too have matched or bettered my younger sister.

Fishing is a noble pastime, for did not the Lord Jesus recommend it? We first tried it on a trip to Plombières, where we went several years ago to take the waters at the spas. We fished in the Moselle; it was very pleasant. In fact the whole trip was very pleasant—I can still hear, and perhaps forever will, the sweet acclaim that greeted my sisters and me as we traveled through the country.

"Oh good, the chairs!" says Frannie, greeting the footmen bringing an array of chairs down from the palace. I frown; the chairs are all the same and we should not be sitting on them alongside our ladies, without distinction for our rank as daughters of France. I decide I shall lead by example and not sit, but my sisters are distressingly heedless of my sacrifice.

Victoire flops down, still complaining about the heat and talking wistfully about wading into the river. Preposterous! As if we were children. I have never swum—of course—but I ran once, across a wide-open field, at the little château of Meudon, where we sometimes visited with our brother the dauphin. Those were happy times, but they did not last. When he was seven, and I four, he was taken into the world of men and our little visits were also taken away. Everything ceased then—it was almost as though we, his sisters, ceased to exist.

I shake my head. The problem with fishing is that it leads to introspection, which often appears in the form of a lady who questions and mocks me. Introspection is a form of self-indulgence I cannot countenance; it is far better to focus on the task at hand and the demands of the immediate world.

"Look! Another one!" cries Louise, and sure enough she reels out another flapping carp. I glare at my stretch of the river but nothing tweaks my rod.

"When are we leaving, sister?" asks Victoire, rising and coming over to fan me. "I hope we will travel back tonight? I do so wish to see Burgundy." Our nephew the Duc de Burgundy, only ten years old, is terribly ill—a tumor in his leg, say his doctors. Not long now, and what heartbreak for my brother and his wife, Josepha. Though if truth be told—and I believe it must—Burgundy's younger brother, Louis-Auguste, is more to my taste, a solid, steadfast boy of six who rarely laughs and who knows well the obligations imposed upon him as a son of France. His brother Burgundy was—is—a more flighty, snippy child, who once complained he did not want to kiss my cheek, claiming I smelled of old.

Thinking of him, my mood turns as dark as the depths of the river before me. My family has seen so much sorrow these past years. My sister Henriette, dear sweet dreamy Henriette, died eight years ago in 1752; so sudden and so tragic. Never have I seen my father more devastated, and he turned to me in his sorrow. For a while, in the wake of her death, we enjoyed a closeness that was as fleeting as it was bittersweet. And then last year my sister Élisabeth, back at Versailles on another one of her escapes from Parma, caught smallpox and died. She was only thirty-two years old.

Before she died, we had fought; I hate to think of it now but it is true. Élisabeth had begun a *rapprochement* with our father's hated mistress, and she wanted us to follow suit. She even claimed that my continued resistance to the Marquise de Pompadour was driving Papa away, and that I was being irrational in my hatred. Much to my disgust, Louise had the temerity to agree with her; I often think my youngest sister must learn to be more *sororal*.

Élisabeth even said, speaking of the Pompadour: *Better the devil you know.* A distasteful quotation that smacked of heresy, and Sophie had squealed in terror at the implication that more than one devil might exist. Such nonsense, I think grimly, staring down at the water.

The deaths of my sisters led us down a path through a dark wood and now we are four: myself, Victoire, Sophie, and Louise. A sadly dwindled number. Though of course I miss Henriette dreadfully, her departure left me the eldest of the king's unmarried daughters. I am now *Madame*, the title significant in its brevity, second only to my mother the queen and my sister-in-law the dauphine at Court, and with a significantly increased household. History is not made in the way we might wish, or want, but when one is called to greatness, one must oblige.

"His Majesty! His Majesty!" cries a man, running down the hill from the château. We all turn to look, and sure enough, there he is on the terrace. What excellent luck, I think, pinking with pleasure. He must have decided to stop on his way back from hunting. Perhaps to see us? Me? My pleasure dims when I see who accompanies him—the Marquise de Pompadour, whom we call the fish woman, blowing like a bitter wind down the lawn toward us. With him as always, tarnishing our precious moments with Papa.

We had thought her hour had come three years ago when that madman Damiens attacked my father. As the king lay close to death, my sisters and I nursed him back to health and pleaded with him to return to a life with God. He looked to take confession and even apologized to us, with such daintiness of expression, for the scandals and the suffering he had caused us.

But then he survived and slipped through our net and went back to *her*, and since then she has continued to reign supreme.

She plays the role of procuress for my father, and manages broth-els in town where she induces him to sin. I am the steward of this disgusting information and keep it to myself; were my sisters to know, their health would never survive.

"Oh, look, Papa is coming! And Pompadour," says Victoire. "Louise, he can admire your fish! Perhaps he wants one for supper tonight? Do you think he will stay for supper? But if not, perhaps I might ride back to Versailles with them?"

I grimace at my fish, looking as small as a sardine on the pier beside me. "Tell Louise to give me one of her fish," I hiss to the Duchesse de Brancas, but Louise overhears me.

"Oh, I don't think I can, sister," she says. At twenty-three, Louise does not consider herself fully out of matrimonial danger, and one of her shoulders still continues higher than the other. She doesn't care that people whisper that she is a crippled monster. "It wouldn't be right, to pretend to have caught a fish when you haven't? I'm sorry, but I can't aid in such deception."

Papa and the woman arrive and greet us heartily; he is in a good humor and wearing a new summer jacket, which he shows off proudly. The Pompadour takes one of the chairs and sits her-self down, comfortably, in a way that makes my teeth hurt. Sitting in front of me, Madame, the first daughter of France! She is a duchess (though everyone still calls her Marquise) and it is her right to sit, of course, but she was born a *bourgeoise*, as too many people seem to forget these days. I had reproached Papa when he bestowed the title on her, but he had proceeded nonetheless.

In truth, my relationship with Papa is a little strained these recent years; since the death of dear Hen, it is almost as though he were pained by our presence. We still see him every day—his visits after Mass last only a few minutes, though occasionally—twice last month!—he stays for almost an hour. But I do notice, and not only on these days when the Lady of Introspection threatens to rise from the deep, that we are no longer as close as we once were.

And now our brother's five children occupy his time, and of

course little ailing Burgundy commands much attention and pity. He loves to take his grandchildren on his knee and jostle them, and though it is ludicrous to be jealous of children, he hardly ever did that with us. And of course now it would be inappropriate, I think. He does occasionally take grown women on his lap—he bounced the little Comtesse d'Amblimont, who Victoire says reminds her of a kitten, on his lap last month. I frown.

"Fishing—what a delightful occupation," says the Pompadour woman enthusiastically. "I have never tried it myself, but how I would like to." I think, as I often do when I look at her, how unfair it was of God to give one woman so much. Even though she is older now—almost forty—she has the complexion of a much younger woman, and her eyes are still bright, and she is, as always, perfectly dressed. Her soft summer gown flows around her like a peach sorbet, elegantly trimmed with petals and a matching sun hat.

"Don't you have anything to say, dear Madame?" she inquires after a pause, daring me to comment on her love for fish. But it is an old game, and in truth it is getting tired. A certain acceptance is required, I see that now. She is embedded in our lives, as thoroughly as though she were a brick in a wall: impossible to displace.

"Fishing is an occupation best done in silence," I reply, then add, more by rote than with any real malice, "One would have thought *you* would know that."

"Ah, my dear Narbonne! Let me see your face, dear Comtesse," says the Pompadour woman, ignoring me and motioning to the Comtesse de Narbonne, another one of my attendants. Narbonne returned from Parma with my sister, then fell ill with the same dreaded smallpox. She survived, but her looks are ruined.

"Frannie, just look at our poor Narbonne's face," murmurs Pompadour kindly, motioning to her friend the Duchesse de Brancas. "But I see much improvement! The asbestos and apricot cream? Is it not working wonders?" The countess submits to the inspection passively; she was a great beauty before the illness, and I know my father admired her for it, but that life is now gone forever. I find ugliness breeds a certain humility, and she is now one of my favorite ladies.

The Pompadour is looking at Narbonne with an odd mix of triumph and concern, which I cannot place, and she seems to be saying something other than her kind inquiry. I vaguely recall a slight rivalry between the two women, but I am not sure of its origin. There are so many undercurrents to court life that I prefer to ignore; I hate to appear ignorant. To be ignorant is almost as bad as being ridiculous, and that I will never be.

"You may take my rod, Narbonne," I say, moving over to my father, who is chatting with Louise and admiring her fish. "How was Bellevue, Papa?"

"Delightful, as always," he replies. "By Jove, that must be ten pounds at least! Man," he says, motioning to one of his attendants, "show this fine carp to the Marquise."

"What did you do there, Papa?"

"Ah, a little hunting, yes, not much." He smiles at me, but his eyes are blank. "Billiards." I am about to launch into a discourse on the Austrian advance on the Elbe—for my father's sake I interest myself in current political issues—but before I can, the Pompadour inserts herself smoothly between us. "We must not tarry, dear, if we want to be back at Versailles by nightfall and see our dear Burgundy."

"We'll walk up to the château with you," says Louise, motioning to Victoire. "And see how Sophie is doing."

"Poor Sophie," says Papa, with a touch of real concern. "I imagine she fainted upon catching a fish?"

Everyone laughs.

"I shall come as well," I announce.

"But, Adélaïde, you swore you would not move until you had caught at least two fish! And you've only caught one—though I'm not sure it's even a fish, more like a tadpole," says Louise with a laugh, and Papa laughs too and then to my horror the Pompadour squeezes my arm—what on earth is happening today?—

have the sun and water made people mad?—and murmurs something about the needs of duty.

They all set off up the lawn and I watch them retreat back to the palace, the Marquise hanging off Papa's arm, so close, and then there is a peal of laughter and I have that awful feeling they are laughing about *me*.

Nonsense—what would there be to laugh at?

Grimly I turn back to the river and stare at my reflection in the water. Wavering but unchanging. No fish rises to bite, but the dreaded Lady of Introspection does, again. I see now, perhaps too late, what my sister Élisabeth had been trying to tell me: my resistance to the fish woman, rather than impressing Papa with its piety and conviction, has only driven him farther away.

Chapter Five

In which Jeanne comes to life

"But I don't want to work with chickens!" I say, for what seems like the hundredth time. And I don't—I have nightmares of plucked chickens, their flesh rubbery and foul under my hands. Only dead fish, glassy and cold, disgust me more.

My mother tuts and continues her plucking. "You can't lie around waiting for something to fall from the sky."

I shake my head; that is precisely what I plan to do. I don't see why I should worry in the meantime, or keep myself busy with awful work; better to lie and await my future with an open heart so that I can be ready when it arrives.

When I left the convent we had hoped Monsieur Dumonceaux would take an interest in me, but he did not—Frederica's hand, no doubt, sniffed Ma. There followed in quick succession a disastrous apprenticeship to a hairdresser; one day as a ribbon seller on the street; another few months as a companion to a crotchety old lady, until her household was upended by her two young sons falling in love with me.

I was dismissed. I am learning of the effect my beauty has on others, and of the blame that is attached to it. I now know what a fallen woman is, and it involves men. Lots of men, or one man at the wrong time. I think of the two sons of Madame de Corneuve: their insistent caresses and overeager kisses, the embellished locket one gave me as a hopeful gift. It might have been nice to marry one of them—the older one was pleasant and had excellent teeth and their château was comfortable, though too far out in the country—but it would have caused the old lady too much heartache. I would not want to distress her with a marriage that was unequal to the hopes she had for her sons.

So here I am back at my mother's house. Reluctantly I help my mother deliver her cooked chickens—I refuse to work with the uncooked ones—and wait for my future to come for me.

It does, one day while I am delivering a dozen capons to a fancy store on the rue Neuve-des-Petits-Champs. I go by the back alley to the kitchens, but there the owner of the store sees me, and through the grime of the streets and the odor the poultry has attached to me, she sees something she likes.

The next day I gather a bag with my few items, kiss Ma and the monk Guimard good-bye, and get into the carriage that Madame Labille has sent for me. My first carriage ride! I only rode a cart to the old woman in Corneuve: she had two carriages but never deigned to send one for me.

Outside the store on the fashionable street, lined with jewelers and fabric stores, hatters and stationers, the coachman opens the door of the carriage and holds his arm out for me to step down. I smile in delight and skip over the cobblestones into the store. I sink into a plush plum-colored carpet that welcomes me back like a dream remembered. The hats and bonnets hanging on the walls whisper in greeting, and the tables piled high with laces and ribbons glimmer their approval.

I'm back in Frederica's boudoir.

Artificial flowers, ribbons, bands of sequins and pearls, sleeves and stomachers, muffs and gloves of fur and leather, scarves and shawls of floating airy materials and capes of colored fur, feathers and jeweled butterflies, bolts of fine fabrics in every printed pattern and color.

Or am I in heaven?

Buckles and shimmering fichus and aprons, pockets and tippets and divine little parasols made of lace, toile and gossamer.

Both, I decide.

The store is called *À la Toilette*, and it is full of all the fripperies to make the plainest gown sing. All the trimmings to make even the drabbest of dresses into a concoction worthy of a queen. Not our queen: Julie, one of the other shopgirls, tells me she hasn't worn anything but black or brown since '44. But worthy of a queen of fashion, I think, twirling around and laughing in delight.

"Follow me," says Julie, and leads me up a narrow flight of steps to a room with three beds. "You'll be sleeping here, with Adélaïde, that's Labille's daughter, a very charming girl, only thirteen." Julie has an odd way of speaking, a mixture of grub and grace. "The convent at Saint-Maur—I had a cousin there— Félicité Bertin, you knew her?"

"Oh yes, a lovely girl," I lie, putting down my bag and sitting on the bed. "Oh, what a fine mattress!"

"Certainly—Madame Labille believes in a good night's sleep. We must look perfectly pretty in the morning, pretty enough to match her wares." Julie smiles at me: she is a lovely girl with a mass of brown hair tied loosely back and her thin body is swathed in fine pink silk.

I am furnished with a trousseau, as though I am a bride to be married: two dresses, a beribboned corset, a handful of soft chemises. Labille picks out a beautiful peach-colored silk for one of my dresses and she chooses perfectly: somehow the color catches my soul and lights it up. I am allowed to pick out the trim for my new dresses, and Madame Labille even permits me a small pair of hoops that lift the heavy skirt and petticoat. I giggle when I remember the nuns railing against such hoops, that send skirts swaying to catch men's fancy.

Madame Labille is a hard-faced woman; her husband has a lottery boutique next door but she runs this store all by herself. "Calls herself a 'woman of business,'" says Julie, and we both laugh at the strange image the word conjures.

Madame Labille decides Mademoiselle Rançon, as I am known, is not a suitable name.

"A new name? Oh, I'm not sure," I say. Is such a thing allowed? "But I was baptized . . ."

"Were you? I thought your father was . . . well, never mind. Besides, it's fun," says Monique, another of the girls and as pretty as a rosebud. "Name means nothing in our world, so pick one to suit you. I was Gollier before I came here and now I am Mademoiselle de Beauvoisin. *Miss Good Neighbor*. What is the harm in changing your name, as you would your dress for a new season?"

I've only ever had one dress, and now I have three, so . . . I decide on Mademoiselle l'Ange: *Miss Angel* and I am ushered into a new life where anything is possible.

"I could stay here forever," I say dreamily to Julie, who has just finished selling a pair of green gloves, embroidered with seed pearls, to an older gentleman. Eighty *livres* he paid for them and he even gave Julie a *livre*, for her beautiful service, he said. Imagine that: a pair of gloves that costs more than twenty chickens! The prices in the shop amaze me, though Julie, who has been here almost a year, says I'll soon lose my charming innocence and realize that everything has a price.

Julie says it is we who keep the customers coming, like meat attracts flies. Or ribbons attract female heads. We are the most valuable product in the store, even more valuable than the two ermine muffs Madame Labille ordered from Russia, one white sewn with pearls, the other black fur banded with amber beads. The Marquise de Rouilly sighed over the white one last week but finally decided that four hundred *livres* was too outrageous a sum. Imagine—a muff even a marquise can't afford!

"I could stay here forever," I repeat, and twirl a soft velvet ribbon around my wrist. Julie deposits the glove money into a box in one of the cupboards, then comes to sit beside me in the window.

"Forever—one as beautiful as you couldn't stay here forever," she says playfully, unpinning a paste brooch from my hair so that a lock tumbles down. Two soldiers passing in the street stop to salute us, and we giggle and blush before they bow and go on their merry way.

"You must be more ambitious. There will no doubt soon be a kind gentleman to spirit you away." Julie has many admirers, including one who buys her a new pair of stockings every single week. She sells most of them, along with anything else she can pilfer from the store, to the peddler woman who comes by on Mondays. *Not like it's worth anything*, she said airily last week, picking up the foot of sequined band left over after Madame de la Popelinière had left.

"Ah, ambition," I say lazily. "Not for me." One should be content with what one has, I think, looking around at the store; the sequins wink back in agreement. The days soon settle into a soft and luxurious routine, and the nuns and their remonstrations fade into the shadows where they belong. And serving in a shop isn't like work, really: what greater joy than to count pretty buttons or neatly fold scarves and ribbons? Madame Labille quickly determines I have no gift for numbers and Julie continues with that dull duty.

"Two strips of this fur, here," says Madame de Soissons, pointing to long yards of fine ermine, "and six for the skirt." Six for the skirt! Imagine that. She doesn't even inquire the price, and I study her cool nonchalance, her elegant air of indifference, the delicate gestures she makes with her hands to the two maids that stand behind. She is one of those hallowed ladies who steps directly from their carriages to the store, wearing only the slimmest of kid shoes in any weather. I guess she has never known rough cobblestone under her feet, never picked her way over a puddle without someone's arm or cloak to assist. The half-finished gown that will bear the fur trim lies over one of the tables, a resplendent cream brocade.

She turns to look at me and a slight sliver of a frown pinches her features. "That is a very charming fichu," she says, coming over to finger the soft gauze at my throat. "I'll take some of that—it will be just the thing with my turquoise silk." I know what she is thinking: a gown in my color, a fichu in my style, will restore her faded skin and smooth her wrinkled eyes. Peach is a most popular color this spring, and all because, says Madame Labille in satisfaction, "You wear it so well."

Other times brown-clad women, with a bustling air of business, pick out merchandise for grand court ladies, picking up their wares on a Tuesday and heading off to Versailles. One, it is even whispered, is the dressmaker to the Marquise de Pompadour. Pompadour is the most elegant and powerful lady in the land, and she rules France, and the king, from behind her perfectly perfumed and constructed façade. One day her dressmaker decides on an enormous selection of chartreuse silk flowers, just arrived from Lille.

Madame Labille has come out from her lair to serve the august woman, and bows and scrapes before the dressmaker as though she were the Pompadour herself.

"Will she return the ones she doesn't need?" I ask, after she is gone—eight hundred *livres* just on silk flowers! I try to imagine what the Marquise looks like and what she would do with two hundred silk posies—the entirety of the order. There are paintings, of course, and prints, but most of them are unflattering, as portraits generally are.

"No, she won't return them," says Madame Labille in satisfaction, making neat notions in the account book. "Keeps the ones she wants, then gives the rest to friends, or charity, or throws them away. I don't really know, but the arrangement is satisfactory."

Not all our customers are women; there are plenty of men who come to purchase for their wives, daughters, and mistresses, as well as to ogle and charm us. Highborn gentlemen come themselves, or else send their lascivious lackeys, who prowl the streets for their masters.

Julie teaches me how to laugh and be charming and coy while seeming to encourage. Men, she instructs me solemnly, are the key to everything and you never know what door they might open. She gives me lessons in coquetry, and soon I have plenty of suitors and admirers myself, offering me tickets to the Opéra, boat rides on the Seine, picnics in paradise or the Palais Royale.

All the wonders of Paris are unfurled for me, like the cloak of a handsome gentleman laid gallantly over a puddle. I am ushered across, my feet in delicate calfskin slippers, never yellow, and never getting dirty.

☙

"The Hôtel de Richelieu, mademoiselle," says the guard grandly as two others open the gate. I carry my basket into the courtyard, and another man, extravagantly dressed in purple livery, ushers me into the house and through a succession of gilded reception rooms.

In the last one he leaves me alone, instructing me to wait. We often make deliveries to clients: to fine ladies too sleepy or too proud to travel the streets; to new brides anxious before their weddings; to recalcitrant lovers, needing a quick fancy to soothe a discontented mistress.

I suddenly feel nervous, for this is the grandest house I have been inside. The men and women who inhabit such places are unknown mysteries to me.

"Indeed. You have brought the gloves?" comes a voice from a shadowed corner. I jump and almost drop the basket.

"La, sir! I thought I was alone. What are you doing, sitting in the shadows?" I peer into the corners, but it is a dull afternoon and the evening candles are not yet lit. Madame Labille constantly impresses upon us the need for formality when making deliveries, especially to the grander houses, but I have found that a smile and a bit of a jest is also well received.

"Shadows are best for observation," comes the voice of an older man, husky and worn. "Now show me one of the gloves. Slip your hand inside."

I oblige, the soft leather greeting me like a friend.

"There, yes, now, put on the other one. How do they feel, mmm?"

"Warm and comfortable. As soft as cream."

"Tight?"

"Yes, sir. Well fitting, snug, like a . . . a glove." I turn my hands this way and that for his benefit.

"Warm and tight, ah yes, excellent. Pull your hands out slowly—slowly, I say! Yes, that's it . . . mmm. Now, put your basket on the floor, dear, and go stand by the window."

"Now, do you want to see the gloves, or me?" I say, doing his bidding. "Oh, but what a lovely statue! Who is she?" I cry, my attention caught by a delicate marble lady in the gardens before me.

"The goddess Hebe. Do you know your goddesses, child?"

"I don't know my goddesses, only my saints. And I'm not a child, sir, I'm already nineteen!"

"Turn around. You are charming, charming." A shuffled creaking and the man emerges from the shadows, older than his voice and a little stooped, but with a certain bright energy. He is wearing a home robe of quilted blue velvet and a gold-tasseled cap.

"Ah, charming, delectable. Do not be afraid," he says, creeping closer.

"I'm not afraid, sir, for I know you to be a gentleman."

"Ha! How strange you should think yourself safe with a gentleman. Come here, my dear, and give me a kiss." He beckons me with a curled, beringed finger.

"Very well," I say, for kisses are free and give so much pleasure. I peck him on the cheek and his arms catch me, surprisingly strong and grasping, and suddenly I am afraid. I push him away, and he releases me.

"Ah, now, twenty years ago, you would not have escaped so easily, I can assure you, mademoiselle," he says, staggering over to a stuffed sofa. "You would have succumbed, and been the more pleasured for it, but alas these days I must conserve my energy." He coughs and spits a phlegmy wheeze.

I suddenly feel sorry for him, though I am not sure why, and impulsively lean over to kiss him again. I see with a giggle that he has fallen asleep and is snoring. I am unsure whether to leave the basket or not; I decide I will and Madame Labille can send a bill for all of it. He can certainly afford it, I think, looking around the magnificent room.

I tarry before leaving, look out over the fountains and the statue of Hebe, then twirl around on the soft carpet. I imagine living in such a house; I am his mistress, this harmless old man is my protector, and every day I wake to the charms of this beautiful life.

If I hold very still, I can imagine it's mine, all mine.

Chapter Six

In which Jeanne falls, but lands quite comfortably

It's been raining for six days and all of us shopgirls are cooped up inside like a brood of ruffled pastel chickens. Madame Labille has taken the carriage to visit the lace merchants in Lyon and we do not want to ruin our cloaks and slippers by walking out in the rain.

Adélaïde, Labille's daughter, is sitting on the floor in front of me, sketching me. She follows me around like a puppy dog and says I am the most beautiful woman she has ever seen.

"Madame Gourdan's is the house of highest repute in Paris," says Julie, fingering a purple bow. "Well, perhaps second to Madame Sultana's." Monique has left to go and work at that famous brothel, enticed there by money and promises.

I shudder. "I'd rather be a mistress than work in one of *those* houses."

Julie shrugs. "The number of presents increases with the number of different admirers, and there is, of course, no chance anyone will tire of you."

"I think to be married would be far nicer."

"Not I," dismisses Julie. "The most we could hope for is a coachman, or a shopkeeper, and then you have to live in a garret for the rest of your life, and have too many children and scrimp each penny. Better to be a mistress: if he mistreats you, you can simply leave."

I look out at the street: it's November and winter is coming. How lucky I am to be in this warm and beautiful house. "But where would you go?" I ask.

"You could come back here," offers little Adélaïde from the floor. "Look—isn't it the perfect likeness?"

I glance at the sketch and ruffle her hair. "It is indeed, pet. You are very talented."

The street door opens and I startle; I hadn't seen or heard the carriage. A man enters, followed by a tall footman holding an umbrella over his head. Adélaïde scuttles out—she is not permitted in the front of the shop when there are clients.

"But Monsieur du Barry! We haven't seen you for almost a year!" exclaims Julie in what appears to be genuine delight. "How is Félicité?"

"Ah, the lovely Félicité," says the man, and I note how handsome he is, with large eyes and a sensuous curve to his mouth. Very handsome. "Some mistakes are best forgotten. And so you must be Mademoiselle l'Ange!" he says, turning away from Julie and offering me his hand. I put mine in his and he kisses it, then almost pulls me off the chair, but in so elegant a motion that I am unaware of what he is doing until I am standing before him.

"Magnificent," he says, and leans closer, and my legs feel a little weak and I almost swoon. I'm going to fall, I think in amazement, even though I have never been one to faint.

"The rumors do not lie," the man continues, fixing me with the full force of his smile. "Enchanting, simply enchanting." I sense something powerful and attractive coming off him, and I smile at him under half-lowered eyes, with the look that the younger Corneuve boy declared drove him to distraction.

"Jeanne is one of our newer girls," says Julie, edging herself back into the conversation. She likes him too, I think. Who wouldn't? He's so handsome. The man she calls du Barry ignores her.

"Now," he says, releasing me. I sit back on the window seat and giggle, for what has passed between us is something rather extraordinary. "I have not come on behalf of anyone else, but entirely for you, mademoiselle."

"La, sir. Now what would you mean by that?" I say, feeling

deliciously flirtatious. It is as though we are alone in the shop, Julie of no consequence, nothing of any consequence except for him and me.

"I came here because of you. A woman's charms are more exaggerated than even money, but I declare you are more beautiful than the rumors. Since you have not disappointed me, in any small measure, I would make you a present—of anything in this store."

"Oh!" I exclaim, smiling up at him.

"And do not hold back on any account of the price—I want to be assured that you will remember me favorably."

"Very well," I say, noting the curve of his mouth, the brushed elegance of his coat, and the gleam of his sword handle. "I already know what I want."

"And what would that be, most charming mademoiselle?"

Some part of me wants to say *you*, but instead I say, "The Russian muff. The white one."

"Bring it here," the man instructs Julie, and when she does he takes my hands and fits them inside the snug warmth. My fingers curl in delight, and I can't stop staring at my new admirer.

After he leaves, Julie snatches his money off the counter and whispers low: "The most debauched man in Paris, a provincial adventurer, some say tainted."

"Well, you seemed rather keen on him when he first came in," I say, stroking the snow-soft fur of my new muff. "Don't be jealous."

"I'm not jealous," she snaps, but I know she is.

That night I can hardly sleep for thinking of him—how handsome! And the look in his eyes when he appraised me, the sincere and mutual admiration. Then more presents and gifts, notes sealed with sprinkles of gold leaf, nights at the Opéra and the Comédie-Française. He woos me with an intensity that I find immensely flattering. He is so very good-looking, and charming. And a *comte*! And he must be very rich to have brought me that muff without hesitation.

He is the first man to sweep me off my feet, but I'm still in the air: I haven't fallen yet. But soon? My stomach wobbles like a jelly when I remember the way he caressed my hands last night, before slipping a perfect emerald ring on one finger, paste but still beautiful.

What better life than to be loved by him?

☙

After seven long years of war, peace has come at last and Labille closes the shop so that we may all attend the celebrations. Du Barry fetches me on foot, the streets too crowded for a carriage to pass. His footman goes on ahead, carving us a course with his cane, toward the Place du Paix where two urchins have reserved our places in the stands. Du Barry throws some coins at them and shouts above the crowd: *"Reserved, for you, my princess."* We squeeze in and wait for the royal procession.

"Do you think we'll see the Pompadour?" I shout in his ear.

"Too sick," he shouts back, shaking his head. "Dying, they say."

A magnificent new statue of our king is unveiled in the middle of the square. Louis XV as Victory on a horse, surrounded by statues of the four virtues. Four vices, whispers Paris, and names the ladies who sustain him: Mailly, Vintimille, Châteauroux, and Pompadour.

A man held up by his mistresses.

"And why should he pose as Victory?" hisses someone in the crowd behind us. "That man has only ever killed stags, not enemies." The rain starts to beat down and someone else whispers that even the heavens disapprove of this man, our king, and his scandalous, wretched ways.

Finally the royal procession arrives, the king in an open carriage, ignoring the rain. I catch his eye, or at least I think I do, and a flicker of what seems like recognition passes between us.

"I think he noticed me!" I say in astonishment, turning to du Barry. "Imagine me, being noticed by the king!" Our king was once the most handsome man in France but now he is very hated. I thought he looked nice enough, not the monster I was expecting.

"Now, why are you so surprised? Even someone as ignorant as you, my little dear, must know the king enjoys his women. And you such a fresh beauty of twenty," he says, slipping off one year to show his manners. Du Barry puts his arm around my waist. Heaven. "I know men in his employ—I shall see if you have made an impression."

I am flattered, but what do I want with the king? I know who I want, and he is right beside me.

There are no cheers for the king, but when the queen and his daughters pass, the crowd applauds. The queen looks old and sad, and then we see Madame Adélaïde looking regal and rather fine in a starchy red dress, her three younger sisters cowering in her wake. After the last of the fireworks, the crowds start to get drunk and rowdy, and du Barry insists we leave the danger of the streets. Finally—the invitation I have been longing for.

His apartment on the rue Neuve Saint-Eustache does not disappoint. We sit down to supper in a gold-paneled room, his footman serving us silently.

"Do you own the whole house, sir?" I inquire, sipping my soup, my insides tightening. It is the first time I am alone with a man, and what a man! Tonight he is wearing a dark green coat, the color of old moss, that perfectly matches his penetrating eyes.

"Ah, what a question, my little one. Try an oyster."

"And this is such a fine dining service!" I finger the porcelain. "Is it rented, or do you own the lot?"

"You have a charming bosom," he replies instead, and I blush at the inappropriate compliment. I'm too nervous to eat much, but I do drink quite a bit, and once the oysters and caramel cream are finished, he rises and offers me his arm.

"Let me show you my paintings."

I take his arm, reassured by its solidity. With him, I'll be fine. He leads me through to the next room, and shows me the grand paintings that adorn the panels.

"You are quite the collector, sir," I say politely.

"I like collecting women more," he says, and stares at me. A strong riptide of danger pulls me forward. What do I want with boring men?

"And that one is a Caravaggio, and I do admire this one," he says, pointing to a painting of a serene woman.

"Oh, she's beautiful!"

"She is called the *Mona Lisa*, from the great master da Vinci. You know Leonardo da Vinci, my dear?"

"Of course," I lie.

He takes my arm and steers me into the next room. "No, you don't, silly girl. Now, now," he says, raising a hand, for he knows how I pout when he calls me thus. "A paltry education is no hindrance to one as lovely as you. And it has left you so free and natural."

I laugh. "I'm never accused of being timid." I lean closer, willing him to put his arm around my waist as he did earlier.

"Delightful, in many ways. A woman as beautiful as you are can be forgiven many, many sins." He takes a step back and I can't help myself: I step forward.

"Now, mademoiselle, I have shown you all my paintings but one. In my bedchamber hangs the greatest treasure I own—*Christ and the Fallen Woman*, by Cranach the Younger. Do you wish to see it?"

Though it's dark in the room, I can see his eyes glowing and the lust that is starting to ooze off him, joining with mine. I know where we are going, and suddenly I want to go there. Very much.

"Yes, show it to me."

∾

"Oh, had I known, had I known," he says, his face flushed, his hands caressing my naked body. I am trembling, filled with so many strange emotions. The black-wimpled faces of the nuns rise, then sink down again and disappear into the sheets, and all I can do is giggle. Such pleasure! How mistaken they were, how mistaken the whole world is. *This* should never be bad.

"What a mistake," he says sadly, shaking his head. "Had I but known."

"Known what?" I ask, marveling at his hardness and muscles and coarse hands, so different from my own softness and curves. I lean in and kiss a nipple. How extraordinary—I had never considered men might have nipples! "And you have made no mistake—I too desired this."

"But I had not thought you a virgin! Who would believe an angel such as you would be untarnished at your age? What a missed opportunity." He sits up and shakes me off him. "Ten thousand *livres*," I hear him mutter. "At a minimum."

I'm not sure I fully understand. "You jest? Of course you're jesting. I think I love you."

Barry—as he insists I call him—shakes his head and his wonderful smile reappears. "Mmm, of *course* in jest. I am not one to brood over spilled milk, not when the future awaits in all its magnificence. Ah, my dearest Angel—I was a man searching for gold in these dreary streets and then I found you, so exquisite, so pure. Are you mine, dearest Angel, all mine?"

"I am," I say in adoration, pulling him back toward me, eager for his touch and the newness of his embrace. I wonder if we'll do *it* again?

Within days, I am quit of Labille's—what do I want there now? Madame is sad to see me go, but she kisses me and even allows me to keep my peach dress. I hug little Adélaïde and she presses a sketch of me to her heart, and then a carriage comes—his own carriage, and a handsome one at that! With two horses that almost match—and I am carried off to my new and wonderful life.

Barry is charming, exquisite, funny, fascinating. I don't miss Labille's at all; strangely, though I loved it while I was there, all I can remember now is the jealousy of other girls, Labille bickering over the accounts of the day, the envy I felt when a customer bought something I coveted but could not afford.

Barry makes me an allowance. To dress myself in the grandest fashion, that I might be a compliment to his ancient and proud name. The Barrymores! Above the mantel hangs a giant coat of arms—he tells me he is descended from that ancient Irish family—and I feel flushed and excited.

Life is suddenly perfect. I am the mistress of an important man. My life is beginning and in what a grand fashion! I am, as they say, swept off my feet. And straight onto my back. It is a fall, but a fall cushioned by pillows and a duck-down mattress is no hard fall at all.

Yes, I have fallen, but into the middle of a fairy tale.

Chapter Seven

In which Madame Adélaïde says good-bye to the fish

It has been raining for a week, as though Heaven were crying, and now her funeral cortege has left Versailles. The Marquise de Pompadour breathed her last yesterday on Easter Sunday: how fitting, say her friends, and what an abomination, say her enemies.

Though I despised her and all she stood for, there was a certain harmony of opinion that she served a purpose. She kept my father happy, and possibly out of the hands of more heinous women. My mother the queen even visited her on her deathbed, and today a curious feeling hangs over us, as though all is unmoored, the palace a giant ship that had just pulled anchor and is creaking off into seas unknown.

Papa is devastated—he remained in his apartment all day—but there is no official mourning. I consider this to be a great day for France, and her death is a blow for our enemy the minister Choiseul, an evil man out to destroy our country and break the power of the Church. It is unimaginable that he has not been excommunicated by our pope for his banishment of the Jesuits, the most holy of orders.

Choiseul was the fish woman's crony—her limpet, I think in satisfaction, and applaud myself for my witticism—and now that she is gone, he will have nothing to cling to. The *dévot* party, led by my sainted brother, with ourselves as his godly foot soldiers, will once more rise to prominence.

While it is unchristian to delight in death, I feel that without that pernicious leech at his side, Papa will return to the godly life. Her death is also an opportunity for my sisters and me to regain the favor and the intimacy with our father that we have lost in recent years. Sometimes I think he is growing bored with us, but such thoughts are nonsense: How can one be *bored* by family?

Now my formal *couchée* is done and I am alone in my bed. I cannot sleep and I get out to roam the room, curiously restless. I sleep alone; unlike Sophie, I am not tormented by night terrors and do not need women sleeping at the foot of my bed. My lips curl at her weakness, for I can't image where her fears come from, though Victoire told me the nuns once locked her up in a crypt as punishment. I scoffed at Victoire's foolish lies: impossible that bland little Sophie could have done anything worthy of punishment.

I circle the chamber a few times then hover over to the window and peer out, cautiously, in case the guards pass. She died at Versailles, and there have been processions day and night but now all is quiet, and so it will remain. She might be mourned by her friends but I know that life moves quickly on. I saw it with Henriette and Élisabeth: everyone crying that their grief will never end, then somehow, and quite suddenly, forgotten as life rolls on.

I must broach the matter of her apartment, next door to my own, with Papa. It would be suitable for Louise, whose rooms remain far from us in the Aisle of the Princes. It might be nice to have us all together; Louise still needs watching over.

A crunch of gravel outside and I shrink back from the window, but it is just a guard on horseback, riding slowly around the terrace. I gaze out at the night gardens; all is in blackness save for the lights gleaming from the second floor of the palace at an angle to my wing.

Where is she now? Yes, she confessed, but aren't there some sins that cannot be forgiven, no matter if confession is made? But then my father . . . I quickly squash that line of thought. No, she is in Heaven, of that I am certain.

She was only forty-two, not old at all. Sometimes I have to strain and remember I am already thirty-two—only ten years younger than she—and the sad realization that time, which I once thought I had so much of, is passing fast, with no way to stop it.

I stare out at the black night, resisting my bed. I have a strange urge to flee, to open the windows and step out into the great unknown of the rest of the world. Foolish thoughts. A movement on the second floor, from a lighted room where a window opens and outlines the shadowy form of a man and a woman. A peal of laughter, the woman pushing the man away, then his arms tightening again around her.

A memory rises, unbidden, of a small girl. A foolish girl, but one with determination to spare. Many years ago, when she heard the English were her father's enemy, she decided to go and fight them. I had read the story of Salome, and had thought to bewitch the English king, then cut off his head while he slept. I blush at my folly—I didn't realize what *bewitch* meant. I was a fool, but an energetic one, I think sadly, and one beloved by my father. Vivacious even.

That little fool made her way out of her sleeping chamber, over her woman who snored too much, and out beyond her apartment into the halls, past sleeping guards and indifferent idlers. Papa would be angry, but after I had killed the King of England, I knew he would be proud of me.

I had almost made it as far as the stables when one of the guards recognized me. What a commotion there was! But I gained my father's admiration—indeed, in a way I had not done before, nor since. I can still remember his indulgent laughter and sweet concern as I was admonished the next day.

My hand is on the gilded brass handle of the long windows. I feel its cold metal beneath my fingers, and I slowly turn. I remember that night so vividly, as though it were yesterday and not seventeen years ago. The emptiness of the sleeping palace, that curious feeling of being completely alone. A magical time. Slowly I turn the handle of the window, then realize I don't know if it is locked or not—I have never thought to ask. Then a rumble of thunder in the distance and a pair of foxes run across the gravel,

skittish and afraid, and disappear down the steps of the terrace.
I release the handle and draw back, and realize I have been holding my breath.

ɔ

"*Strappare il* tuo *occhio*—pluck out *thine* eye," I correct Victoire.

We have started studying Italian—Sardinian princes still menace, but only faintly. Louise, the youngest of us, is almost twenty-
seven and can confidently say she has never, in all her study of
history, found a French princess married at that late age—the
eldest she has uncovered was twenty-two. Her shoulders have
straightened out completely, and I thought the time prudent to
turn from Greek to Italian.

"Don't you think we've done enough?" says Victoire, flinging
down her book and stretching out on the sofa, her skirt falling
back to reveal two mismatched shoes.

"Madame de Civrac!" I cry, calling over her *dame d'atour*, who
rises rather slowly from her chair by the fire. "Look at Madame
Victoire's feet!"

"Oh, it's not Civrac's fault," says Victoire, sitting up so her
skirt covers her ankles again. "I just have a corn on my left foot,
and my red shoes are rather tight and I thought a larger shoe
might be more—"

"Enough! I do not need the genealogy of your foot com-
plaints. Now we must finish this verse. Monsieur Garibaldi will
be here tomorrow," I say, referring to our Italian instructor, "and
we must impress him with our reading."

"Why?" asks Louise. Louise once said she thought our study
sessions a "waste of time" but I had no idea what she meant—how
can the meaningful pursuit of knowledge waste time?

I gape at her—she never ceases to confound me. "Why must
we impress him? What sort of question is that?"

"A true one, sister."

"You are most vexing, Louise," I say, and turn back to the
Bible, where Matthew is commanding us to gouge out our eyes.
But in truth it has been almost twenty minutes since we started,

and even I will admit it is quite hard to concentrate in the midst of such a momentous week. It is not five days since the Marquise died, and it is quite possible we have not examined the matter to satisfaction.

"Very well—a short break that we may discuss the current situation," I announce, and Victoire sighs happily. Not gossip, I tell myself, but the mere art of being informed; as the first daughter of France, the one and true Madame, I feel this is within the purview of my duty. The Court can talk of nothing else than who will replace the Pompadour. Every brain is busy; such a matter has not been equaled in importance since we wondered who would replace Benedict as pope.

We close our Italian Bibles and I call to Civrac to join us, as well as my lady Narbonne. Civrac has an infuriating ability to ferret out information, far surpassing my Narbonne's abilities. Her base blood no doubt contributes to her gossipmongering talents: she comes from a very minor branch of the Durfort family, a twig really. Narbonne sometimes disdainfully calls her Grubble, because she has managed to worm her way into the very highest of circles.

"Come now," I say, "we shall discuss this matter of supreme importance. We have been the laughingstock of Europe for having a *bourgeois* mistress in the palace, and we must ensure this never happens again."

"Are you sure that's why we are the laughingstock?" asks Louise, in her infuriatingly calm voice, placing rather too much emphasis on the *we*.

I look at her in astonishment. "What else would Europe have to laugh about? Father's sins are for reproach, not laughter." I think of England, where George III sits on the throne, faithful to his wife. Distressing, really, that the model of morality should be an Englishman, and a Protestant to boot.

"So, who's at the top?" breathes Victoire, opening a cupboard herself and gathering a bottle of cherry cordial and a plate of Malaga raisins. Victoire is a lost sheep as far as decorum is concerned and her ever-present vial of sickly cordial—which she insists is just nectar and not wine—is an indulgence that should be a foreign concept to a daughter of France. She knows my disapproval, but she pays it no heed.

She pours herself a glass and looks around eagerly. "Is it the Duchesse de Gramont? She was at Mama's *cavagnole* yesterday and looked rather flushed and happy."

"No, she's far too old," I dismiss. "What a crone!" I speak of the minister Choiseul's sister Beatrice; a viler, more barren woman I cannot imagine.

"She's about your age," observes Louise. "I believe."

Narbonne shakes her head, picking at her pox scars as she does when she is excited. "No, there is no doubt that the Gramont woman is out. Especially after that incident . . . the forced . . ." she hisses in a low voice, reserved for the greatest of scandals.

"Really, Narbonne, you must remember you are in the presence of sheltered ladies," I say, gesturing to my younger sisters. That we live in a palace of bestial vice is without doubt; equally without doubt is my role as protector of my sisters' virtue.

"Oh, everyone knows that story," says Louise with a giggle. "Such a funny one about that woman raping Papa!"

"Rape," breathes Sophie, choking on a raisin.

"No need for words like that!" I glower at Louise. In truth, I was confused by the story, circulated even before Pompadour's death: the libertine duchess—best known for her seduction of her twelve-year-old nephew—ensured my father had too much to drink one night and then, by force . . . had her way with him?

I confess myself confused.

Civrac nods as though in agreement, and continues: "I heard Madame d'Esparbès is currently at three to one down at Roche's in town."

"Madame d'Amblimont had a dream the king gave her flowers, and we all know what that means," adds Narbonne.

"Of course." I nod sagely, though I don't know what it means.

"What does it mean?" asks Victoire, looking at me.

Narbonne jumps in: "Flowers mean many things, but of course in this case they symbolized lust."

"Lust," squeaks Sophie.

The names and attributes, chances and fortune of many other ladies are thrown into the mix:

"The Duchesse de Mirepoix's niece? I can scarcely countenance it."

"Gabrielle de Rohan? She looked rather fine in that pink shawl last week."

"But the child is only thirteen!"

"I believe we are forgetting someone," I say, when I judge the conversation has reached a silly low point—the Comtesse de Livry? With her mole-ridden forehead? Ridiculous!

"Who, sister?" asks Victoire eagerly, taking another sip of her cordial, her face almost as red as the cherry liquid.

"Our sainted mother, the queen." Although she is past her sixtieth year, last night she wore a new green gown—I cannot remember ever seeing her in anything but drabber colors—and appeared enlivened with hopes. "We must remind Papa of the joys to be had in the bosom of the family."

"Bosom," murmurs Sophie.

Now it is Louise who appears to choke on her raisins. "Though the list of contenders is long," she says dryly, "I am not sure our mother's name is on it."

"Louise-Marie! Remember your place! Your sardonism"—I say it smoothly and confidently, though I am not sure it is an actual word—"is sadly misplaced. We must wish for what is in the best interests of our father's soul."

Louise snorts and stands up suddenly. "I promised Clothilde I'd come and see her this afternoon, then I'm going to Mass again," she says, referring to our little niece.

"Oh, I'll come as well!" exclaims Victoire eagerly, jumping up and nudging Sophie along too. "To Clothilde's, I mean, not to Mass."

"But have we quite finished? The list of ladies?"

"I believe we have, sister," says Louise firmly.

"Well go, then," I say in irritation. Certainly we must keep a close eye on our nieces and nephews—their mother's Saxon influence must be contained, and I suspect their governess, the Duchesse de Marsan, of flightiness and worse—but I do not approve of visits at any hour of the day. Order and schedule must be kept to, or the world will fall flat.

My sisters leave with their ladies and I motion that mine may go as well. I sit back with my Italian Bible and attempt to resume my studies, but I cannot concentrate on the words.

"It is better for you to enter the kingdom of God with one eye—*É meglio per te entrare nel regno di Dio con un occhio solo*," I read over and over again. "*Con un occhio solo.*"

There was one name missing from the list that we discussed. Myself. The Marquise kept my father entertained as a companion, a marvel of platonic friendship, and in that role I am confident I could replace her. Of course I would not be the procuress she was, but all her other roles I could gladly—and capably—fill.

I had Narbonne seek out Collin, the Marquise's steward, and she obtained from him a list of the Marquise's books. My plan is to read all of them, and thus provide my father with the same level of conversation and companionship that the fish woman did. I smile in pleasure at my cunning.

I shall start with *The Grammatical Dictionary of Geography*. No, perhaps *The Ecclesiastical and Civil History of the French Cities and Provinces*? *The Kingdom of Vegetables*?

Chapter Eight

In which Jeanne descends

Ma comes to keep house for us, and concedes that the kitchen is a good size, with a nice window looking into the courtyard. Barry is all charm to her, but despite his efforts, she's not as enamored of him as I am. She says the magnificent paintings are copies, not originals, and bad ones at that: surely Jesus never wore breeches. The monk Guimard is suspicious as well, and tells me that all the magnificent books in the library are uncut.

I had thought Barry was the owner of the whole house, but he only has two floors; nonetheless the upstairs family are quiet and of good character. I also find the furniture is rented—there was a loud argument over a marble table, carried away by two men in gray that happened the week after I arrived—but those small worries are easily forgotten.

"But he's a *comte*. And he loves me. He'll take care of me." I smile and think how safe I feel in his arms. Safe, and wonderful.

"I was thirty when I fell," sighs Ma. Though past fifty, she is still very beautiful. "But you—you're so young." But she doesn't protest too much; she is a pragmatic woman and knows the value of a roof over her head.

"I'm not too young! And would you have me rot away at Labille's forever?"

"I thought you liked it there!"

"I did, but this is pounds better. Pounds and pounds! Besides, I am the *Comtesse du Barry*!" I say in satisfaction, leaning over to dip my finger into the mound of almonds my mother is chopping. That's what he calls me, and I accept the title with delight. Imagine me, a countess!

"Turn the spit there, dearest. Madame Paquin wanted hers delivered an hour ago."

I do as she bids, holding an apron over me to shield my cream satin robe, trimmed with soft tickly rabbit fur, from the chicken grease.

"This life could give you the world, or the gutter," sighs Ma, suddenly looking old. "I always feared you'd take the flowery path, but you must beware the thorns and bees."

I laugh at her words: of course I take the flowery path! Who would walk amongst barren fields when one can skip in the sunshine of a flowered meadow? There's only one street I want to walk down, and that's the easy one.

There are others in our house—the footman Bonnet, as silent as he is tall, and a woman called Dorothée, her nose rotted away from syphilis. She used to keep house, and perhaps more, for Barry, but now her world is much reduced and she mostly lies on a pallet in a corner of the kitchen; Barry complains she is as useless as a button without a hole.

"But why can't she take the mercury cure?" I demand, aghast at the young woman's face. She must have been very beautiful, once.

"No use, no use. The whole world knows her ills and none would touch her again. She has already cost me a great deal," he finishes grimly. Sometimes I think I see glimpses of a harder and crueler man, but those shadows flit so quickly across his face that I can never be sure. "And she's on the list for a free cure at La Salpêtrière; they'll get to her soon enough, I'm sure."

I put away my doubts; there is no use in looking for shadows in the sunlight. And there is so much to enjoy about my new life—opera, theaters, parties, and balls—and everywhere I am feted as Barry's mistress.

There is work, too, for this sweet gay life must be paid for.

Barry's official income is from a contract to supply food, uniforms, and munitions to three regiments in Corsica, but he always says that is paltry money compared to where the real fortune lies: he runs a gambling table several times a week from our salon, and keeps the local police well oiled with money to turn a blind eye.

I act as hostess at the table. It reminds me a little of Labille's, only the men are of a much higher quality and include many court nobles. Among others, I meet the Duc d'Ayen; the Duc de Lauzun; the Duc de Duras and the Marquis de La Tour du Pin. The old Duc de Richelieu is also a good friend of Barry's. I didn't think he recognized me, but then one night he made a wicked comment about debauching a glove of mine.

Other ladies come and stay for a few days, and help me at the table; sometimes the gamblers flirt with them so successfully that they retire to a private room together. Once I heard Dorothée whisper, in what was left of her voice, that Barry was nothing more than a common procurer.

I'm sure not; he is a kindhearted man, and how can a count be common?

Business increases in the wake of my arrival, and what a fine thing it is to be admired and praised, the men slipping me coins when they win, accepting my consolation and offers of wine when they lose. Which is quite often; Barry has dealings with a man who delivers him new packs of cards—with special markings only he understands—every week.

My manners are improving, though Barry says I am still too free and easy. I shrug (something he hates) and tell him that none of our guests have ever complained.

"Darling, you saw the Duc de Lauzun last night—he went positively pink with pleasure when I grabbed his arm after he won!"

Barry snorts. "If you're going to manhandle the men, Jeanne"—he doesn't call me Angel very much these days—"at least do it where it counts."

I hate it when he is in a bad mood, but it seems he often is these days.

"And the way you laughed, throwing back your head like that, we could see quite down your throat."

"And do you not enjoy the view?" I say archly. Barry has taught me many things and now there is no part of my anatomy that does not hold memories for me. He introduces me to pleasures, some of which threaten to blind me with their unbearable sweetness, and even insists we make love in the Turkish fashion. He always declares himself delighted with me and my sexual training, though I think *training* an odd word.

ᴄⁿ

"I didn't know you had a son!"

"I do," he says proudly. I don't ask after his wife; he has implied she is dead and the memory pains him too much. If she is dead, might he marry *me*?

Adolphe, Barry's adolescent son, has arrived from Toulouse. With the backing of the Duc de Richelieu, Barry was able to secure a post for him at Versailles as one of the king's pages.

"We'll get Adolphe in there, he'll cultivate all the right people, and then that scoundrel Le Bel can suck my sword, and then we'll get you there."

"Oh, la, what do I want with Versailles?" I say in irritation. We have this conversation far too often. When Barry drinks, he rails at Dorothée in the kitchens, and moans about how his chance with her was blocked by the king's valet Le Bel, and since then none of his girls has succeeded.

Why, how many have you had? I want to ask, but then decide I don't want to know.

"What do you not want with Versailles!" scorns Barry. He goes to Court once a month, always in a fluster about which coat to wear and whether his stockings are decently darned and if his sword is rusty. He doesn't get on with the king's ministers, especially the powerful Choiseul, and he always returns in a bad mood, his contracts in jeopardy and never having achieved what he hoped for.

Now, with Adolphe there, he feels the tide is turning.

"So, what news, boy?" he asks when Adolphe visits us in Paris. Barry is lying on a sofa, stewing over his account books—last night the Duc de Duras had spectacular and unexpected luck at *comète*.

"Certainly, Father. I heard that Madame Adélaïde is now studying Italian." His son is very handsome and very young; the image of his father, had I known him twenty years before. Our like is instant and mutual.

"Oh, not about her, my boy," says Barry with a shudder. "Tell me something of consequence, something important to *me*."

"Sorry, Father," says Adolphe mildly.

"So who is the king with now?" demands Barry. The king's mistress Pompadour died a few years ago, and ever since the Court has played a merry game of guessing who will replace her. Though betting on each lady's chance is more exciting than even *beriberi*, as the Duc de Lauzun declared last week, no one ever seems to win.

"Well," says Adolphe, blushing and looking far too young, "they say there was a certain Madame d'Esparbès, but she was indiscreet and Choiseul banished her."

"That man is determined to deny the king every pleasure," says Barry grimly. I've never met the great minister, but Barry describes him as an orange, blobby toad who only wishes to thwart his ambitions. "Besides, that is old news."

"They also talk of a Comtesse de Séran; she's rather old but the king finds her good company," says Adolphe. I smile at him and he blushes yet again—what a charming boy. Sixteen. So like his father, but without the faults and grumbles.

I wonder what it would be like if he came to my room later, and by the way he stares at me I know he is thinking the same. It's past noon but I am still in my pretty lace robe, so I shift and allow it to fall away, just a touch. I take a lock of my hair and twirl it, and regard him from under my lids. I've never done *it* with anyone but Barry.

"They say the king has three houses in town now," says Adolphe, staring at me, a bright cherry flush creeping up his throat. "But that might just be exaggeration."

Barry shakes his head—for once I am glad he is a self-absorbed man—and says he wishes no talk of those houses, not after the fiasco with Dorothée. I'm not sure why he cares; it's not like he has another girl he wants to place there.

"The Pompadour had a toucan," says Adolphe to me, sticking a finger through my canary's cage. The Lord Fitz-James presented it to me last month and I call her Fifi. She trills prettily at Adolphe's waggling finger. "It—the toucan—only understands Portuguese. She left it to the Prince de Soubise, and we are tasked with its care."

He takes a grape from a dish on the table and pushes it through Fifi's cage. "Poor bird," he says suddenly.

"Why?" I ask, motioning for him to feed me a grape too. I take it straight from his fingers, causing him to blush purple and dart his eyes at his father, still absorbed in his account book.

"Trapped in a cage. No freedom." Adolphe gulps, staring at me in fright and adoration.

"Oh, be a man. You are too kindhearted," grunts Barry, throwing the account book on the floor and stretching back on the sofa. The afternoon is passing away as so many do; we rise late, nibble on the remains of the food from the night before, watch while Dorothée and Ma prepare the tables for the night's pleasure.

"But you shouldn't feel sorry for Fifi! She has all she wants."

"But she is trapped—birds are made to fly!"

"Perhaps it's because you're a boy," I say kindly. "A man, I mean to say." I am sure Fifi is as happy as I am, safe here in this house, not scrounging for scraps on the dirty streets.

"Well, I would let her go free!" declares Adolphe with the passion of youth, and his father tells him to shut up, he's trying to take a nap. I get up and put a wool throw gently over Barry, kiss his forehead, then go to stand by Adolphe at Fifi's cage.

"Do you want to set her free?" I whisper, putting my hand on his arm. I imagine doing with him all the things that Barry has taught me, and my grip on his arm tightens.

☙

"With him?" I am confused. It is late and I have drunk more than usual; every time I turned around Barry was there, with another glass.

The Baron de Jumilhac squeezes my hand and Barry smiles at me, and I sense he is alert and watchful under his sloppy mask of drink. I am confused; why is he pretending?

"Bu—"

"Now what objection, my dear?" says the baron, leaning closer, and I smell old snuff on his coat. "Such a morsel as you should be shared." I try to smile at him, but then his eyes remind me of that man at Frederica's.

"Like the lemon sorbet," slurs Barry. "Everyone must have a bite." Ma spent all day preparing a rich cream sorbet and had asked Dorothée to help grate the mound of lemons. I can't touch the stuff for fear she might have grated in her scabs, but the other guests lapped it up.

I look at Barry, unsure what is happening, trying to read his expression in the gloaming of the corner. The two men lean closer around me. Behind us a group gambles on; the Chevalier de Soissons is now betting with his rings. But I had better focus on me, for I think there might be danger here. Danger? In my fair gilded cage? I giggle and shake my head. "What is going on?"

"Here," Barry says, suddenly spinning me around and presenting me with another glass. "Drink this."

I do, and the room spins some more. I lean on the baron to stop myself falling, then he is leading me into my chamber—how does he know where I sleep? I feel his hands on my body, his fingers heavy and cold with rings. Not like Barry, I think with a long sigh the color of the darkest, deepest green that matches my sheets. Then he is on top of me and moving against me, but I am not; my legs are so heavy they will never move again.

I sleep.

"Not like that. Not again!" says Barry, pulling back the curtains and my covers. "Not like that again!"

I pull my covers back around me as the brightness of the morning assaults my pounding head.

"It won't be like that again," he repeats grimly, and relief floods me that he regrets what happened. Though what did happen? Little winks of memories flash back, the baron on me, the heavy weight of his body—who undressed me and why am I in this robe? I look down at my hands and see small blue bruises on my wrists.

"He paid good money for you, a fine bundle, but complained later you were not what he had been led to expect! As cold as a fish, was his complaint, and after I'd talked so highly of your virtues, and by *virtues*, I mean skills, and then you embarrass me like this. A fish—is that how you wish to be known? After all our arduous training?"

Oh. An unpleasant truth scuttles beneath the sheets and threatens to come out.

"Answer me!"

"No," I say sullenly, still clutching the sheets around me.

"Not again—I shall not be embarrassed again. Is that clear?"

I gaze up at him.

"Why—is this something that will happen again?" I say in a small voice, hoping to appease the glaring monster before me, and hoping he will reassure me that no, this will never happen again.

"Of course, my dearest," says Barry kindly, now smiling at me in the dazzling way that used to make me weak with desire. "I couldn't keep a pearl such as yourself all for me, now, could I? You are far more valuable in the hands of others." He sits on the bed and strokes my hair tenderly, and to my relief the glaring monster is gone. "Why do you think I have been parading you around for the last year? I have never been a jealous man. And I don't believe you have the makings of a jealous woman."

I gaze at him.

"Now, the baron is a nothing," he continues hurriedly, as

though to get an unpleasant business done and out of the way. "A tax farmer but not a rich one, though how such a thing is possible is quite beyond me. But there are others—there is a certain duke who is keen to try your angelic delights. He'll visit next week."

My stomach lurches and I gaze at him, trying not to blink.

"Now, if you want to lie in," he says, getting up and giving himself a self-satisfied stretch, "I'll send Dorothée up with some chocolate and you can ask her to close the curtains again." He's acting like he is giving me a special treat, but I never get up before noon.

"The Duc de Duras," whispers Barry to me the next week as we prepare the table for the evening's entertainment. "An intimate of the king, and of no better family. He is a fine gourmand, one of the best, they say. You'll show him a good time, won't you, Jeanne?"

He grabs me around the waist and pulls me tightly to him. "You'll show him everything, dearest, won't you? Everything I've taught you."

I bite my lips and take a deep breath. There is no escape from this cosseted cocoon—what would I do without him? How would we survive, me and Ma?

"When?"

"Tonight! Is that not clear?" He pushes me away. "Don't be disobedient, Angel. You'll be out on the street tomorrow if you are."

I stamp my foot. "You misunderstand me! I was asking: When tonight? Before or after the games?"

"Ah! I knew you'd quickly see reason," he says, smiling at me. "You're not as silly as you sometimes pretend." Barry's smile is pure joy, and I think how my knees used to weaken at it. Now I just regard it coolly, and a little sadly. He's a procurer, I think, just like Dorothée said, and that makes me a . . .

"Chicken with honey, in a pot," says my mother, coming in with a huge porcelain dish. I wonder if she knows what happened with the baron. I didn't want to tell her and see the knowing disappointment in her eyes. Besides, she'll know soon enough.

"Do him twice, if he can bear it," Barry whispers, sniffing in appreciation at the tureen, then striding out of the room. He calls to Bonnet to come help him dress, and I can hear the triumph in his voice.

He believes he has won, and perhaps he has, I think as I dip a finger into the sticky sauce that glazes the birds. I thought he was my slave, but I see now I was only fooling myself. My future, which has been waiting in the corners of our house, flitting through the guests' eyes and the worry in my mother's, that future has finally come out of the shadows to meet me, and I find myself looking it squarely in the face.

Chapter Nine

In which Madame Adélaïde comforts her father
and achieves great happiness

L ouis de Narbonne spins around proudly, showing off his
smart red coat with its glittering bronze buttons.

"Wonderful!" Victoire claps as the young boy gives a
courtly bow and his mother looks on indulgently. Narbonne's second son is a very handsome young boy of ten; he is my godson,
and I am ravishingly fond of him. He is so very handsome, almost
as handsome as my father, whom he looks very much like.

As we all compliment the boy on his new coat I grimace,
remembering the horrible rumors that circulated about the child:
that he was the son of my father and Narbonne, even though
she was in Parma at the time of conception; and then, worse—
far worse—that he was the son of my father and . . . and myself.
I choke up, remembering the ugly rumors that took something
so wonderful, my intimacy with Papa in the wake of Henriette's
death, and turned it into something unthinkable and foul, something one could not even bear to say the name of, something—

"Incest," squeaks Sophie, as though reading my mind.

I glare at her. "What did you just say?"

"Insect," she whispers, and points in fright at a spider climb-
ing one of the rose-trellised bookcases. I shake my head to clear it
of the fulsome disgust that had taken hold of me.

"Narbonne," I hiss in irritation, "get one of the women to get
one of the men to—"

"I shall kill it, Mesdames," says little Louis gallantly, and
flicks the spider with his miniature sword onto the parquet, then

finishes it with a satisfying squelch under his shoe. We all applaud in admiration, yet the boy does not even turn pink; even at so young an age, he has admirable presence and control of his emotions. Narbonne is raising him according to the precepts of Rousseau, and though I care not for that freethinker—and have admonished Narbonne many times on the subject—I have to admit he is a fine young man, free and easy but in the most polite way, full of confidence and blossoming manly vigor.

"Now show Mesdames your dance," says Narbonne, smiling at her handsome son. Beside us, Civrac sits winding a spool of thread around her wrist in jealous discontent; her children have none of the fairness and grace of this Louis, and her youngest son has an unfortunate stutter that we cannot countenance.

As the boy prances around the room, I sense movement above. Yes, footsteps above us, in my father's private apartments. Papa must be back from the state council! I shall go and see him, for I—and I alone amongst my sisters—have the right to enter at will. An immense honor and privilege, and one that demonstrates the high regard my father holds me in. Me!

After the fish woman's death, he was ravaged by grief, and it was a most satisfactory year. A wonderful year, even. As I had hoped, the death of the Pompadour left a hole in his heart that he filled by turning to his family. We encircled him with love, and the force of us all together—my brother the dauphin; Josepha, his wife; we four daughters—created a powerful web with him nestled in the center. While daily prayer meetings were quickly abandoned—much to my pious brother's dismay—we still hold private suppers that Papa attends with what appears to be sincere enjoyment. I take pains to keep myself apprised of politics and current events, and he listens, and once last month he even complimented me on my advice!

"That book you recommended, Adélaïde," he said. "The one from Confucius? I read it and found it most useful." And then followed a satisfying discussion about the comparative merits of French and Chinese thought! What a triumph and an honor! At the time I wanted to melt, simply melt in happiness, and even today the memory of that sweet intimacy makes my heart sing.

Perhaps, I sometimes think in satisfaction when I am in my bed and alone, with my deeper thoughts allowed to run unchecked after the last stays of my bodice and the constraints of the day have been removed . . . perhaps it has even been the happiest year of my life.

I rise in pleasure and little Louis de Narbonne frowns and stops his dance.

"I must apologize, my dears," I say, happiness making my voice magnanimous, "but the privilege to see Papa when I want was only extended to me." Of course, everyone knows that, but reminders can be so very satisfying, especially in front of my sister Louise.

"Didn't we just see Papa this morning?" Louise asks, perfectly unruffled as usual.

"Of course," I say shortly, motioning to Narbonne to bring a hand mirror from one of the attending women. "But I do this for him, for I know how he values my company."

Louise just raises her eyebrows; jealousy, I have decided, comes in many forms, and from my little truculent sister, it appears wrapped in nonchalance and veiled threats about overstaying my welcome. Nonsense. Once a welcome is extended, how could it be overstayed?

I finish fussing with my hair—the summer heat has made it bristle more than usual—and walk up the small set of stairs that connects one of my antechambers to Papa's private apartment, those intimate rooms that had last been open to me after the death of my sister Henriette in 1752. Thirteen years ago. And though my father still grieves for the fish woman, this time I need not share his sorrow.

"Adélaïde!" Papa looks up at me in astonishment. "How did you know I was here? I took pains not to disturb you."

"I can always hear you, Papa," I say with a broad smile, and he smiles briefly back.

"But I did not expect to see you here this afternoon—do you not have your trumpet lesson?"

"Indeed, Papa," I say, crossing the room to curtsy over his hand, "but Victoire is so far behind, not to mention Sophie, that I thought it best to leave them to the care of the master for extra practice. So they may attempt to advance to my level." I sidle a glance at the stack of papers on his desk. "More dispatches from Vaudreuil?" I ask.

"Indeed. The Americans continue to resist paying their taxes to the British Crown."

"A travesty," I murmur. I keep myself well abreast—well ahead, I mean to say—of events unfolding around the festering American revolt.

"Of course we must side against the British, but Choiseul does admire them in some measure," continues Papa, looking lost in thought.

"Choiseul admires the British? That man does not have France's best interests at heart!" I say before I can stop myself. Papa still cleaves to that unholy man, but unlike with the Pompadour, now I try to hide my antagonism. Sometimes I even feel superior to Louise, whose religious convictions are so strong she will not say the man's name or tolerate hearing it without crossing herself, and looking as though she would like to spit.

Papa shakes his head. "I too admire the British," he says. "Able to pass new taxes. Their Parliament at least serves a purpose, unlike our wretched Parlement, which refuses to pass—"

"But our Parlement does pass new taxes!" I say in astonishment. Admire the British? "Was there not a new one on firewood, and another on rags, passed just last week?"

"Yes, but taxing the poor, again? Choiseul says we cannot wring water from a stone—it is the wealthy who must pay more. But our dear parlementarians resist imposing taxes that inconvenience them. Whereas with the British model, the men of Parliament are elected to their seats; they do not inherit them."

"But that results in common men in the government!"

"They might be men of merit."

"But men of noble birth are by rights men of merit," I say, not sure I should be arguing with my father, yet at the same time relishing the liveliness of our conversation. Certainly, the men in our Parlement are not of the highest nobility, but at least they are not *bourgeois* like the men in the British Parliament. My father just raises his eyebrows and something deep and weary passes over his face.

"Sometimes I am not sure, Adélaïde, not sure at all. Men of lower birth can be most capable; I remember my dear old Fleury."

I frown, and rack my brain to think of another example in order to agree with him. Unfortunately the only one of low blood I know is Civrac—her pretensions to gentility are as thin as a strand of hair and just as weak—but her ability to uncover gossip and untangle relationships is rather noble, and—

Papa rises rather abruptly. "Was there anything in particular you wished to see me about, Adélaïde?"

"Well, no. That is to say—we are planning another supper tomorrow," I improvise, "and would be most honored if you could attend. Monseigneur le Dauphin is feeling better." Our dear brother's health has unfortunately been declining all year: he has a troublesome cough and appears to be getting fatter by the hour.

"I am afraid he will pop," Josepha cried last week, the anguish on her face almost unbearable to see. We are all very fond of Josepha, despite her Saxon blood, and consider her as a sister.

"Nonsense," I told her, to calm her fears. "He is no danger, surely, perhaps just partial to the pasta and sweets he loved as a child."

"Yes, the news of Monseigneur le Dauphin's improving health has gladdened me, but I do not believe I will be able to attend your supper, my dear," Papa says, and though I fancy I hear some regret, there is a sheepish and buoyant undertone to his words. I search his face, feeling my breath growing shallower and tighter.

"A prior engagement—a friend, in town. I have promised to visit her. Him."

"Of course, Papa. Friends are all the more necessary as we grieve."

"Yes—grieve," he says, rather absentmindedly, and suddenly smiles. "Dearest Adélaïde, there is no need to inconvenience yourself by coming up again tomorrow. I shall visit you and your lady sisters in the morning, and would be most pleased to hear your progress on the trumpet."

He leaves, and as I descend the narrow staircase back to my own rooms, I try to brush away my faint fears. Is he withdrawing from us again? Have we bored him? My intimacy with him is my most dearly beloved treasure, and the thought that he might be leaving our fold is unbearable. I shake my head and push my silly thoughts aside. Certainly, it is good he has friends, and did not Civrac mention something about an old friend returned to town, that the king was wanting to see? An Irishwoman, now called the Comtesse de Flaghac?

A friend. Yes, surely.

Chapter Ten

In which Jeanne experiences grim times

"A milk cow," my mother says sadly. We are in a new house on the rue de la Jussienne—the whole house now!—equipped with handsome furniture in the upstairs rooms and a large, modern kitchen. Ma adds cream to the sauce she is stirring on her gleaming new iron range. "A milk cow. I never thought I'd say it."

"Then don't," I reply curtly. For all the grand rooms upstairs, the kitchen is my favorite place. I yawn and take a sip of my coffee and watch my mother start pounding a pile of chicken breasts. It was a hard night yesterday with the Prince de Ligne. I am stiff and sore today, but I would wager, I think with a smile, that he won't be riding his horse for a week.

I recognize now that Barry is just a scoundrel dealing in secondhand women, but my new future is not all disappointment. The bets are better placed at the gaming tables, and I reap the rewards as my admirers progress from the bonds of petty admiration to full-on worship.

Barry allows me some choice in my men and soon I have a select list of regular clients—admirers—as well as certain others that pay grandly for the privilege. I need only sleep with one man a day, never two, and it is rare that Barry forces me back to someone I do not care for. And making love to other men—well, it seems there is quite the variety in sizes and experiences, and some not altogether disappointing.

The warts on the frog have made themselves known, the warts

Ma saw all along, but he is good to me, and declares himself still enamored of me, though I know he isn't: he's more enamored of the easy life I give him.

"You know how I fear for you," says Ma. "You should find a patron to take you out of here. Stop being a milk cow for that farmer man and start being someone's treasured hen."

"And be kept in a small apartment, perhaps with no kitchen? And then what would you do?"

"Don't you worry about me, child," says Ma grimly, giving one of the breasts a hard whack.

"The Prince de Ligne ate six of your capon pies last night," I tell her, hoping to put her in a better mood. "And declared your *poulet aux amandes* beyond compare."

"What about that new gentleman, the Comte de Montbarrey? The one who visited twice last week. You told me he was in raptures."

"He's short and vain. Finishes too quickly," I say. If I'm going to have a patron, it must be someone I admire. Love even. Some of my admirers are fine men, but none matches my early feelings for Barry, and that makes me sad. Sad and tired.

"Don't hide from me." Barry strides into the kitchen and lifts me by my hair. He releases me but slaps his riding crop menacingly against his thighs. "I've been looking everywhere for you."

"I'm sorry." I know his anger will be over soon; it never lasts. "You're in a bad mood, and already with the brandy? Don't forget you have supper with Richelieu tonight."

"Don't worry about me, girl, let's worry about you. I want you wearing the blue gown, and make sure that wretched girl does your hair properly." He switches me once with the crop and it stings through my thin robe.

"Oh, stop it, I'm not a horse," I say crossly as Barry herds me upstairs.

The future is starting to unfurl before me, rather unpleasantly, in an endless succession of men and wearisome entertaining. I'm getting tired of this life, and of his bullying. I tell him as much while Henriette starts to dress my hair.

"And you raging at me like a bull all the time; it's bad for your health. And for mine. I'll leave," I say, and it is more than an idle threat—I haven't told Ma, but the Comte de Saint-Foix promised me an apartment and an allowance. I'm not sure I trust him, but perhaps I should.

"Pish—you know you are nothing without me," says Barry, flicking his crop over my philodendron plant, shredding the leaves.

"But it seems that *with* you I am still nothing, so where is the good in that? And leave my plant alone."

"I'll throw you out onto the pavement if you don't mind me."

"Oh, throw me out," I say in irritation. "Or I'll walk out myself."

"I'll make sure you don't walk half a block before Sartine claps you in the Bastille," he says, referring to the head of the Parisian police.

"You don't have that power."

"Try me, girl, try me."

We glare at each other, the air in my boudoir as stale as this life. Henriette intently combs one ringlet, over and again, waiting for a break in the hostilities.

"You're never getting rid of me," hisses Barry, completely contradicting himself. We have these conversations far too often. I know he is a frustrated man with hopes for more, but the glittering doors of Versailles remain closed to him, and therefore to me.

He leaves my shredded plant and sits down on the bed. "Now, Ayen is an intimate of the king—you will charm him, you hear?"

"Of course I'll charm him," I say, patting my head and admiring the height of my coiffure. I remember Ayen as an older man, kind, with an affection for wigs of all sorts. Certainly he will appreciate this new hairstyle. Henriette fetches a jug of hot water from the kitchens and I wash at the stand in the corner while

Barry watches. I rouge my nipples and dab my nether parts with a new scent I bought last week. I dab some on Henriette and we both sniff in appreciation.

"Patchouli—isn't it fabulous?"

Henriette helps me into my chemise and a beautiful green beribboned corset, and ties my pink silk stockings with pretty blue ribbons. I pull on a simple gown of gauzy white cotton—I can never abide big, heavy dresses, and for one in my position . . . best to save the ruffles and puffles for what lies beneath.

"You look fine," says Barry grudgingly. "Still fresh and radiant, though you're as used as an old slipper. And no coarsening or stretching," he finishes, alluding to my lack of pregnancies. I smile, a little wearily; it's true there have been no inconveniences or even messy failures. Rather ideal for one in my position, I sometimes think; perhaps I am simply not one of those women that God has graced with fertility.

I pull a ringlet from my head and let it curl around my shoulders. I wish I could leave my hair loose and run through the streets with it flowing all around me, but of course I can't: I'm not a common prostitute. I wrap myself in a magnificent cape of dark blue wool, armor against the chills of the dark March day, and out I go to work.

৶

The house is small and private, hidden behind a narrow courtyard. A man in livery helps me down from the coach and ushers me inside. The little house is plush and voluptuous, a small jeweled aerie. From somewhere on the floor above I can hear a child laughing, the sound out of place amidst the discreet elegance.

A footman leads me into a small room with a bed, a sofa, and a table set with a giant tureen in the shape of a goose. I lift up the lid and smell—goose stew, delicious. And the delicate porcelain box in the shape of asparagus also reveals asparagus.

"Ah, you are hungry, mademoiselle, hungry?" says the Duc d'Ayen, coming into the room, followed by a slack-eyed lackey. "And look at you—ravishing!"

"Why, thank you! And congratulations, Monsieur." His father recently died and he became the Duc de Noailles and head of that powerful family.

"Yes, yes, indeed an honor. Now Richelieu was insistent I meet with you again; he claimed the years have only increased your loveliness. Unusual in your profession, but his words ring true."

I smile at him and regard him from under half-closed eyes. Men always think themselves so witty, but I find them as transparent as angel wings.

He is dressed in a quilted velvet robe and his slippers have bells on their toes that tinkle softly as he moves. Without his wig and the fine costume of the gambling house, he reminds me of the monk Guimard, and I feel a sudden rush of tenderness for him. Ma can't understand how I can love everyone, but I do.

"Now, has your man spoken of my little project?" he asks, referring to Barry.

"Not at all," I say, sitting down at the table, hoping we can eat.

"Well, I have a great many interests, mademoiselle," he starts, sitting down and motioning for me to serve him. He starts to drone on and I regard him with a look of fixed interest. He is a kind man; one can always tell by their eyes. I wonder if he will want me to stay the night? I should rather like to be home and in bed, and I said I'd accompany Ma to Les Halles tomorrow . . .

". . . a quiet evening at home," Ayen finishes up, and I smile at him, to cover the fact I have not been listening. "Now, about this project."

"Yes, sir, I am certainly intrigued. This stew is delicious, and the asparagus so well prepared."

"Suck one for me."

I do as he says. It won't be long now.

He swallows, but continues talking, shoveling in his stew rather quickly. "I have long had an interest in wigs."

I nod; at the table last month, he wore an elaborate wig of dyed red hair, and looked quite ridiculous, but you could tell he thought it was the most fashionable thing.

"Not just the styles, but wigs of different hair interest me very much. Horsehair, of course, and human hair, and I even have a wig made from rabbit hair—fur, I suppose. I am very proud of it. Very white, and no need for powder, and feels most comfortable on the head. That acquisition led me to think of another form of hair, and my friend, the Marquis de Merquin . . ."

My thighs tighten as I understand where this is going. At least . . . at least this is a fair demand, and not one that will try me either morally or physically.

"A clipping, just a clipping, and then I will mix them all together . . . gathered together as though in a stew . . . such pleasure."

I congratulate him on his wonderful idea, and giggle to think of these private moments when the great men of this land are revealed for what they really are: men. Avid and greedy and ruled by their passions and desires.

"What a wonderful, naughty idea!" I exclaim, as though in delight. "And where would you wear this wig?"

"Ah, an excellent question, indeed. I think only at home. It shall bring me private joy, for I like the idea of the different hairs mingling, of all the ladies whose pleasures I have sampled." He checks himself: "All the *women*, I should say, for my wife is a lady and her hair will certainly not be included."

He stands up and I take a last bite before I rise as well.

"Now, if you permit?" he says greedily, looking at me as though I am more of the goose stew. I lift off my dress and continue stripping in response to his hand that waves me toward nakedness. The room is hot and cozy, and soon I am naked but still pleasingly warm.

"Excellent, excellent," Ayen says, tickling his hands through my patch as though it were a pet cat. "This is a fine bushy arbor. None of that baldness associated with mercury cures. Charles!" he calls loudly, making me jump. The same slack-eyed lackey returns.

"The equipment," commands Ayen, and soon a salver is brought with a miniature pair of scissors and a large silver box.

"Can I open it?" I ask, and before he answers, I lift the lid to reveal a large nest of curly hairs, of all different colors and textures. "Oh, you have so much already!"

"Indeed, indeed," he says proudly, picking out a handful. "You see, this white stuff, very fine, from an albino—have you ever seen an albino? Most astonishing and rare. And this bunch here, from a Negress indeed, a most astonishing texture. Now," he commands, taking my hand and forcing me to put the clump back in the box, "stand still while I trim your exquisite bush."

Chapter Eleven

In which Madame Adélaïde is pursued by the beast

I look critically at the rosebush, then snip off a deadhead with my scissors and drop it into the basket Narbonne is holding. In truth, I am not overly fond of gardening, but it does provide a small diversion, a nice complement to the life of the mind my intellect steers me to.

We are in our little garden in a corner of the Stag's Court, separated from the rest of the courtyard by a grilled fence. Here we have a private garden with a fountain, orange pots, several rock gardens, and planters. On the walls a hundred stag heads, which give the larger courtyard its name, watch over us, and above them are the windows of the king's private apartments.

The gardener is supervising his men as they bring out the pots; they wintered in the Orangery and now they are being brought out to welcome spring. In addition to our usual flowers, this year Victoire wants to grow more vegetables. I am thinking tomatoes. I have a yen for their lush red fruit, and though their name makes Sophie blush—love apples—I think a planting would do.

But tomatoes. How can we think of tomatoes—or even marrows, as Civrac so inappropriately suggested—when our dear mother is dying?

I abandon my scissors and twist another deadhead off the rosebush with my hands. It didn't die over the winter, I think. The flowers may have, but not the plant itself. Beside me, Victoire is complaining of the cold; inside, Sophie is crying and Louise is praying for our mother's soul.

Outside, the air is fresh and crisp as spring arrives, but inside all the windows are shut, the Grand Apartments draped in black, the chapel bells tolling day and night. For many months we have known the end was near; her fever continues unabated and now she is increasingly frail and forgetful. Last week she could barely open her eyes, and when she did, she smiled and greeted me as Saint Polycarpe.

I twist another deadhead off the rosebush. I could twist it away to nothing, I think, shivering as a gust of wind causes the dead leaves from the past winter to skitter around me. Sometimes it seems as though the whole world is dying. Or already dead. These are grim times indeed, our years filled with sorrow.

"Can't we go inside?" whines Victoire. Her eyes are red and she has been weeping too much, and now she is shivering under her thin wool cape. Usually she loves our garden—I have to grudgingly admit her thumb is quite green—and last year her daffodils far surpassed mine. "Let the men do this. And how can we think of planting when Mama is dying?"

"Oh, go!" I snap in irritation. I cannot bear to be inside, to be reminded of my mother's impending death, and of all the other deaths. Perhaps a carriage ride this afternoon? But no—we are expected at Mass again.

Life passes from one disaster to another; what a trial these last few years have been. Not two years after the passing of the Pompadour my dear brother, future King of France, the hope of all who were godly in this world, died at the age of thirty-six. When he breathed his last, it was as though the whole world stopped breathing. Then Josepha, his wife, died last year; tuberculosis and grief sent her to an early death.

Those blows hit my mother hard—she gave birth to ten living children, yet now only four are left. And now she too lies on her deathbed. I twist another deadhead then move on to the next bush. She was always critical of us; never ceased to remind us of our duty and of our religious instruction, but in other matters she remained mute and distant, preferring the company of her close friends.

I snap off seven more heads. Seven. One for each person I knew and loved, taken from me too early, I think viciously as I throw them into the basket Narbonne holds. My brother, his wife, Henriette, Élisabeth, the little Duke of Burgundy, more dead babies of the dauphine . . . I could have a hundred heads, I think in horror, and that might never be enough.

Never enough. I curl my hand around a stem and feel the sharp pinch of thorns through my gloves. Ghosts everywhere.

"Madame, your gloves," says Narbonne in concern. I shake her away and continue my pruning, aware that Narbonne and the two other ladies are watching me, and that even the men bringing in the pots have chosen this moment to stand and gawp.

"Leave me!" I say suddenly. "Everyone, go. I would be alone."

Under the watchful eye of Richard, the head gardener, the men shuffle off and Victoire and our ladies reenter the palace. I can hear the Comtesse de Chabannes laughing with Civrac, something about a rosebush. So unsuitable, I think, narrowing my eyes. How dare she laugh when our mother is dying? Narbonne stops beside the mullioned doors; when I said leave, she knew it was just my grief talking.

I am never alone.

"I'm going into the gardens," I announce, opening the grilled gate of our little enclosure and walking swiftly through the courtyard, then through the palace to the back terraces. Narbonne shuffles after me, calling frantically to one of the guards. I pull the hood of my cape down around me. I make no show; all are dressed in black and somber colors.

I stalk down the steps of the terrace and past a group of courtiers without slowing for them to greet me. I am alone, I think, hurrying along, the sudden wild idea coming to me to break into a run. I am aware of Narbonne hurrying behind me, joined now by one of my equerries and a guard. I enter a yew-framed alley and my pace slows; I am ashamed now of my rash decision back at the palace. It was just . . . it was just . . . I need to be alone, I need to be gone from that place.

I stop at the entrance to the Labyrinth and find myself impelled to enter.

"Don't follow," I call to Narbonne, and as I disappear into the maze I can hear her telling the guard that Madame wants to be alone.

Madame. I am the one true Madame now; it has not escaped me that with the death of the dauphine and now my mother, it is I who shall lead this Court and be first in precedence and dignity. A burden and responsibility I shall rise to, for Papa's sake. I now do the honors of the Court and host the weekly card parties that my mother used to hold; attendance has decreased—out of respect for her illness, I am sure.

I wend my way through the Labyrinth, past statues representing the animals of Aesop's fables, each adorned with a fountain, the basins now dry and filled with dead leaves on this cold April day. The high walls of the hedges narrow my world and reduce the sky above to thin strips of gray. Does one find comfort or terror in walls? I wonder, then realize I am not alone in here: the dreaded Lady of Introspection has followed me in.

I must concentrate on more immediate matters, I think, hurrying onward, past the fountain representing the Fox and the Stork. We have our music lessons this afternoon, with my beloved Beaumarchais; then another Mass, then another visit with our dying mother. Yesterday, she mistook my sister Louise for Saint Paphnutius, and her smile, full of such love and adoration, was one I had never seen before.

I stop in front of a fountain depicting the Ape and the Dolphin. The dauphin my nephew is the spitting image of his father and a model of piety—through him our darling brother lives. They are talking of his marriage to an Austrian archduchess—I am against the match, and favor instead another Saxon princess.

His future wife, the new dauphine, will certainly have precedence over me, but she will be just a child, ready to yield to my wisdom.

I turn a corner and find the statues of the Cock and the Jewel. I read the inscription:

> *A hungry cock, searching for food*
> *Found instead a pearl.*
> *Had your owner found you, how happy he would be!*
> *But give me a single grain of corn before all the jewels in*
> *   the world.*

For small mercies we must be thankful: there has been no one else for my father, no official mistress, since the death of the fish woman. The ladies of the Court tied themselves in knots trying to win that coveted position, but my father preferred to hunt in town—I shudder at the euphemism—and keep his bestial side away from the purity of the palace and his family. None of the does from that hideous house—houses?—has ever breached the palace walls.

Of course not—unthinkable.

I wish I could say that with the lack of an official mistress, my influence with Papa increased, but it seems that the opposite has happened. The slight, sweet intimacy fostered by sorrow in the wake of Pompadour's death dissipated as quickly as dew in July. I slow down to stare at a statue of a serpent with many heads. Sometimes it seems as though he is bored with us . . . I hurry on, fleeing from the Lady of Introspection.

But Papa seems bored with everyone, and everything, these days. Nothing I can do seems to bring him out of his mood of ir-ritated despair. My hand trails over a porcupine facing a nest of snakes adorning an empty basin, and I notice with irritation that Narbonne was right: my glove is shredded.

I sit down on a small bench and relish the quietness of the scene. When one is surrounded by people, silence is hard to come by, and indeed it can be golden. A crackle of dead leaves and my heart stops. Suddenly I am aware of how alone I am, how isolated. In the gardens, I mean to say. Narbonne standing at the entrance that now seems so far away, with only one guard beside her. The gardens so quiet and deserted on this cold April day, and I, deep inside this twisted maze, alone. What had I been thinking?

Another rustle and the hedgerow in front of me sways ominously. My heart thumps twice. Oh. The gardens are not well guarded. What if it is a man, a stranger? Or worse?

They caught the Beast of Gévaudan last year, a ferocious wolf monster that tore the throats of children and villagers and others who dared enter its forest lair. It was killed—but though it is dead, there are rumors it had a son, or a brother.

Of course, it was caught in the Margeride mountains, many miles from Versailles, but they say it could run as fast as the wind, and perhaps it could travel as far. I imagine it closing in on me through the path of the maze, its fetid furry paws over my body, its jaws on my thighs . . . Oh. Who will save me?

Another rustle in the hedgerow.

"Narbonne!" I squeal. Something dreadful is coming, I know it.

Another rustle and then a yellow bird emerges from the hedge. Just a pretty bird, a finch probably. I follow it as it flies up and disappears into the gray-lead sky, my breath coming slower now. Just a pretty yellow bird.

Still, I can't shake the feeling that something dreadful is coming.

Something horrible is going to happen.

Chapter Twelve

In which Jeanne meets her match, and her destiny

"Something wonderful has happened! Wonderful, wonderful!"

I startle to see Barry in such a good mood. He grabs me by the waist and twirls me around, knocking over a chair in his frenzy. "Our big chance!"

"What's happened?"

"Versailles, my dear, Versailles has happened!"

"You're going to Versailles?"

"*We're* going to Versailles! Finally, the gilded gates have cracked open." Barry beams at me, and in his flushed face I see traces of the handsome man I once loved.

"But is this not an awkward time?" The queen is dying and in Paris the bells toll mournfully throughout the day for a soul not yet dead.

"It is precisely the gloominess of the times, and of his master, that has induced Le Bel to seek answers. Richelieu was finally able to persuade him and I have the invitation here—we are to dine next Tuesday!" Barry's features darken. "And Richelieu has assured him that despite your harlot's life, you are as fresh as a daisy."

"Of course I am," I murmur, thinking of Dorothée dying on a pallet in the kitchen.

"And so this is it! Great good glory!" He picks me up and swings me around again, and I can't help but giggle. Fancy me, going to Versailles! And meeting with the legendary Le Bel!

⁕

I break into a run and sprint through an enormous pair of gilded doors, almost skittering over on the waxed floors. Versailles! Such elegance, grandeur, as though the world were made entirely of crystal and gold. Gloomy black curtains are hung everywhere—the Court is mourning the death of the Duc de Penthièvre, Barry tells me, as well as anticipating the death of the queen—but I can see beyond the gloom to the heavily shrouded magnificence.

"Get back here!" cries Barry, trotting behind me. I almost collide with an older woman, her skirts four feet wide, a thick inch of powder caked over her face. I skip over a pile of what looks like dog shit and run down a slippery marble staircase. I poke my head through an open door and a lady in a fur wrap frowns at me coldly and asks if I have the bacon. I giggle and run on.

Barry catches up with me and grabs my arm. "What are you doing, little fool?"

"Seeing the palace!" I stick my tongue out at him. "We've got plenty of time!"

"We do *not*," says Barry grimly, and I can see he is nervous.

"Oooh, the great Comte du Barry—nervous! Look, you're sweating!"

"Enough! This is my most important night, do you not understand?"

"I want to see more of Versailles," I say with a pout. "Let go of me or I'll scream."

"We'll come back another day, I promise; please, Jeannette, please, Ange, come now."

Oh, fine. I yield to his gentler tone and he steers me back up the stairs. As we approach the landing a large group of courtiers sweeps by, carrying at their center a richly dressed man with bulbous blue eyes and an odd, lumpy nose. His eyes sweep over me in strange disinterest. Barry releases my arm and attempts to leap into the man's path.

"Monsieur de Choiseul! Such a pleasure, such a—" The man Choiseul jerks his head in annoyance and one of his retainers pushes Barry roughly away. The entourage sweeps forward like

a grand wave, leaving detritus and an embarrassed Barry in its
wake.

"A busy man, a busy man," says Barry, following the group
with empty eyes.

"Come," I say kindly. "Let us go to Le Bel's rooms. But promise I can look around after? I've heard the chapel is more magnificent than Heaven."

Barry glares at me.

In a wood-paneled room—cozy and elegant, each panel painted
a soft jewel-like hue—I am introduced to the appreciative guests as
Madame de Vaubernier.

"Oh, is that who I am tonight?" I giggle and take a chair at the
small round table, joining the men who have risen to bow to me.
There is the Duc de Richelieu, smiling at me kindly, and I am delighted to see the handsome Comte de Saint-Foix, one of my constant admirers. Then I am introduced to the famous Le Bel, a tall,
hawklike older man, looking rather nervous and sweaty.

"And the Duc de La Vauguyon, the tutor of the dauphin's children," whispers Barry, a restraining hand on my arm. He's going
to keep it there all night, I think in irritation.

"Those poor motherless beasts," I say to Vauguyon. When the
dauphine died last year, she left three sons and two daughters, the
eldest only fourteen.

Vauguyon smiles thinly. "I am not sure I would refer to my divine charges as *beasts*, but you have the charm of good intentions."

"Oh yes, it's a term of endearment, such as we use in . . ." I
babble on, knowing Le Bel is watching me from across the table.
And Barry as well—his disapproval is curling around me like a
snake. But even if he can no longer see my charms, others certainly can. A pair of footmen bring in several plates for the table
and soon the aroma of oyster loaves and snails pickled in vinegar
and cream heat up the small room.

"I am afraid we are a somber Court these days," remarks Le Bel
as another round of bells starts tolling. His nervous aura has settled somewhat and I know he will soon be under my spell.

"La! The poor lady," I exclaim. "I should hate to hear my death being knelled on every hour."

"If it is of the queen you speak," says Vauguyon smoothly, "she is the most Christian of souls and does not shirk her coming duty."

"Oh, I absolutely adore snails," I say, picking one from the dish and sucking on it greedily. Each of the men leans a little closer and the room gets even warmer. Like living inside a jeweled snuffbox, I observe, and Saint-Foix declares he has never heard prettier words.

Soon I forget I am supposed to be on display and start enjoying myself. The champagne is good and life is good and I decide Versailles is wonderful. After the stuffed calves' tongues and the talk of Guibaudet's latest scandal, and before Barry can upbraid me for pinching Vauguyon when I disagreed with him, Richelieu and Le Bel excuse themselves for the king's formal *couchée*.

"I am sure he will want to see you," whispers Richelieu to me before he leaves, "but just remember the king is having a soft time of it lately; after fifty, the flesh is not always as willing as the heart."

I allow Saint-Foix to fondle a ringlet that has strayed loose from my hair as I tell him a funny story about the Lauzun's losses at *beriberi* the week before. Across the table Vauguyon gazes at me in drunken admiration while Barry pours himself more champagne, his face growing gradually darker. Midnight passes and still no summons. I sigh and know it will be a long carriage ride back with him in this mood.

Well, nothing doing; I take another helping of a delicious sorbet. At least Le Bel is charmed.

"Come and see me next week, and we'll play more than cards," I whisper to Saint-Foix. I suck a spoonful of strawberry sorbet and enjoy his look of complete and utter rapture.

Le Bel returns, looking pleased with himself. He announces to our little group that there is a certain gentleman who would be delighted to make my acquaintance, should I be so interested. Barry thumps the table and bellows in triumph. I smile; I was beginning to wonder myself.

"I did it!" exclaims Barry, thumping the table again. Vauguyon and Saint-Foix rise and bow in reluctant farewell.

"Now I told you to stay away from the champagne," hisses Barry, grabbing my arm as Le Bel grabs his. "After all I have invested in you, all my hard work, you'd better not . . ." I stick my tongue, stained bright strawberry red, out at him as Le Bel hustles him away.

Alone in the small room, I circle the table, sipping champagne and grinning in excitement. He must have been watching—the King of France. And he's about to meet *me*. A movement in the corner and a door hidden in the paneling opens. An older man, wearing a patterned robe of plum velvet, his head unwigged, with two large yellow slippers on his feet, enters.

The king.

Older than I was expecting—of course kings age though their portraits don't. He hasn't had a good time of it recently, with his son and daughter-in-law dying, and now his wife, and it shows in his empty eyes and on his yellow, disillusioned face.

"Madame, you are as lovely as promised." His voice is soft and cultured but rather weary. He looks me over but without much enthusiasm, then sits down at the table and helps himself to a spoonful of the melted strawberry sorbet.

I frown—can he not see how beautiful I am?

"Well, Le Bel isn't going to lie to you, is he?" I say.

"Ah, you have a saucy mouth. All the better, all the better," he says rather indifferently, and pats the chair beside him.

"Come." I extend my hand, and for an instant he looks puzzled; I think he meant I should go to him. Nonetheless he rises, with a weariness beyond his years, and comes toward me. I see a man jaded and lost, younger than Richelieu but without that lecher's *joie de vivre* and virile energy that still remains, despite the weight of years.

"Why such a sigh?" I murmur, pulling him close. "You're walking like you're eighty."

He stiffens, and I remember Richelieu warning me about the king having a soft time of it recently. Not with me, I think, and quick as an earwig, I kiss him on the mouth. The king startles as though I have just shot him. I kiss him again, and suddenly I want this man, so weary and sad in my arms, to know all the pleasures of the world that I can see are missing from his life.

∞

"My angel," he says in wonder the next morning. "My dear, never have I known such a night! You have transported me! Before, I was a man in the galleys, toiling away at dull life; now I am a man reborn."

"Of course you are," I say with satisfaction, thinking how I will crow to Barry. Ha! I stretch on the soft blue sheets, and run an appreciative finger over a lace cushion, then over the king himself.

"Such pleasures you have shown me!" he continues in wonder, grabbing my hand and kissing it. "And that sweet hole of which I have hitherto been in ignorance; that such joy could be derived from such a dark place."

"There are other, even better holes," I whisper in his ear, though there aren't really. It seems the king is a morning man; married chickens, we call them, ready to go when the rooster calls. I would rather sleep a bit more, but the look on his face is very gratifying.

"Oh no, my angel," he says as I reach for him. "No, I am afraid we have no time." He shakes his head but pulls me closer, his arms telling me he never wants to let me go.

"It'll be quicker than a wink," I whisper wetly in his ear, and it is.

Chapter Thirteen

In which Jeanne rides over a bump on the road to happiness

"I am in the arms of an angel," he declared, over and again. "What kind of angel are you?" he asked me, then answered himself: "A saucy, dirty, lovely, kind angel. But an angel, my dearest: never have I awoken to such delights."

I savor his words and the memories, trying to catch every little detail before they disappear. That look of delight when I showed him the way; how he turned from a jaded old man into one filled with tenderness and energy; his doting words (*I have been waiting for you all my life*); the feel of his skin; the smell of verbena on the pillows; the softness of the down mattress; and his childish delight in all that I offered him.

"I have been wandering in the desert for four years," he murmured. "Not forty, as Moses did, but four years is a long enough time. Now I have found you."

I stayed two days and two nights nestled in a room under the eaves of the palace. Then Louis—as he says I must call him—had to prepare for the imminent death of the queen, and I was sent here to this discreet little house in town, just steps from the palace. Barry joins me, flustered and nervous. He promised me—the king, I mean, not Barry—that he would send for me soon. "As soon as I can, my angel," he said, holding me tighter than any man has ever held me.

And now I sit, and wait, and remember. The house is small, but clean and smartly furnished. I wander through the rooms and look at the naked nymphs painted on the salon walls, smile in recognition at a gilded chair with straps, now sitting in an empty bedchamber. It is so quiet here, after all the noise and bustle of Paris—almost like being in the countryside.

I sigh in contentment. The King of France said he loved me! *Me.*

"He is so kind and has the nicest eyes and his voice is so soft and deep, as soft as . . . as . . . a cushion." My eyes fasten on the sofa, then on the delicate tortoiseshell box that arrived that morning, containing a beautiful pearl necklace. "And, oh," I continue, jumping up onto a chair and sticking my tongue out at Barry: "Did I mention he is the king? The King of France?"

Barry puffs his cheeks and watches me silently. He's worried; it's been three days now, and apart from the necklace, no word from the palace. In between worried puffs, he chews on a great pile of candied hazelnuts.

"Three days," he says sharply. "Three days—you're a fool to be dancing around like you own him. He's forgotten you already."

"Oh, la, shut up!" I cry, jumping down and going over to ruffle his hair. "The king loves me. Loves me," I repeat. "Don't be worried." I take a handful of the hazelnuts and scatter them around the room. A cat—there are several in the house—jumps off the mantel and follows one under the sofa.

"Now," I say, leaning down to peck Barry on the cheek, "instead of worrying, you should be planning which government post you want! Or would you like another five supply contracts? Ten?" Or maybe an ambassadorship, I think, twirling away and going to sit by the window; it might be nice to have Barry firmly gone.

"I did consult my lawyer about purchasing a house on the rue de Varennes," he says, puffing out another long sigh then shoveling more of the hazelnuts into his mouth. "But perhaps that was premature, two nights is a flimsy foundation for a lifetime of dreams to hang upon." His voice turns sharper: "And you weren't even looking your best—I told you that yellow dress was too simple! But of course you didn't listen to me, and now see where we are."

"Oh, poof, Barry, you do talk nonsense sometimes. I'm going out for a walk." I grab my cloak and hurry out the door, eager to get away from his sour mood. I want to walk forever and absorb the amazing turn my life has taken, but instead my footsteps lead me toward the Place d'Armes, the giant esplanade in front of the palace. All roads lead here. Ahead of me the palace sits in its golden, spreading glory, hundreds of windows glinting back their secrets, the majestic iron and gold gates hung with great black cloths for the queen's mourning. He is in there, somewhere . . . What is he doing? Is he thinking of me?

"No, no, I'm not buying," I say, pushing the tinker woman away, but then a length of aquamarine chiffon, flimsy and exciting, catches my eye. "Oh, but that's beautiful!" I exclaim, and can't stop myself from touching it.

"The color of your eyes," purrs the woman. "From a lady of the palace, real it is."

Stolen, most likely, but oh, how magnificent. Draped over the bodice of one of my white gowns . . . I rub the fabric between my fingers and it conjures up a soft, luxurious dreamworld. The world of Versailles and the world of being loved by a king. And aquamarine *is* the color of my eyes.

"Five *livres*?"

The woman peeks at my shoes and appraises my cloak.

"Twenty."

"Fine." I grab the chiffon and bury my face in it; it yields a faint trace of roses. From a duchess, no doubt, and I imagine her wearing it in one of the magnificent rooms of the palace, carried always in a magnificent chair, her feet never touching the floor, her life as fine and fleeting as this scarf.

Versailles is a fairyland, a land of mythical beings, Frederica's boudoir but one that spreads for miles and miles. That is the life that I want. Barry always accuses me of being lazy, and without ambition, but suddenly I feel it, a craving so intense and so sharp it stops my heart with longing.

I want that life, and all that it offers.

Le Bel arrives at the house the next day. I am delighted to see him: I had been dreaming the king would ride down himself and claim me, but Le Bel is certainly a good alternative. He stands as though in confusion in the salon, his face white with worry, an ugly sheen turning his complexion gray. He appears to have aged twenty years in less than a week. Worry scurries around the back of my mind and I feel a sudden tingle of foreboding.

"Have a seat, have a seat, monsieur." Barry ushers him over to the grandest chair in the room. Le Bel sits down, and his dazed and terrified look reminds me of a young boy I saw once in a tumbril, on his way to the hangman. A look of bewildered terror; not understanding what was happening, but perceiving somehow the horror to come.

"Are you ill, sir?" I ask kindly.

"My good man, too many brandies at the gaming table last night?" jokes Barry in forced exuberance. He claps the man on the shoulder but Le Bel absorbs the thump without even moving.

"Don't! Can't you see he is unwell?"

Barry ignores me. "Well? Was the king not charmed? Is the king not delighted with his newest angel?" he demands buoyantly, as though to steer Le Bel back to cheerfulness through the force of his will. Le Bel stares dolefully at the floor.

"I knew it," says Barry, turning on me with a sudden vicious sneer. "I knew it, you did not tell me everything. You're a silly girl and could never hold his interest! You lied to me!"

"No, no. The king . . . the king is smitten," quavers Le Bel, rocking slightly now, his eyes still fixed on the floor.

"Ha! But that is good news. Cause for celebration, and brandy!" Barry claps his hands as relief floods over me. He wants me. He loves me.

I smile at Le Bel. "And then so what, monsieur, would be the problem? You seem a little out of sorts, though the news is good." To put it mildly: the man looks as if he's about to have a fit of apoplexy. I saw something similar once, a guest at Barry's gambling table. He was a nobody, really, and was ushered quickly out onto the street, for fear he would fall ill in our house and become our responsibility.

Le Bel takes a huge breath, one hand blindly groping for his knee. "I have made a huge mistake." Still the quavering, trembling voice.

"La, but what mistake, sir? The king is well smitten, as you yourself just said, and I know men when they are . . ."

Le Bel raises a shaky hand and I trail off. His light green coat is now splattered with ominous dark patches where his sweat is seeping through. "I have made a huge mistake," he repeats, shaking his head slowly; a bead of sweat rolls off his nose and onto his chest. "I risk being arrested for this new development. Yes, the king is smitten—but with the lovely *Madame de Vaubernier*, daughter of a baron, widow of a noble."

"No, he's not!" I say. "He's smitten with *me*. Never mind that false name."

"Shut up, Jeanne, and listen to the man!" cries Barry, understanding something I haven't yet.

"The king . . . the king is talking permanency, an apartment in the palace, presentation . . ." Le Bel clutches his chest, gasping for air. I smile and want to skip in happiness. "I tried to tell him the truth about Madame de Vaubernier's past—but he did not seem to care."

Of course he didn't, I think smugly.

"The king is talking thus, thinking the young lady a woman of good family, a widow, or married at least, not a . . . not a . . ." Words fail him and he clutches at his chest again. "Treason, treason. To lie to the king! Oh, I will be hung and quartered as that Damiens fellow, and where is the chicken?"

"What? I think we should get him some wine," I say, looking at the old man's face, now going from gray to red. "Or a doctor."

"A prostitute to become the mistress of the King of France!" he blubbers. "No offense, madame," he adds with effort.

"None taken," I murmur, but I do want to clarify that I am not a common prostitute.

"A trifle, a trifle," Barry says, and though his voice is confident, I can hear the worry beneath. "She will be married, quickly, to a member of a good family . . . There is no need for the king to know the details of her background."

"Oh, he knows," says Le Bel dolefully. "As a chicken knows. He knows everything. He is the King Chicken."

"Come, monsieur," I say, stretching out a firm hand, "come and lie down. You are overwrought." He follows me meekly into the next room, where I lay him across the dining table. His dry creped hands clutch weakly at mine and he mutters some more about the chickens. I stroke his cheek, worried—the man is past seventy—then rejoin Barry in the salon, where I find him drinking brandy.

"This is a bump, a trifle," mutters Barry to himself, staring down at his glass. "We are so close . . . I will not be turned back when we are already at the gates of Elysium. We must not drown ourselves in a glass of water."

"Oh, stop talking in riddles! I'm worried about Monsieur Le Bel—I think he needs a doctor."

"We'll get you married. I would marry you myself . . . but my wife unfortunately lives."

"So you do have a wife!"

"Of course I have a wife! Who do you think Adolphe's mother is?"

"I thought she was dead," I mutter, going out into the hall. "Rose!" I call toward the kitchens for the serving girl. "Send for Dr. Pigot! Our guest is not feeling well."

"There is a solution, there is always a solution." Barry drains his glass and pours himself another.

Who's going to give the summons if Le Bel is unwell? I desperately want to see the king again, to have him hold me in his arms and assure me that I am going to have the finest future in the world. Assure me that he doesn't care about Madame de

Vaubernier, or Mademoiselle l'Ange or any of the dozen other false names and pretenses of my past. I pick up Le Bel's cane and twirl it slowly around. But he said he loved me, and I know he does. I smile; that is all that matters.

"Do you not realize the gravity of this situation?" roars Barry. "What are you smiling for?"

"I just don't see the point in getting upset when, as you said yourself, everything has a solution." I poke the cane as close to his face as I dare. "All that matters is that he is smitten, and wants to see me again."

"I doubt he'd be smitten if he knew your past!"

"Oh, he knows!" I retort. "Please. You don't learn tricks like that at the hands of a dutiful husband." *Only at the hands of debauchers like yourself*, I want to add, but don't.

Suddenly Barry sits up straight and thumps the table.

"I've got it!" he exclaims. "Guillaume!"

"No—don't wake him. Poor old man. Rose! We need the doctor."

"No, not Le Bel, another Guillaume. My dear, you shall be married and you shall be the Comtesse du Barry!"

"You just said you're already married."

"That is true, Geraldine is unfortunately the picture of health, and so I myself am unable to oblige. Fortunately, she is content to languish in Toulouse and makes no more than the usual demands of a discarded wife. However, there is more than one Comte du Barry."

"You're not proposing I marry your son Adolphe, are you?" What a strange marriage that would be. Though not entirely displeasing.

Barry shakes his head. "No, but you are close."

"Oh, just tell me." I stomp my foot.

"My brother!"

"I didn't know you had a brother."

"Yes, indeed, I do—two of them, in fact, both unmarried, as well as two sisters, also, alas, unmarried, though I am sure they are

a comfort to their mother. Yes, that's the ticket. I'll ride out now!"
He jumps up and grabs me around the waist. "Posthaste to Toulouse. And I shall return with one Comte Guillaume du Barry—
soon to be your lawfully wedded husband."

I giggle. "So I really am going to be the Comtesse du Barry?"
I've called myself thus many times; funny how the world works.

"Yes, indeed you are, my darling! I shall get Mother's approval,
the signed papers, and one bridegroom, and be back here within
the week. A fortnight at the most. Rose! Rose!" he cries, exiting
out into the hall. "No, don't go for the doctor, get back here, you
witless girl. Monsieur Le Bel is tired, nothing more. Start packing
my bags—I leave for Toulouse within the hour!"

Chapter Fourteen

*In which Madame Adélaïde makes a
disgusting, and disturbing, discovery*

Though the bells toll on every hour, there are not enough Masses or requiems in this world to adequately honor the queen. Our sainted mother is dead; the length of her illness makes the final passing sad, but not unexpected. A fortune-teller in Paris says that this queen will be the last Queen of France to die in her bed, and in peace. He is hanged for his profane and silly words.

Good Queen Marie. The grief of the people is profound, that of those at Court less so.

Our father hides his grief well and is surprisingly buoyant. Today, when we greeted him on his return from the hunt, he hugged Victoire, attempted to engage Sophie in conversation, exchanged a brief sally with Louise, and even smiled at me.

"How wonderful to see our Papa thus." Victoire sighs in contentment when we return to our rooms. "Papa King must be so delighted that Mother is now in Heaven," she continues, taking a plate with some ham and cheese out of the cupboard and sitting down happily. I am a little dubious—Victoire's silliness only increases as she ages—and much as our sainted father did love our mother, the explanation seems not quite right. I wish it were, but I cannot approve the idea.

He was in a good mood from the hunt, I decide, and share my conclusion with the rest of my sisters. "Did his eyes not glow when he talked of the tenth stag he slaughtered?"

"Still, it did seem a little—ah—disrespectful of Father to be laughing and joking so. And hunting already? It has only been a week."

"Louise-Marie!" I snap at my youngest sister, who, as usual, is looking placidly well pleased with herself. "You shall *not* criticize our father. Especially not at a time like this, when his sorrow is unbounded. Now I would retire, and we will reassemble at seven for the second Mass. Then we shall have a small supper, served in . . ." I look around at my sisters. "Served in Sophie's rooms."

Sophie whimpers and whispers something that sounds like *meat*.

"No, not meat," I say impatiently. "Narbonne told me we're having duck tonight."

I wake the next morning feeling vaguely unsettled from a dream half remembered. Unfortunately the particulars escape me, and though Sophie and Victoire were most eager to know the details (my dreams are invariably more interesting than theirs), I could recall nothing except a vague sentiment of threatening fairness, blondness of hair or such. For some reason I think of the yellow bird that almost attacked me on that frightful day in the Labyrinth—was it in my dream?

At breakfast, I receive a note from the Duc de Choiseul, my father's chief minister and a most hateful man. The note requests an audience! With me!

My routine with my sisters is to take a light repast together, before our formal *levées* and Mass, then go to greet our mother, and then our father. Just Papa now, I think a little sadly, though the walk to Mother's apartments was quite far, and the polished marble on the east staircase apt to be treacherous.

"Choiseul? What do you think he wants?" asks Victoire in astonishment, leaning over the table to help herself to a great dollop of jam for her pastry. As she leans over, her robe falls away to reveal the outline of her chemise, barely covering the outline of her second chemise, barely covering the outline of her ample breasts. I motion frantically to her, but she looks at me in placid confusion, her spoon still poised over the jam pot.

"I'm sure there's more apricot jam if you want it," she says, her robe falling away even more.

"No, no," I hiss, hoping the attendants will not hear. "Your br . . . br . . ." Oh, I cannot bring myself to say the immodest, hateful word.

"Breasts?" breathes Sophie, her knife clattering down on her plate.

"Shhh!"

"Oh!" Victoire laughs. She sits back again and pulls her robe around her and takes a large bite of her jam-laden roll. I glance around but the servants remain at a distance, their eyes respectfully examining the rugs.

I take a deep breath, the crisis averted, and turn back to the matter of the curious note.

"Perhaps now that I am the first lady in the land—the one true Madame—Choiseul seeks to involve me in policy and such." Certainly, the duke is a heinous man. My brother the dauphin was firmly at loggerheads with him, and I continue the feud in his memory. He is known as a detested liberal, and even seeks compromise with Parlement. But father is oddly dependent on him, and I decide that if France needs me, I must agree to a meeting.

"But, sister, might I remind you, Choiseul expelled the Jesuits, the holiest of orders, from France! He is a godless man, practically a *Protestant*." Louise's eyes hold a challenge as she takes a prim sip of her chocolate. While I cannot refute the truth of her words, I ignore them and smile into my cup: he asked for an audience with me, not her.

After breakfast I shoo my sisters out and put on another robe—there must be no repeat of that dreadful scene with Victoire. I receive Choiseul sitting in my salon, my lady Narbonne safely by my side.

After the preliminary pleasantries, most delightfully delivered—though distasteful and rumored to have orange hair beneath his wig, the man is of course of excellent lineage—Choiseul asks if the Comtesse de Narbonne might be excused.

Oh. I try to hide my fluster and look to Narbonne for guidance.

"I may wait in the next room, with the door open?" says Narbonne doubtfully. "Both doors?"

Oh. Oh, well.

But I am the *Madame*, I remind myself. The first lady of France. I must be fearless. I incline my head that Narbonne may go and then I am alone with Choiseul. Alone, in a room, with a man, only an open door between myself and the possibility of . . . I breathe a little deeper, willing myself to calmness. Suddenly the room seems larger and colder. Alone, with Choiseul, who despite his rather puggish looks, is a man that few beauties are cruel to. A man who is not my brother, not even a rela—

"Madame," says Choiseul, bringing his chair toward me; the possibility of a ravishment inches closer. "Might I approach, Madame, and speak in lowered voice?"

"Of course." I hold my breath as he moves the chair closer until he is sitting but a few feet away. I should have received after my *levée*, I think in a panic: the panniers of my court robes three feet wide and known to keep even the most ardent of lovers at bay. Those that approach from the side, at least.

"I have some bad news, I fear, Madame," he says, looking suitably stricken. I feel my heart beating and my thoughts fly to my father, my own precarious situation forgotten.

"It concerns Our Majesty."

"My father has been looking well recently. He has come out of the shadow my dear mother's death imposed upon him," I whisper, proud of finding my voice, though I speak low as this occasion demands—this appears to be an *intimate* meeting. "He even laughed yesterday at the *débottée*."

Choiseul coughs delicately. "Yes, His Majesty's light demeanor has been well remarked upon. So well, in fact, that I had my men seek and confirm the source of it."

Before he can continue, I know what he is going to say. Suddenly it all makes sense: the smiles, the kind inquiries, the boyish bounce in his step, the *bonhomie* that fair radiated off him.

A woman.

Oh, my father, how can we keep you strong?

A woman.

I am disgusted, of course, but secretly pleased that Choiseul has chosen to share the news with me. But who? My thoughts fly to the Princesse de Chalais. Or is Esparbès, recalled? The Comtesse de Flaghac?

"Who?" I breathe.

"You are very astute, Madame, while remaining the epitome of discretion."

"Valenciennes? Brionne?" I spit out.

"No, it is none of those ladies. It is far, far, worse."

"Who could be worse than the Brionne?" I demand. "Oh! The Duchesse de Gramont?"

Choiseul looks taken aback. Of course; the hideous duchess is his sister.

"No, Madame, it is not, though Madame de Gramont remains good friends with the king. But alas, it is no lady that has bewitched our sovereign."

"No lady?" I gasp. But . . . a man? Oh. I grip the sides of my chair and find my breath coming in short, ragged waves. I have heard rumors, of course, of such things, mainly in pagan countries or in the Bible, but here, in Christian France? But Choiseul is still speaking; I must pay attention.

"Though I hesitate to say the words before your most august and innocent highness, I must tell you the whole story."

Sodom, I think with a squeak, then wonder what fainting will feel like.

And so he tells me. Not a lady, nor a man, thank goodness. But a prostitute. A common prostitute. How even the word fills one with horror! A woman with a debauched history, a police dossier an inch thick, full of her misconduct and many vices.

When Choiseul takes his leave, I sit in stillness; outside a storm is coming and the world turns dark as though in sympathy. The king will not hunt today, and there will be no ceremony for his return. Thank goodness. I need time, I think, time to assimilate this most awful of news.

Certainly, my father has been with low women before, but now Choiseul tells me that Papa is thinking of bringing this one to Versailles. A prostitute to darken the doorstep of this magnificent palace! Surely this is only temporary manly madness, brought on by that unfortunate piece of their anatomy that impels them (far too often, it seems) to rashness? A beastly *bourgeoise* was one thing; a common prostitute quite another kettle of fish. I am pleased with my metaphor, and must remember to use it when I share the dreadful news with my sisters.

I take a deep breath. Choiseul was right to tell me and enlist my help. I will not fail him. Though the monarchy is of course unshakable, the idea of a king with so low a woman—what would that not destroy?

I take the night to compose myself, then breakfast alone as I prepare. I gather my sisters around me after Mass. We all are dressed in white and black and wearing veils; mourning for our mother, but also suitable for this occasion.

"No, keep it on," I command as Victoire flings herself down on the sofa and sets to work on her veil. "I would have you suitably attired for this news."

Victoire shrugs—how many times have I told her?—as Sophie and Louise arrange themselves around her.

"Now," I say, "terrible news has come my way. You must guess what it is." I settle back and a pleasant hour or so stretches before me. I shall divulge the scandal to my sisters, piecemeal, in a way so as not to overly shock or offend. Then I will share with them the course of action I have decided upon.

"Papa has a new mistress," says Louise.

I glare at her. "How did you know?"

"It's fairly obvious, isn't it?"

"*Mistress*," breathes Sophie, looking like a frightened black beetle.

I shake my head in dismay. Why does Louise have to ruin *everything*? "Well, you'll never guess what kind of mistress," I snap.

"The woman that calls herself the Comtesse du Barry is known to be a common prostitute," says Louise calmly.

I gape at her.

Sophie swoons and mutters what sounds like *whore* but surely was not; she was just asking for *more* . . . of something.

"Oh! Oh! I think I need the smelling salts!" says Victoire in distress. "Or my cordial might do." She reaches for the ubiquitous bottle on the sideboard.

"Unfortunate, certainly, but we all know Papa has a weakness for our fair sex," says Louise calmly. "Apparently the woman has a dossier full of vice—my equerry has a copy and has promised to bring it to me, once he has finished with it."

"Who told you?" I ask through gritted teeth.

"Who didn't tell me? It's all anyone can talk of."

I take a deep breath and attempt to regain control of the conversation. "As you all know, the Duc de Choiseul—yes, an enemy of the Church but also Father's most cherished adviser—requested an interview with me. He begged for my help in saving our dear father's soul."

"But how can we help him?" wails Victoire, choking on her sip of cordial. Sophie pats her back with a timid, fluttering hand. "Oh! A prostitute! Oh, Papa!"

"Yes," I say firmly, "though I am not sure we should say that word here. *Prostitute*. I think something a little more delicate . . ."

"Tramp?" suggests Louise. "Whore? Trollop?"

"'Indelicate lady,'" I decide. "No—'indelicate woman,' for she is scarcely a lady. Now, this is what Choiseul proposes we do. Listen carefully."

Choiseul had suggested we approach our father to reproach him; remind him of his duty to France and to his subjects, and invoke the peril to his soul if he does not abandon the woman and his shameless project of bringing her into the palace.

"Letters," I finish up. "I have thought long and hard, and have decided that letters are the best way. That way our reproach retains permanency."

"Letters to the prostitute?" squeaks Sophie, her eyes alive with fright.

"No, silly," says Victoire, "letters *about* the prostitute. Right, sister?"

"Indelicate woman!" I almost shout. "Letters about the indelicate woman!"

Louise raises one eyebrow. "It rather seems that Choiseul is getting you to do his dirty work. You know how Papa hates reproach."

"Nonsense!" I sigh in exasperation. "If you do not wish to participate in our letter-writing campaign, Louise, then you may be excused. Those of us who care about our father's soul shall remain here, and start the letters. Sophie—get Civrac to tell Mercier to tell someone to bring in our writing implements."

Quills, inks, scratch paper, and parchment—the weapons of the righteous, of those who do battle for France against indelicate women.

⁂

Once I am satisfied with my letter—a delicate missive that professes our desire to lead Papa from the desert of sin to the rivers of spiritual harmony, as Moses led the Pyramids—I decide that I shall hand-deliver it. I request an audience with Papa; it has been a long time since I have done so and he receives me warmly in one of the rooms of his private apartments. I note with relief he is in a good mood.

But of course he's in a good mood.

"Dearest Father." I curtsy and stand before him.

"What is it, Adélaïde?" he asks kindly. We are in the Wig Chamber, and he sitting beside the window at a small desk with a stack of papers. He has dismissed his men and now it is just he and I alone in the small room, the smell of powder and bear's grease almost overwhelming. I try not to breathe in these threatening odors of masculinity, reminding me as they do of my interview with Choiseul, the way his chair approached mine. Did it touch—his chair—touch mine?

But I must focus on the task at hand.

"My dear father." My fingers tighten around my letter. "You know how much I—we—love you."

"Of course, dear. And you know how fond I am of you."

"Papa, it has come to my attention, to our attention, a distressing matter, most distressing, Father . . . reproach, in the desert . . . Egyptians . . ." I stumble over my words, unsure how to begin.

"Are you worried about the new horses from Limoges?" he asks pointedly. A certain hardness plays around his beloved eyes. "I've already ordered Fourget to replace them."

"No, certainly, they were distressing, but there is something even more distressing—"

"The illness of Madame de Castries?" he says, referring to one of my sisters' ladies. His voice is now hardening to match his eyes. "Certainly, smallpox is distressing."

"No, Father! My concerns are more—spiritual—my distress for your soul. Your eternal soul . . . the desert of sin . . ." I trail off as his face changes from hard to black. He holds up a hand and suddenly the room is terrifyingly cold.

"Enough. I know why you have come, Adélaïde, and I do not wish to hear it. Do you understand?" His words are as hard as iron and just as heavy. "I shall not have you comment on, or even think about, my private life. I shall not suffer reproach for it, least of all from those in my own family. Is that clear?"

I gape at him, suddenly wanting, more than I have ever wanted anything, to take back my words. To take back this visit.

"Is that clear?"

"Yes, Papa," I manage to croak. I don't know what to do. Why is he so angry? Why is he looking at me like that? Almost as if . . . almost as if . . . Oh, I am shaking and the tears are falling fast. Why is he so angry, when all I care about is him?

"Are you crying?" he demands, his voice heavy with disgust. "Get ahold of yourself. You're being a fool, and you look quite ridiculous."

He stands up and regards me, and through my tears I can see his face soften. He sighs, still looking at me with a mixture of disgust and annoyance. "I'm off to Marly tonight for a few days. I believe we will be dining together next Saturday—please wish your lady sisters a pleasant week."

He strides out of the room and the doors close behind him with terrifying finality. I cannot move. His words, so horrible; more distressing was his tone, that coldness I have never heard before. Is that who he is? I stagger over to sit in his chair, still warm from the imprint of his buttocks, and I think again of the coldness in his voice—I have never heard him speak in such a way. Never, not even when we reproached him about the Pompadour.

And what does he mean, his private life? What is a *private life*? I want to put my head in my hands and sob forever, but for the stone-faced footman who stands inside the door, I keep my body erect and gradually stop my sobs. I should return to my apartment, but I do not trust my legs, nor the carping courtiers I am sure to find along the way.

Gradually the afternoon—this horrible, hated afternoon—dims around me and the balls holding the wigs darken into shadowy outlines, and it is as if I am surrounded by a hundred headless courtiers.

A passel of dogs bark in the antechamber then the doors open again.

"And then she said, get him off me, and he—"

"The presence of Madame de France!" cautions the footman, and the men stop. It is the Duc de Richelieu with the Duc de La Vauguyon, laughing together.

"Madame," says Richelieu, stopping and presenting me with an extravagant bow. I hate men, I think suddenly, men and their stupid follies and pitiful lusts. "Madame, I did not expect to find you here. What a pleasure this is."

"I was just leaving, I say coldly, glad the candles are not yet lit and that my face remains in shadow. "Man, get my equerry, I need his arm."

Back in my rooms, I retire to bed, complaining of a slight headache. Narbonne pulls the curtains around me, and inside the darkness and through my sobs I relive, again and again, Papa's terrible words that I fear will never leave my thoughts.

What have I done? What have I destroyed? What has *that woman* destroyed?

Chapter Fifteen

In which the Comtesse du Barry becomes the Comtesse du Barry

Within a fortnight—a fortnight of happy days and dreamy nights (and also a fortnight during which Monsieur Le Bel died of apoplexy, poor man)—Barry arrives back in Versailles with his prize. I'm upstairs in my room when I see the carriage pull up. Barry emerges first, sneezing dreadfully, followed by a tall, heavy man who radiates surliness. Finally, a small woman in a badly made red dress, picking straw out of her hat, emerges blinking into the sunlight, looking as lost as a needle in a haystack.

"Not even two cushions, and both of them straw," I can hear her complaining through the open window. The big man—that must be his brother, Guillaume—stops suddenly in front of the door.

"And once more, before I enter into this house and into this ignoble agreement—six thousand *livres* is simply not enough. Not enough for the ignominy of being offered up like a trussed chicken. I must insist, once more, before I cross this hearth—"

"Oh, shut up," says Barry wearily; his voice tells me they have been having this argument for the last many hours. "The whole street can hear you." He pushes his brother rather violently over the threshold. I giggle and run down to greet them.

I kiss Barry and present my hand to Guillaume, who takes it roughly without even a bow. I note his provincial manners with amusement: so this is what my superior Barry would have been had he stayed in Toulouse. Guillaume is big and heavy, a hastier sketch of his more refined brother. He's dressed in a badly cut black coat with pink stockings, the whole outfit with the look of one worn only for best.

"Mademoiselle de Vaubernier, I present Monsieur le Comte du Barry," says Barry dryly. "And vice versa, if you please. Where is Rose? There are crates of brandy in the carriage that need to be unloaded. Rose!"

"Hello," says the little woman in the red dress, appearing from behind the angry bulk of Guillaume. I note her kind eyes and sharp mouth. "I'm Françoise Claire du Barry, but everyone calls me Chon. My brother . . ." She gestures to Guillaume, who is now staring at me with an open mouth, a hint of drool threatening to slide down his enormous jaw. "I'm the sister." She attempts an awkward curtsy, which makes me giggle, and I sweep her up in a big embrace.

"Welcome!" I decide I'll like her, though Barry never mentioned anything about bringing a sister back. "Are you to be married too?"

Barry returns from the carriage with an opened crate full of brandy bottles. He pours himself and his brother two great glassfuls. Guillaume takes his as though in a daze and downs it without taking his eyes off me. Suddenly he begins to talk. "This scheme is the most capital idea. Versailles! I shall visit Paris tomorrow, perhaps with my lovely wife? I take back my words of ingratitude, brother." His voice is a rough growl and I note with distaste the unfashionable wide cut of his coat. "I am most desirous of assisting in this scheme, and as our mother always says, fraternal love is the most elevated of emotions."

"She never said that," scolds Chon, taking off her hat and picking up the bottle of brandy. She takes a swig. "That was a ghastly journey."

I giggle at her manners. "Let me get you a glass. Rose! Rose!"

"Don't get any ideas, brother," drawls Barry, draining his glass. "She's the king's now—even I haven't dared a poke since she met him."

"But I shall be her husband!" declares Guillaume. I look at him coldly. It's nice not to have to be polite to every man I meet, especially boorish provincials.

"Oh, what lovely flowers," says Chon, admiring an enormous bouquet on the side table. She leans in to sniff and I indicate the ribbon they are tied with, studded with diamonds, finer than anything we ever sold at Labille's.

"Oh my, are those real?" she says, fingering the pink and blue satin.

I grin and nod. "From the king," I whisper, as though it were a secret, though I suppose it isn't.

"Chon is to be your companion and teach you the ways of the world, and of the Court," announces Barry in satisfaction. "And we needed a woman on the journey to fetch things and wake us when we got to the inns."

"But you've never been to Versailles, Chon," I say kindly. *And even I don't drink straight from bottles*, I want to add. Not anymore, at least.

"No, I never have. I've never been anywhere. I am that worst of creatures, a dowerless girl," she says wryly. "And from Toulouse to boot." She sits down on a chair, finds a candied hazelnut behind a cushion, and pops it in her mouth. "Must keep these away from Guillaume—he has a dreadful reaction to hazelnuts."

"But you are a noble," I say in surprise. "Surely someone would marry you?" Even if she is hunchbacked and rather ugly, surely her birth puts her above the sorrow of spinsterhood?

Chon shrugs. "My mother would not sully our name with a base man, and a poor man with the right name would not sully himself with a penniless woman. It's just how the world is."

"You sound remarkably wise for one who has never, until this week, even traveled outside Toulouse," remarks Barry, taking off his coat and dropping it on the floor. His fingers grapple with his neckcloth. "God, I'm tired. My bones feel like they've been cracked in two."

"My wisdom comes from books," retorts Chon. They look

nothing alike, I note, watching them argue. Barry is still hand-some, despite his forty-six years—and the brandy, which has coarsened his features and reddened his nose. In contrast, Chon is small and neat, thin and secretive. As for the brother . . . well, I won't waste another thought on my future husband.

⋈

My mother and the monk Guimard come from Paris to the church for the wedding. I hug them both, and then hug Barry, and even Guillaume, who grabs at my bodice and has to be roughly bundled, weeping from too much brandy, into the car-riage that will take him straight back to Toulouse.

The priest who performed the ceremony looks on in sharp disapproval and stares straight ahead when Barry tries to engage him in conversation.

"A toast to Jeanne!" cries the monk Guimard in something close to ecstasy; the cases of brandy from Toulouse have even made their way into the church. I'm not sure how the carriage car-ried all of us and that many crates. "A toast to my lovely daugh-ter!" The priest's head snaps around in horrified censure.

"I speak in general terms," mumbles the monk Guimard, looking down at his bottle in fright. "Daughter of Eve, that sort of thing. Daughter of fortune?"

A great roar bellows forth from the priest. Barry quickly bun-dles us all off into another carriage and we repair back to the house on the rue Saint-Louis to continue the celebrations.

Barry, Ma, and the monk Guimard settle themselves on the sofa—I doubt they'll be getting up again today—while Chon and I sip our drinks and giggle over the fantasy that Barry has had prepared for me. Guessing that the king's genealogists would accept any fabrication without demur, Barry invented an illustrious family history for Mademoiselle de Vaubernier, one that would make a prince proud, and one that contains, many times over, the required degrees of nobility for a court presentation.

"Cost me a pretty penny—the rules have tightened since

Pompadour's time. But a wise investment, I'm sure," says Barry proudly, surveying the papers.

"Oooh, look, Ma—you're now the Marquise de Montrabé."

"No bleeding way! Me, a *marquise*?" says my mother in astonishment, her mouth gaping, her hair falling rapidly out of her cap. "And Montrabé—that's the little village where I used to help with that old man's harvest—what was his name? His son was my first lover."

"What's that, now?" demands the monk Guimard, turning to her in astonishment.

"And look, Monk Guimard," says Chon quickly. "Even a nod to you—Jeanne's uncle is now a cardinal. The *Cardinal of Cardillon*. Doesn't that sound grand?"

I giggle. "The name of a hamlet close to Vaucouleurs where I was born. No more than two farmhouses."

The serving girl Rose comes in with another two bottles of brandy. I motion to her to sit down with us on the sofa, and she does so, nervously touching her face scar—a hot poker in childhood, no doubt.

"Drink with us, Rose, it's a day for everyone to celebrate," I say gaily, and she giggles; she is a sweet girl and I dread to think what her life is like with such a deformity.

"Ah, my little girl, you've become quite the lady," says Barry in satisfaction. "I always knew you were special, and everything is happening perfectly." He is betting that with the passing of Le Bel, the houses in town—or was there just this one?—will remain shuttered. "Great good fortune. You have done well, Jeanne!"

I incline my head and sweep down in an elegant curtsy. "Indeed I have. A true countess I am now, with a lineage dating back to 1355, and never a more refined lady will you meet." I execute my curtsy perfectly, then twirl around in a pirouette and collapse in happiness next to my mother.

"Fit for a king, is my little girl," says Ma proudly, stroking my hair.

The monk Guimard raises his glass. "Now, without that per-licky priest looking on—what, has he never sinned?—a toast! A toast to my lovely daughter!"

"To Jeanne," all chorus.

To me, I think happily.

Chapter Sixteen

In which the Comtesse du Barry
vexes over her presentation

I call him France and treat him with that mixture of mother, nurse, and whore that men, especially as they age, seem to enjoy. He is—was—a jaded man, but I turned him around. He says I make him young again, and I do: I have restored life into him. In turn he calls me Angel and sometimes "my little jade." He gifts me a magnificent toilette set made entirely of that fine stone, but that is just one of my many presents, and soon my coffer is full of jewels of all kinds.

"We fit together so well," he muses one night, watching me finish up the remains of our supper. We dined, a small group: Chon, Richelieu, Saint-Foix. Barry is back in Paris—the king has conveyed very clearly to him that it will be the Bastille if he so much as shows his face at Court. Riches for him, yes, but glory, no.

I push him to the very far reaches of my mind and only remember him when Chon reads from one of his endless letters. I don't miss him at all, and only now from afar do I realize how he suffocated me.

"We fit together so well," Louis repeats. "As though we were two pieces of this spice set: salt and pepper, perhaps. I am the old gray pepper"—and it's true, beneath his wigs his luxurious brown hair has turned half-gray—"and you the fresh young salt, as white and fine as the day." He fingers part of the magnificent porcelain cruet set, the two little jugs and two little pots fitting together perfectly.

"Salt makes old meat sing," I say.

"Ha! Indeed it does, and indeed you do. But who is the vinegar?"

"Oh, that would have to be Chon," I say, popping a strawberry into my mouth and savoring the sweetness—as sweet as my new life.

"Come here, Angel, surely you have had enough strawberries?"

I go and sit on his lap and he unpins my hair until he is draped in my curls. "You make me so happy," he whispers in my ear, as he whispers so often. "You are so free, and simple."

"Simple?" I pull back and pout in mock affront.

"Simple, I mean, my dearest, free of intrigue and politics. Do you know," he continues in a small, sad voice he uses when he wants sympathy, "can you even begin to imagine, dearest, what it is like to be surrounded by intrigue, all one's life? A living hell, it is."

"Well, pinch me, everyone's life is hard."

"None as hard as mine," he says, complying and pinching me gently.

I caress his neck and murmur something in his ear, which he thinks is sympathy, but isn't. I don't have time for his melancholy and his dark moods, for the vacancy in his eyes when he sets to snuffle in self-pity. So many have lives so much harder than this king, I think, remembering the scourge of hunger in my belly on the days when the convent couldn't feed us, the endless cold that seeped through our thin shoes, Dorothée's sightless eyes and ruined nose.

"But you were sent to rescue me. Heaven cannot be entirely displeased with me, to send such an angel. I was getting tired of the house in town," he muses. "Pleasure, lots of it, but no friends, no companionship. Ah," he sighs, "indeed I must be getting old."

I snuggle against him. "No, everyone needs a friend."

He holds me closer. "You remind me, a touch, of my dear Pompadour; she was a true friend. My only friend." His features draw in again, back in the past. "But a trifle annoying at times—

she tried to be perfect in everything. But I know she loved me, for me."

I'm silent. I never ask about her, but when he does wander down memory lane, I follow him gladly.

"Not as sweet as you, dearest," he continues, stroking my arm. "There was a coldness to her, the heart of seagull beneath her beautiful dress. No, you remind me in your sweetness of another lady, my first Louise."

I don't ask who she is but instead: "I'm warm," I say, guiding his finger into the heat of my insides. "I'm fire."

"No, not fire," he says, gazing at me tenderly, moving his finger inside me. "A slow, gentle burn, the flames just enough to warm my soul. How I love you, my dearest."

We spend the autumn at Fontainebleau. When the Court returns to Versailles, he leases me a house in town on the rue de l'Orangerie, and I leave the ghosts of the little house on the rue Saint-Louis behind.

I pass my nights with him at Versailles, but not the days. When I walk through the halls of the palace, with Chon or Richelieu, I am like a ghost, a nameless creature no one sees or acknowledges. I am not presented, so I am nothing at Court and I must spend hours or even days away from the king, our lives cleaved in two by the power of etiquette. Were I presented, I would have the right to take part in the journeys of the Court, to get in royal coaches, to live publicly with the king, attend concerts with the royal family, show myself at Mesdames' card parties.

And have an apartment in the palace.

"A painted prostitute," Chon says the ladies of the Court call me, and my heart hardens—they don't even know me, yet it seems they are determined to hate me. And I don't even wear rouge. Chon has become my confidante; she has her brother's scheming ways but in a much more pleasant package. When she tells me about her life in Toulouse, it is as though she speaks of my convent days. I shudder. I'm never going back there, and neither is she.

She is very resourceful and beetles around the palace, befriending members of the second tier at Court, a large and vast group generally ignored by the ones above, yet who hold all their secrets. She determines that I need to be presented.

"Presentation is like a baptism. Welcome to the church of Versailles!" she says.

I agree. The Christmas and New Year's festivities are coming up and in my current state I cannot be a part of them. I pout and cry at Louis—I think he would be perfectly happy for things to continue as they are—but eventually he agrees. Yes, I shall be presented.

Ha! I shall be not just the queen of his heart, but the queen of Versailles. And then maybe those starchy old ladies will talk to me.

But those starchy ladies . . . it seems none is prepared to present me. And without a lady who herself has been presented, I cannot be. Louis insists Richelieu will take care of it, and that I must not worry.

"Promise me."

"I promise," he says sadly. "I shall redouble my efforts with Richelieu—he must know it displeases me greatly that he has not been able to take care of this."

"Soon, you promise?"

"Yes, my dear, you have my word."

"And after your presentation," he announces to me one night, with the air of one who is about to grant me an enormous and unhoped-for favor—possibly the emerald parure I wished for? "You are to spend several months . . . preparing yourself."

"Oh!" I sit up in fright. "What do you mean, preparing myself?"

"I mean to say, my dear, you must prepare yourself . . . for this place," he finishes grandly.

"What place?"

"Versailles, dearest."

"What exactly do you mean?" I ask again, my suspicions growing. I remember an excruciating conversation with Richelieu last week, about how a prince wasn't a prince, if a prince and a duke, and that to call the Duchesse de Valentinois the Princesse de Monaco would be an insult, the magnitude of which could never be rectified. I grew bored with the conversation and decided life was too short and sweet to worry about such things. For me, etiquette is like Latin: a language I have no wish to learn.

"You must learn etiquette and our ways; the position of a royal mistress is a heavy role and a burden."

"You would send me to school? No! France, my only burden should be to make you happy."

Louis shakes his head, laughing. "No, peaches, you don't understand. There are many rules and obligations, many customs to learn . . ."

"Oh, flumadiddle! Who am I supposed to be fooling?"

"Well, yes, I concede you have a good point there, but—"

"I shall not be sent to school! You cannot make me."

"Not to school, dearest, but—"

"I shall run away. Run away right now, without any clothes on!"

Louis chuckles. "Well, fine then, we'll leave your tutelage alone. Perhaps it is not a bad idea to ask the courtiers to adapt themselves to you. It would be rather amusing to see them learn new tricks."

I give him a big wet kiss, and promise to show him a few new tricks of my own.

∽

I sweep down, and up, a literal lead monster on my stomach and back. Chon has sewn my bodice with silver from the table, saying it will mimic the heaviness of the jewels that I will surely wear at my presentation.

My curtsy is perfect, but still no lady has been found who is willing to do the honors. In their resistance, the depth of the courtiers' hatred for me is revealed. Songs circulate about me, one even claiming my sexual depravity began before I was ten, and that Saint-Maur was a brothel, not a convent.

A carriage pulls up outside—Richelieu. Chon's face darkens. She says she does not trust the duke as far as she could throw him, but I tell her not to be silly: Richelieu is our friend. One of my only ones, I think grimly, for it is an awful thing to be on the outside, and despised, and simply for being me. A fly on the wrong side of the glass, and no one is opening any windows.

I'm not sure I like Versailles very much.

Richelieu sweeps in, setting his gloves and sword on the sideboard.

"Watch me." I sink down in an elegant curtsy and rise up again.

"Lovely, madame, lovely. Are those forks on your bodice? Spoons?"

I smile at him. "Some good news, I hope?"

"I am afraid not, madame." He sighs and sits down rather heavily, his face the color of pressed cheese. A wave of premonition—I don't want to be the cause of any more harm, I think in alarm, remembering Le Bel. And Richelieu, though enlivened by the last few months, is still an old man. "So many excuses I have rarely heard. The death of the queen—as if anyone was afflicted by that! A sprained wrist; a forbidding husband—no end of useless excuses."

"Oh, la!" I cry. "Why are they being so hateful?" I yank a fork off my bodice and throw it on the floor.

Richelieu shakes his head. "I hate to say this, but we need the Pompadour; she had the most amazing gift for taking care of even the thorniest of problems."

"Really, sir?" asks Chon. "I thought you were one of her keenest enemies?"

"Ah, in this life there are few worthy opponents . . ." muses Richelieu with a sad and distant look in his eyes, then shakes himself. "But what am I saying? She was a *bourgeois* nothing, with scales beneath her skirts. I never countenanced her presence at Versailles."

"Yet you support my dear sister?" challenges Chon. "Jeanne is many things, but she is a far cry from even a *bourgeoise*."

The duke winces: he is unused to being challenged, and certainly not by one as insignificant and female as Chon.

"Do not be worried, Mademoiselle Chon," he says smoothly. "Our dear Madame du Barry is what the king needs, but I never saw the use of the Pompadour. I had many superior substitutes, but in her fried and battered way, she satisfied his appetite."

"So who is going to present me?" I demand, turning the conversation back to what is important. "The king demands to know." Richelieu is more at Court these days, and in the king's presence, and all because of me. Now he has to repay the favor, I think grimly, playing with one of the spoons secured to my chest.

"I have tried so many, but all remain intractable. This insubordination of the female sex is very vexing—it is as though they do not consider the effect of their independence on the men! Even Mirie—I mean to say the Duchesse de Mirepoix. I had my man procure a very rare rabbit from India—at least it was supposed to be a rabbit, though it looked more like an overgrown rat—but the duchess is getting so old she wouldn't know the difference. Yet still she refused.

"Even my daughter," he continues, "denied me in a most unfilial manner. But she is married and no longer under my command, so what can I do? And my mistresses; I have a long list of them, you know." Here he attempts a leer, which devolves into a coughing fit that leaves spittle on his fine lace coat. "I have asked all of them, yet to no avail. I had thought to have some traction with my nephew's wife, Félicité d'Aiguillon, but it seems she has forgotten the two best nights of her life."

"What about someone from d'Ayen's family?" demands Chon. "Surely the old duke can help? Can't you find him a wig of spider silk or some such thing?"

"Sadly, no. His daughter-in-law the Comtesse de Noailles

is such a proper woman and he fears her health would never recover were he to command her obedience. The same for his wife." He sighs, looking back and forth between us, shaking his head. "The king is not used to not getting his way. As you know, that toad Choiseul is decidedly against our cause, and that is not helping."

Choiseul. I have met him, of course; Louis even arranged a small dinner for us, but his frosty air and superior mien remained. Chon tells me he calls me a strumpet and is responsible for many of the salacious poems circulating about me. He is still living in the past, when he and Pompadour regented the king's fancies, and I know he wishes me to stay in town, and never breach the walls of the palace.

"We need someone old and in penury," continues Richelieu. "There is a certain Diane, the Duchesse de Lauraguais—de Brancas, now. She is retired from Court since the death of the dauphine, and in terrible debt, but I fear her health is so bad that such a proposition might send her over the edge. I cannot be responsible for the death of such a dear, dear friend," he finishes, with a little leer, successful this time. "And none of Mesdames' ladies: they are threatening instant dismissal should anyone even consider it. Disgusting old harpies."

I grimace, thinking of the old ladies as I saw them at Fontaine-bleau: the eldest, Madame Adélaïde, almost forty, with a heavy, masculine face as rigid and expressionless as stone. She wore a choker of pearls around her plump neck that dug into her flesh and made her face red. Madame Victoire, who looked for all the world like someone's kind and frumpy aunt, and then Madame Sophie, as terrified as a squirrel. They all carefully elevated their noses and averted their eyes when I passed, except for the youngest, Madame Louise, who looked at me with what appeared to be amused nonchalance.

"What about someone in her second infancy?" suggests Chon. "Isn't the Prince de Ligne's mother as mad as a batfish, and not far from here in Passy?"

"Already considered, my dear Chon, but guardians can be such troublesome people," says Richelieu, looking at Chon with new appreciation and respect.

"Well there has to be someone!" I stomp my foot, frustrated. "Surely, out of that vast palace of a thousand souls, there has to be *someone*?"

Chapter Seventeen

In which Madame Adélaïde's world ends

"I know who it is! I know who it is!" Victoire comes barreling in, her hair threatening to slip out of her cap, which is threatening to slip off her head. "It is confirmed, it is confirmed," she pants, slumping down on the sofa.

"Sit down properly, and calm yourself," I say crisply, setting aside my morning reading: *The Taxonomical Order of Vegetables*. "Lisette, get Madame Victoire a glass of water."

"Better some of the apricot cordial!" says Victoire quickly. "My nerves, my nerves. But it is confirmed!"

"What is?" I say in annoyance. I had a dream last night that left me unsettled and unable to concentrate properly on cabbages.

"The presentation," breathes Victoire.

Oh! Damn my Narbonne woman, always leaving me in the dark and being lax in her duty of keeping me ahead of the facts I need to know at Court.

"But we must send for Sophie and Louise," I say, rising and trying to contain my excitement. "Narbonne! Now, calm yourself and do not tell me, not yet. We must all be together." I get up to circle the room in mounting excitement; war is meaningless if the enemy is not known. Who could she be, this traitor to our blood, who will present that unspeakable woman whom no one can stop speaking about?

Only when we four are gathered do I dismiss the women and allow Victoire to tell. Sophie is almost overcome with the gravity of the situation, but Louise only looks rather annoyed at being summoned! She affects great piety, but how irresponsible that she should not care when our father's soul is in peril.

"Yes, yes," said Victoire eagerly, looking flushed and not only from the news, "it came from Civrac herself, she heard it straight from her daughter, who heard it from Belsunze, who heard it from—"

I hold up my hand. "We are not interested in the genealogy of this information, just in the facts. And I propose we guess!" A pleasant hour stretches before me, and I will be the one to—

"It is the Comtesse de Béarn," says Victoire, and I could throttle her.

"Who?" asks Louise curiously.

"Yes, she's frightfully obscure, but was presented to Mama—and probably to you too, Adélaïde, in '38, more than thirty years ago. Distantly related to Villars and Ségur, I believe. She is apparently very poor, and there are debts involved . . . Civrac says she used to go to that creature's house in Paris and gamble."

The enemy, identified. Well, not the real enemy, that of course remains the indelicate woman, but enemies can be a many-headed Hydra. A many-headed Medusa?

"We shall stop her!" I announce. "The Comtesse de Béarn is a traitor to the entire noble race."

Sophie murmurs something that sounds like poison.

"What?" I say sharply.

"She might die. Poison. She's very old already," she whispers in a tiny voice, and buries her head in her hands.

"Pity she's not indisposed; then she might die in childbirth," says Victoire solemnly, "but she's got five children already and they're all grown up."

"How you have such a memory for these insignificant facts, Victoire, yet can never remember the pluperfect of Greek verbs simply astounds me. But back to the task at hand: the countess must be stopped."

"Which countess?" asks Victoire, pouring herself another glass of cordial.

"De Béarn! Well, du Barry too, but to stop that indelicate woman, we need to first stop Béarn. Letters! Yes indeed! We shall all write her letters."

"And what will we write in these letters?" asks Louise. "For her to desist in this undertaking?"

"Of course," I say in astonishment. "What else?"

"Don't you think she already knows that we are displeased with her decision to present that woman?"

"Well, yes, if she is not half-witted, though wasn't there a Villars who was mute from birth? But I have no doubt a letter coming from me, from *Madame de France*, will certainly bear weight."

"We must be careful not to make Papa angry," warns Louise. I haven't told anyone about the dreadful scene with him, but sometimes I suspect Louise knows, and now there appears to be an irritating pity under her warning. Even though it happened more than six months ago, time has not erased the crushing cruelty of his words.

"But we are trying to save him from making a dreadful mistake! Choiseul said the entire monarchy risks being undermined by this indelicate woman."

"But will Papa see it like that? And he's happier these days, and it is his decision, really."

"It is *not* his decision," I say through gritted teeth, struggling to control myself. "He is not in his right mind, he is simply held captive by that part of his anatomy, by that p— Oh, Sophie, I am sorry," I say as Sophie squeals in fright. I glare at Louise: "Look what you almost made me say!"

Louise apologizes calmly and rises. "My dears, I must go. I shall see you later."

Oh, go, I think in irritation, then turn back to the matter at hand. "Civrac! Have our writing desks brought!"

We will make this Comtesse de Béarn understand she risks our eternal enmity if she does goes ahead with the presentation.

We shall not fail.

༄

We failed and the infamous day dawns, a pretty spring day to herald the end of Lent and the coming summer.

It should be hailing.

Papa returns from the hunt, but this evening at his *debottée* he looks harried and irritated. As though this is an onerous duty imposed on him, and not one of his own creation, I think sourly, then curse myself for my disloyal thoughts.

We follow our equerries back to our apartments, fighting the way through the prodigious crowds; there are rumors there are more people here than there were even for the fish woman's presentation. Du Barry's coming has united everyone in common dislike, enemies embracing erstwhile friends as the palace closes ranks against this disgusting interloper.

Voltaire joins the protest and publishes a satire entitled "The Court of King Topsy-Turvy." Though I must officially detest Voltaire as a dreaded atheist and *philosophe*, I nonetheless applaud his efforts. And topsy-turvy indeed, I think sadly: a daughter of France agreeing with an atheist.

The world—our world—will never be the same. Why must our father persist so? I believe Choiseul spoke the truth when he said the monarchy would never recover: our father with a harlot—yes, I use that word now—presented to the greatest of France's families. Forcing his children to speak to a common prostitute.

We wait in our rooms as the afternoon light fades, yet still she does not appear. A murmur of hope runs through us: Have we won? Has the harlot changed her mind? The servants appear to light the candles and the torches. But no, she is just delaying her arrival, no doubt waiting for that evening hour when the candles enhance the dusk to make a woman's beauty shine. She keeps the King of France waiting from sheer female vanity!

The palace holds its collective breath, and then her carriage is spotted coming through the gates. Sophie starts to tremble so much that I call for more cordial—what has this day wrought?—and then I realize in horror I have been worrying the lace on my sleeves and have unpicked one of the bows.

It is coming. It is really happening.

"Get ready, now! Stand!"

"But she will be a while in the Marble Court, and then surely—" says Victoire from the sofa, grasping her cordial as though it were a shield.

"We must prepare! And how can we with you lounging on the sofa like a, like a—"

"Beast," whispers Sophie, and I feel like crying.

"There are worse things in this world, I suppose," says Louise.

"I dare you to name one," I snap as we fall into line, myself at the head, Victoire beside me, Sophie, then Louise, each shuffling over.

"War? The deaths of thousands of Frenchmen? Starvation?"

Is she mocking me?

One of our women rushes in with the news that she has been presented to the king: she winked at him as she rose from her curtsy. Winked at him!

"And she is not even wearing rouge," says Marie in wonder, breathless from running. "But my, how beautiful she is!"

"Beautiful, indeed! Such foolishness! Now, at attention, all of you! She is coming."

It is coming, the force of all that is evil and unaccepted in this world. Worse than the Beast of Gévaudan. I say the small speech I have prepared: "Come, my sisters, we must be strong, this is a battlefield, and though we may welcome this woman into our home, we only do it to bring the enemy closer. Then we shall cut off her head, as Salome did to the enemy."

"So we are the dancing harlots now?" asks Louise, smoothing her skirts, as annoyingly composed as always.

"What?"

"Salome was a dancing harlot. It strikes me as odd that you would compare us to such a low class of woman; I would have thought she would be better as the Comtesse du Barry. Perhaps it is she who is coming in to cut off *our* heads?"

"Surely not?" I fumble.

"I think you are mixing your stories again, dear sister."

Victoire giggles.

"Enough! You are quite aware of what I am trying to convey," I say tightly. "Which is: the ends justifies the means."

"The end," whispers Sophie in fright.

Movement outside and the murmur of hundreds approaching our rooms, then three raps at the door before they are opened and there they are—the two women, framed by an enormous crowd.

"Oh, so pretty!" gasps Victoire, and Sophie lets out a long sigh of admiration.

"Silence," I hiss as they advance toward us. I keep my eyes off the harlot and on the Comtesse de Béarn, who is smiling as though she is enjoying herself. Traitor!

As they advance, something like shock shadows over the Comtesse de Béarn's face. "Oh, how they have aged," I think I hear her gasp. Then the wretched woman sweeps down in a creaking curtsy and I bid her rise.

"Madame la Comtesse de Béarn. Such a long time. It has been how many years?"

"Since 1738, Madame."

"Indeed." I must keep the conversation going, delay the inevitable. "I do not remember you, I am sorry to say."

"You were just six, and how charming you were! With your two sisters, you were so pretty then in your matching pink gowns, like little—"

"Thank you, madame," I say curtly. "We all grow old." I close my eyes and take a deep breath as Béarn steps back and the harlot steps forward.

The moment is upon me. *Be strong, be valiant. For France.*

"Madame, it is my honor to present to you Jeanne-Marie de Vaubernier, the Comtesse du Barry." The harlot steps in front of me and sweeps down in a curtsy. I contemplate her bowed head, the fresh golden locks, the enormous diamond brooch on top of her curls. No powder, no rouge. An insult to the Bourbons, to the very core that makes Versailles great.

Two seconds, then three. *Face the battle, identify the enemy, and emerge victorious.*

"Madame du Barry," I say in my iciest voice. We will wait, and attack when the time is right. "You may rise."

She does and our eyes lock. She smiles at me and then I find myself . . . dazzled. An angel, I think before I can stop myself, an angel with the sweetest face, who has come to show me home.

Be strong, Adélaïde. Avoid the temptation of Satan, for he works in mysterious ways.

"Welcome to Versailles," I say in a voice that I urge not to shake as I quash my weak and scandalous thoughts. "We welcome you to Versailles."

Part II

Collision

1769–1774

Chapter Eighteen

*In which the Comtesse du Barry is
saddened by her cold reception*

I punch him on the shoulder. "You deliberately misunderstand me, France," I warn.

The king steps back in shock. "My dear . . . you just *punched* me."

"I'll punch you again if this continues." I dazzle him with a smile to soften the blow.

"You punched me! You should be grateful you have much that I desire, Angel. To punch me! Like a, like a . . ." Words fail Louis and he sits down heavily, shaking his head at the way his world has turned.

"Of course I have much that you desire. I am *perfect*."

"You are, you are," he says sadly.

"So make them talk to me!" I cry, referring to the ladies of the Court, who, despite my presentation, remain vexingly obstinate and silent toward me.

"Richelieu," he says, rubbing his arm. This year Richelieu is on duty as the First Gentleman of the Bedchamber and is in charge of overseeing court entertainment. "He wanted to bring in bare-knuckled boxers, for our entertainment, but I do not see the charm in such spectacles. How it must hurt, to be a boxer! What an affront you have given my arm!"

I ignore him and continue my railing, stalking up and around the room, the snubs of the evening still raw. "So I may enter and play, but have no right to conversation? What am I supposed to do, pass my life in silence while they ignore me?"

After my presentation, the cold reality of Versailles closed around me. The Comtesse de Béarn, unable to bear the ice field of disapproval that slid her way, disappeared within days. I have plenty of male admirers, but few—if any—ladies. While Chon's friendly face and shrewd mind are always waiting for me back at my rooms, she has not the entrées for the concerts and card parties. There, I find an impenetrable wall of arrogant, painted faces. It's not my beauty that causes this jealous female spite, but rather it is disdain for a fault I cannot erase: my birth. And perhaps my Paris life.

I've never been hated or despised before, I think sadly, and I really don't like it.

Daily, Louis grants requests for ladies to retire to Paris or to their country houses; a sudden vogue for summer in the country seems to have come upon all and sundry, along with a plethora of sick aunts and grandmothers.

The Comtesse de Brionne, a member of the powerful Rohan family, recently started a trend of wearing her left sleeve slightly off her shoulder, still within the bounds of propriety but showing clearly her desire to give me the cold shoulder. I heard Beatrice de Gramont, Choiseul's sister and perhaps my most ardent enemy, even hosted a debate: Was conscientious objecting, popularized by the Quakers in England, suitable? Could etiquette be ignored for reasons of conscience?

I have become the common butt of a rampant dislike. I kick over a small table and it crashes to the ground, shattering a porcelain bowl filled with berries.

The king's hooded eyes follow me as I stalk around the room. "Ah, my dear, not more unpleasantness," he pleads. "My soul could not bear yet another sigh today."

He doesn't like these scenes; he confessed once that he had no idea that women were capable of raising their voices. And shouting. "I never knew nature allowed a woman the capacity to scream, outside of childbirth, I mean," he said in wonder.

"Can you not be content with our little circle?" he pleads. He says the hours we spend together, alone, should compensate for the slight irritation of our public hours. "Dearest, can't you see: my hands are tied. I cannot *force* the ladies to speak to you."

"Your hands are not tied!" I retort, then smile, remembering a night last week. I turn grimly back to the matter at hand. "You don't know what I suffer! Yesterday Richelieu's daughter said I was like a cloud—when I disappeared, I made the day brighter! And right where I could hear her!"

Louis chuckles, appreciating the wit.

"Don't laugh!" I scream. "They are hateful, hateful! You don't know what it's like to be despised." I start crying. In a minute, the tears will make my eyes as turquoise and brilliant as my robe.

"Ah, there you are wrong," says Louis. True; Paris certainly despises him, and I was surprised to discover, in soft whispers and veiled innuendos, that many of his courtiers do too. I might once have imbibed the resentment common on the Parisian streets, but now I see that he is just a man, and a kind one at that, and what can one man do?

I float back to him, softer now, and embrace him. "I'm sorry, France. I didn't mean to yell. Or, ah, punch you. All I want is for them to like me."

Louis pulls me down onto his lap and caresses my hair. "Don't cry, dearest. Oh, your lovely, lovely eyes!" Louis kisses me and promises me he will take care of the matter.

He does so, by placing the problem once again in Richelieu's hands.

Chapter Nineteen

*In which the Comtesse du Barry finally
makes some friends of the fair sex*

The château at Bellevue was once the favorite house of the
Marquise de Pompadour. Instantly I love the delicate
little rooms and the symmetry of the formal gardens that
lead down to the river.

"Do you like it, Angel?" asks Louis as we stroll the terraces.
"Do you want it?"

"Of course I want *it*," I tell him with a giggle. It's a glorious
summer morning, brilliant and perfect. And it's true—every time
we make love, I can't help but think in satisfaction that he is my
lover, and how perfect my life is, even if his skills are not perhaps
what they could be. But is not desire the sum of all parts of a man?

Indulgent exasperation from Louis, who can't stop himself
from flushing in pleasure. "You are so childish, Angel, I can never
tell if it is on purpose, or if you really mean it."

"A bit of both," I say airily.

"I talk of the house. And gardens. Would you like it? Them?"

"Oh, France, no. It was hers—it can't be mine." The Pompadour's presence is everywhere: in the frescoes painted by Boucher;
in the green tiles of the bathroom; in the parterres filled with
purple roses and lilacs. We stop in front of a statue of Philotes,
surrounded by a circle of stately irises that sway lazily in the slight
breeze.

Louis sighs. "Philotes—the goddess of friendship. You're right,
my dear, it *was* hers. But we could redo it to great effect; everything can be changed."

"Too many ghosts," I say firmly, and pick an enormous purple iris from the base of the statue and stick it in my hair. "Look—the flower of friendship."

"We'll find you a new home, then," says Louis, and puts his arm around my waist. We lean on each other as we make our way down the path. I inhale happiness and the beginnings of a perfect day. Richelieu worked his magic and tonight there will be a small supper party here. The guest list was carefully developed, and by focusing on those old enough and poor enough, Richelieu has managed to finagle a selection of well-placed ladies that will attend, and speak to me.

Richelieu joins us down on the lawn, wearing a striped summer coat and looking remarkably pleased with himself.

"Save your self-congratulations for after the meal, perhaps?" suggests Louis mildly, and I realize in astonishment that he is nervous. Louis—nervous? I give him a big wet kiss and tell him not to worry.

Rimming the parterres in the garden stand fifty or so sullen shepherds and shepherdesses, looking rather silly in frilly yellow outfits.

"What are they for?" I whisper to Richelieu.

"Decoration," he says curtly.

"But why are they dressed like that? Look at that woman—she looks like a yellow meringue! And are those real sheep?" Louis goes over to a lamb, its fur yellow and sticky, and pats is cautiously.

Richelieu looks at me as though I am half-witted. "Rustic effect," he says dismissively. "We are in the country, after all. And they will hold the torches as the evening progresses; most satisfactory, really, as torch stakes blow over if the wind mounts."

Louis rejoins us, still looking worried. I kiss him again and tickle the nape of his neck with my little finger; Richelieu looks discreetly away.

"And be nice to Choiseul," warns Louis, picking a piece of yellow lamb fluff off his arm. "I cannot have my most trusted minister and my most loved woman at war with each other."

"Certainly, if he's nice to me," I say, taking the iris out of my hair and securing it in his wig. "I have no quarrel with him." Choiseul's sister Beatrice is also invited tonight. Choiseul remains a thorn in my side—one that will only grow sharper, warns Chon—and I am getting tired of his resistance. We even enlisted the help of the Duc de Lauzun—a young nephew of Choiseul's wife and an admirer of mine from my Paris days—to plead my case, but the minister remains stubborn, egged on by his sister.

"Sometimes, France," I say archly, "I think you like to watch people fight. Putting us together as though in a cockfight!"

"A cockfight?" splutters the king. "What on earth is a *cock-fight*?"

"Two roosters in a ring against each other, to the death."

"Ha! I see. An interesting notion. Now, let us say you and Choiseul were in the same ring—no, wait, that does not a good image conjure. Perhaps you and the Duchesse de Choiseul?" he says, referring to Choiseul's sweet and lovely wife, Honorine. All say that malice could find no foothold in her, but even *she* is cold to me. "Now, who do you think would win?"

"That you can even ask that question, France! Of course it would be me."

Soon the guests arrive and join us on the lawn. My debut; I giggle, thinking of my presentation day. At least I'm more comfortable now—my gown is plain pink muslin, trimmed with white lace. But my jewels are anything but simple, I think in satisfaction, fingering an enormous sapphire-and-emerald necklace that glitters like brilliant butterflies around my neck.

Richelieu introduces the guests, handpicked by himself and, he assures me, eager to please, their tractability neatly correlated with their poverty. I had wanted Chon and Adolphe to be invited, but Richelieu had spluttered and said that though I might willfully defy etiquette, we cannot expect our august guests to mingle with nobodies.

"The Marquise de Flavacourt," says Richelieu with a flourish.

As a lady of the late queen, Flavacourt is Richelieu's biggest triumph. Chon finagled the guest list from him—they have become fast friends, in a way that rather concerns me—and insisted we go over it. Hortense de Flavacourt: one of the infamous Mailly-Nesle sisters, and the only one of her sisters not to succumb to the king. I'm not terribly interested; it all happened so long ago, almost before I was born. And thinking of them makes me realize how *old* the king is—he will turn sixty next year.

"Thank you so much for coming," I say, curtsying to the marquise. I remember something Chon told me. "I heard your nickname is Hen—my mother loves chickens so, and I am also partial. What is your favorite chicken dish?"

The marquise blanches, then closes her eyes and says very carefully: Chicken *à la Mazarine*. She is fifty-five, but still very beautiful, her complexion soft and pink. In truth, she reminds me a bit of my mother. I tell her so, and the great lady's eyes fly open and her face turns an awful shade of gray. She staggers and motions to one of her attendants.

"You are not well? If my mother ever comes to visit, I'll have her make it for you, she says there is nothing a good chicken dish can't cure." I smile and stifle a giggle; I know I'm shocking her but I am enjoying myself immensely. They are all here to please *me*. And they might even be nice, under their thick rouge and the weight of their family names that they carry around so heavily.

"What a pity my sister Diane, the Duchesse de Lauraguais, can't be here," says Flavacourt, patting her brow with a crisp lace handkerchief, one of her attendants fanning her vigorously. "I think you'd like her immensely. So . . . *frank*, both of you. But alas, she is ailing."

A more matronly lady approaches.

"Madame la Maréchale de Mirepoix," introduces Richelieu. "A great friend of His Majesty"—here there is no leer, attempted or otherwise—"and also of our dear departed Marquise de Pompadour."

I smile warmly at the old lady, but she only returns a tight curl of her lips. Her head shakes slightly—from drinking too much tea in England, Chon said. A small black boy dressed in the maréchale's livery comes forward with a lilac cushion, a miniature rabbit seated nervously on it. The boy extends the cushion forward and the rabbit's nose twitches.

"Oh, how delightful! What is her name?"

"His name," says the maréchale firmly. "Male rabbits are far more convenient—no risk of messy, inopportune births. His name is Jonas."

"Jonas! La, how adorable! Can I have him?"

"No, but I will tell the breeder, and may present you with one shortly." The maréchale's voice is firm and motherly, and instantly I feel at ease. I am about to tell her how she also reminds me of my mother, but then I remember the unsettling gray of Flavacourt's face.

"And oh! I want one like him!" I say instead, pointing at the little black boy who lowers his lashes shyly.

"Ah, that can be more easily arranged," the maréchale assures me.

I meet the other guests that Richelieu has managed to acquire, including Félicité d'Aiguillon, the wife of the Duc d'Aiguillon. Aiguillon, Chon solemnly informed me, was the first lover of Marie-Anne de Châteauroux and is a distant nephew of Richelieu's. He shares his uncle's hatred for Choiseul and is therefore a possible ally of ours. I look at Félicité's teeth curiously; apparently she has the most impressive set of false ones in the palace.

I also meet the beautiful Princesse de Talmont, and the Duchesse de Valentinois, married to the Prince of Monaco, but lovers with the Prince de Condé. Her jealous husband is threatening to keep her locked up in their castle in Monaco.

"Straight out of a novel!" I say, and the duchess raises her eyebrows and remarks that she has never thought of herself as a tawdry heroine, but presumes I meant it as a compliment.

More guests arrive and great quantities of plum wine circulate, and soon we are as merry as spring magpies. One of the yellow lambs gets chased into a fountain, where it turns the water a sickly yellow, and the Prince de Soubise entertains with a rendition of the lamb's chorus from Handel's *Messiah*. Louis sits apart from the amusement, watching from the terrace above.

And if my guests are here under duress, well, so be it! I think, smiling at Catherine de Valentinois and complimenting her on her pale green gloves and matching parasol. They will see, once they get to know me, that I am not that bad. And how lovely it is out in the countryside! I regret saying no to Bellevue, but then I decide Louis can buy me another country house, a château with a garden as lovely as this one, that I'll fill with myrtles and roses and honeybees.

Near the end of the afternoon, Choiseul and his sister arrive. It would be nice to have Choiseul's friendship, for I know he is a capable minister and a good friend to Louis—but it takes two to dance a minuet, I think as they make their way down the steps to the garden.

"Madame la Comtesse du Barry," says Choiseul through clenched teeth, and I appreciate how his tone makes *Barry* sound like something found on the bottom of one's shoe rather than a noble name. "What a pleasure to attend you."

No cockfights tonight, I determine as I present him my own warm greetings, but my pretty words are met with nary a sign of warmth in his puggish blue eyes.

Choiseul's sister Beatrice steps forward beside him. She is in her late thirties and was languishing in a convent, unmarried, until her brother found Pompadour's favor. He then married her to the debauched Duc de Gramont, and she came to Court as a duchess. Chon tells me that though Pompadour was a friend of Choiseul, she cared little for his sister.

"An ice field of ambition and greed, they say," Chon told me, and I thought I detected some admiration in her voice. "Very powerful in her influence with her brother," she continued rather wistfully. A pity Chon couldn't be here; perhaps she and the duchess might have found some common ground, for I sense the duchess and I will not.

"Madame la Duchesse de Gramont," presents Richelieu, smirking. Though I am not sure if the two have been intimate—Chon declared herself completely unable to compile a comprehensive list, for either—it is well known that Beatrice's predilections do not run to her husband.

Beatrice inclines her head coldly, and I quell the urge to giggle at her attire. She is dressed in a heavily beaded purple and gold court costume, completely out of place at this informal country gathering where etiquette maintains only a hovering presence. Hoping to make me cower before her magnificence, I think in amusement.

"What a delightful gown, Duchess!" I say merrily. Chon says that she is the key to unlocking her brother's enmity, but I know I will get even less quarter from her: I generally have more success with men.

"Only the finest Venetian brocade," she replies tightly. "The *noblest* of cloths."

"It takes a woman of great independence to be so heedless of current fashion," I can't resist retorting.

After some more forced pleasantries, they both stalk away and stake their ground near the fountain, accompanied by two yellow lambs. A small crowd gathers around them as the merriment continues on its way.

The Prince de Soubise drags one of the frilly shepherdesses onto the lawn and dances a jig around her, and then I show everyone a dance we called the Moutonnière—the Sheep's Dip—and everything is rather jolly and fun. Even the Marquise de Flavacourt puts away her disapproval and her fan, and partakes of the plum wine.

Gradually all the guests gravitate to me, as though being pulled, slightly against their will, in my direction. Dusk falls, and as the torches are distributed to the sullen shepherds, Choiseul and Beatrice are left standing alone by the fountain. They engross each other in what appears to be lively conversation, but they must be acutely aware of their isolation. I usually have no truck with outlandish rumors—now that I am the butt of them—but seeing them together, so completely absorbed in each other, one has to think of the rumors of incest that swirl around them. Surely not?

Louis comes down from his perch on the terrace and walks by them. He pats Choiseul rather sadly on the shoulder, as though to console him, and comes to stand by me. Well, at least he sees I made an effort, I think, and happily he was too far away to hear my words to Beatrice.

Richelieu announces that supper is ready.

"Come, everyone, down by the water! We have the tables set there, and you may sit where you wish!" I cry to the guests. I halloo extra loudly to the lonely brother and sister, over by the fountain, but they only stare back imperiously. Richelieu leads everyone down to the river, where an enormous table stretches and another hundred frilled shepherds stand.

"You have quite the talent for this," murmurs the Maréchale de Mirepoix, motioning for one of the shepherds to seat her. She looks at me with approval and this time she is smiling with her eyes. I may have a new friend! The maréchale is a coup indeed: her brother is the Prince de Beauvau and her sister-in-law is one of Choiseul's mistresses.

"You may call me Mirie," says the old woman. "I stand on no ceremony with my friends. Ah, lovely—roast lamb, my favorite."

Chapter Twenty

*In which Madame Adélaïde considers
the sad state of her world*

"Betrayal, and by the Maréchale de Mirepoix!" breathes Victoire.

"Not surprising," I say tartly. "The woman is a scandal herself. She married a nobody as her second husband, and entirely lost her rank and her place in the world. What sort of woman willingly displaces herself? It would be like one of us marrying . . . marrying a . . ." Words fail me.

"A lace merchant?" offers Victoire helpfully.

I tug at my thread and it runs out of the fabric in a satisfying line. We are working on last year's chair cushions, pulling the gold thread out of the green-and-gold fabric—*parfilage*—in order to donate it to the poor. Charity is most important, and though I am not sure what the poor will do with their spools of gold thread, I am sure our work will be much appreciated.

"I heard Mirie—I mean to say the Maréchale de Mirepoix— was paid a hundred thousand *livres* by Richelieu to attend," says Civrac.

"Do not mention that man's name in here!" I snap. "How many times must I tell you? That man is a simmering cauldron of sin." But he is everywhere these days, riding to new prominence on the back of the harlot.

"Simmer," repeats Sophie, picking slowly and ineffectively at her piece of chair cover. I note with satisfaction that my pile of gold thread is larger than hers.

"I would have expected more of the Marquise de Flavacourt," says Louise sadly. "Such a good, pious woman."

"And so very nice," sighs Victoire. "Once, when Mama was ill, she pretended to be the Virgin Mary, and Mama was so happy, though a little surprised that the Holy Mother had such good manners, being a peasant and all."

"Piety does not always equal goodness," I snap. In truth, Flavacourt is not my favorite lady. I fancy she thinks herself more judgmental than even I, and they call her the last of the great ladies once known as the Pious Pack and once a force at Court. I yank at a particularly obstinate piece of thread, but it refuses to come through.

"Let me," says Narbonne helpfully, and I relinquish the fabric to her. Our ladies on duty this week are with us, helping us with our charity, but I note with suspicion that some of the younger ladies' piles of thread are rather small. And the Duchesse de Broglie—is she not even trying? I fix her with a beady eye but she only gazes placidly back, as though I am honoring her with my look, and rubs her belly—she is indisposed *again*.

"Those ladies that attended that supper of infamy and dared to consort with the Barry woman must know they have earned our limitless enmity." That phrase has a nice ring to it, so I repeat it: "Our limitless enmity. Even the Marquise de Flavacourt, pious as she is. We set the scene at Court and we shall shun them, and others will follow."

"Do you really think we set the scene at Court?" asks Louise mildly, and from behind her I hear what I think is a snicker from the Duchesse de Laval, very young and very pretty, and very much disliked by me.

"What a question! I am first in precedence, am I not?" It is a hot August day, the sun beastly and unrelenting. The windows are open, but the breeze doesn't enter, only the flies, despite the flock of valets poised by the windows to beat them back. Perhaps we should have gone for a carriage ride, as Victoire suggested, but with the Feast of Saint Monegundis coming up—one of my mother's favorites—I had thought it best if we devoted the afternoon to charity.

"A sad, sad state of affairs," says Thaïs, the Comtesse de Montbarrey and one of my favorite ladies. Her husband, the Comte de Montbarrey, is a small and pompous man but excellent with the compliments: last week he declared that he felt most intelligent and superior when seated next to me. "With that indecent woman everywhere," she continues. "Perhaps the old days were best, when we were served fish, and not chicken and entrails."

I bristle for not having thought up such a quip myself. Yet sadly, her words ring true—who would have thought that we would ever look back fondly on the days of the Pompadour?

After the infamous dinner—plum wine from their own orchards, sighed Victoire as though in envy—the harlot settled into court life, happily lodged in the old third-floor apartments of the pimping fish. Always laughing and in a gay mood, showing herself everywhere, and even attending my card parties. Chattering away with her new friends, with the men circling her like a flock of hungry birds.

After being forced to attend the dinner at Bellevue—no thaw was reported—Choiseul departed from Court in order to register his disapproval. A fine move, but Papa does not appear to care. I wish I could also retire to register my disapproval, but I am not sure where I would go. And besides, Papa would miss us too much.

"Please add this to your pile, Madame," murmurs Thaïs de Montbarrey, handing Narbonne an enormous spool of gold thread. A great bead of sweat runs down my neck and I shift uncomfortably; I feel as though I am swaddled in a wool blanket, though my dress is as light as formality allows.

Behind me there is a scuffle and another giggle. I whip my head around, but not fast enough to catch the Duchesse de Broglie at whatever it was she was doing with her thread. I narrow my eyes and she looks back placidly, winding the thread around her elegant white wrist, yet still somehow managing to rub her belly.

"We must reproach Papa," says Louise sadly. Louise has often complained about this work, for she believes donating money would be more appropriate and does not understand how much better it is for the poor if we devote our time to their cause. Today, though, she does not complain and appears quite tractable and happy to be pulling out the threads and passing them to Civrac, who then twists them into neat spools. "His soul is in peril," Louise continues, "and we cannot sit lightly by while that woman takes away his chance of Heaven."

I look at her with suspicion, but she does not meet my eyes, just quietly continues picking out her thread to add to her distressingly large pile. We still see Papa every morning, and most afternoons, but these days his visits are quick and routine, as though something to be submitted to, like the barber or the wig powderer. He no longer makes coffee in our apartments, and rarely embraces us. Me. And hasn't since that dreadful day . . .

On those nights when the harlot is with Papa, it is extra torture, for though I wish to engage him in conversation, I cannot bring myself to talk to him in her presence. What if she were to join—interrupt—our conversation, and then I would be in the awkward position of having to address her . . . but it does not bear thinking about.

"For his health, we should not mention the matter," I say, still staring at Louise. Is she trying to trick me? I have not told her about the dreadful scene, but somehow I think she knows. I see again my father's dark eyes flashing and that awful look of pity mixed with disdain. I inhale deeply and pull viciously at a particularly stubborn thread. "On the surface we must appear calm, but beyond that we must do all that we can to unseat this dreadful woman."

A large fly starts to buzz around my head, and Narbonne calls a footman over, but he is unable to catch it with his net. Suddenly I feel as though I am baking in boredom and irritation.

"I think our piles are large enough," I snap. "Narbonne, you may gather the threads, and you, Brionne, the fabrics. Now we must prepare ourselves for Monsieur Marvette. He will be here shortly, and we must devote our attention to him."

Marvette is Papa's astronomer; next month Venus will eclipse the sun and I wish us all to be prepared for this historic event. Papa has a keen interest in astronomy, and I imagine a select group of us on the roofs, enjoying the moment together. I myself will point out the trajectory and talk knowledgeably about orbits—he will be most impressed.

"I don't want to study astronomy," says Sophie, standing up and wiping her neck with a handkerchief. "It's too hot."

"What?" I turn to her in astonishment. Sophie's voice was clear, and high, and had a strong timbre to it that I hadn't heard since . . . well, since . . . ever.

"I don't want to study astronomy," she repeats, her voice reverting to her usual whisper.

"My dear? I know it is difficult, and hard to understand, but that is precisely why . . ." I trail off. I don't think I have ever heard Sophie speak so clearly. Or speak at all. What on earth is happening? "But Louis-Auguste is joining us?" I say, referring to the dauphin and our favorite nephew.

"I don't think I will stay either," says Louise calmly. "Stargazing somehow smacks of the heathen. Come, Sophie, ladies, walk me back to my apartments." They exit, and I think I hear a whisper about someone "never finding Venus."

I turn to Victoire in astonishment.

"What was that? What on earth is wrong with Sophie?"

Victoire can only shake her head, looking terribly flustered, and motions to Civrac to get the cordial from the cupboard.

Well. Well. I stand up and circle the room, not sure where to stop. My goodness, it is a hot day; I feel as though there is a roiling river of sweat inside me. I pick up my fan and start fanning myself.

"It appears Madame Sophie has had a bad turn," I announce, to no one in particular, "and does not wish to participate. We shall . . . we shall prepare ourselves, nonetheless . . ." I sit down and frown, unsure of what I was trying to say.

Victoire settles beside me with her glass and pats my arm lightly. "It is a pity Sophie has gone; I know she was wondering what colors she should select for her autumn wardrobe."

"It's astronomy, not astrology," I snap, wishing I could take her cordial and fling it all over the face of the Duchesse de Laval, still smirking in the corner. I smooth my skirts and take a deep breath. "Monsieur Marvette will be here soon and we must . . . we must . . ."

The dauphin and his attendants are announced. Dear Louis-Auguste. Such a darling boy. The Court makes fun of him, of course, and calls him *pudding*, as they called his dear father, but to me he is perfect. So solid and serious, channeling his energy—I am sure he has some—into studious pursuits. And so shy—always a sign of a good heart.

"Aunts," he says, fumbly bowing and sitting down, his tutor, Vauguyon, beside him. Louis-Aug—as we call him—is fifteen and slightly awkward. He has been too long in the company of men—I dart a glance at Vauguyon, one of *her* creatures—and we provide the essential goodness of female life that he and his two younger brothers, the Comtes de Provence and Artois, are missing. Provence—only a year younger—is cut from the same mold as his older brother (though if possible, even more stolid and fat), but Artois is too confident and charming by half.

Dear Louis-Aug will be married soon, but we can't rely on his wife to provide much for him: she will be Austrian, after all.

"My honored pupils," announces Marvette, coming into the salon, accompanied by his men carrying the tools of their trade. "We shall prepare to chart the course of Venus!" I note with satisfaction that Louis-Aug blushes suitably at the mention of Venus—so very inappropriate of the Greeks to name the planet after a female goddess associated with the immoral side of life.

ℰℬ

Sophie's intransigence subsides, thank goodness—I never could determine what had caused her outburst—but now I am convinced something is happening with Louise. She is so complacent, and at peace, and her usual acerbic wit quite diminished.

A dreadful thought swaddles itself around me and refuses to unwind: she has a lover.

As much as I cannot countenance the idea, I become more and more convinced it is the truth. She has long been jealous, no doubt, that I am the only one amongst us with a romantic history. She is thirty-two, and though I am loath to admit it, she is still rather pretty. I find myself staring at her, noting with suspicion the serenity of her countenance, and even her apparent sincere enjoyment of our trumpet lessons, which she had hitherto resisted.

But who?

I corner Victoire. "We must find out what Louise is doing in the evenings!"

"Certainly," says Victoire, her eyes widening and starting to look flustered. "I'll ask Civrac. What do you think she is doing?"

"I suspect . . ." I purse my lips, then utter the dreaded words: "I suspect a man."

"Oh! Oh no," breathes Victoire, her eyes popping. Civrac is instructed to glean what she can, but she only comes back with the news that Louise is praying and spending more time in the chapel.

Unlikely, I think. Or perhaps . . . praying her sins away? My knees weaken at the thought of the scandal that would hit us were my suspicions to be true.

Sometimes, I think glumly, watching Louise one morning at breakfast as she calmly butters her toast, it is as if the whole world is turned upside down. Prostitutes in the bed of our father; Louise's sudden secretiveness; Sophie's rage. Surely such a state of affairs cannot last?

Chapter Twenty-One

In which the Comtesse du Barry happily ensconces herself in the largest apartment in the palace

"Oh, beautiful, beautiful!" I run through the finished rooms and stop counting after eight. Peach, yellow, pink, blue, delicate rooms of light and love. "Beautiful!" The Marquis de Marigny, the Director General of Buildings and the Pompadour's brother, is proudly showing us the results of the yearlong renovation of my new apartment. In his stubborn, full-cheeked features there is no hint—at least none I can discern—of the beauty of his dead sister. Louis is relaxed and comfortable around him, and I decide I like him too.

"Thank you, Marigny! They're beautiful." They call him Mariné—Marinated—but apparently he doesn't mind. Even though he looks to be well past forty, he married only a few years ago. His wife is rumored to be one of Louis' bastards, by a woman called Irene Filleul—Chon says she is finding so many past paramours her head is dizzy with girls. Marigny could therefore be considered Louis' son-in-law, though Louis has never acknowledged the connection.

Marigny bows. "I am delighted you are content, madame."

"More than content!" I confirm. "Now you may go."

"Madame?" asks Marigny, looking at the king. Louis shrugs slightly, as I have taught him.

"Thank you, we would be alone. We have some work to do."

"And what work is that, Angel?" chuckles Louis after Marigny takes his leave. "Certainly, the bathing room is unfinished—you heard the man, the Tuscans are—"

I kiss him. "No, not that kind of work, silly." I drag him through a small door into a large reception room, sunny and pink, and explain to him the need to christen each room.

"I like the sentiment, but there are thirteen rooms," protests Louis with a muffled groan. He once complained, in admiration, that he had finally met his match: someone with a stronger desire than his own. "An admirable sentiment, but could we not find something a little less . . . sacrilegious than 'christen'?"

"Baptize?"

"I am not joking, Angel," he says patiently. "We must remember God can see us at all times."

"Of course, dearest. Bless? No wait, I'm sorry, that won't do either, far too religious-y. How about . . ." I twirl around the room once more. "How about *anoint*?"

He groans and I giggle; there is no escape.

I pull him down beside me onto the perfectly parqueted floor. "Now, you lie back," I say, straddling him.

He complies, shaking his head. "I used to think this position so sacrilegious—la, all roads lead to God this morning. La!" He chuckles. "Angel, I'm even starting to *talk* like you! What would I do without you?"

"La, what *wouldn't* you do?"

I love everything about my new apartment. I am seven years old and back in Frederica's boudoir, only this is ten times more luxurious. Taffeta hangings, Turkish sofas, giant mirrors, carpets as plush as birds, rooms of intimacy and delight, scented with potpourris and fresh flowers. A nest—or a cage—for the most beautiful bird of paradise: me.

I revel and roll on my luxurious bed, the mattress a foot thick, then get up and wander for hours through the furnished rooms, marveling at my good fortune. Since the party at Bellevue, my life at Court has become infinitely more enjoyable. Mirie is a firm friend, and the Marquise de Flavacourt was even quite pleasant to me last week over *beriberi*.

When Choiseul absented himself in disgust after the dinner,

the Duc d'Aiguillon took that opportunity to worm his way into the king's favor, and is now constantly at his side. He must have been very handsome when he was younger, to have won the heart of Marie-Anne de Châteauroux, but now he has receded into middle-aged dumpiness. Nonetheless he is always full of flattery; he is quite the poet, and once even said he would like to drink my sweet nectar, were I not taken by his master.

He tried the same line on Chon, who told him very clearly that she was not a honey farm.

Of course there are plenty who still disdain me at every opportunity. The young Comte de Lauraguais, apparently as big a lecher as his father the duke (or so Chon tells me), brings a flower seller from Brittany to Court. He parades her around and calls her the Comtesse de la Tonnerre—the Countess of the Barrel, a pun on my name of Barry. I think it rather funny, and even stopped to greet the girl one day; she blushed and looks frightened in equal measure.

The prank incenses Louis and he suggests to young Lauraguais that he spend some time in England, and immediately. His mother has just died and I think the punishment over-harsh, but Louis assures me I needn't be so kindhearted—Diane was only his stepmother.

"The Duchesse de Lauraguais, a part of my past," Louis says sadly; she was one of the infamous Mailly-Nesle sisters rumored to have slept with him many years ago. "She was his stepmother, never had children of her own who lived, poor woman."

"Still . . . it seems cruel to send him away now, when he must be grieving. I know how I would feel if the monk Guimard died."

"Who?" asks Louis.

"The monk Guimard," I repeat, and explain that he is a friend of my mother's.

"A monk? But surely—not anything more than a friend?"

"No, of course not!" I lie. Chon is constantly urging me to be more cautious in what I share with the king. Ma is now ensconced comfortably in a convent in Paris and I visit her quite often. It is

a very aristocratic convent, and my mother is now known as Madame de Rançon de Montrabé.

☙☙

Ma greets us with a hug and treats Chon and me to a plate of
chestnut-coated chicken wings fresh from the fryer. Of course she
doesn't have to prepare and sell chickens anymore, but she still
enjoys cooking. The kitchen is respectfully empty for my mother,
and the monk Guimard is here. I wonder, briefly, how the nuns
explain his presence.

"You know what you should do," he says, when I tell them the
story about the Countess of the Barrel, "is take one of those high
noble friends of yours, and have them pretend they're a fishwife
for a day!"

"Oh, they'd never accept that," says Ma.

"Ha! You might be surprised at what they would do," I say,
delighted with his suggestion. "For the right amount of money.
Chon, do you think the Maréchale de Mirepoix would consent
to play a fishwife for a day if I gave her my new emerald necklace?
She did so admire it last night."

"Don't press your luck," says Ma, crushing a great mound of
chestnuts under her rolling pin. "Tread carefully. It's like hens
when the cock is rampant—you think they are docile, but they're
just scared into submission."

I take another chicken wing. "Mmm. Will you give my chef
the recipe for this? I would serve them at my supper. My *first* supper," I clarify, "that I will be giving in my *new* apartment."

My first supper at Versailles, I think in excitement, as a presented lady and as an *accepted* lady. Ma wraps up a few of the
chicken wings for the ride back, and in the carriage Chon and I
plan the guest list and entertainment.

"Should I put on a play? Or have a poetry reading?" I say, a
little dubiously. Mirie has told me about all the cultured enter-
tainments Pompadour used to stage. I've seen her portraits—I
am definitely prettier—but Mirie says she was the most elegant
woman she ever had the pleasure of knowing; not a stitch wrong,

not a word out of place. "She was always onstage, it seemed, some might say the essence of artifice, but at heart she was a good woman." Mirie's face got rather red when she talked, and it appears she genuinely cared for the woman.

Chon shakes her head. "No, that's not your style. Just be yourself. That's the way the king likes you."

"Fine," I say happily. "We'll have good food, and lots of wine, and just our own wit for entertainment. Nothing else!"

Back at Versailles, Louis greets me with the news that he has found the perfect house for me: Louveciennes, the palace of the young Princesse de Lamballe, widowed last year.

"Syphilis, and advanced," whispers Chon. "Heard it from the princesse's own reader."

"The princesse has syphilis?" I say in astonishment, thinking of her angelic face, perfect nose, and extreme piety; she crosses herself every time she sees me.

"No, not the princesse, silly," whispers back Chon. "Her husband had it. Though of course . . ."

"Well, it sounds lovely," I say to Louis, feeding him one of the wings we saved from the carriage ride. I riffle through the floor plans unrolled on a table. "But how does Madame de Lamballe feel about me taking her house?" The princess only arrived last year, from Italy, and is constantly weeping. Very sad about her dead husband, or relieved—one can never tell which.

"So charming, charming, my dear, always concerned for others, above yourself," says Louis, taking me in his arms.

"Don't be," hisses Chon when we are alone again. "The Princesse de Lamballe isn't concerned for you, and never will be, so why should you care about her? And Louveciennes is perfect—my source tells me it has wonderful gardens, and is most conveniently placed—just over an hour from Versailles."

My dreams are so vivid and intense, and so interesting, that I cannot help but look to them for inspiration. It is a flaw I have prayed long and hard against, but still I dream. Last night I dreamed of a giant blue egg, a robin's, I suppose, that rolled over and then . . . I can't remember much else.

Choiseul, his disapproval sufficiently registered, returns to Court to oversee preparations for our new dauphine's impending arrival. When he seeks another audience with me, I acquiesce graciously. These days, old rivalries are best forgotten as all join in common cause against our enemy.

This time his sister accompanies him; the man is gallantry personified.

I nod to Beatrice, who sinks down in a stiff curtsy. We are close in age, but she is most unattractive and I believe looks far older than I.

"I have a plan, my dear ladies, to defeat our common enemy. I must seek your approval and help in its implementation," says Choiseul, after the pleasantries have been exchanged.

I nod my head in perfect understanding.

Beatrice nods as well. "Yes, we are in need of a fresh plan, for that woman's hold shows no sign of lessening. I heard she does exercises, down there," she hisses, and shakes her head in disgust. I too look suitably aghast, though I have scant idea what she is talking about.

"She has tried hard to win my approval," continues Choiseul, "but it is not to be had. She even tried using my nephew Lauzun to intercede with me." I sneak a peek at Beatrice, rumored to have been the young man's lover, but she seems unflustered at the mention. Unflustered! "She wanted him to plead her case. Needless to say, I was unmoved."

As he orates on I think what an odd-looking man he is; such a lumpy nose. He caused a scandal last month by attending the state council with no wig or powder, his orange hair showing for all the world to see! Modern and radical, I think with a shudder, wondering what my dear brother would think were he to see me now, chatting away with this man he once called a liberal lecher.

Such a pity the man is an atheist and freethinker who tries to compromise with Parlement, that body that so vexes my father. Choiseul even considers himself proud to be progressive— as though that were a good thing! Had he been on the right path, he might have done much for France, for by all accounts he is a capable man and my father thinks highly of him. And he is, of course, of superior birth; in recent years there has been a distressing trend for the Nobility of the Robe, the newer nobility who generally assume the lower ranks of administration, to ascend to the highest government positions in the land—I think of men like Maurepas and Argenson, and shudder. But Choiseul: his family traces its roots to 1215, and I know he jealously guards the prerogatives of the ancient Nobility of the Sword.

"—and no matter how many overtures, I shall never consort with that woman," he continues grimly.

"Certainly, brother," agrees Beatrice, and their look of mutual admiration makes me almost choke, though I am not eating. I have heard the rumors—I did not understand them at first, and had scolded both Victoire and Civrac for spreading such calumny, entirely contrary to nature. I must make sure Sophie doesn't hear of those rumors, I think, getting flustered, and suddenly wishing for some of Victoire's cordial. Were Sophie to—

". . . of that minx," finishes Choiseul, raising an eyebrow at me. I hide the fact I was not listening with a quick reprimand.

"I am sure such language is not appreciated here, monsieur," I snap.

"Of course, of course," he says, "how remiss of me to use such a word, with your known delicate sensibilities. Now, Madame, I know you have much of importance to attend to today—I saw Figliari in the antechamber, for your lesson in ornithology, no doubt—so I will be as brief and blunt as manners allow. I have a new plan for your father's happiness. And ours."

I nod that he may continue.

"I am commonly known as the *Queen Maker*."

"Are you? I have not heard that expression before."

"Indeed, because of the instrumental role I played in arranging our dear dauphin's marriage."

"Of course." I am surprised to hear Choiseul speak of it so proudly, for surely he knows I—we—disapprove of an Austrian on the throne of France?

"And the success of that marriage," he continues, as self-satisfied as a man, "has led me to think—why not a similar bride for your father? The King should marry again."

Oh.

Beside him, Beatrice's gray teeth are bared in feral agreement.

"I am thinking one of the sisters of the Archduchess Marie Antoinette might indeed be the ideal candidate," continues Choiseul. "I have already commissioned a portrait of the Arch-duchess Élisabeth, an elder sister of our future dauphine. Not an etching—a charming pastel—but I could show it to you in my rooms, should you be so inclined."

Is he inviting me to his rooms?

"You see, at heart the king is a man moved by family"— here he reaches over and caresses Beatrice's hand—"and though there has been strain lately, I believe that as he ages he will only turn more to religion, and to the warm bosom of his family." *Bosom*—my hand loses its tenuous grip on the side of my chair and I almost fall down, but the man continues as though he has said nothing untoward: "The king turns sixty in a few months, an age when the thoughts of men, and even kings, must turn to mortality."

He says it so smoothly, it doesn't sound at all treasonous.

C/D

Upon reflection, I decide Choiseul's idea is excellent in its simplicity: Papa must marry again. The sanctity of marriage, and the scourge of sin erased, for a new queen would never countenance the Barry woman.

Perfect.

And since I will have already lost precedence to the coming Austrian child, I am open to considering the idea. I am not enamored of Choiseul's choice—another one of the fluster of archduchesses, another Austrian—but the wife herself is immaterial. The *concept* is what matters.

"A new Queen of France!"

"A new mama?" says Victoire with a worried frown. "I'm not sure about that." She pours herself a glass of cordial—how did it come to be on the table?—and sips with a worried frown.

"Well, it is a little surprising, but I think it the perfect solution. I must insist on a united front when we talk to Papa." Oh—did Choiseul wish me to broach the subject with Papa? We had not discussed it, but I hope that is not his intention.

"There is our father's soul to be considered, balanced against his"—a delicate shudder for Sophie's benefit—"earthly desires." I look around. "But why is Louise not here? She was summoned hours ago!" I should have waited, but was too impatient to reveal the news. And Victoire had no idea! Civrac failed in that one, I think in grim contentment.

Louise enters, looking distracted as usual. "You called, sister?"

"Indeed, I did." I look at her hands. "You have an ink stain on your glove."

Louise looks down at the small blot, seemingly without remorse. "I was writing a letter."

"You should have changed your gloves," I say pointedly. I wait for an apology, but none appears.

"I can send for a fresh pair of mine," says Victoire, reaching for the bell to summon one of the women.

"No, don't bother," I say in irritation. "Louise-Marie, sit down. We have momentous news."

"Carriage," breathes Sophie.

"Really? The carriage is fixed—that is what you called me for?" There is real irritation in Louise's voice. "And I already told you, I don't want to ride out tomorrow."

"No, no. Sophie, you really must speak more clearly! Marriage . . . marriage is what she meant to say."

A hunted look blossoms across Louise's face and her left shoulder inches up as she slumps down. "But I thought . . . Papa? My deformity?"

"No, Louise-Marie, it's not *your* wedding we are talking about! You're far too old."

"She's only thirty-two," protests Victoire.

Relief floods Louise's face and her shoulders straighten. "So," she says casually, rubbing her forehead, exposing her stained glove again, "who is getting married? One of Broglie's children?"

"Not at all. It is in fact our dear father—the king—who is to be married." My words sound very important and pleasing.

"Really?" Louise finally looks interested. "And who is the bride?"

"Well, the details are not certain. Perhaps one of the new dauphine's sisters, there are so many of them."

"Strange, isn't it—there are always so many daughters," observes Victoire.

"It is well known we women are of hardier constitution than the men, and that is why there are more of us," I say. It sounds right, but then I think of my dead sisters and dead nieces and I am not so sure.

"And what does Papa think?" asks Louise.

"Well . . . that is to say . . . he has not yet been informed. Choiseul chose to take me into his confidence and he proposed—"

"Choiseul—that infidel? I didn't realize you were still cavorting with him," says Louise.

"Cavorting," murmurs Sophie.

"Cavorting! What strange words you choose, sister. Cavorting!" My hands start shaking. I—a daughter of France—to be
accused of *cavorting* with a man. And my sister said it so calmly,
almost as though . . . she were the one cavorting. I narrow my
eyes. My suspicions remain, and I consider briefly if the time is
right for a good accusation.

"Oh, calm yourself, Adélaïde. One badly chosen word. An
interesting idea, to be sure, but I can't imagine Papa submitting
to a dynastic marriage, to an unknown archduchess. Why not a
French lady of good birth?"

I gasp in horror. "A French lady—*of good birth*? Of inferior
birth to ourselves? To be Queen of France and overtake us in precedence? Have you quite lost your mind?"

Louise stands up. "Well, thank you so much for sharing
the news, and we will have to see how it develops. Now, if you
will excuse me, dear sisters, I have to get back to my correspondence. And I shan't be supping with you tonight or attending the
Comédie—I am receiving the Abbé de Luynes."

When I tell Narbonne the news, she considers it thoughtfully
then suggests we go see the portrait of the Archduchess Élisabeth
for ourselves. We make our way to Choiseul's rooms and order the
footman to open the doors. I look around in distaste at the lair
of masculinity, the dark green paneling on the walls, the shelves
lined with books. Almost as if he has no wife, though Honorine
is often at Court, where she spends her days weeping about his
many infidelities.

We find the portrait leaning against a wall in the salon; beside it, two open doors lead into his bedchamber, where a pair
of maids are working on something on the bed. Of course, entertaining in a bedroom is certainly proper, though it is done less
and less these years, of which I must be glad.

I focus on the pastel portrait. Mature years—our new

dauphine is only fourteen, just a year younger than our dear Louis-Auguste—but her sister Élisabeth is already twenty-six. And she would be the Queen of France, and become her sister's stepgrandmother . . . Papa would become his grandson's brother-in-law . . . it is rather ridiculous. But still, ridicule is preferable to sin.

Almost.

And a queenly archduchess would make short shrift of the harlot.

"She looks a bit like the Marquise de Fleury," remarks Narbonne, referring to my most hated and flighty lady-in-waiting.

"Mmm, in a certain way. Though perhaps it is just the color of the dress—Brionne had a similar one, the color of a robin's egg. I remember Madame Victoire rather admired it, and fashioned one of her new spring gowns on it."

"And her choker is odd, a bit high."

"Perhaps that is how the Austrians wear them," I say doubtfully, agreeing it is very ugly.

As we turn to leave I suddenly recollect my dream, the large rolling blue robin's egg—was this a premonition?

Chapter Twenty-Three

In which Madame du Barry makes a difficult decision

"L a, how I hate politics! And intrigue. Well, intrigue can sometimes be interesting," I concede, picking up a shawl and floating it around me. As light and airy as an angel's wing, the draper declared. My morning toilette is dedicated to commerce—throughout the day I may welcome petitions and such, but my mornings are devoted to my tradesmen.

The room is now littered with their debris—samples of fabrics, shoes, and jewels. A particularly dainty-looking hat. A new style of bodice with buttons. Yards of gold trim hung over the back of the sofa. Labille's shop, after a great storm. I pick up a cream kid shoe and turn it in the sunlight by the window—beautiful, and the real gems on the soles so cunning and unexpected.

"Ah, Jeanne, you may hate politics, but politics loves you," observes Chon, running a length of red ribbon through her hands. Despite my entreaties, she only ever wears dark colors. "You are a cipher for the games men play."

"What's a cipher?" I drape myself in the beautiful shawl. The tradesman left two—a pink and a green—and I promised to decide by tomorrow.

"A cipher is a person who does the bidding of others, and appears to have no will of their own. Someone other people can put their desires and dreams on."

Put their desires and dreams on. Yes, that's true, I think: all my life men—and some women—have put their dreams and especially their desires in and on me.

In a surprising turn of events, the *dévot* party of the Court—the champions of conservatism and religion—have become my allies. The hatred they feel for Choiseul, the man who banished the Jesuits, who compromises with Parlement, and who openly quotes from the freethinkers, is so intense that they are willing to ally themselves to me. Cardinals and courtesans, allied against Choiseul. How funny!

Politics is indeed a strange beast.

Led by the Duc d'Aiguillon, we are called the *Barriens*. It is rather a heady thing to have a political party named after oneself. Not a formal party, of course—there is no such thing in France—but Chon says the *Barriens* and the *Choiseulites* are like the Whigs and Tories in England.

"What a funny name for a political party, in English. Wigs!" I think of the Duc d'Ayen. "Did you see d'Ayen's wig last week at Madame Sophie's ball? And the Marquise d'Arcambal wore one too!" *Not only for men*, she told me. Fashion is starting to dictate height for hairstyles and not every lady is as blessed with abundant hair as I am.

"I doubt I'll ever need to wear a wig," I say in satisfaction and to no one in particular. I run my hands through my hair, still undressed and only pinned up loosely. I washed it yesterday and the scent of lemon and verbena is heavenly.

"Now, what do you think of this wrap, should I get it in the pink or the green?" I say, steering the conversation to brighter pastures.

Chon ignores me and starts directing the women to clear away the debris of the morning and to bring the articles I wish to consider into an adjoining room. Outside, it starts to rain. I frown; I like a daily walk around the gardens, but not in wet weather.

The door flies open and Louis enters.

"Darling! I thought you were dining in public today!" I say, giving him a kiss and wrapping him up in the green shawl.

"No, no," says Louis, looking a little sheepish. "I have such a headache, Angel, and it only increased at Mass, that man blathering on about brimstone and bushes." He sighs. "I suppose I shouldn't talk thus of a man of God. Ah—that's lovely."

"Do you like it?" I take the shawl back and twirl around with it.

"Marvelous, yes. I thought I might come here and take a little rest. And Adélaïde and Victoire will do our duty admirably, won't they?" he says, referring to his daughters who were to dine with him.

Louis often gets headaches on days when he must dine in public. I completely understand, for the ceremony is long and dreary and the food always cold when it reaches his plate. And my Louis hates being on display—like a monkey in a menagerie, he once complained.

I lead him to my bedroom and unbutton his jacket, take off his shoes, and tuck him into bed. Outside, the storm rages and the rain beats harshly down on the roof.

"I love being up here in the rain," says Louis, grasping my hand as I turn to leave. "Down in my rooms you can't hear it, but up here . . . I feel closer to the skies. To Heaven." I kiss him once then go to leave. "Don't let Maupeou find me," he pleads, referring to his chancellor and important minister.

"Madame!" It is Richelieu, chatting with Chon in a corner.

"Hello, Rich," I say, sitting down on the sofa and picking up the pink shawl again. "I can't decide—pink or green?"

"We've got good news, Jeanne," says Mirie, coming in from another room, her rabbit, Jonas, loping along behind her on a velvet leash. Chon sometimes says I have too many rooms, and she can never keep track of my guests.

"Tell me!"

"Madame," says Richelieu, coming to stand in front of me. "Certainly, the green one. No question. But now . . ." He takes a letter from his pocket and bows with a flourishing sweep. "Madame, I am happy to present you the invitation you have long desired, given to me by the Duc d'Aumont himself; he wished to deliver it, but I claimed the honor."

"Ha!" I exclaim, leaping up and snatching the paper. I know what it is: the invitation for me—me!—to greet the new dauphine at Compiègne. The Court has been buzzing about this matter for weeks, wondering whether the king will be indecent enough to foist his harlot on his new daughter-in-law.

Well, now we know the answer.

"I'm so very curious to meet her," says Mirie, settling down and telling one of my women to bring some tea. "One hears such conflicting reports. But we know Choiseul hopes she will charm the king into restoring order at Court."

I snort, knowing what she means.

"More than a fourteen-year-old can manage, certainly, no matter how charming she may be," observes Richelieu. "And I doubt she really is that attractive. I have seen the arrival of three dauphines in my time, and I remember they even waxed eloquently—well, slightly—about the poor Infanta Rafaela, back in '45."

"I've heard she's rather silly and immature," says Mirie. "Not surprising, really. I remember when I was fourteen—I was married, but I was just a chit-headed girl from a convent. Thought that when I closed my eyes, the whole world went dark, and I was always worrying over spiders."

"Fourteen—I was still in the convent too," I say, thinking back to Saint-Maur and to my silly fears of falling. I giggle. "Did you know when you were fourteen—about life? You know, that side of life?"

Mirie chuckles. She is a very pleasant woman, supremely unflappable, and indulges me to no end. "Well, I was married, so in some ways yes, but I thought it was just something my husband did. I was astonished when I found out all men did it. Extraordinary."

"I was twelve," recalls Richelieu in a faraway voice, stroking the pink shawl, "when I first discovered the delights God saw fit to bless upon men. The ladies of the Court used to pet me, thinking me no more than a boy, and it took them a pleasant while to realize I was playing with their breasts, and not their ribbons. A world of possibilities opened up—literally."

"How sad it is that youth must leave us," says Mirie with a sigh, staring into her teacup. She is a few years older than the king, and as I look between my friends, I suddenly realize how old they both are—Richelieu is seventy-four this year. I am surrounded by age, I think in despair. How will that help keep Louis young?

Mirie motions for Zamor, my little page (she helped me secure him from Bengal, via Bordeaux) to help her off the sofa. "I must get going; I promised Félicité I'd help her go through her jewels for the wedding festivities."

"I shall accompany you, my dear lady," says Richelieu, rising with some difficulty from the deep chair he had sunk into. "Jeanne, don't let the king sleep too long—I shan't tell Maupeou where he is, but I know he'll be pestering me."

After they leave, I wander over to Chon, hard at work on a letter. The rain continues to beat down; there was a leak in the corner of the blue room last week, and it fair stained the paneling.

"Who are you writing to?"

"Ah, people," Chon says, her pen busy, her brow furrowed in concentration. Chon passes her days writing, to whom and for what I know not.

A commotion in the next room and Zamor comes in to say Chancellor Maupeou's undersecretary is looking for the king.

"Tell him he's not here," I whisper to Chon. "Tell them he rode to the Trianon before the rain came; that'll confuse them." Chon giggles and bustles out. She keeps the demons at bay, the castle safe. A crack of thunder startles me. I hope the storm does not wake Louis.

I slowly open the door to my bedroom, careful not to disturb. Louis slumbers on, his mouth open, snoring lightly. I settle in a chair by the fire and watch him sleep. Occasionally his limbs twitch and once he mouths what sounds like *bijou*. Dreaming about jewels, no doubt, like I often do.

Such a kind man, I think, looking at him tenderly. He refuses me nothing. Not just material things, but requests for mercy and kindness as well. Last month I saved a young girl, accused of infanticide, from being burned alive, and then an army deserter destined to be hanged. Chon says my kind heart means I will forever be besieged by petitions, but I am happy to oblige.

I think about my invitation and the new dauphine who is coming. Will she be a friend? I hope so, though unfortunately she will be Choiseul's creature, and will no doubt do his bidding. Politics, intrigue, how it makes my head hurt.

I should start planning my dress, I think, turning to more pleasant thoughts. The king coughs then turns over in his sleep. Something magnificent. I must remember to get the merchant Perrot back again; he showed me some wonderful fabrics last week. But it's hard to think of spring clothes when it's so cold and dreary outside.

I go to sit by Louis on the bed and stroke his head, careful not to wake my sleeping prince. We are just the same: we both hate obligations, and both hide away from all that is unpleasant. Me like the King of France? But why not—he's just a man, born of a mother, living and dying like the rest of us. My thoughts wander over to children, as they occasionally do these days. I used to revel in my barrenness that allowed me freedom, but now small twinges of regret, that we have no child together, sometimes prick me. When they do, I try not to think about them. I snuggle down beside him, then a ferocious crack of thunder wakes him from his nap.

"Ah, you are here," he says sleepily, and reaches for me. "Come closer, dearest." He falls asleep again and I doze alongside him as the rain beats down over us. Heaven is a place on earth, and it is in my rooms, I think. I have created a home for him, in the middle of the grandest, nastiest palace in the world.

The pink, I think suddenly, before sleep pulls me down in its warm embrace. Yes, definitely the pink shawl.

Chapter Twenty-Four

In which Madame Adélaïde is betrayed, again

"The king, the king," says a chambermaid, rushing in. "He's here!" It is not gone six and I am still in bed, trying to remember a dream . . . of ducks, or was it dogs?

"What? Here? Oh, goodness, goodness! My stays, but Fourdan has my morning gown, no I'd better change it, what? What does he want?"

"Shall I get Madame de Narbonne?"

"No time, no time, I—"

"His Majesty said no need to stand on ceremony."

"Why didn't you tell me that first, dratted woman?" I sit back down on my bed, breathing heavily, confusion addling my morning brain. "Bring my black robe, and we'll tie it over my chemise."

She helps me into the enormous black habit and I wash my face and paste on a nervous smile, but I cannot quell the fear that mixes with my excitement. What have I done? What if he is not pleased with me?

"My dear, I would speak with you alone." My father looks rather old and worried in his plum-colored dressing gown, his nightcap still on his head and two bright yellow slippers on his feet. Like two ducklings, I think, distracted. My dream . . . He puts his arm on mine, and embraces me, and I want to weep in pleasure—he hasn't done that for years.

He draws back and I search his face: he looks tired, and sad, but also somewhat peaceful. Not angry—but then he never shows his anger until the minute. My heart starts to thump uneasily. Choiseul decided to wait until the new dauphine has charmed

Papa—I was dubious—before broaching the subject of a new marriage. But still . . . has he found out? Does he think I was meddling? Oh, why did I ever consent to see Choiseul?

"My dearest Adélaïde," says Papa, and I see he has been crying. But he hasn't cried since Mama—no, not then, it must have been when dear Josepha, our brother's wife, died.

"Papa—the news! Is it not good?" Would he cry on sending *her* away? Perhaps; I do not understand, nor even attempt to, the ways of men and their lusts.

"My dear, come sit beside me." I do, and a memory rises of the days when I used to play on his lap, when I was a little girl. How I wish I were still that little girl. "My dear, your sister has gone away."

"My sister? Who?"

"Louise-Marie, my dear, she has left us."

"With who?" I blurt out, beginning to shake—such scandal—a daughter of France, a sister of mine—run away with a man. My premonitions were correct! We will all be tainted! Will I be blamed? Oh, pray it is someone worthy! "Conti?"

"Conti? What? No, no . . ." Papa shakes his head, as flustered as I am.

"Orléans? Another man?" Oh, pray it is a prince of the royal blood, yet one unmarried—

"No, no, my dear, there is no man. What a ridiculous idea! Louise has left us, with my permission. She has entered the convent of the Carmelites at Saint Denis. She has done it . . ." Here his voice catches, and he buries his head in his hands for a moment. Should I pat him? Stroke his arm? He looks up again, his face agonized anguish. "She has done it for my soul. She has sacrificed her future for my redemption! There can be no greater love."

"Oh!" I search his face for a sign he is joking, or that the convent is a code for something more unpleasant. "A convent? She's to take the veil?"

"Indeed." He shakes his head again, not looking quite so pained now that he has revealed the news. "Darling Adélaïde, I knew you would understand. I must get going—I promised d'Aumont he could do the honors with my wig this morning. I shall see you at Mass—the priest is informed but will not mention it until tomorrow. Now, you'll tell your sisters, won't you? You know how much I detest unpleasantness, and I know you are just the one to share it with them."

"Of course, Papa!" I cry, but he doesn't embrace me before he leaves.

So that was it. Not a man . . . of the earthly sort. I sit quiet and still in the empty salon, the silver early-morning glow suffusing the room. Louise will be a bride, but of Christ, not of Conti. Suddenly it all makes sense—the newfound calmness, her happy demeanor, the sarcasm diminished. And to do it for our father's soul! That is a debt that can never be repaid.

A raging jealousy rises up in me. Trumped, again, by my crafty little sister.

Two footmen come in with the breakfast table, laughing: "And after she rode it—" When they see me sitting on the sofa, they drop the table with a clatter and back out quickly.

I must face this day with fortitude. I must tell my sisters before they hear rumors, or before Civrac can trump me. When I share the grim news, Victoire starts crying and asks why Louise could not have told us. Sophie grows bright red and flustered and whispers something about a bride.

"Perhaps she'll be like the Duchesse de La Trémoille and come out after five days, complaining of the convent discomforts," I say, unsure how to comfort my weeping sisters. But I know Louise would never do that. She is, I must admit, made of stronger mettle and has done a fine and clever thing. I think of Choiseul's words: as Papa ages he will turn more to religion. And there will be Louise, radiant in her black habit, just the person to help him return to the rightful path.

"It was a crafty move, well played, and will keep our father forever in her debt," I mutter.

"Our Father—God—can never be in anyone's debt," says Victoire, sniffling.

"What? No, I speak of Papa."

"She will save his soul," whispers Sophie in wonderment. "Soul."

After my sisters leave, a desolate emptiness spreads through me. We were once six, and now we are three. Halved. Cleaved in two. Élisabeth dead, Henriette dead, Louise not dead but disappeared into the clutches of the convent and God, and with my father's undying admiration.

Fleeting wings of despair brush me and a sudden urge to take to my bed overcomes me. Nonsense! That I cannot do: there is Italian to study, a trumpet concert to prepare for, a games night to host. So many duties, so many responsibilities. I cannot take to my bed; France needs me.

At least I still have Victoire and Sophie, I think as I trail back to my bedchamber. And they need me, even if Louise didn't.

Chapter Twenty-Five

In which the Comtesse du Barry awaits the arrival of the dauphine

"It was so dreadfully cold," the Marquise de Flavacourt sniffs, "and I remember Gilette—the Duchesse d'Antin, dead now poor dear—her nose was quite frozen, and remained red for days."

The Marquise de Flavacourt is talking of the arrival of the last dauphine, the Princess Josepha of Saxony in 1747. Twenty-three years ago; I was only four years old then. I'm half listening, watching the parade of stiff nobles, the cream of French aristocracy, circling around the grand salon of La Muette, where we are gathered for her arrival.

Fast messengers arrived with the news that she stepped onto French soil safely seven days ago; she should be with us within the day. The small château is aglitter, overstuffed with courtiers and their attendants, the dressmakers run off their feet, and the sound of construction on the pavilion in the courtyard is endless.

"We all laughed at her," continues Flavacourt, still speaking of Josepha, "though in private, of course; she had her hair done in this very strange manner, all sort of puffed up with ribbons, and even though she was changed into French clothes, somehow she managed to make them look . . . Germanic. I can tell you, the Court was not overly impressed."

The Marquise de Flavacourt takes a minute to pick a speck of ash off her magnificent silver skirt. She is dressed, as is everyone else, in grand court costume, her silver skirts shimmering as she talks and a string of lucent pearls, five rows deep, circling her neck. She continues: "Well, this one is supposed to be charming, at least."

"They say she is very dainty, and most high-spirited," I chip in, thinking of the rumors that have been swirling around for months.

"La," snorts Mirie. "See how I pick up your mannerisms? Remember how they gushed about Josepha? And let me tell you there was not much to gush about there. *Of course* she must be praised and admired, that is the nature of what it is to be a dauphine."

"She was a pleasant enough girl," murmurs Flavacourt. "Though nervous, always sniffing around like a silly rabbit." Mirie stiffens and the two older women exchange an icy look.

"I hear she walks so daintily, it is as though she has wings," enthuses the Duc d'Ayen from his perch by the window, his new triple-pigtailed wig resplendent and polished, as smooth as porcelain. "And Richelieu wrote that he would, ah, certainly be delighted to, ah, be with her, were she not an archduchess." Richelieu is with the entourage that met the dauphine at Strasbourg.

I giggle. A stamp of approval indeed!

Beside me, the Marquise de Flavacourt stiffens and says coldly, "He talks of our future queen."

Our future queen, I think. But only when my Louis is dead.

"Oh, he likes to say that about all the dauphines," dismisses Mirie, laughing. "Poor man, it must be difficult to be getting so old and so impotent."

I watch Madame Adélaïde circling the room like a tower, wearing a new gown of deep blue, both her face and her hair gray with powder. Beside her, Madame Victoire is in a fluster of excitement, her cheeks high pink to match her gown.

"I'm so very excited," I can hear her prattle as they sweep by us. Madame Sophie follows, clutching the arm of the Duchesse de Duras and looking as frightened as one of Mirie's rabbits.

Their sister Madame Louise entered a convent last month, in a process so secret not even my Louis told me about it. Our first secret. He cried after he told me, cried at how he feared he had disappointed his family and taken the wrong path, and cried at the devotion his daughter—his youngest and most intelligent—displayed for him.

Well, one thing I know, I think, listening to the women as they continue comparing the old dauphines to the new: she won't be as beautiful as me, and Louis remains firmly devoted. But I have to admit to some apprehension, mostly installed in me by Chon, who can't stop reminding me that Louis likes young, pretty girls. I'm almost thirty, though I know my complexion still blooms like that of a much younger woman. But it is true he is susceptible to youth and charm, wiles and simpers. The newly married Marquise de Caillot, all fourteen years of her, enjoyed much attention when she was presented last month.

The coming of the dauphine has also sparked new life in Choiseul and his cronies; they sense a change is coming. A little squirrel of worry scrabbles around inside me, and won't be quelled. I start playing with the Duc de Croÿ's spaniel, half listening to Flavacourt and watching Mesdames still circling around the room, Madame Adélaïde's nose leading the way.

"Still, one can't compare a little Saxon princess—no disrespect to our late dauphine—to the daughter of an empress. The blood of Caesar flows through our future dauphine's veins," remarks Flavacourt approvingly.

"And the blood of murderers," murmurs Mirie lightly as the Marquise de Colbert approaches.

"Good morning. Ladies," says the old marquise, nodding to Mirie and Flavacourt. Though her gown is magnificent, she is wearing something approaching black, in order to protest the death of her husband at the Battle of Dettingen in '43—against the Austrians.

"Marquise," murmurs Flavacourt as the old woman sweeps away, then adds: "The king will certainly be displeased if he sees her wearing *that* tonight."

"There's no chicken on the menu tonight, thank goodness,"

sniffs Mirie, and I start, fearing I have missed something. "My valet told me he thought they were putting rabbit on the menu, but thank goodness . . ."

A commotion in the courtyard as riders clatter in with the news—the procession approaches! Louis and his grandson rode off yesterday to meet the carriage in the forest of Compiègne nearby. He has hardly had time for me these past days, I think, feeling something queer and sinking inside.

I fancy some of the courtiers are growing colder to me, as though they sense another sun rising. The Marquise de Colbert did not greet me just now, and I overheard a remark yesterday about harlots making for revolutions. And what did Mirie mean just now, gibing about chicken on the menu?

It was an enormous triumph for Louis to have invited me here, for even at Versailles, I have never dined with the royal family. Of course not. I feel oddly alone and suddenly wish I was back in Paris, with Ma and the monk Guimard and their kind words. Or that Chon were here with me. Perhaps I shouldn't have pushed for the invitation. But no; my place is at Louis' side.

I don't join the crowds that rush to fill the courtyard, falling over themselves for a first glimpse. I'll see her soon enough at the dinner. I climb the steps to my room, feeling vaguely uneasy and disheartened. I only saw Louis briefly this morning, and he was in a bad mood, muttering about his oafish grandson.

"Great dolt," he declared, grimacing. "He will be the ruin of France and of himself, but at least I won't be here to see it." He shook his head grimly. "Had to straighten the boy's coat myself—what are his attendants doing, I ask you?"

Up in my room—a small chamber in one of the outer wings—my attendant Henriette is brushing my gown. I hate feeling like this, I think, lying down on the narrow bed: sour and unhappy. Uncertain.

"It's so beautiful, madame," gushes Henriette, fingering the silver and red tissue, the fine fabric spangled with strands of tiny rubies that will wink and glitter in the candlelight.

"It is," I say, hoping it will cheer me up. I have a new ruby necklace to wear with it, the center stone as big as a duck's egg, the color as rich as blood. I must shine and show the world that the arrival of this girl changes nothing, that I am not frightened of this new Austrian threat.

I will look so beautiful tonight, and Louis will remember he loves me, and the new dauphine will love me, and all will be fine.

A clap of thunder—it has been threatening rain all day. Not a good augury for her arrival, I think, a little smugly; in times like these, even the smallest of omens takes on grand significance.

"Did you see her?" asks Henriette eagerly, unwrapping a pair of sheer satin stockings, red to match, from my chest.

"No," I say shortly. How excited everyone is. Everyone except me. I roll off the bed and seat myself before the mirror—warped and faded, I note in annoyance. Even though the Duc d'Aumont is a friend and in charge of the room assignments, I was certainly not given a superior apartment.

Henriette starts to comb out my coiffure. Usually, thinking about my hair puts me in a good mood, but not tonight. In a strict breach of etiquette, I'm going to leave it unpowdered: I want the dauphine to see my crowning glory first.

Again I wish Chon were here, ready with a quick crack or wise observation. Even Barry, I think dully, watching Henriette as she starts to curl my hair into ringlets. I certainly don't miss him, but he was always so galvanized by a challenge or a problem, and always so confident they could be overcome.

Chapter Twenty-Six

*In which Madame Adélaïde proudly welcomes
the new dauphine to France*

The hall is magnificent, draped in miles of royal purple cloth, a hundred footmen in their magnificent blue livery lining the walls, fifty gueridons ablaze with candles. The courtiers glitter to rival the chandeliers; every family jewel and ancient heirloom is worn proudly tonight, for the glory of France.

The Princess de Guéméné's bodice was so laden with jewels she fainted and had to be carried out. The train of the Duchesse de Chartres was so long and heavy it took four valets to carry the diamond-dripping velvet. The Comte de Matignon's coat was so stiff with pearls he almost knocked over a lackey when he bowed in greeting to the Prince de Ligne.

An excellent first impression of France, I think with satisfaction as we prepare to be seated in the great salon. The new dauphine will soon realize that though her mother might be an empress, the kingdom of France is the finest in Europe.

"She's soooo pretty," whispers Victoire, standing beside me. "I am so happy for Louis-Aug!"

"Louis-Auguste," I snap. "Appreciate the solemnity of this occasion!"

But I have to agree with Victoire, I think as I watch the archduchess being led to her seat by Papa; she is rather charming. For an Austrian. Choiseul and Count Mercy d'Argenteau, her Austrian adviser, are dancing around her and cannot stop beaming, and even Choiseul's sister Beatrice seems to shine in satisfaction.

We make our way to our table in ceremony, the finest flowers of France gathered around the room sweeping in bows and curtsies at our progress. Except for *her*, of course. My gaze slides reluctantly over to the harlot. She is wearing a dress that shimmers like red water in the candlelight. Could those be real rubies? Tasteless and vulgar, I decide, almost colliding with the Comtesse de Noailles' four-foot panniers, covered in cloth of gold.

But still, despite that one sullying stain, what a magnificent spectacle! What a resplendent race we are! As befits my rank as the first lady in France, I am seated to the right of the dauphine at the ladies' table. Then I remember that now I am second. But not to worry; the girl may precede me, but she is so young, and rather frightened looking, and will doubtless want to be guided by her elders.

The dinner commences and an enormous quantity of food is brought in; soon sixty dishes are laid out on the tables. Ten whole peacocks, stuffed with peas and chickens, their tails reassembled with feathers made of marzipan; enormous baked turbots surrounded by fried calves' ears; skate swimming in black butter; piles of mussels in cream sauce; too many other magnificent dishes to count. I'm sure they don't have food like this in Austria, I think in satisfaction. Around us, the lesser courtiers range themselves, standing respectfully; tomorrow, at Versailles, there is sure to be an even grander crush.

Over at the men's table, Papa is looking happy and relaxed, resplendent in his velvet coat with the sash of the *cordon bleu* wrapped proudly over him. He looks twenty years younger, and the favor he showed to the dauphine was well remarked upon. He will no doubt be charmed by the girl, I think a little sourly.

Seated next to her, I make steady, banal conversation—a grand ceremonial dinner such as this is not a time for pleasure, but for show. I notice with a frown that the girl has trouble pronouncing her *r*'s. A future Queen of France, stumbling over her words—disgraceful. And her manners—a trifle too much fork on the teeth, but only I, thankfully, am close enough to hear that. I think about what the Comtesse de Noailles, the dauphine's new *dame d'honneur*, whispered to us earlier: that instead of greeting her most senior attendant with the dignity her rank required, the girl embraced her. *Hugged* her. Like a . . . like a . . .

"Oh, who is that lovely woman over there?" exclaims the dauphine, following the king's eyes. Papa is transfixed by the sight of the harlot at the other end of our table, her bodice glittering with what appear to be a hundred rubies, waving a fork and laughing gaily at something the Maréchale de Mirepoix has just said. "She is so very beautiful!"

I almost choke on my turbot.

"Now, that, Madame la Dauphine," says one of the younger Noailles standing behind us, quickly and smoothly, "is the woman who entertains Our Majesty."

"Well, then I will be her rival, for I too desire to entertaining His Majesty!" A morsel of fish slides down the wrong way and a few places away Sophie is suddenly taken by a fit of shaking. "I will please him more than she does." The girl's voice is high-pitched and her unfortunate words are heard by too many.

"Of course, Madame, of course," says Mercy, his face reddening not a touch, deftly pushing the Chevalier de Noailles away. "Now, have you greeted the Duc de Croÿ? I shall call him over; an ancient family indeed."

As others catch and relay the dauphine's heedless words a great wave of mirth and smirk rolls down the table. The child remains oblivious; as innocent as a yellow lamb, I think in disgust. And what a terrible thing to say: as if she would ever entertain my papa like the harlot does.

"Like a jester, we had those in Vienna," the girl continues happily, oblivious to Mercy's attempt to steer the conversation to a new subject. "They weren't so pretty, and we didn't have them all the time. New Year's, mostly."

She turns to me, still talking. "And I do so admire that dress. I have always loved red, though Mother said it is not a good color on me and—"

"Red is the color of sin," I hiss. I glare at her. Does she not know how and when to stop? "That dress is vulgar."

"Oh! Certainly, yes," replies the dauphine in fright and confusion. At least she understood my tone; they may not have much in Austria, but I am sure they have disapproval.

"And, Madame," says Mercy again, skillfully slipping in and leaning over, "as I was saying, the Duc de Croÿ . . . allow me to present . . ."

ᴇᴏ

The next day we all travel back to Versailles in a slow progress, the roads lined with thousands of well-wishers crying their acclaim for the marriage, and even for Papa. How happy he will be! Once at Versailles—the dauphine was suitably (or unsuitably?) openmouthed at her first glimpse of the palace—the marriage ceremony is performed. More festivities throughout the day and evening, capped by another grand round of too much food and fine entertainment.

I am determined to be strong as the moment approaches, both for my sisters as well as for my soul. Lucky Louise, I catch myself thinking, that she does not have to witness the deflowering of our precious Louis-Auguste. Of course, we're not going to actually *witness* it, but the thought pains me as much as the spectacle would have.

The girl, who has been burbling in a frothy and rather annoying manner all day—I am beginning to be concerned about her circumspection—grows silent as her ladies start to cut and unlace her out of her formal wedding gown. As expected, her new household is composed largely of ladies from the Choiseul party, but there are a few disgusting *Barriens* among them, I think, glaring at the Duchesse de Piney. But be they Choiseuls or *Barriens*, only the finest flowers of France are present tonight, I think in satisfaction—no harlots welcome here, though the Duchesse de Picquigny is included.

The Comtesse de Noailles takes off the last of her mistress's chemises, and now she is quite naked in the bedroom. The Duchesse de Chartres has the honor of handing the dauphine a white nightgown of the softest Alençon lace to cover her virginal body. When she is dressed, we gather around her to lead her to the nuptial chamber, where she will join her husband.

My poor Louis-Auguste, what a trial this will be for him. He has never—I am convinced of it, for the boy is a paragon of virtue. How these vile deeds that he is required to perform in the name of duty will sully his virtue and trust in the goodness of life! I thank God again that I and my sisters were spared what my nephew is about to experience.

We arrive before the men and help the girl into the magnificent bed, draped in crimson. Then the doors open and the men burst into the room, Papa fair pushing his grandson forward. He is whispering a dirty joke in Louis-Auguste's ear, leaving our poor nephew stark red and troubled. Papa repeats it sotto voce to a few of the men—I only catch the words *belt* and *nipple*—and then he leads the nightshirted dauphin to the bed.

All fall silent as the Archbishop of Reims sprinkles holy water over the couple and blesses the nuptial bed. Then gracefully we back out of the room, leaving the two children behind and alone.

Chapter Twenty-Seven

In which Madame Adélaïde encounters a vexing problem

Victoire is pink with pleasure at the impending arrival of the dauphine. "She will honor us with her presence! It might even become a regular morning visit!"

"I rather think it the other way round," I snap. Really, it is too early for Victoire's foolishness, though it is pleasing that the new dauphine has decided to make us part of her morning routine. And our rooms are cozy; the perfect setting for an intimate chat and the start of our new friendship. She will be like a daughter to us, I think in satisfaction. An obedient, tractable daughter, one who will look up to us and follow our guidance, and one who will, with the right charm and guile, persuade our papa to rid himself of the heinous harlot.

Narbonne whispers to me that Choiseul is in the antechamber; would I take a minute?

Choiseul bows, looking frightfully pleased with himself. He is dressed in a coat sewn with double-headed eagles; symbols of Austria is taking things a bit too far, I think in disapproval. The sooner we forget her origins, the better.

"Madame, would you be so kind—delicate female touch— inquire—progress of France's future—the dauphin—madly elusive—" Choiseul effuses in his flowery way, his words slipping smoothly over themselves, his demeanor unflappable.

"Indeed," I say, holding my breath until he backs away and I can reenter the salon. Narbonne, seeing my face, rushes over to fan me, calling as she does for the smelling salts. I sit down, breathing heavily. The way Choiseul broached the subject, so composed and calm. I don't like to imagine my precious Louis-Auguste having such carnal pleasures, but within the bounds of marriage, such activities are necessary. Duty must come before prurience.

Too soon the dauphine arrives, still looking more like a frightened child than a future Queen of France.

"Brioche *dorée*," I announce as Narbonne offers the dauphine the plate. "You must know French pastries are the finest in the world?"

"Of course," says the dauphine politely. She really has the most amazing complexion, I think, my hand creeping over the soft folds of my neck. Like porcelain, really. I'd like to get up and range around the room and absorb the task before me, but I hold my seat and smile at the young girl.

"And your husband?" I finally inquire.

"Oh, he is very nice!" exclaims the young princess, and I do believe she is gushing. I frown lightly. One does not "gush" at Versailles. I do not believe I have ever *gushed* in my life.

"Indeed he is," I assent, modulating my voice that she might follow my example.

"I'm sorry, Madame, I did not hear—"

"Call me Tante, please, as your dear husband does. Most nice," I agree, reluctantly raising my voice. "He is, and certainly we—the French—are. Nice." Another pause. "So, your new husband . . . you are well pleased with him?"

"Oh yes! He was most considerate; he wished me a good night, then slept. And I did have a good night."

"Slept?" I inquire, my voice a trifle thinner than it ought to be. I stare at the young girl: if innocence could be painted, her face would be the very picture of it.

"Oh yes," says the dauphine rather wistfully, and pauses awhile, as though thinking of something. "He was very tired, and after he wished me good night, he went straight to sleep."

Ah—perhaps my question was not clear enough; perhaps she misunderstood, or meant to use another word instead of *sleep*. A delicate matter, indeed. I cough, wondering if perhaps Victoire or Sophie will aid me, but of course they won't; Victoire is giggling into her tea and Sophie's ears are quite as red as the stripes on her silk gown.

"Oh, Tante Sophie," exclaims the dauphine. "What is the matter? You are frightfully red!"

"Our dear Sophie is of a delicate turn of mind," I explain hastily. "Even such light conversation as we attempt now . . . unsettles her."

The girl looks puzzled.

"So . . . the dauphin . . . He was tired, you say?"

"Yes, he yawned twice, and said he had eaten of the mussels, many, then went to sleep. I also ate of the mussels and slept. Is it not the custom in France to sleep?" finishes the dauphine, looking between me and Victoire with a worried look.

At least she's confused, I think bitterly, that she might understand a portion of the trouble she is causing me.

"Ah, no, no, dear child," I say, reaching over to pat her hand, which lies limply on her lap. Ungloved—I shall have a talk with Noailles later. "Of course we enjoy our sleep as much as the next country. We are most excellent sleepers, perhaps the best in Europe." I wish I could stop, but I cannot and I am only glad Louise is not around to mock my efforts. "So you were pleased? You are his *wife*?" I put a delicate little trill on the last word, that surely cannot be misinterpreted. My cup clatters down and I realize I have spilled some of the milky mixture into my saucer.

"But of course I am his wife," says the dauphine with a worried look. "We are married. You were not at the ceremony, Tante Adélaïde? No, forgive me, of course you were."

I take a deep breath.

"Indeed, indeed. Please take another brioche. Did I mention these brioches are the finest of France?"

"You did, Tante," she says, taking another and chewing on it. Is her mouth open? She, the daughter of an imperial house!

Extraordinary. Or is she just mimicking Victoire, perhaps thinking the French way is so? Oh! I should have been more firm with Victoire and her dreadful manners!

I take up my fan and flutter awhile, still smiling at her, not sure how to proceed. Either the child is completely oblivious, and has failed in her duty, or she is too delicate to even understand what I am talking about. The former, I think, fanning hard, Victoire smacking her lips beside me. I shall have to inform Choiseul that the dauphin remains in a pure state of innocence, and his wife as well.

I take a deep breath. One more matter, then this distasteful interview will be over.

"Now, there is something I must advise you upon. You wish my advice, my dear?"

"I do, Tante," says the dauphine, still chewing on her pastry, and I realize in horror she has taken two bites without placing it on her plate in between. Impossible!

"That woman—that woman at the dinner at La Muette, that you so admired."

"Oh yes, the Comtesse du Bar, I think?"

"Du Barry, yes. Well, I must warn you . . . We must warn you . . ."

I let the words dangle, inviting her to take the bait.

"Whore," breathes Sophie.

"What? I'm sorry, Tante Sophie, my French, I did not catch . . . ?"

"What Sophie means to say is that the Comtesse du Barry is not a *suitable* woman at this Court."

"Not suitable? But she is a friend of His Majesty," says the dauphine stiffly, a little of the imperial daughter appearing to cover her confusion.

"Yes, my dear, but we mean friend . . . in the French fashion? Friend?" I stare at her. Of course, I think bitterly: the Austrian Court is the very model of propriety.

The dauphine now looks to be on the verge of tears. "But she is your father's friend? His special friend? I should hope to hold in high esteeming all those that the King . . ."

"Don't worry," says Victoire, interrupting my efforts. "Everything must seem very confusing to you."

"Oh yes!" The girl exhales in relief. "You know how it is . . . well, I suppose you don't, I mean you never had to leave France. It's all rather different. So different . . ." she says bleakly, "and French is rather difficult . . ."

Is she insulting our language, the glory of Racine and Montesquieu?

"I do like your sleeves," says Victoire kindly, reaching over to fluff at the dauphine's silk-trimmed flounces.

I clear my throat and guide the conversation back to the matter at hand; Victoire shall be admonished later.

"The Comtesse du Barry is a woman of *sin*," I say firmly and grandly.

"Sin," whispers Sophie.

"A woman of sin?" The dauphine processes the words, then finally understanding blossoms over her taut, pale face. I sigh in relief and finish my brioche; what a time it has been.

As the new dauphine and her attendants take their leave, the Comtesse de Noailles raises her eyebrows at me. I would like to raise mine back, but of course that would be entirely unthinkable. Instead I bow my head in sympathy; what a trial this girl will be for her.

I sink back in exhaustion on the sofa, the magnitude of the problem temporarily overwhelming me. At least she knows about du Barry, but the purity, the blessed purity of the child!

"This is a grim matter," I say to Victoire and Sophie when our guests have departed. "She is an innocent! A babe in the woods!"

"It sounds like Louis-Auguste didn't do much," says Victoire, and I realize she is as apprised of the delicate facts of life as I am. How on earth does she know the dark secrets of men and their desires? And what if she knows more than I?

"Don't put this on our dear nephew," I snap. "The girl didn't do her duty. And while we should be happy Louis-Auguste remains pure, the demands of state . . . This is a delicate matter," I finish grimly. "A very delicate matter. As delicate as a . . . as a . . ."

"Hymen?" whispers Sophie.

"As delicate as a hymn," repeats Victoire in satisfaction. "What a pretty phrase. Are we all going to Mass now? Or shall we wait and go with the dauphin after dinner?"

Chapter Twenty-Eight

*In which the Comtesse du Barry and the king
discuss a certain lack of progress*

Louis is pleased with the new dauphine and pronounces her charming: "A little flat on the bosom, but it promises to develop well."

He makes a special show of attending to her assiduously at all the marriage festivities, and the dauphine plays him with all the guile of youth and charm. I can't deny that right now, in this spring of her youth, the dauphine is quite delightful. Not beautiful by any means—her hair is faintly ginger, she lacks eyelashes and has an oddly protruding lower lip—but all together her freshness, vitality, and complexion are an attractive package.

Not to worry, I think, observing her one night at cards in Mesdames' rooms—her pale insipid looks are the kind that will fade very quickly. A few babies and a few more years, and she'll be as charming as Madame Adélaïde.

Though babies might be in short supply.

News of the dauphin's inadequacies are greeted by the gossips as though they were dying of thirst in a desert, and have finally reached the oasis.

"I can confirm—cream pudding never gets hard, no matter how old it is."

"Loves tinkering with his lock sets, but it seems this time he can't find the keyhole."

"Well, the saying isn't 'like grandfather, like grandson,' is it?"

"Strange, because he always has such a hard time of it *outside* the bedchamber."

A part of me is gleeful; since her smiles to me during the first dinner, the dauphine has retreated behind a glacial mask and has not said a word to me, nor even looked in my direction. Chon confirms that Mesdames have taken her entirely under their wing—poor girl—and I have no doubt they are poisoning her against me.

And of course, the new dauphine is allied with Choiseul, who worked so hard to make the marriage happen. While I might smirk at Mesdames' evil plan—it is quite obvious they want to use the new dauphine to effect my banishment—Choiseul is always a more worrying enemy. As long as he is around, I fear the dauphine will remain cold to me and there will be little hope for a friendship.

"And then apparently she told Ad—I mean to say, Madame Adélaïde—that her husband kisses her good night and leaves, and she is confused as to why he would want to stay!" I report to Louis gleefully. It is almost two weeks since the wedding, and the Court can talk of little else.

"Oh, I know, I know," he says irritably. "Both Mercy and Choiseul have told me, and the news is on its way to Austria. Dratted cowhand."

He smacks his riding crop against a statue of Dolores. We are in the gardens at the Grand Trianon; I have spent a pleasant day here gathering flowers, and he has stopped by on his way back from the hunt. Zamor stands behind me holding a large basket of pink roses, perfect in their abundance.

"Who is a cowhand, my love?" I ask, taking one of the roses from Zamor's basket and securing it in Louis' hat. Louis should be in a good mood—after the excitement of the wedding, the palace is settling back to its familiar routine, and the hunt, his favorite activity, resumed today.

"My grandson is the cowhand. Never—never, I say—was a man more suited to tending cows and less suited to governing a kingdom. Don't go repeating that, dearest, but it is the truth."

I am silent; I know there are a great many who would prefer

the dull solidity of the dauphin to what they call the debaucheries of our current king. But time enough for all that, I think as I often do these days; let Louis enjoy himself while he can. I remember Barry once said the king had gone too far to ever reclaim the love or respect of his people, and so why try? And that was even before he took *me* as his mistress.

"His father was the same," continues Louis, puffing in frustration and taking the rose out of his hat in irritation. "Well, not the same, there was a little difficulty at first, and Raphaela certainly did not have the charms of Antoinette, but then all was quickly resolved."

"Give them time," I murmur, thinking I shouldn't have led him down this path, for the distress it causes him. "Come here and look at the new rosebushes—Richard found me another twelve varieties."

"I simply cannot understand! When I was his age, I was a morbid box of near-constant arousal. A trying time: my tutors wished to fill my head with the glory of history and literature, while all I wished for was time alone with my, ah, hand and my guilt. I still often wonder if my slight myopia was caused by those youthful years of excess. You cannot imagine."

"Oh, but I can! Barry's son, Adolphe, was the same. I once found him fu— having carnal relations with one of my garters." I giggle at the memory, and remember our little flirtations, Barry oblivious in the corner. Dear Adolphe—he has not suffered his father's exile and remains in the service of the king and is well favored by His Majesty. We must get him married; Chon promises me she is hard at work finding a suitable bride.

"With your garter? Ah, my dear, I cannot imagine these constant shocks are good for my health." Louis sighs again. "Luckily, Fleury recognized my state and married me off quickly—seven times on my first night with the queen. At last, a sanctified outlet for my impure thoughts and deeds."

"What did you like best about her?" I ask, hooking my arm in his and leading him through a parterre of yellow lilies. I only saw the queen from afar, that one time during the peace celebrations in Paris. A large portrait of her—looking regal and sad—hangs in the Salon of Diana, and Mirie told me one day that she thought Madame Victoire was the spitting image.

"Ah, it was so long ago, almost another lifetime. She was soft, and fair—and there. I never left her alone, poor woman, her womb was full of my sticky seed."

Louis stops in frustration, back in the present. "And yet with that cow dolt it has been seven weeks!" he peeves. "I assumed the dratted oaf was a virgin, and Vauguyon confirmed that there had been no dalliances, but still—what is he waiting for? The health of a nation is the health of their sovereign—the people will never respect a king who is not a man!"

"The dauphine must be devastated," I commiserate, smiling inwardly and imagining the depths of her humiliation. Last night she twittered at the Comtesse de Tavannes, standing next to me, that a certain woman reminded her of a crow, always pecking around for shiny objects. I swallowed the insult, but I could feel my cheeks burn. "To be spurned by her own husband! Not to be able to give it away."

"Dearest, do not talk of our daughter-in-law in that manner," says Louis in a mild, reproving voice. "The daughter of an empress and your future queen."

"But *you* called the dauphin a cowhand."

"True, indeed, but I am his grandfather and the family connection gives one certain prerogatives."

"And you are the King," I concede. "Perhaps the dauphine doesn't know what is supposed to happen?"

The king sighs. "It may be, it may be. Vauguyon assures me the dauphin is instructed in the mechanics of the thing, but perhaps Antoinette's mother—the empress is a woman of profound morals—did not choose to inform her daughter. Were that the queen were alive, that she might undertake the task! It seems an unfair burden to place on the Comtesse de Noailles' shoulders; I have heard she is quite suffering from an outbreak of hives brought on by the strain of her position. Perhaps I may trust one of my daughters to help the dauphine . . . understand."

"Those raddled old virgins?"

"Hush, dearest, they are as pure as nature intended. But they are of mature years and certainly . . . aware. There was a book, a rather smutty one—I must ask Richelieu to get me a copy that we might enjoy it together," he says, getting a little flushed and picking at the rose in his hand. "Yes, perhaps they should be the ones to guide the little dauphine, who, I fear, is quite naive."

We turn back toward the palace, and Louis kisses me goodbye. "I must be off, back to the palace—I'm thinking Vallette shall have the honor at the *debottée*, he speared six boars this afternoon, and the pleasant squealing of the sow with the piglets—boarlets?—was most enjoyable."

He rides off and I turn back to the cool interior of the Trianon; I'll walk back to Versailles later with Chon and Zamor. It will be a good summer, I think, suddenly determined. It will be. And surely the dauphine cannot continue cold and silent toward me forever?

Chapter Twenty-Nine

In which Madame Adélaïde undertakes a task
as delicate as a . . . as a . . .

The hymns are finished and we return from the chapel. I am deep in thought and contemplation, and mull over the words of the sermon—the subject was servants, and their gratitude—as I make my way back to my apartment.

I settle in with my sisters and prepare for the morning visit of the dauphine. While her dependence gladdens my heart, this strange situation is abhorrent to me. The dauphin, my pure, lovable Louis-Auguste, is being mocked. Consummation—it is all the Court can talk about, and I fear I will never enjoy my consommé again.

Antoinette—she has insisted I use her Christian name, quite against our conventions—extracted a promise from her husband that he would make her his true wife while we were at Compiègne this summer, but the longed-for coupling did not take place.

Now Vauguyon tells us that the dauphin needs more time; such sensitivity of feeling is certainly commendable in his virginal state. And there is a growing consensus that the fault lies not with him, but with the dauphine. It is unthinkable that Louis-Auguste be at fault, for he is a man, and men always seem to know the ins and outs of this delicate matter.

The dauphine is distressingly naive, and, I fear, not of the highest intelligence. We tried to include her in our afternoon astronomy lessons, but she pleaded that they were too hard. I was tempted to rebuke her and remind her that if Sophie could learn, then so could she, but the girl looked so distressed I gracefully permitted her absence.

It has not escaped me that if the little Austrian is not the true wife of Louis-Auguste, then she could quite easily be sent back to Austria and a new, more suitable, and less Austrian dauphine might be obtained. Despite these thoughts—and they are not only mine—the girl seems oblivious of the danger she is in, almost as if she has never been exposed to intrigue before. Extraordinary. What on earth were they doing at the Austrian Court?

But the situation is distressing to Papa, and he kindly asked my help in resolving it. I take a deep breath. If France needs me, I shall not shirk my duty.

Narbonne, knowing my task, suggested I seek an intimate time alone with the dauphine to broach the delicate subject. Ah, my dear Narbonne, I think fondly, she is becoming more and more of a rock. When she was in my sister Élisabeth's household, I thought her a trifle loose and sluttish, and of course there were those preposterous rumors about her and my father. But now that she is firmly ugly, she has become a kindred spirit and I believe we see the world in a very similar way. Though I am not usually partial to children, her two sons are quite charming, and Victoire used to dote on them rather heavily when they were children. Myself too, if I am to be honest.

My dear Narbonne also in some ways knows what the dauphine suffers, for her husband lost that vital part of his manhood in battle, even before their wedding. I pause, making a connection I have hitherto ignored. But I shake my head; now is no time to go wandering down side paths—I must focus on what is important.

"My dear." I rise and greet the dauphine before she can sit down. I peer at her suspiciously—it is almost as though she is not wearing stays, her yellow morning gown heeding rather too much to the contours of her body. "It is such a delightful morning—I thought we might take a stroll around the garden, walk down a side path . . ."

"Now?" The girl jumps, as nervous as a hare. A little of her fresh bloom has already worn off, I note with pleasure.

"Indeed. Now. It is quite proper, I assure you, I have already apprised Madame de Noailles." I hold up my hand at Victoire, who is happily reaching for her gloves. "Just the two of us. Our ladies may follow, but there is something I would discuss with you, alone."

A frightened lamb of an archduchess follows me out onto the terraces. "Come, I thought we might walk down here," I say, steering her down the steps toward the gardens.

It is early morning and the gardens are quite empty; inside the palace, toilettes are still being performed, Mass attended, the great rising for another day, the beehive humming to life. I take a moment to gather my thoughts, and as though sensing the importance of the occasion, for once the girl is silent and doesn't start blathering on about the flowers or chasing butterflies. Though she does stoop down to pick up a peacock feather, missed by the early-morning sweepers, and does not heed my warnings that it is dirty, and that she should wait for Noailles to give it to someone to clean.

We walk briskly down a yew-framed alley. This is a fearsome task, a delicate task, but one for which my unique combination of femininity and strength is well suited. The very future of France and of the Bourbon succession is now in my hands. I think happily of when my father approached me: the kind request; his dependence on me, unstated but obvious; the relief in his eyes when I quickly understood what he wanted.

"My dear . . . Antoinette. We must talk of a delicate matter." I take a deep breath, thinking of Sophie's foolish words. "A very delicate matter indeed."

"Yes, Tante?" says the dauphine meekly, biting her lower lip and looking very white and thin. Victoire is always going on about how difficult her position is.

"She's so young," said Victoire sadly last week. "I remember when I was fourteen." I think to when I was her age: I was per-

fectly in control of my emotions and surroundings. It was 1747—
the year Josepha arrived, a time when the Pompadour was still
firmly in power. I compare myself to the dauphine at that age:
certainly, my French was better, and I was more in command of
my person, and never thought once to complain.

"Now, let me start with a homily, from the Greeks, on duty
and marriage." I had thought long and hard about how to begin
this interview, and had fastened on the story of Atalanta, reluctantly wed, as an excellent starting point.

"And so you see, Atalanta, who had derided her female duty,
was finally compelled to marry, and her husband Hippo . . .
Hippo . . . Hippocrates? Yes, then he made an oath to serve his
patients faithfully, I mean his wife, wait—"

The archduchess is becoming confused, and in truth, so am
I. In such situations, it is always best to be direct. "In sum, what
I am trying to say, my dear: we must all do things that require
sacrifice, and the act of . . ." I raise my eyes to the heavens; the
skies offer me no help, but I take a deep breath and steel myself:
"The act of penetration within the bounds of the marriage bed is
sanctified by our Lord."

The sentence was well practiced, and I believe it came out
admirably.

"Tante Adelaide," says Antoinette slowly, and I notice she is
not blushing, though I feel my own cheeks burning. "Tante, I
understand . . . I understand *it* . . ."

Oh, thank goodness! I feel the need to collapse, and steer her
into the Bosque des Reines, rimmed and private. A rabbit startles
and dashes off into a dewy hedge, and I sit down heavily on a
stone bench.

"But"—she is still speaking; thank goodness I do not have
to—"I do not understand what is expected of me . . . He, ah . . ."
A delicate pause, and I am aware, for the first time, of a certain
dignity she carries, intrinsic to her person. "A few times he has,
um, climbed on . . . on me, but nothing . . . nothing happens.
Oh, it is so very hard . . ."

"What is hard?" I ask sharply.

"Everything. I do not know what I am supposed to do." Finally, the dauphine's face is starting to show some distress. "You know he promised me at Compiègne, but nothing happened, and he does say now he is fond of me, but . . . but . . ."

"Good!" Fondness is certainly a start. "Good—you understand what needs to be done, you are just not doing it well enough."

"Yes, Tante," says the girl dully. She sits down beside me and stares blankly ahead of her, twisting the peacock feather in her gloved hands. Outside the copse, I can hear the faint crunch of gravel and the sound of someone greeting Narbonne.

"You must try harder. To . . . entice him. A young man will not respond to a . . . a . . . cold woman, so you must entice him." Entice—I am not sure that word is quite proper. I realize I am starting to breathe rather heavily. A statue of a Greek hetaera gazes over me in cool marble judgment, and for some reason I am reminded of the way the harlot stared at me across the *beriberi* table yesterday evening. She was laughing in her vulgar, throaty way, and the Prince de Soubise's eyes followed her, his mouth gaping open, looking as though he would like to *eat* her.

"I would offer you advice . . ." I remember a picture from that smutty book, the one that the Comtesse d'Andlau foisted on my unsuspecting purity when I was a child. Henriette and I looked through it and tittered—so long ago. The woman was dismissed, of course, and put in the Bastille, but still, the damage had been done. I remember one of the pictures. "Bare buttocks. Show him your bare buttocks."

"Yes, Tante." Antoinette starts crying, softly, and I see the unhappiness etched on her face, the tears running rivulets through her face powder.

I lean back, tired and spent, not wishing to see her distasteful tears. I close my eyes but the image of bare buttocks, lined up in a row, does not leave my mind. If I open my eyes and stare directly at the sun, I could be blinded, and then perhaps the disturbing images would leave. The sun is weak on this September morning, but perhaps still sufficient? One of my women, the Comtesse de Chabannes, has a brother who is blind from birth. Of course he does not come to Court—such a thing would be unthinkable—but how extraordinary it would be, never to see and never to know—

"Tante Adélaïde?" It is the dauphine; I had forgotten where we were, and who was beside me. What we had been talking about. "Might we go back to the palace now? The king said I could ride out with him this afternoon, and I do not wish to be late?"

I open my eyes slowly. It has been a good conversation, I decide, and smile heartily at the young dauphine, and note with pleasure she has dried her eyes well and looks composed. How long have we been sitting here?

I rise, proud of having accomplished my mission; fortitude and forbearance have been my friends throughout my life.

"Certainly, let us return. But I would be leery of riding too much." Antoinette accompanies Papa on the hunt several times a week, sometimes wearing a distastefully masculine riding habit. "It is an unsafe activity, if there is the risk of your being preg— *indisposed*..."

"But, Tante, there is little likelihood..."

"No, I shall not be contradicted on the matter. It is well known that riding causes miscarriages. Follow in a carriage, if you must, but not on the horse. Now, come, we don't want you to be late, and it would be unseemly to be rushing. *Rushing*—that is something we the French do not approve of. I am not sure what happens in Vienna, but at Versailles, it is never appropriate to have the appearance of haste. I do believe haste is a..."

Chapter Thirty

In which the Comtesse du Barry watches Choiseul ride away into oblivion

T he dauphine's star is hastily fading; she still hasn't been able to get the dauphin to fulfill his duty—in my kinder moments, I wonder if she really is to blame, as everyone contends—and some of her behavior shocks the older members of the Court. Her list of crimes grows daily, and she is unfavorable compared to Josepha, the last dauphine, whose legacy as a paragon of virtue only grows as the Austrian girl trips merrily through the quicksand of Versailles malice.

"Chasing butterflies," the Marquise de Flavacourt says in disgust. "Riding donkeys. Walking through a door without waiting for the second one to be opened, as though she were a mere countess without the honors!"

"Larking around with the king's younger brothers!"

"Romping on the carpet—the carpet!—with her maid's children!"

"Trying to get out of wearing stays, even with court costume!"

The consensus is that she is acting more like a shopgirl from Labille's than a future queen, and I sometimes think sadly that were we not pitted against each other, we might find much common ground in our zest for life. But she remains frosty and silent and has yet to address a single word to me. It is well known that Mesdames—well, Madame Adélaïde, at least—have the girl firmly under their rather dismal and expansive wings and have even allied themselves with Choiseul in their mission to get the girl to unseat me. They are using the pathetic girl as their weapon, and even suggested that she lecture the king on the filth that surrounds him.

Me—filth! Needless to say, Louis was not pleased. Nor was I.

"The effrontery! That chit of a girl, to try and moralize with me. I was greatly displeased. Well, you know, you saw me after."

"I did," I murmur; Louis' purple face had quite alarmed me. The girl is greatly misguided if she thinks that the king would respond to piety and sermonizing. I can definitely sense Adélaïde's clumsy and rather large man-hand behind this matter.

Last week one of the ladies of the dauphine's household, the Comtesse de Gramont (a sister-in-law of Beatrice's husband), deliberately stepped on my train as I was leaving the chapel, and didn't even apologize but just tittered alongside her mistress. After I complained, Louis quickly banished the countess, and signaled his displeasure to Count Mercy at the dauphine's treatment of me. Yet still she remains stubborn and does not speak to me.

Despite the fading star of his protégée, Choiseul is as arrogant as ever and continues to resist my overtures.

"Choiseul's greatest strength," Chon observes one afternoon, "is that he is the only man of any substance surrounding the king. Well, apart from Maupeou and Terray," she finishes, referring to another two of the king's chief ministers.

"The king likes a man who is both courtier and adviser," observes Richelieu, "and much as I hate to admit it, only Choiseul plays both parts well." Richelieu is getting older—well into his seventies now—but intrigue still invigorates him.

"I fear we are stuck with him," I say. It is inconceivable to me that he has not succumbed to my charms. He is a well-known aficionado of the female sex, which makes my lack of progress all the more puzzling. Dratted man. "But unfortunately, Louis would be lost without him."

"The king only *thinks* he would be lost without him. We must stop trying to placate Choiseul—compromise is overrated. He's a thorn, and might I remind you: thorns only grow," says Chon impatiently.

"And thorns need to be cut off," observes Richelieu.

Chon and Richelieu look at each other and smile; they have decided that the Duc d'Aiguillon, Richelieu's nephew, would be a perfect replacement for Choiseul. I suddenly realize that Chon's new dress is made from the same fabric as Richelieu's coat. Extraordinary—what are they doing?

Their plan works, and by September the Duc d'Aiguillon is fully integrated into the king's favor. He sides with the king against the Parlement and Choiseul, and even secures the prestigious position of Commander of the King's Guard.

Choiseul, in a rage over Aiguillon's appointment, has his men drag an effigy of me—me!—through the streets of Paris. I am piqued but a little curious. I wonder how they dressed me? What happened to the effigy—made of stuffed wool, someone told me—after it was dragged through the streets? Not much, I'm sure: despite the wicked songs and pamphlets that circulate, and even the claims that I am undermining the very foundation of the monarchy and the country, the people of Paris can't dislike me that much, for I was once one of them.

Louis is greatly displeased with Choiseul over the effigy, and everyone, apart from the man himself, can sense a showdown is coming.

In times of war, a minister is more valuable than in times of peace. Hoping to solidify his position, Choiseul seeks to involve France in a quarrel that Spain and England are having over some distant islands—the Falklands. Choiseul even sends a letter directly to the Spanish king, without the king's knowledge, pledging France's support. In direct contradiction to my war-weary Louis' wishes.

The letter is intercepted, and the battle lines are drawn.

"Oh, he'll have his war all right," says Richelieu gleefully.

Louis is persuaded, by Aiguillon and Maupeou (who conveniently changed sides over the summer, a rat leaping from the old ship onto the *Barrien* new), to write a *lettre de cachet* for the man who was once his most trusted minister.

Louis does, then spends the night circling his rooms in unease, unable to give the final word. In the morning, all of Choiseul's supporters try anxiously to see the king, but he hides from them in my apartment and another day passes. Choiseul keeps to his rooms as well, and the Court is hushed and wary, suspended between two different futures.

Finally the letter is delivered. On Christmas Eve—the villains were thrown out of the inn, remarks Aiguillon wryly, for the Duchess de Gramont will share her brother's exile. It is the hour of the *Barriens'* greatest triumph.

"What a wonderful New Year's present!" says Chon in satisfaction.

Perhaps, but I prefer the tortoiseshell box full of sparkling sapphires that the king gifted me.

As Choiseul leaves Versailles and travels to Chanteloup, where he will spend his exile, the roads are lined with people cheering him and crying at the injustice. *There goes the man who could have saved France*, they cry, and there are riots in Paris to protest his dismissal. Versailles empties of courtiers as half the Court travels to Chanteloup to give allegiance.

Chanteloup—nothing to do there but sing to the wolves. Choiseul will be very bored, I think sadly. Really, if he had just been nicer.

"Such open demonstrations would never have happened before," says Mirie, referring to the riots in Paris. She is looking old these days; the death of her favorite rabbit, Jonas, has hit her hard.

"They are saying it is a revolution," observes Chon, looking, if possible, a little worried. The riots in Paris took us all by surprise, including her. "I don't usually have regrets, but the depth of his support surprises me."

"Anything that Paris does surprises us," says Richelieu with surprising sagacity. "We're two separate worlds; how on earth are we supposed to know what the other one is thinking?"

After the New Year's festivities—what will 1771 bring? I wonder—Louis and I retire to my apartment on the third floor, empty of courtiers and friends who still revel down below. The rooms up here are dark and cozy; only a few candles in the sconces, the chandeliers unlit, a fire roaring in the hearth.

Louis has an evil, snuffling cold that has afflicted half the Court, and I am in a sour mood. Earlier, at the ball, the dauphine looked straight through me, as she has been doing almost since her arrival eight months ago. I stood almost beside her at a table in one of the buffet rooms, but she barely looked my way, then made a disparaging remark about a platter of stuffed chickens. When she moved away, all the other ladies did too; even Mirie. It is my right as a presented lady to be addressed by the dauphine, yet she continues to defy etiquette and even the king's orders, and refuses to speak to me.

It all reminds me too much of my early days at Court, when I was shunned by everyone. Of course, my position is stronger now, but Chon always warns me that friendship at Versailles is never to be trusted; one day a friend, the next day you turn around, quickly, and find you have been stabbed in the back.

Like Louis just stabbed Choiseul in the back.

But Choiseul asked for it, I remind myself, settling Louis by the fire and pouring him a glass of brandy, murmuring sympathetically when he complains of his stuffed nose and aching throat. I throw a fur wrap over my shoulders and go to stand in one of the window alcoves overlooking the Court of Honor.

Merriment from the ball below floats up and through the thin glass of the windows. Earlier, I danced and Louis watched me with pleasure. It starts to snow, the thick flakes falling dreamily through the black air. Some of the guests spill out into the winter courtyard. I can hear a woman saying over and again, *No, no, no,* but her voice is open with laughter and longing.

I have a sudden sharp desire to be out there, an angel in the snow, and not stuck in here being a nursemaid to a sick old man.

Oh! Such horrible thoughts, when he has been nothing but good to me. Brandy—it always brings out the worst in me. Feeling penitent, I rejoin Louis by the fire.

"A mistake, a mistake," he mutters, and I know he is thinking of Choiseul's dismissal. "The people will never forgive me, nor perhaps should they. But the reckoning will be after my time, I do believe."

"You're talking nonsense again, France," I say softly, passing him a fresh handkerchief.

"Pomponne—the Marquise de Pompadour, I mean to say—when she was dying"—his voice catches—"she said: *Après moi le déluge*. After me, the flood. And it rained so hard the day she died."

"La, what a funny expression!" I say with forced joviality. "There won't be any floods at Versailles. Well, apart from my ceiling in the blue salon, but that has been fixed. And look at the pretty snow falling!"

"Yet strangely prophetic," muses the king, ignoring my words but reaching over to stroke my arm. "She was a very intelligent woman, the Marquise, so rare in a woman. Though I must say, I prefer your warmth and kindness."

I bristle, just a tad. "I am smart!" Last month the Prince de Ligne joked that the only way to get politics into my head would be to use state documents as curling paper for my hair. Everyone agreed it was tremendously witty, but I thought it rather cruel.

"I'm sure you are," Louis says kindly, winding my hair and tugging me toward him. We kiss awhile, then he releases me to mop his nose.

"Why do you never get sick, dearest?" he complains, snuffling. "Always so radiant."

"Daily walks," I say promptly. "And plenty of baths."

"Baths . . . yes, you bathe even more than I do. So much water," he continues to muse, taking a draft of his drink. "I often think of her words. *After me, the flood*."

"A long way away, a long way away," I murmur, tired of this talk. Besides, I know Louis doesn't really care; he has long since stopped worrying about his lack of popularity or even the state of his country.

"My only comfort is that I won't be around. But when I think of that buffoon boy who is coming after me—did you see how awkward he was during his minuet?—my heart sinks even deeper. France, as you would say, is in a fine pickle."

Out in the courtyard I can hear that woman laughing again, and pleading *no* with the same high-pitched excitement. Who is it? The Duchesse de Picquigny?

"Do you know the Baron de Champmars has just turned ninety-two?" I say suddenly. Chon has started supplying me with stories of longevity, designed to cheer Louis.

"Ninety-two, you say? I knew his son, before he died of that cat bite. Ninety-two: how extraordinary. Funny, some should live so long and others pass so quickly through this world. Come here, dearest."

I go and sit on his lap; he is grown stouter with age, not wasted like some old men. Some *older* men.

"You make me so happy, dearest," he says, fumbling at my breasts. "You are so beautiful." He falls asleep with me on his lap. His wig is askew and I slip it off—he looks much younger without it; he still has a fine head of hair.

Chapter Thirty-One

In which Madame Adélaïde displays great fixity of purpose

W e are here to witness this triumph of the Bourbons and of the monarchy. My father at the center of the hall, high above the lesser men on his *lit de justice*—bed of justice—a literal bed from which the word, and law, of the king is dispensed.

Maupeou is beside him as they face the recalcitrant parlementarians, their heads rightfully bowed in shame, their hats clutched to their chests in contrition.

"I will never change," declares my father in a voice full of command and majesty. "We will never change." In the wake of Choiseul's dismissal, there was a bloodbath of his supporters, and Maupeou has emerged triumphant. He quickly discontinued the compromise policy that Choiseul favored in dealing with the Parlement. Back to the glory of the monarchy and absolutism!

I am inspired, as I always am, by the sight of my father and I think with fervor how much I admire him. My sisters and I are in Paris to witness this seminal occasion, cooped up in a little balcony far from the government of men. Victoire appears to be sleeping, but Sophie is alert and nervous.

The dauphin, of course, is also at the *lit de justice*, looking rather sleepy, but his wife is absent; she has no interest in politics or governance. Little Philistine, I think in disgust. I heard a troubling rumor she was in Paris last night, dancing at a public ball. Without her husband, and only returning when the dawn rose.

She shows little interest in any of the weightier matters of life, and even spends the hours when she should be reading engaged in idle chatter.

"Your duty to France is not to impede progress, but to ratify our demands!" continues my father, scolding the parlementarians for their disobedience. Never has he been more regal or resolute. Such mettle! Such fixity of purpose! "*My* demands," he thunders in clarification.

"You have failed at your duty and failed France," the tongue-lashing continues. "You will learn my will, and it will be done. You will no longer impede our attempts—*my* attempts—to reform the tax code." When he is finished, he has dismissed the Parlement and it is as though order has been restored, once again, to the world.

"Certainly the harlot has tried, hard, to bring the monarchy low, but look how our father elevates it!" I announce to my sisters as we watch the men below us file out.

"Why, is the harlot influencing the Parlement?" asks Victoire, waking up and stretching. "I didn't think she cared for politics. Look at Maupeou's wig—it looks like a bear pelt."

"Not the harlot," I snap, "but the men who surround her." Then I remember most of the *Barriens* are opposed to compromise with the Parlement, just as my father and Maupeou are, and I straighten my mink cape with a huff.

Instead of returning directly to Versailles, my sisters and I stay in Paris and visit Louise in her convent. She took her vows last month, but may still receive visitors. There has been a gradual thawing between us—we now write—and I decide it is time for reconciliation.

Louise greets us in her simple black habit. Ugh—coarse wool.

"Come," she says cheerfully, "we will all dine together and you will see what my life has become!" In the vast, freezing refectory, we sit on cold wooden benches, and though we have our own table, I watch in astonishment as the nuns sit at the other tables. Seated in the presence of daughters of France!

Louise sees my outrage. She leans over and whispers content-edly that we are all children of God in here, and rank is not to be respected. She radiates calmness and serenity, as though she approves!

A servant places a great clay dish on the table.

"Potatoes stewed in milk," announces Louise in satisfaction, and ladles us out our portions. Herself.

"I'm not sure I shall like this," whispers Victoire, on the brink of tears, and it is all we can do to gulp down the sordid fare. Louise just smiles and tells us, proudly—though pride is a sin, I think, as sour as the milk I must force down—that she receives no special treatment here.

"There isn't even anyone to help me up and down the steep stone steps. And so I walk them by myself!" she says. "I practiced the first few days, with one of the other novices, and then I tried it myself—there is a *rope* that one may hold on to, attached to the wall. A poor substitute for my equerry's arm, but it is a trial I have faced and conquered."

"Rope," murmurs Sophie, looking distressed.

"And my bed—a straw mattress. Apparently that's what you fill a mattress with, if there are not enough ducks. Though I am not sure why there are no ducks available, as we do keep many chickens—I even gathered an egg last week! I wonder why chicken feathers can't be used—for the mattress, I mean. All this to say I sleep like everyone else," she concludes in satisfaction. "The love of Our Father makes even the most painful of burdens easy to bear."

It is true, I think sadly, pushing a piece of potato in the disgusting milk slop. Papa's love makes anything bearable.

"Do you think she's happy?" asks Victoire anxiously during the carriage ride home. "Potatoes in milk! How horrible it was."

I snort. "What is happiness? We should be more concerned with duty." But she is, I think in surprise—she is happy. Little smart, secretive Louise has finally achieved what she wanted. Whereas we . . . whereas we . . .

Victoire sighs and snuffles into her handkerchief; she has had a cold for almost a month now and I am tired of her hacking cough.

"Paris always makes me sad; so much human suffering," she observes as we pass a man shivering at the side of the road, crouched in a position of defeat. Such scenes are thankfully absent from the palace and the gardens, though last month our carriage going to Choisy was delayed by a corpse on the road, frozen solid into one of the ruts.

I shiver and press my feet against the warming stove. It has been a hard winter, and though we are now in April, spring remains elusive. There is a ridiculous rumor going around that the king is deliberately hoarding grain, in order to starve his subjects and take their wealth for himself.

Preposterous! As if the peasants would have anything my father desires. And why would he bother to starve them, when they seem to do a good enough job of that themselves?

Back at Versailles, I am lost in the thoughts of the day. Papa, so resplendent. Louise, so radiant and contented. Potatoes slopping around in milk. I visit Narbonne in her apartments, and on my return I stop at the top of the staircase that leads down to my rooms. I raise a palm to my equerry as he comes to assist. The steps stretch long and winding before me.

"I shall descend myself." I can do this, I think grimly. I can.

The young Baron de Montmorency looks confused but backs away, poised to return should I need him.

I look down the stairs. I can do this, I think again, but the way is long and badly lit; we are at that uneasy hour between dusk and the lighting of the candles. Perhaps not the best time for an undertaking of this magnitude. At the bottom of the dimly lit cavern, two guards are lounging, unaware of my presence above.

"And then she stuffed . . ." I hear one of them say, laughing.

Perhaps I should undertake this adventure in daylight, when the way is brighter and the steps more welcoming. But then I think of the crowds that might surround me, and the gossip and sneering comments should I fail. I back away and wave Montmorency over.

Besides, I'm sure the steps in the convent aren't nearly as high and treacherous as these at Versailles.

∽

Antoinette's entreaties with the king to banish the harlot have not been successful. His admiration for her has certainly cooled; as I well know, he dislikes lectures on his private life. It was worth a try, and worth sacrificing Antoinette's reputation, but her influence was not sufficient and now Papa is displeased with her.

Nonetheless she remains cold to the harlot, and refuses to address her or speak to her. The correct course of action, and one that I continue to commend to her. Together, we resist the presence of that woman.

A tough trial, for sometimes it seems as though we must choose between Papa and what is right: he is excluding us from visits to Choisy and Marly because of our rudeness to her. Narbonne even implored me last week to be kinder to the harlot and said I was cutting off my nose to spite my face, but I thought her words ill-chosen and silly: my nose remains perfectly intact.

The dauphine is under great pressure from her advisers to talk to the harlot and keep the king's favor, but so far she has remained strong and refuses. Though her stays remain worryingly absent, there appears to be a spine beneath the frothy gowns she favors. Then we hear that even her mother has become involved, exhorting her to talk to the Barry woman. For a mother to wish her own daughter to defy her conscience and speak to a prostitute!

I decide I do not hold the Empress of Austria in high esteem.

But with all the pressure from Count Mercy and from her mother, and without Choiseul's support, I fear Antoinette's resolve is fading. One morning she broaches the subject with us. She sits on the edge of the sofa and I am aware that underneath her skirt she is rhythmically swinging her foot, her little pink-clad slipper peeking through her skirts.

"If you want to walk, you need only get up," I say coolly.

Antoinette bites her lip and tucks in her foot, then looks at a point over my shoulder, and presses again: "Mama is getting frightfully angry?"

"Your lady mother can only approve of your moral backbone," I say firmly. "Never—you must never speak to her. The people will lose all respect for you if you do." I know the dauphine's refusal to speak to her is causing the harlot no end of frustration and Civrac told us there was a disgraceful screaming episode last week. My poor papa is suffering, but the solution is simple: banish her.

"Do you think they care? The people? Mama cares most awfully. As does the king."

"My dear, you must not falter! You are the first lady of France, queen in all but name—these are causes worth sacrificing for! You must have fixity of purpose," I say, thinking of my father at the *lit de justice*. "Be firm and resolute. Compromise will gain you no pearls."

The girl only looks confused; her French has certainly improved, but it is by no means perfect. "But they only want me to say a few words to her. Perhaps a sentence or two next week?"

"Your silence is the right approach, and you must take strength from that."

Antoinette chews on her lip, and behind her I can see the Comtesse de Noailles shaking her head. Though dim, and rather stupid, the dauphine, I suspect, is becoming aware of her rather precarious position—a king who is increasingly displeased with her, and an unconsummated marriage.

Yet despite our stern counsel, the dauphine weakens and promises Mercy and her mother that to please the king, she will address the harlot.

She is about to capitulate, but that can never happen. Fixity of purpose!

We risk the harlot's polluting presence and deign to attend a card party in the suite of the Duchesse de Valentinois, where the conversation is rumored to take place. Valentinois is a distressingly immoral woman; she caused a scandal by refusing to live in Monaco with her husband. Though understandable—apparently in Monaco everything is wet and riddled with sea salt, even the wine—last year she displayed great moral laxity in running away from her husband and taking up quite openly with the Prince de Condé. A supporter of Choiseul, Condé was exiled with him, but the duchess remains at Court.

With Victoire and Sophie, one at each side—my lieutenants—we ensconce ourselves in a corner of the room, ready to spring forth into battle when needed. The harlot is dressed in a white-and-green-striped dress, her hair piled high like an actress's, only a hint of rouge on her face. She is barely visible, surrounded by a flock of male admirers; Papa is supping with the Cardinal de Luynes tonight, and does not attend.

At the other end of the room the dauphine plays at a table of *comète*, her voice too high-pitched and too excited to truly be decorous, and she cries out like a child when she loses. She is gaining a reputation as a flighty flibbertigibbet—well deserved—but she must show the world she does have a backbone. Fixity of purpose. Resolution. I remember my father's steely voice as he addressed the Parlement. We shall not waver, we shall not capitulate.

"Ah, look, there she goes," whispers Victoire in a voice of tiny excitement. And it is true, the dauphine has finished her game and is now walking rather stiffly toward the harlot's cluster, Count Mercy nodding her forward. The Duchesse de Valentinois grins and flutters her fan and the room falls silent. The crowd of men around the harlot parts to reveal the treasure in their midst, the Prince de Soubise holding her arm as though to protect her. The way between the two women is now a straight line, free of impediments and people, a smooth strip of parquet showing the dauphine the way forward.

No, it shall not be. No compromise. The harlot must not win.

I hurry over, my feet sturdy in low-heeled mules, chosen just for tonight. My armor as I enter the battle.

"Come, my dear, come, I am sure the king is waiting for us. He would like us to wish him good night before he retires." I place a restraining hand on the dauphine's arm. The whole room is watching us. Admiring us. Me.

"Tante?" Antoinette stops and her face is a mixture of fear and relief as she looks between me and the harlot.

"Come," I say more firmly, pulling her away from the path of compromise she has chosen. "Come and let us go and give our good-night blessings to the king. We must not keep him waiting!"

I steer her out of the room, Victoire and Sophie scurrying after us. As we leave, I cast a look of triumph at the hated harlot, Soubise now solicitously fanning her, her face as red as the felt on the table behind her. Beside her, Count Mercy is looking at me with what can only be described as hatred.

Triumph.

Chapter Thirty-Two

In which the Comtesse du Barry hears an intriguing idea

"Not so tight, man," complains the king as his dresser attempts to button his breeches. I peek into the room and smile at Adolphe, now the king's chief equerry.

"Ah, my dear, come here and tell me what you think," says Louis, his face lighting up when he sees me. "I'm not sure about the coat—a little flamboyant? Ridiculous?" His valet slips it on and he turns around to model it.

"Never," I say, giving him a kiss and winking at Adolphe. The king's coat—ordered by me—is of patterned silver, sewn with thousands of bright lilac sequins. "You look magnificent. And it's perfect for this heat."

I'm dressed in a thin summer gown of rose-colored taffeta; here at my château of Louveciennes we stand on little ceremony, even for a formal dinner. Earlier, Chon said that I looked as though I was in the Caribbean, in Saint-Domingue perhaps, where even Frenchwomen forget propriety and dress in chemises.

"Indeed," I said. "I'll take that as a compliment!" Besides, jewels can make any gown magnificent: cascades of diamonds fall off my ears, and around my neck a magnificent rose quartz choker gleams.

"Rather tight." Louis sighs again as his valet closes the buttons of the coat over his belly. He is starting to put on a little weight. I think his belly adorable, and tell him as much.

"Ha! Well, I have never been very proud of that part of my

anatomy," he says, giving his stomach a sad jiggle, "but it pleases me that you like it."

Against all protocol, we descend together to the salon. This dinner is to honor Aiguillon's appointment as minister of foreign affairs—the *Barriens* are more powerful than ever—but it is also to celebrate my lovely house, finally finished and ready to show off.

Life at Louveciennes is heavenly and I come as often as I can. Here, there is no need to get up for Mass, no need to dress in uncomfortable gowns, no need to suffer the silent reproach that still lingers around me at Versailles. Here, I am surrounded by fresh air, not the stale miasma of the palace, and I am far from the squabbles and endless intriguing, and the icy silence of the dauphine.

Louis and I enter the magnificent dining room, a temple of luxury. Giant mirrors adorn the gilded panels and from the ceiling hang dozens of chandeliers. On a balcony above, a light orchestra of harps and violins fills the night air with its sweet music. Guests—friends—already crowd the room, including Adolphe and Chon. They won't be at the main table, of course, but I was pleased to be able to include them. My Louveciennes, my rules, I think in satisfaction, and I know that my little scented invitations are in great demand.

Later, when the food is mostly a memory and the guests satiated with the wine and rich food, a troop of monkeys is brought in to perform. Some guests watch idly, while others chat amongst themselves, and a few even fall asleep and snore loudly. Those guests kept standing attempt assaults on the main table when the occupants of the chairs excuse themselves.

Anarchy, I think, and smile. The footmen come in bearing great platters of fruit pudding, made with apricots and cherries from my own orchards. Unfortunately, the puddings remind Louis of his grandsons, and his mood turns dark. Louis' second grandson, the Comte de Provence, was married in May. His bride, the new Comtesse de Provence, is a rather dull Savoyard princess with poor personal hygiene—Chon tells me the Italians are notorious for never bathing. Though the Comte de Provence boasted, often, of his sexual prowess and skillful deflowering of his bride, he is even fatter and more torpid than his older brother, and no one believed him.

The sad amatory state of his grandsons vexes Louis to no end, and he cannot stop wondering what he did to deserve them. Though they say the dauphin has progressed to partial insertion with his wife, it's been over a year since their wedding and nothing final has happened.

"Two unnatural grandsons," he thunders as I try to interest him in the monkeys or the delicious pudding. "Find me two men in all of France who would not be all over those virgins, charmless as the Savoy girl is," he rails, stabbing at the wobbly mess on his plate, his mood dark despite the gaiety around him.

"La, leave your family troubles behind at Versailles," I admonish, "where they belong. Look at the monkeys!"

At the end of the table, one of the monkeys, dressed in a lilac jacket—resembling the king's coat, I realize in alarm—performs another somersault. The guests applaud and Louis just shakes his head; I don't know much about etiquette, but I do know that clapping in front of the king was once prohibited.

Things change, I think in satisfaction, things change.

I call Richelieu over. "Tell him about the Duchesse de Mazarin and her dinner," I command, and leave the king with him. Richelieu is always ready with spicy stories to lighten the king's mood, and the story of the duchess's dinner party will surely amuse him. Wanting a pastoral theme, she had her chefs place live birds inside an enormous pie. When the pie was served, the enraged birds broke free and attacked the guests and their wigs with venom.

I go to stand by one of the open windows and look out over the July night. The song of hundreds of nightingales from the myrtle hedges outside trill in the dark night, complementing the orchestra within.

"A triumph, my dear, a triumph," says Mirie, carried over to me in a chair, her head wobbling rather rapidly. Her gout is acting up this summer and she has difficulty walking when it is too hot. "Truly magnificent. You have such the talent for entertaining!"

"Madame, an exquisite night, a night to remember, a night to live in my dreams," says the Duc de Duras in his usual overwrought manner, shaking his head as though stunned by my beauty, and the beauty of the dinner.

"My dearest, we thank you from the depths of our hearts," says Félicité, Aiguillon's wife, smiling and curtsying to me. Her ivory teeth glow yellow in the candlelight. Beside her, her husband bows smugly; Chon says I must be glad to have such a firm supporter. In truth there is something about Aiguillon I do not trust completely, and even Richelieu admitted his nephew was a man of outstanding mediocrity.

I let the waves of admiration wash over me and look around in happiness. What did Chon say to me? *That the fumes of adulation intoxicate me.*

It's true. They do.

The next day the house empties of courtiers and Louis leaves as well; Maupeou, in the wake of the dismissal of the Parlement, is determined to push through a new tax, and that matter has quite occupied him these last months.

Chon and I stay on for a few days. We walk out to see a pavilion that is being built by the river: smaller and more intimate than the big house. Zamor follows with a basket to fill with wildflowers. When he first came he could scarcely walk in the shoes we gave him; now he minces prettily behind us.

We stop to contemplate the half-finished pavilion. It will be very simple but proportioned and will be the perfect place to hold summer suppers. A cleared lawn, still bereft of flowers and grass, leads down to the water's edge.

"What a wonderful breeze!" I turn to the river and extend my arms to catch the wind wafting up from the Seine. "Do you feel it? It got so hot last night—did you see how Felicité's rouge melted and dribbled?"

"What?" shouts Chon. The pavilion is just above the mechanical fountains that pump water from the Seine to be delivered to Versailles, and the pumps make a continual hum in the background. "What a dreadful *industrial* noise!"

"Come, let's go this way," I shout. "Arnould says if we plant more linden bushes, the noise will be deadened. And you do get used to it—it does fade in time."

We trail through the peaceful serenity of a wooded path by the waterfront; all this land is mine. Across the river the spires of Paris rise on the horizon, and down to our west lies Versailles, an easy hour's gallop away.

"So—you're looking very pleased with yourself," I say to Chon. "Was it the Prince de Ligne? He scarcely left you alone all evening. Or Aiguillon—I saw him dancing attendance on you." I am determined on a romance for Chon, but she doesn't seem in the least bit interested.

"I have found a solution," she announces smugly. "To our intractable problem."

"I don't believe you," I say, impatient that thoughts of that ginger-haired girl should impinge on the peace of Louveciennes. Despite pressure from her mother, from her advisers, and even from the king himself, the dauphine remains surprisingly stubborn: she will not talk to me. How distressing, I sometimes think, to have discovered she has a spine of steel. And that it had to be about me.

Silly girl.

Last month it seemed she had finally succumbed to the pressure and was about to address me, but then Mesdames extracted her from the room. Not Mesdames, I think grimly, just Madame Adélaïde: I can still see her broad and uncompromising back as she whisked the dauphine out of the room. Louis was so angry he even talked of banishing his daughters from Court as a permanent display of his displeasure. I had to talk him down from that rash idea; I don't like banishing people, and what happened to Choiseul still makes me uneasy.

Louis is equally annoyed with the dauphine. He only likes females who smile and purr, not pout and cry and cause difficulties. Chon tells me that she—the dauphine—is terribly unhappy, and that a chambermaid caught her crying in the night last week. Another night when her cowhand husband didn't visit her. I wonder sometimes if she clings to her hatred for me as the one thing in her life that gives her satisfaction.

"So, Chon—what have you come up with? When will she speak to me?"

"Now, you see, Jeanne," begins Chon pompously, "you're so focused on small details—like having the dauphine speak a sentence to you—that you are entirely missing the bigger picture. You are not seeing the forest for the trees."

"La, what a stupid expression!" I declare. "How can one not see a forest when one is in it?" I gesture at the trees surrounding us. "Mostly oak, I think. Chestnut."

"You know all that talk of the king marrying again."

"Not all that talk," I say sullenly, my mood turning dark. I take a posy of wild roses that Zamor has gathered and inhale their fortifying scent. The idea scared me, but talk of it lessened in the wake of Choiseul's departure.

"You know the story of Madame de Maintenon?" asks Chon.

"Well, certainly. Louis XIV's last mistress, whom he married. What has she got to do with anything?" Richelieu remembers her and says a more pious, sanctified hag could not be found. "You're not suggesting Mass three times a day, are you? I don't think more piety will make the dauphine speak to me."

"Jeanne, you must focus on what I am saying," says Chon, stopping and taking the roses from my hand and throwing them down. "Think: if you were queen, the dauphine could hardly ignore you, could she?"

"Of course not! Why, if I were queen, that red-haired chit would curtsy to *me*!" I laugh in delight as I imagine the look on the girl's face, then realize what Chon is suggesting. "Me—marry the king? But I am already married! To your brother, no less."

"Married—pishposh," says Chon cryptically. "Divorce can be considered."

"Divorce?"

"Think about it, Jeanne! It's perfect!" Chon's little face is flushed and animated and I realize she has put some thought into her plan. "You were never Guillaume's true wife. All he has to do is declare that it was never a real marriage, never consummated. We'll get Terray on board. Richelieu has already spoken to Maupeou, and we would only need the pope's approval, and then . . ."

Oh! I sink down onto the muddy forest floor, my legs as weak as rope. "Do you think . . . ?" I whisper. "Do you really think . . . ?"

"I do," says Chon firmly, and not for the first time I think what an extraordinary little woman she is.

"You're a genius."

"An evil genius," she corrects me proudly.

"What would I do without you?" I get up, shaking my head and my skirts, the idea starting to delight me.

"Spend your days trying on clothes and selecting jewels, no doubt," replies Chon promptly.

Chapter Thirty-Three

In which Madame Adélaïde hears of an abhorrent plan

A small word, but an important one. It was once the entirety of my world, my identity bound within it. *Madame*. Now I am no longer the Madame I have been since the death of my elder sister Henriette. So many years—almost twenty. When I think of how quickly the years pass, it makes me panic; it is best not to think of it at all.

The Comtesse de Provence, my nephew's new wife, now has my title and all the prerogatives of Madame. I mull and stew, and stew and mull, and wonder if I should beseech Papa to change the rules, but a glum voice tells me there is no use. I must bow before the immutable rules of etiquette. The rules are made for our protection; if we ignore them, it is at our peril.

That is what the Comtesse de Noailles said to the dauphine last week after she refused to wear rouge; such true words, I wish I had thought of them myself.

And so I accept in outward silence, with dignity as befits my station, the loss of my position.

No longer *Madame*; I am now *Madame Adélaïde*.

Since the marriage and this unfortunate turn of events, I have been in a sour mood, so unlike my normal benign mien. My ears are still blushing from Provence's lewd boasting all over Court, designed entirely to shame his brother, of his lovemaking with his new wife. I can no longer make eye contact with him, and poor Sophie was so distraught she took to her bed for a week.

The dauphine continues within our tutelage, though daily my

disdain for her grows. Instead of her becoming more French and more refined, the opposite is happening. It is almost as though she is eager to flaunt her informality, yet at the same time she can be surprisingly haughty. A haughty hoyden—a dreadful combination. She freely attends masked balls, returns to the palace at dawn, chatters like a river, and is even rude to some of the more moral, older ladies that must serve her. She treats informality as a virtue! Almost like . . . the harlot.

But with regard to the harlot, at least, she retains her will. Great fixity of purpose, I constantly remind her, and though the pressure on her is great, she listens to me and thus far has not addressed a word to the woman.

Triumph.

I may no longer be the one true Madame, but I still wield much influence.

My father's chief adviser, Maupeou, even seeks an audience with me. He asked that I attend him in his offices in the Ministers' Wing—a place for serious reflection, he assured me in his note, and I thought the sentiment agreeable. But as I proceed to his offices, a small doubt niggles at me: Is it because I am no longer Madame that I am to *be* summoned, and not do the summoning?

Maupeou rises and bows as I enter. A lackey brings a most imposing armchair, upholstered in crimson-and-gold silk; procured solely for the honor of receiving a daughter of France, says Maupeou smoothly, though it does remind me somewhat of a set I saw in the Comtesse de Matignon's apartment.

Maupeou offers a quick compliment on my brown cap, then begins: "Madame, the king is most distressed, and indeed all of Europe is distressed . . . With all that is happening in Poland, now is no time to be alienating the Austrians. You understand?"

"Of course I understand," I reply, disliking his tone. "I am most conversant in politics and state affairs. Why, I have studied geography and know where Poland is."

"As it seems," he says cryptically, and stares at me. In truth, I am a little afraid of Maupeou; Civrac told us there are rumors he once killed a man, or shouted at him, and he certainly has been ruthless in his dealings with Parlement. Through the open doors of his office, I can hear my ladies Narbonne and the Marquise de Fleury, reassuringly close, chatting in the antechamber.

"It is our deepest wish that the dauphine be more amenable about this delicate matter," continues Maupeou. "The king is greatly displeased with her that she does not address the Comtesse du Barry; how can we consider France and Austria to be united when the dauphine clearly disobeys the king?"

Though he has just suggested something of great impertinence, I keep my dignity: "I have never influenced the dauphine. She is young—and Austrian, and flighty, heedless, and I suspect slightly stupid—but she must form her own moral judgment about that scandalous woman. She has decided that it is beneath her dignity, as a future queen, to address a common prostitute."

Maupeou leans back and contemplates me. There is a faint look of menace in his eyes, almost as though he is judging me. Judging me! Of course, he is a man bound to the *Barrien* cause, and thus an enemy of mine. His eyebrows are preposterous, I think: like two black caterpillars stuck to his face.

The minutes tick along. What does this dratted man want? I regret agreeing to this meeting, when my time might have been better spent preparing for my woodworking lesson. Suddenly he leans forward and points to a high stack of papers bound with a green ribbon sitting on the corner of his desk.

"The expenditures of your household, Madame Adélaïde," he says, tapping on the pile of papers with a stubby, accusing finger. "Provided to me by Terray. Clothes, food, servants, those carriages that are always breaking down. And the household of your sisters? Why, I believe the cordial bill for July alone exceeded eight hundred *livres*."

"Indeed?" I say coldly. "And why should I be interested in that?"

"It reminds me, it just reminds me . . ." He sighs and rubs his eyes as though distressed. "Forgive me, Madame, I am just a trifle weary today. Family problems."

I stiffen; it is never polite to divulge family secrets. Though I would be curious to hear about his cousin's rumored bout of madness last year.

"Yes, indeed, my sisters, though I love them dearly—I have three, no four, if we count Gabrielle, who is quite bedridden." He laughs apologetically, then continues: "All of them unmarried, yet expressing no desire for that state, nor for the veil! They continue to live at home, and the expense of their households and trifles is wearying me down. Yet when I make one simple request of them, they refuse it. Unnatural, indeed, and not a problem one imagines being burdened with."

He raises one enormous eyebrow at me, as though expecting something. Why the man thinks I should be interested in his sisters, who have not even been presented, is quite beyond me.

I rise abruptly, deciding the man is infuriating and I shall have nothing further to do with him.

"I have much to attend to."

"Of course, Madame, of course, I must thank you again for visiting me in my humble offices," he says meekly, but his fingers continue to drum menacingly over the stack of ribbon-bound papers.

I sweep out of his offices, feeling restless and irritated, and complain to Narbonne about his impertinence and his ridiculous family stories.

"But, Madame Adélaïde," protests the Marquise de Fleury, the youngest and most flighty of my ladies; her weeks are days of holy terror for me. She inserts herself alongside us as we hurry back to my apartment. "I know Maupeou's family well—his uncle is my father's cousin's uncle's stepson, so we are close kin—and he has no unmarried sisters. I would remember such a strange and monstrous thing."

❧

"Tantes, I must share some distressing news with you," says Antoinette. I frown, for it is our role to impart news to the dauphine, to guide the guileless lamb, and not the other way around. "I have heard quite extraordinary news."

"Oooh, tell us," says Victoire, leaning in, her cheeks more flushed than usual. I narrow my eyes at her untidy cap, the pastry crumbs gathered in her lap. I think of Mauepou's words—eight hundred *livres* on cordial? Surely not? It sounds like a very large sum, though I have scant to compare it to. Did Narbonne say that the new carriage her son wanted was thirty thousand *livres*? Or was it just three hundred *livres*?

"The Princesse de Chimay," Antoinette continues, motioning to one of her ladies, who nods with wide eyes, "she heard . . . that the harlot is seeking a divorce!"

"Divorce," squeals Sophie, dropping her cup with a clang.

"A divorce! For what purpose?" I demand. "So she may be known as the vilest woman who has ever walked this earth?" I am shaking in indignation. To bring the taint of divorce beneath the hallowed roofs of Versailles—when will this calumny end?

The dauphine stares at me, as though willing me to understand something. "I think . . . I think she wants to be as Madame de Maintespan?"

"Who? Do you mean Montespan, or Maintenon?" I snap.

"Ah, Maintenon, yes, my Laure—"

"Who?"

"The Princesse de Chimay?"

"I see." How vulgar of her to call her ladies by their first names!

"Laure says the harlot wants to be the next Madame de Maintenon, and would divorce her husband in order to . . . in order to . . ."

Oh, calamity! The harlot thinks to marry Papa, to put herself on the throne and above all others. Suddenly my distress at the loss of my position seems rather pale and trifling next to this momentous news. A divorce! Marriage to my father! Base and sacrilegious, and completely preposterous.

I stand up, unable to contain myself. "Impossible, impossible," I mutter, circling the room and wringing my hands, imagining how it would feel if I swooped the spice boat off the mantelpiece.

Impossible yet true—shortly, Civrac confirms the dauphine's news. Now we hear envoys to Rome are dispatched and that even Terray, a new *Barrien*, has been helping the harlot. Then we hear that our sister Louise in the convent is in support of the project— if married, my father will cease to live in sin. Yes, but there are better ways to achieve that happy state.

I write Louise a firm letter and happily imagine her discomfort upon receiving it.

Then the husband of the wretched harlot presents himself at Court, to dispel rumors he is dead, as well as to testify to the lack of consummation of their marriage, on the basis of her consummation with his brother. Soup, of any kind, no longer holds any appeal.

The husband stays a week, longer than anticipated, for he fell sick when he was served a hazelnut pudding one night, specially prepared by his sister. The Court held its collective breath, as did he—apparently the nuts stopped him from breathing—but he recovered and left, but only after signing a document testifying to his lack of intimacy with his wretched wife.

I dream of kittens and soft purses, ribbons of silk. It is coming closer, the threat of an impossible plan closing around us. The imperative is clearer than ever: we must get our father married, but not to *her*. The Archduchess Élisabeth is no longer an option; she has been stricken with smallpox and is now a monster.

"I'm not sure *monster* is quite the right word," says Narbonne, running a finger over her pitted cheek. "You can hardly tell, sometimes."

Certainly, with an inch of powder, I think sourly. "Someone else, someone else. There must be someone else." I feel frantic, faint, as the specter of a marriage with that harlot slides closer. If such a thing came to pass, I would seek Papa's permission to retire from Versailles. I would forsake even him, if *she* became queen.

"Lamb," whispers Sophie, clutching at a cushion.

"Lamb? No, we had that yesterday, they won't serve us two days in sequence," I reply in irritation; some days Sophie can be so trying.

"Lam*balle*. The Princesse de Lam*balle*," she whispers with more effort. "For Father."

"Indeed, Choiseul also suggested that," says Narbonne, then seems to regret her words.

"You are writing to Choiseul?" I ask with narrowed eyes, and she makes a noncommittal gesture.

I consider the Princesse de Lamballe . . . a young widow, very pious, with just the loveliest neck. She was brought from Italy to marry our close cousin the Duc de Penthièvre, who promptly died. She has remained a widow, as finding a new husband with the same or higher rank is near impossible—the duke was a prince of the blood. The Prince de Condé's wife was ill last year, but then she recovered, and her only hope was gone.

Though to concede precedence to her, were she to marry Papa, would be annoying, it would not be the calamity of bowing to the harlot.

Lamballe as Queen of France—certainly.

Anyone, as long as it is not *her*.

Chapter Thirty-Four

*In which the Comtesse du Barry hears seven words
to delight, and sadden*

"Madame la Comtesse du Barry," says the king, accepting my curtsy. I rise up and he smiles at me in adoration. "We have missed you this last hour."

I stifle my giggle out of respect for the solemn occasion. "I will do my utmost to make myself more available to His Majesty in the coming year."

The king grins and moves past to greet the Duc and Duchesse d'Aiguillon beside me. He is part of a solemn procession, following a fixed trail through the grand staterooms as the sovereign and his family offer New Year's greetings to their courtiers. The Hall of Mirrors is crowded but icy, the chandeliers blazing though it is not yet noon, the wax fumes overwhelming. This is the day it will happen. Everyone knows it.

The Princes of the Blood pass through with their wives and retainers, and then a murmur runs through the crowd: the dauphine approaches.

She makes her way closer now, her thin, haughty nose slightly red from the cold. Her lips are tighter than usual and a certain stubborn pride radiates off her. I heard she was out in Paris again last night, dancing like a common whore, and there are even rumors starting to circulate about her preference for the Comte d'Artois, the dauphin's witty and handsome youngest brother.

I shiver lightly inside my fur-lined court gown. I know the dauphine is being forced against her will to do this. She is humiliated, bound and trussed, a pawn in a European game that knows her shame and her silliness.

But I mustn't feel sorry for her; she has brought this on herself. If only she'd been pleasant to me, a few rote words of politeness now and then, all this could have been avoided. I've never understood people like her: Why didn't she just try harder to please? Why couldn't she see that the king loves me, and that I am part of this Court, and that she should just have submitted to the etiquette that requires acknowledgment of a presented lady?

She draws closer and all eyes shift in cupidity; even those greeting the king stop to turn and stare. There are two hundred people crammed into the hall, and each one leans a foot closer. The dauphine stops in front of Mirie, downwind of me, and mutters some platitude, then advances to stand before me. Chon told me the bets are five to one in town that she still *won't* do what is expected of her.

A hush the size of the universe fills the great room, and all fall silent, suspended between the past and a new future. I stare into her blue-gray eyes, and from behind the pale frosted glass, I sense some of her pain and humiliation.

"Madame du Barry, there are many people at Court today," she says in a clear, high voice, and I can almost hear the lackeys running off down to town to share the news: the Dauphine of France has spoken to the king's harlot. Finally. She has capitulated, and I have won.

I murmur my agreement. Then she is gone, giving Aiguillon beside me a stiff compliment on his starched cuffs. Farther down the line, I can see Mesdames approaching, bowed and crooked under the weight of their heavy pride, dressed in black and white as though in mourning. Madame Adélaïde leads their grim entourage, edging closer.

&

There are many people at Versailles today.

I enjoy gossip as much as the next person, but really: How long and how often can seven words be dissected? I avoid the king, or he avoids me; all of this is unpleasant and awkward. And unnecessary, I think, the carriage jolting forward over the ice-rutted road as I flee the palace and the gossips.

Now that I have all that I wanted, I'm not as happy as I should be.

There are many people at Versailles today.

It is a hollow, empty victory, and I feel the same unease as when Choiseul was banished. All this silly intrigue, and for what? Why must people hate me?

The steam and warmth of the convent kitchens embrace me.

"Perfect! I was hoping you'd come." Ma's breath is bright and beery. "Have a taste of this filling. I've been making these delicious duck pies all morning."

"Happy New Year, Ma," I say, hugging her.

She admires the present I brought for her—a set of jade bracelets and a fine satin jacket—and we chat about little nothings as she stirs her sauce. She doesn't ask about the dauphine, and I don't tell—either she doesn't know (though it seems the whole world does), or she knows how it would distress me. She's looking older, though plump and content, and on her head she wears a garish turban of blue silk and glass beads that I gifted her last month.

"Why do I have enemies, Guimard?" I ask finally, leaning over Ma and dipping a finger into the delicious sauce. "Doesn't the Bible exhort us to be kind to all people? And I've never hurt anyone."

"Never a soul," says my mother proudly. "My kindhearted little chick. Shall I prepare a few pies for you to bring back?"

"Ah yes, indeed, the Bible has many such verses," says the monk Guimard, nodding at me kindly.

"Tell me one." I see again the dauphine's frosted eyes, their unblinking hate. She'll never forgive me, I think suddenly.

"Ah . . ." Guimard takes a draft of his ale. "Yes, the Bible has many, many verses. Ah . . . *Be kind to your enemies,* I mean *thine enemies.*"

"I *was* kind to her," I say sadly. I never did anything against her. Well, I did call her names, but only in private. "Yes, what more?"

"Have a glass of sherry," says my mother kindly. "I hate to see you so unhappy."

"Ah . . . *Love your enemies. Love* thine *enemies*," says the monk Guimard. "*And trouble ye not about the haters.*"

I frown; I'm not sure the Bible ever said anything about *haters*. What does it profit me, I think sadly, if I gain the whole world but then lose my soul?

"Is it true, the rumors?" asks my mother suddenly. "About the divorce?"

"Yes, they are," I admit.

"My dear, there are sins, but then there are greater sins. I did hope the rumors were not true," says my mother in concern.

"But I am not really married to that man! Ma, you know, you were there. And it would secure my place after . . . after . . ." I can't bear to think of Louis leaving me, but he is so much older. "After the king is gone."

It's an improbable, fantastical plan—Richelieu actually choked on his spit when he heard it—and I can't quite believe it myself. I haven't discussed it with Louis. I'm afraid to: there are some things that love and desire cannot overcome, and I know how sacred he holds the throne of France.

The palace is invigorated as the rampant race to get him remarried starts, and I even heard him lauding the Princess de Lamballe after a concert last week.

"Why don't you marry *her*?" I asked him sourly, after he had praised her piety and serenity.

"I could do worse," he murmured, and my blood ran cold.

"But I think it's just a dream, Ma," I say sadly. "Just a dream, and then . . . ah, who knows?"

"You must come to Louveciennes, Ma," I say, kissing her when I take my leave. "Come after Easter when it's warmer. And the kitchens are so grand—tiled sinks and a winch for the spit—you'll love it."

"What sort of poultry are you raising?" says Ma, tucking two small duck pies into a basket for my journey home.

"None yet—you will have to advise me." I don't get back in my carriage but instead pull my hood down and walk, the carriage following slowly behind me. I lose myself as I move down the silent side streets, the whole world still sleeping from the excesses of the previous night. The first day of the new year.

Walk as I might, and try as I might, I cannot remember why it was so important that that girl speak to me. I hate feeling melancholy and uneasy—what a sad way to start 1772. I think of her humiliation and of the humble pie I made her eat—not the tastiest of treats. Perhaps I should make her a present and offer a letter of gratitude, to show her I bear her no ill will and demonstrate my eagerness to be friends.

I may have won, but I fear I have also won her unlimited enmity.

But perhaps everything will turn out all right, I think, brightening: the divorce will happen, Louis will marry me, and then he'll live for another twenty years, with me beside him as queen.

Chapter Thirty-Five

In which the Comtesse du Barry discovers an unexpected enemy

"'*All France wishes for divorce / Yet hope is ever coarse.*' What does that even mean?" I ask in impatience.

"Ah, pay him no mind; the Abbé de Bernis is a bloated windbag," sniffs Mirie. "Loves his little poems, but no one else does."

I crumple the letter and toss it on the floor; one of my greyhounds ambles over to sniff at it. The Cardinal de Bernis is France's envoy in Rome, and he writes that the pope is not amenable to my divorce.

"A great friend of the Pompadour's," continues Mirie, still speaking of Bernis. "But latterly they fell out and he was banished from Court. '*Fat monk gone / All was won,*'" she finishes with a throaty laugh.

I pick up a pair of red shoes with low heels, and stroke the inner softness—baby rabbit fur. Brollier, purveyor of the finest shoes in France—the finest in *Europe*, perhaps—has just left and his new offerings lie scattered around the salon.

"This lining is so soft!" I exclaim, but Mirie pretends not to hear.

The Abbé Terray, the king's finance minister, had assured us that Bernis in Rome is on our side and will do his utmost to influence the Holy Father to our cause. Terray is now a firm *Barrien*, but I do not like him—he is a cold man who never bothers much with courtesy and the niceties of court life. Though I prefer him to the vile Maupeou, who reminds me of a malevolent bear and always makes me shiver.

I grimace—as I often do when thinking of the ministers—and pick up a pair of delicate citrine slippers. I fear they are too narrow, though Brollier's measurements are usually so exact. Perhaps with a little wear they might be made comfortable.

"If they are uncomfortable," says Mirie, rising and gesturing to the citrine shoes, "have them remade. There are limits to the strains that beauty must impose, and as one gets older that becomes more of a maxim than a suggestion. Now I must go—I'll see you at the concert tonight."

I put on the shoes and totter into the next room, where Chon is writing at a desk in the corner. She has been beetling around the palace, busier than a bluebottle, hard at work on what she calls "our little matter," as well as actively seeking a bride for Adolphe—nothing but the best family will do, she has decided.

"Don't despair," Chon says; she has read Bernis' letter. "There are other ways, apart from the pope, to free oneself from a marriage."

"No, there aren't!" I moan. "If he doesn't sign, all is lost." Several jars of jam are stacked on her desk. Beside them is the stem of a broken goblet and a little mound of crushed glass, ground into a fine powder.

"What happened to sand? Isn't it frightfully expensive to dust your letters with ground glass?"

Chon doesn't answer but continues to scratch away furiously. I try to wiggle my toes inside the tight shoes, bored and discontented, Bernis' silly words ringing in my ears.

"What is the jam for?"

"A present."

"For who?"

"Whom. One jar for your dear husband, Guillaume, and one for my sister Laure. Gérard sent them yesterday from Louveciennes. Gooseberries—last year's crop."

"That's nice of you," I say. "Mmm. I love gooseberries—keep one for me. Why is this jar open?"

"Oh, I needed to sample it—I would hate to send Guillaume a sour batch," says Chon innocently.

I pick up the open jar and stick my finger in for a lick.

"Don't touch that!" Chon grabs the jar back.

"Don't be silly! I adore gooseberries and only want a little bit."

"It's for Guillaume. If you must, try the other jar, the one I'm sending to Laure."

I huff. "You are too silly. Who are you writing to?"

"Now," she says, finishing up her letter and smiling up at me, ignoring my questions as she always does. I don't press, for I am grateful that she takes care of charity and patronage and leaves me to swim in the lakes of luxury and indolence.

"I have a new solution for our marital woes. If the pope refuses, as I am afraid he might."

"What?" I say dully, sitting down on a sofa and kicking off the too-tight slippers. Wretched things. I pat my greyhound, Mirza—a gift from the Prince de Soubise—in distraction. Since planted, the idea of marrying Louis has taken hold of me and has not let me go. Marriage to the King of France. A new Madame de Maintenon for a new century. And imagine me, Queen of France!

Best of all, no dreary exile if—when—my Louis dies: a dowager Queen of France would retain her position. I might even remain at Court, and continue to outshine the new queen, though the idea of that girl as Queen of France makes me shiver in a way I cannot quite understand. Relations have not improved since that New Year's conversation; all she has given me since was a compliment on a dress, and it was a rather backhanded one at that.

Damn Bernis, I think viciously, and damn the pope.

"So what is your solution?" I ask, looking between the jam jar intended for Guillaume and the neat pile of ground glass.

"Saint Uncumber," says Chon, taking a small pinch of sand from her box and dusting it over the fresh ink of her finished letter.

"I thought you were using the glass?"

"What? Oh yes, of course." She sprinkles a touch from the little pile. "There—you see: ground glass works just as well as sand. So—Saint Uncumber, Jeanne, Saint Uncumber."

"Saint Uncumber? Who is he? She?"

"She—the patron saint for getting rid of unwanted spouses."

"Really?" I am not impressed with Chon's solution. Saints have never taken me anywhere I've wanted to go!

"I was speaking with the old Marquise de Flavacourt; apparently, Saint Uncumber was one of the late queen's favorite saints, though of course she could not publicly disclose her preference. But Queen Marie liked her more for her ability to relieve devotees from tribulations general, not spousal."

"So I should pray to Saint Uncumber?"

"You should."

Ridiculous. All of this is ridiculous. Why will the pope not agree? Who does he think he is?

℘

The Abbé Terray takes off his spectacles and polishes them; without them he has the feral look of a hunted animal. He has been avoiding me, but I have tracked him to his office and cornered him here, and insisted on an update.

"I fear our little project has undergone some setbacks," he says, shaking his head, replacing his spectacles but avoiding my eyes. "Some sad news, madame."

"What more do they want? I have testified about Barry, and Guillaume, and received an official separation, and provided all the necessary documents! And though Bernis was not encouraging, he did leave some room for hope."

"I am sorry, madame," says Terray, "but the pope has refused, and now we have little recourse."

"But why?" I demand, hitting the desk in frustration. "This is absurd! Does he not know that the king desires it?" I feel myself blush as I am caught in a lie—does Louis desire this marriage? "Why would he refuse? Is the King of France not one of the pope's most important customers?"

"Madame, I do not think we should compare the relationship of a king and the leader of the Christian world to that of, say, a shop girl and a man buying a muff."

The disdain in Terray's voice, which he tries little to hide, stops me short. I stare at him and he stares blandly back.

"You didn't try hard enough," I accuse, and as I say it I realize it is true. "Why not? Do you think me unworthy of the king's love? Do you think I am unfit to be Queen of France?" My voice rises as the depths of this final disappointment sinks in. "You are a traitor and a fool, going against the king's wishes!"

The door opens and Terray's pretty young daughter skips in.

"Ah, Aglaé, my dear!" Terray rises as the girl embraces him, a smug look of pride on his sharp features. The Abbé Terray's riches and position enable him to openly seat his mistresses at his table, and acknowledge his children. One rule for the rich men of God, and another for the poor ones, I think in distaste, remembering Ma and the monk Guimard.

"Papa—oh, Madame du Barry!" little Aglaé lisps, sinking down into a graceful curtsy then rising. She smiles at me, with all the freshness in the world, and I note how charming she looks in her striped pink-and-green dress, her fair hair piled on her head and adorned with silk ribbons. "How wonderful to see you here!"

The girl is only thirteen, married last month to the grim Comte d'Amerval, and is suddenly everywhere at Court. She is very giddy and charming and I know my Louis is enchanted by her. Rumors are that even Richelieu, despite an attack of gout, is girding himself for an attempt on her blossoming virtue.

Terray beams at his daughter, quite ignoring me. As I watch them, I see something that was invisible but is now as clear as glass. Chon is always accusing me of being silly, but I do have that instinct that serves women well, and suddenly I understand why Terray has never seemed eager to support the divorce: the answer is standing right in front of me, chattering prettily about the bat that her dog Frappie caught.

So Terray wants to put his mincing pie of a daughter in my place.

A foolhardy plan, and one bound for failure. Louis may have a wandering eye—a deranged, unstoppable eye, Chon once called it—but I am sure he has never been unfaithful to me. The houses in town are all firmly closed, and I am determined they will not open again on my watch. Last month I railed at him over the attention he was paying to a certain Marquise de Sillery, a very pretty young widow who had slunk into Court from the colonies. He took me in his arms and assured me I was all the woman he needed, and would ever need.

I brusquely take my leave. I am not really worried about Terray's plan, though it does show the shallowness of those who profess to be my supporters. And how much easier it would be to forget the plotting and the intrigues if I were queen! But now— no. I have an urge to run to Louis and share with him the bad news, but I don't think I can—he is off hunting with his grandsons at Choisy—and besides, I am not even sure if it is bad news for him.

There is a concert this evening at the dauphine's and I should really begin my afternoon toilette. Henriette prepares my bath, and as I sink down in the tub, perfumed with amber oil, warm water and despair wash over me. I'm just a mistress and will never be anything else. Not Queen of France, I think sadly. Not married to Louis. Abandoned by the pope. Betrayed by Terray.

God has forsaken me, I think sadly. Everyone has. Perhaps I should pray to that saint with the outlandish name that Chon was rabbiting on about.

Or perhaps Guillaume will enjoy his gooseberry jam.

Chapter Thirty-Six

In which Madame Adélaïde uncovers a sad truth

"Oh, but I do adore your hair!" gushes Victoire. The dauphine doesn't visit us every day now; she often holds morning court in her own rooms. At her mother's insistence, Civrac tells us, and so it is we who must go and pay homage to her. But this afternoon she has visited us, and Victoire's air of flustered eagerness quite fills our salon with its sad desperation.

"Yes, it is lovely, isn't it?" says Antoinette, waving a self-satisfied hand over a tidy clutch of cream-colored bows. "Louis said it reminded him of a puffy cloud." Despite their continued lack of success in the bedchamber, Antoinette and her husband have developed a fond relationship. Showing, I suppose, that the girl does have a good heart underneath her harebrained ways.

Still, it has been more than two years, though at one point Louis-Aug did claim a half success, after which oysters in their half-shell lost their appeal for me. My father is increasingly distressed by the situation, and even the Empress of Austria has gotten involved in the sordid affair.

"Sent love advice by letter," Civrac whispered, "though what the Austrians know about the art of love would fit in a thimble. And her mother also warned her daughter against bad influences."

Bad influences—no doubt her ladies Montmorency and Mailly-Harcourt, both young and flighty. Though I am loath, after the incident in the garden, to give Antoinette any more romantic advice, I am always ready to provide counsel on her choice of companions.

We, as daughters and princesses of France, must take great care to spread our regard and affection evenly amongst our ladies. It is the reward we give them in return for their service. Why, I am even civil to the Marquise de Fleury. A favorite is certainly acceptable—what would I do without my dear Narbonne?—but such displays of affection are not for public hours.

Unfortunately, it seems the dauphine already has pronounced favorites that she openly flaunts. Though her friendship with the pious Princesse de Lamballe is only to be commended, her familiarity with the flighty Duchesse de Montmorency and the silly Duchesse de Mailly-Harcourt is simply not suitable.

"How many bows?" asks Victoire eagerly. The dauphine waves an airy, disinterested hand over her hair.

"Twelve. Or twenty."

I frown; I have noticed she has a new confidence of manner since the New Year, when she greeted the harlot. I was dismayed, of course, and lectured her on her inappropriate conduct, but she remained unbowed and even slightly . . . truculent. Astonishing. As though I were in the wrong for having counseled great fixity of purpose!

Since then, her visits are infrequent, and when she attends it is almost as though she were bored. Silly Victoire, I think as my sister continues to gush—gush!—over Antoinette's hair.

"You have heard the good news about the harlot?" I inquire, breaking into their frivolous conversation. "You know her divorce has been denied?" Though I detest gossip and talk of the harlot, it always entertains the dauphine.

"Oh yes." Antoinette laughs shortly. "Such foolishness, indeed."

"We heard that she screamed like a fishwife when she heard the news," chips in Victoire.

Antoinette nods. "Yes, we heard the same."

"I wonder why we always talk about fishwives screaming?" asks Victoire. "What do they have to scream about?"

"The odor of the dead fish makes them angry," I say firmly,

grimacing at the interruption. I have prepared a little speech about the dangers of divorce, which I wish to share. I clear my throat. "Yes, indeed, the divorce was denied, and one can never be more content than when the Holy Father upholds the sanctity of marriage. Marriage, even between two of the basest sort, is nonetheless pleasing to his eye."

Antoinette doesn't say anything, just picks a raisin from her pastry and rolls it between her finger and her thumb. Such manners—as I predicted, the Comtesse de Noailles is at her wit's end, fearing she will be held accountable for a future queen with imperfect manners, if such a monstrosity could even be imagined.

Antoinette looks pointedly at the clock on the mantel. It is one from Sèvres that she admired last week; when she did I took the opportunity to instruct her on the superiority of French porcelain. Narbonne directs one of the women round to serve more coffee, but Antoinette stretches—stretches!—and places her cup firmly down.

"Well, Tantes, I must go. We are driving out to Meudon tomorrow and we must plan the picnic."

"Oh, wonderful," says Victoire, clapping her hands. "I do love picnics. And Meudon has the most wonderful geese. Do you remember last year we went and I brought back two; we had them that night with caraway sauce. Or was it caper sauce?"

"Caper," murmurs Sophie.

Antoinette regards Victoire with a fixed smile and a rather empty face. Perhaps she is confused and does not know the meaning of *capers*. We must remember her French is still not perfectly polished, though by comparison with Provence's new Italian wife, she is a veritable linguist.

"Caper sauce is made with capers and sauce. Capers are a fine delicacy, one of France's finest, and indeed my sister is correct: it is an excellent accompaniment to goose."

The girl ignores me and continues to stare at Victoire, who smiles happily back, thinking of geese.

"Dearest Aunt Victoire," says Antoinette finally. "How lovely that you would think to come with us! But the road is rough, and unfortunately I must take the cabriolet with the better springs. There is room for only four, and we are already that number."

"A problem easily remedied," I say. "We will follow in our own carriage. We only have our Chinese lessons tomorrow afternoon, and an excursion to Meudon would be just the thing."

It has been far too long since we have been anywhere, and a drive out suddenly sounds like a capital idea. Papa is at Louveciennes this week, recovering from a fall from his horse. The palace was in an uproar but he survived, then took refuge at the harlot's house. Since her triumph at the New Year, when the dauphine capitulated and spoke to her, it seems the harlot is even more powerful than ever.

"I did hope not to inconvenience you, for the drive is far and the road past Chaville is quite dreadful," repeats Antoinette, her voice matching mine in firmness. "And . . . there is a forecast of rain."

"Well, if it rains, none of us shall go, and then you shall join us in our Chinese lesson, which we will reinstate should the weather not cooperate," I say, equally firmly, and a look of something like hatred flits across the girl's face. I wonder in irritation what is wrong with her this afternoon.

"Excellent! Civrac, we must bring an icebox for the geese!" says Victoire happily.

Antoinette smiles sweetly, though a little grimly, and says she is looking forward to the outing, as one might look forward to nothing more.

She takes her leave after an abrupt curtsy, and as she does, the idea that she didn't want us to accompany her crosses my mind, a mouse that skitters along a skirting board then disappears quickly through a crack in the wood. I dismiss my thought as absurd.

Or is it? She's slipping away, I think suddenly. Sometimes it feels as though the whole world is changing, all the new brides for my nephews, their new households, the easy way the younger people mix together. Marriages being planned for my little nieces

Clothilde and Élisabeth. Artois, the dauphin's youngest brother, getting married next year. A younger generation nipping at our heels, like an irritating dog that refuses to leave one alone.

Everyone is slipping away, I think bleakly, remembering Louise's shining contentment when we visited her in the convent. And Papa, as distant as the moon, writing frequently to Louise, but hardly ever coming to see us at all. Everything escaping, water over rocks, clouds racing across the sky, our happiness disappearing into the hands of the harlot.

"Antoinette's hair is really getting absurd," I say sourly, picking up a coffee cup and putting it down again, then getting up to circle the room. "Only actresses wear their hair high like that."

"Oh, I quite like it. It rather suits her—she has such a noble forehead," sighs Victoire. "I do hope it doesn't rain tomorrow. Geese! I shall ask for them to be prepared with caper sauce, as last time. Or was it caraway sauce? Civrac?"

"Not a noble forehead," I snap. "It is a too-high forehead, and almost as displeasing as her protruding lower lip."

After my sisters disperse to their own rooms, Narbonne directs the footmen to bring in my writing desk. They set it by the window, where I can observe the world outside. I stare out the window, then at my correspondence—a letter to my niece Marie-Louise, my sister Élisabeth's youngest daughter, now married to the heir to the Spanish throne—but then the little table rocks—I am not sure how—and the inkwells spill out in a great splash on the floor, turning the whole world black and blue.

"Foolish girl!" I snap at the chambermaid who rushes in to clean it. "Foolish girl! What a mess you've made! Why can't you do anything right?"

Chapter Thirty-Seven

*In which the Comtesse du Barry witnesses a
painful and rather sordid scene*

"I must be present!"

"No, dearest, that would not be appropriate. Would that my son had not died," sighs Louis, "that the burden of this dreadful conversation might not have fallen on me." We are talking of the dauphin and dauphine; the crisis over the consummation—or lack thereof—has reached a head, and Louis is determined to get to the bottom of their inability. The doctors are vague; some prescribe an operation, while others contend that the dauphin is not yet ready to be a husband. Pish—not yet ready—the boy is eighteen.

"I'll hide behind the curtains!"

"Don't be silly, Angel," he says, rather curtly.

I giggle. "Make them try it in front of you! You should be able to help, with so many years of practice."

Louis smacks me lightly on the buttocks. "Don't be vulgar, little one."

"I know—I'll hide under the sofa!"

"No."

"France! Do not deny me this," I say crossly, sitting up and looking down at him through my tangled hair. I roll off the bed as though in exasperation, then crawl back across the carpet to him. I envelop his legs in my arms, and look up at him with pleading eyes, and even shed a few tears, then lean in and start to play with the buttons on his breeches.

"Oh, dearest." The king sighs as I unbutton his breeches with my mouth, and I know I have won. He never holds out for long. Easier than getting that rock-crystal toilette set, I think as I wash my mouth out with rosemary water, kept by the bed for just this purpose. And even that magnificent set paled before the necklace he has just commissioned for me. The king knew of my distress at the pope's refusal to grant my divorce, and as consolation, he commissioned an enormous diamond necklace, valued at two million *livres*.

Two million *livres*! It will take several years for the jewelers to amass the diamonds required for the most perfect necklace the world has ever known.

Even Richelieu was astounded. "Two million *livres*? No woman has ever been worth that!"

"But the king loves me more than anyone has ever loved anyone, anywhere," I replied. And it's true: he is as infatuated as ever.

Chon muttered darkly that revolutions have been based on less, but Chon is just a natural worrier. And perhaps even jealous? Despite my best attempts—there is one form of intrigue I do enjoy—I have been unable to convince her to take a lover. Though, come to think of it, I did see her last week with a fan similar to the one the Comtesse d'Egmont, Richelieu's daughter, is currently flaunting—perhaps a secret admirer gifted it?

On the day of the interview, Chon insists on joining me and we huddle in a dark cupboard in the paneling, the door ajar but shielded by an enormous vase of tulips on a table in front.

"My dears," says the king, motioning for the dauphin to sit down and grasping the dauphine in a rather long embrace. The dauphine extricates herself from the king and sits beside her husband, her face impassive.

"Oooh, I like her dress," I whisper—the neckline of the dauphine's bodice is ornamented with starched blue ruffles. Chon kicks me to be silent.

"Ah, my children. My dear children." Louis shakes his head,

smiling coldly at the two sitting before him like the wayward children they are. What a funny situation. I start shaking with giggles until Chon puts her hand, surprisingly strong, over my mouth and pinches me. Louis shakes his head and utters some more vague platitudes about dear children. He wanders around the room, his hands clasped behind his back, the dauphin and his wife following his movements carefully.

"So, now. You must tell us what you have been able to achieve thus far," says Louis, stopping and gesturing to his grandson.

"Sire . . ." The dauphin squeezes his eyes shut, his pasty complexion reddening. "Sire. We have, I b-b-believe, achieved"—he is gulping like a fish on land—"the . . . inside . . . of . . . our wife." He lets out a huge breath and bows his head to examine the carpet intently. His wife beside him is as stiff as a meringue, and I notice a faint blush creeping up her neck.

"Yes, as you told the doctors," says Louis impatiently. "A fine erection, but what happens once you are inside, boy?"

"He forgets where he is," I whisper, and now it is Chon's turn to shake with silent laughter.

"Ah, inside, yes, inside." The dauphin chokes over his words and his wife puts a hand on his arm. I can sense humiliation and more pulsing beneath a thinning mask as she struggles to stay serene.

"Sire—Grandpapa," she pipes in, her voice thin and careful. "He does try. We do try. But the pain . . ."

"Whose pain?"

"My husband's pain, Sire." The last tenuous hold breaks and the mask slips off, revealing the frightened, humiliated child behind it. Something in her face melts my heart. That poor girl—caught in a tragedy not of her own making.

"Pain! Pain!" barks Louis, starting to circle the room once more. His voice is perilously close to a shout. "You, leave us," he says, pointing at Antoinette, and in his anger he is unable to even feign politeness. The poor girl dashes out of the room, leaving Louis alone with his grandson and his anger.

"Pain, pain! Mewling as though a virgin never parted! How

is it that you are not able to perform this most natural of acts?" explodes Louis. "You are the shame of Europe, and *my* shame."

Chon and I watch, aghast; I have never heard Louis raise his voice like this.

"Just get in there and move, boy, move!"

The dauphin's face is now a deep purple color. He stares dully at his shoes, breathing heavily.

"Have you at least done it with your hand?" demands the king, going over and shaking his grandson's shoulder, his voice rising ever higher. Any more and they are going to hear him in the antechamber. "Are you at least capable of that? Does *that* hurt?" he spits. "Look at me when I speak to you!"

The dauphin looks up at his grandfather with an expression of terror and hate. Louis catches some of the look and withdraws his arm in disgust.

"Leave us," he mutters, turning his back and staring out the window. "Leave me before I say more things to regret. Get out."

The boy stumbles out of the room, almost tripping over his shoes. Louis remains fixed by the window, breathing heavily. I suspect he has forgotten we are here, and now I regret being a witness to the awkward scene.

Louis stays immobile before the window for a long while, then goes to stand before a portrait of his son, dead almost seven years now. I creep out of the closet to embrace him, and see he has tears in his eyes.

"Oh, France! I'm sorry," I whisper. "That was awful."

"I do not leave much to my beloved country," Louis murmurs, staring at the portrait, "but I thought the succession to be secure. How has this happened?"

"But surely your other grandsons will provide? Between the two of them, there will be little Bourbons aplenty. Do not worry, my love."

"You don't understand," he says curtly. "The dauphin's position is sacred."

"Those poor children," I murmur. "You are upset, dearest, but so are they."

"My tender little dove," he says sadly, kissing me. "What an oaf that boy is. The girl is not to be blamed, for not even half a man would turn down that fresh flower. But that boy—he is unnatural."

"She must be so humiliated," I say, but there is no glee in my voice. I wonder what it would feel like if Louis no longer desired me. If no one desired me.

"The doctors assure me of his generous—well, ample at least, genitalia—why can't he just use it? Pain, what is this pain he minks on about? Pathetic," he concludes, some of his anger returning.

"You'll always love me, won't you?"

"Of course I will, Angel, of course. I'll talk to the doctors again; we'll have another examination, but I'll be present this time, see for myself what the problem is. Perhaps an operation, though I doubt he has the constitution to steel himself for that ordeal. A minor procedure, though—his father had one—a simple snip of a tight foreskin."

I kiss him warmly to take his mind away. I stroke his neck and wrap myself around him like a blanket, to comfort and caress. A sudden sneeze reminds us of Chon, still in the closet. I pull back, but the king is now holding me greedily.

"Leave us," I call out as Chon emerges from the cupboard.

Chapter Thirty-Eight

In which the Comtesse du Barry comforts the aging king

"Another blanket," I say, motioning to one of his valets. "Monsieur le Comte de Chamilly has already been informed about the king's feet," says Madame Adélaïde, avoiding my eyes and staring at a point on the opposite wall.

Normally I would ignore her, but I feel a sudden surge of pity for the fusty old woman in the pale pink dress that is far too frothy for her masculine looks. Though the aging princesses continue to follow fashion in a slavish but awkward way, the new styles do not suit them.

"Your father thanks you," I say prettily, and she casts me a look of venom that would kill a kitten. "Ah yes, here comes Chamilly, accompanied by another blanket for the king's cold feet. Darling, your daughter is to be commended."

Louis squeezes my hand and smiles at Adélaïde, who becomes flustered and takes a sudden step backward. Madame Victoire settles in on the other side of her father, and behind her, like a ciphered shadow, floats Madame Sophie.

"Little Élisabeth is so excited," says Victoire, referring to Louis' granddaughter. "She has been practicing for weeks."

I move aside to allow Mesdames' ladies to settle in around their mistresses, and watch Louis' eyes linger on the pretty Comtesse de Séran. We are in one of the smaller rooms of the king's apartments; outside a harsh winter rages. I snuggle inside my fur cape. Yesterday I went out for a walk, but it took two hours for my nose to lose its redness, so today I stay huddled inside like the rest of the Court. A fire burns merrily and a ring of porcelain stoves warm the little room even more.

Under the tutelage of Madame Victoire, Mesdames Clothilde and Élisabeth are putting on a concert for their grandpapa. Madame Victoire is looking very happy, if slightly disheveled and flushed at the enormity of the occasion. I must remember to have Gérard bring a few bottles of the gooseberry cordial we prepared last year at Louveciennes—I am sure the plump princess would appreciate it.

Only she and her two sisters attend alongside their father; the dauphin, his brothers, and their wives have gone hunting at Marly. Louis would have liked to have gone with them, but since his fall last year, his doctors are dissuading him from the hunt, especially in icy weather.

I stand behind him and pick a speck of ash off his wig. Madame Adélaïde inhales sharply and turns away.

"Ah, you would have me bundled up and bound like a baby, my dear!" he says as Chamilly arranges the mink respectfully over the king's feet. Madame Adélaïde blushes violently—I know he was talking to me, but I let the old woman have her moment.

"Bound," echoes Madame Sophie fearfully, looking for all the world as though she might like to flee the room, should anything happen.

The two little stars of the afternoon entertainment enter with their governess, the Comtesse de Marsan, and their attendants trailing behind them. Clothilde and Élisabeth are both dressed in green damask gowns, their hair piled neatly under matching caps and their faces properly rouged. They blush and giggle as they pay their respects to their grandfather; the elder, Clothilde, is fourteen and as fat and round as her father was.

They are already talking of a Savoy marriage for her; with this generation, there will be no unmarried princesses haunting the halls of Versailles and draining the coffers of the nation.

"You are prepared?" asks Adélaïde, but it comes out as more

of a command than a question and both girls shrink back in fear. They say the older girl is wont to piss in fright when her fearsome aunt addresses her; I do hope she won't do so today, for new carpets from Turkey were just installed last week.

"They are well prepared," answers Madame de Marsan stiffly, putting a comforting hand on the fright-struck girls. Marsan is the daughter of the hated Duchesse de Tallard, Mesdames' governess, and it appears they have successfully carried their feud over to the next generation.

A small orchestra squeezes into the corner of the room. Everyone shuffles closer and I find myself standing almost behind Madame Adélaïde, wedged firmly next to her father. It is strange to be so close to such an avowed enemy. I lean in and sniff cautiously: a sharp odor of prunes and smoke.

I have tried to induce Louis to be kinder to his daughters, but they don't know my efforts, nor do they know how sorely they are needed. The king now takes his morning coffee almost exclusively with the dauphine or with the Comtesse de Provence, and there will be another young bride coming at the end of the year for Artois. Soon the Court will be full of these young wives and they are quite eclipsing their aunts in the king's affection.

Louis likes beauty and freshness, and I know the aging grayness of his daughters, and their continued meddling in his private life, have pushed him away, and perhaps forever. There is desperation now in Adélaïde's overtures to her father, but she does not realize it is too little, too late. I know her heart, such as it is, would crumble completely if she heard the way her father talks about her.

"Meddling old hags," he called them, when he learned of their role in persuading the dauphine to remain silent to me. "Any person in their right mind would do the opposite of what they counsel; they have even less wisdom than the average woman."

Chon always says I am too kindhearted and mustn't worry about Mesdames, for they certainly never worry about me, but what is a heart for, if not for kindness?

"The lutes, where are the lutes?" barks Madame de Marsan.

"Such disorganization," tuts Adélaïde in disapproval, loud enough for Marsan to hear.

"Ah, we are in no hurry," says the king from under his pile of minks. "Élisabeth, come here and show your grandpapa your pretty cap—is that a butterfly?"

Little Élisabeth, only eight and very sweet, climbs shyly onto the king's lap.

"I sewed it myself, Grandpapa," she says softly.

"Well, aren't you a clever little thing!" Louis kisses her forehead. Adélaïde watches them, and from behind, I can see her head is shaking slightly. Élisabeth smiles up at me from around her grandfather's neck, and I stick my tongue out at her. She giggles.

Adélaïde snaps around. "Madame du Barry," she demands, and I almost jump—she has never addressed me directly. "Did you just stick your tongue out at Madame Élisabeth?"

I smile. "I did indeed, Madame."

The king chuckles and Élisabeth giggles, and sticks her tongue out at me.

"I hardly think that is suitable behavior for a granddaughter of France," says Adélaïde, her voice laden with disdain.

"Madame du Barry was just fooling with the little girl," Louis says mildly, though I can detect the irritation at the edge of his words. "Look, and I shall too!"

He sticks his tongue out at his granddaughter; Élisabeth squirms in delight and everyone laughs. Except Adélaïde—she is staring blankly at her father, looking as though someone has just struck her.

"Ha, will you remember this, dearest?" asks Louis, hugging little Élisabeth. "Will you remember the day the King of France stuck his tongue out at you?"

Élisabeth giggles shyly and he lets her slide off his lap. Before she can slip away, Madame Adélaïde stops her with a hand to her shoulder. A fearsome gray tongue snakes out of her mouth and the little girl shrinks back in fear. She looks about to burst into tears, or worse, when Marsan whisks her away; the lutes have arrived.

Clothilde and Élisabeth take their instruments and the great tenor Jélyotte bows grandly. The halting music begins, Victoire clapping in time to the painful rhythm, Louis tapping his foot and regarding them fondly. The choice of music is odd—a funereal piece of Bach—but the two princesses play passably well, and their solos are not as painful as expected.

"Well, that was delightful," says Louis when the concert is finished. His granddaughters, praised and kissed, have been dispatched and he rises creakily from under his mound of blankets. "Simply delightful. Not much can capture the heart as a fine melody does."

Maupeou materializes from an antechamber, flanked by two of his minions.

"Sire, a wonderful concert to brighten even this frightfully cold day." Maupeou tries hard to be a courtier—Louis likes his advisers to mince as much as they minister—but his impatience with flowered niceties causes him to rush his words. "Now, we must beseech Your Majesty to listen to Monteynard's proposal about the Americans."

"The Americans are revolting, they are indeed," says Adélaïde, looming like a dark shadow beside her father.

Louis ignores his daughter and looks at the pile of papers Maupeou is hopefully proffering. He yawns. "Come now, my good man, it has already gone five!" It hasn't—the clock has barely chimed three—but no one dares contradict the king. "I would take a rest—we can meet after Mass tomorrow. Come, dearest," he says, searching for me in the crowd around his daughters. "Let us repair to your rooms and take a nap."

"That was lovely," I whisper when we are up in my bedchamber, the small room heated nicely from a daylong fire, the windows hung with heavy drapes to block the cold. We burrow under a pile of furs and snuggle against each other. "Your granddaughters are charming."

"Élisabeth is certainly a pretty little thing," agrees Louis, absentmindedly picking at a ribbon in my hair. "Sadly, Clothilde resembles her father, and for a girl, that is no compliment."

"And her grandfather," I say, kissing him and unbuttoning his shirt. "You're becoming quite the rotund bear." Since his fall from the horse last year, he is not hunting as much as usual and his paunch, long a source of distress, has increased. He is also troubled by dyspepsia—indigestion—and though he limits his meals, he still grows in girth.

I loosen his shirt but stop there. Yesterday, yes, but two days in a row? Sadly, no. His doctors are urging him to slow down and I no longer share his bed every night, something that pains Louis to no end. Some doctors even insist that abstinence is the only solution, and urge him to unyoke from me. Unyoke—as though I were an ox!

So we lie fully clothed, resting in the waning of the afternoon. Louis is thinking the same, and he murmurs, his face buried now in my hair: "Once I would not have kept my hands off you— could not—yet here we lie like an old married couple. What tragedy when the flesh is willing, but the body is weak!"

"Ah, you're just tired," I say kindly. In Louis' mind, this weakness where he was once so strong and virile portends another kind of death. Chon, able to find the positive angle in any situation, says I should be glad the king is feeling his age, for the doctors would be against a new marriage for him.

"I sometimes wonder if this is God's message to me," he says sadly.

"Nonsense! It is a natural thing. All men are a little diminished in their later years."

"Diminished—what an ill-chosen word, Angel! And not every man," he says. "My stamina may be failing, while Richelieu, fourteen years my senior, maintains his."

"Ah, that old dog is more bark than bite, and has been for many years now."

"I fear I have greatly displeased Him in my life," continues

Louis, slipping down into his favored melancholia. "God, that is to say, not Richelieu."

I am silent; God looms ever larger in Louis' thoughts these days as his health troubles increase. Even a mild case of indigestion sets him thinking beyond the burps and into mortality. And now his sixty-third year approaches, a significant year the Greeks called the *climacteria*, when death was supposed to be on the horizon.

"Didn't the Comtesse de Séran look pretty this afternoon?" I suggest, to distract him from his grim musings. Usually I can keep him aboveground quite easily, but this winter it seems he is ready to slide into the depths of depression at the least provocation. "Her green cape matched her eyes perfectly!"

"'*The years of our life are seventy, or even by reason of strength eighty; yet their span is but toil and trouble; they are soon gone, and we fly away,*'" quotes Louis mournfully, refusing to meet me in the meadow with the Comtesse de Séran. "Seventy is but seven years away, Angel, and how I hate the number seven! *Our days are made to seventy*," he repeats dolefully.

"Pish—look at Richelieu; seventy-seven and still going strong! And your great-grandfather lived to seventy-seven, and Broglie celebrated his eightieth last month."

"Really? The Duc de Broglie? He looks like a young man, not more than sixty!"

Chon even found the case of a butcher in Rheims who lived to be a hundred, a fact well attested to by church records, but Louis was unimpressed: "A butcher; I fear there is no comparison, for his life was spent surrounded by blood and meat, and that strengthens a man."

"We had roast for supper last night," I remind him lightly.

"Ah, pumpkin, if I could have my years to live over again." He dandles an uninspired hand over my breasts, more out of habit than lust. "Though it is true my great-grandfather lived to seventy-seven. We Bourbon men are long-lived."

"Yes, you are, dearest." I do not remind him of the premature deaths of his grandfather, father, elder brother, and son.

"And my Cardinal Fleury," he says hopefully. "That dear old man. He lived to be ninety. And he instructed me so well; might such things be transferred?"

His birthday passes and he eases into his sixty-third year without incident. The *Gazette de France* publishes a list of centenarians to please the king, but then Easter approaches, a time when the tentacles of God reach down from the heavens and the thoughts of men turn to sin and mortality. The Abbé de Beauvais delivers a scathing sermon comparing the king to Solomon, sated with sensual indulgence, and even implies the king's turn has arrived. The dratted monk so scares Louis that he considers giving up sex for Lent.

His visits to his daughter Louise at the convent increase; when he returns, he is thoughtful and sad, sometimes for days after. She corresponds with his spiritual advisers, including the offensive Abbé de Beauvais, and wields a surprising amount of influence. God becomes a permanent and unpleasant presence in our lives.

"Who is the better fighter?" ask the wags, buzzing about the king's rediscovered piety. "Who will win: his daughter Louise on her knees, praying for his soul, or Barry on her back?"

Myself, on my back, and on my knees. Definitely.

Chapter Thirty-Nine

In which Madame Adélaïde receives an unexpected visitor

I regard the Duc d'Aiguillon coldly as he bows and seats himself before me. The duke is one of *her* people and I was surprised when he requested an audience. What—another supplication for my friendship? But no; the harlot has never wooed me, not like she is trying to woo the dauphine—her most recent offering was a pair of magnificent diamond earrings, rightly ignored by Antoinette.

The harlot knows the futility of any overtures to me, I think in satisfaction; she understands my fixity of purpose. Though she did present Victoire with a crate of gooseberry cordial last month, from her estate at Louveciennes. Victoire sang—and drank—its praises, and I deigned a sip, but then recoiled in disgust, for it tasted like whore.

Narbonne fusses over the tea set the footmen are laying out, then leaves with the Comtesse de Lostanges trailing behind her, talking about one of her brood of children. As Aiguillon helps himself to a cup of tea, I regard him coolly, remembering how flustered I was to receive Choiseul alone. But that was years ago; I am now past forty and with that age comes a new sense of confidence and courage.

"Serving ourselves, in the English style," says Aiguillon energetically. "My cousin visited London, and declared it quite a useful system! No need for clumsy servants."

I know my brother admired Aiguillon greatly, and he is still a champion of the religious party, which has become sadly intertwined with the harlot's supporters. Does he wish my forgiveness?

I curse Narbonne again; Civrac would know what he wants, but she is absent in Paris this week.

"Are not the gardens so very fine this time of year?" says the duke, taking a prim sip of tea. "The roses in Diana's Grove cannot be more admired; they say it is the late frost that has produced such a veritable orgy of flowers."

I splutter on my tea.

"Ah, Madame Adélaïde, forgive me! You are too important and too busy a woman to waste time on such frivolities. I shall be direct: We need your help."

"Indeed." *We*—does the harlot need my help? How I would turn down that base supplication, as Arachne turned down the spider! I only wish I had had time to prepare a suitable quote to demonstrate my unwavering hate and firm resolution.

"A dreadful plot is under way, concerning your father's marriage," continues Aiguillon, staring at me as though in understanding, and I see his left pupil is odd, shaped like a star; a defect I had not previously noticed.

A chill sweeps through me. Has Rome changed its mind and agreed to a divorce? But Aiguillon is one of *her* creatures, and so he would hardly call the divorce a dreadful plot.

"The wolf from Chanteloup," he says, referring to Choiseul, who still attempts to wield influence from his exile, "has fixed upon a certain Madame Pater, formerly the Baroness de Neukirchen, as a suitable bride for your father."

"And how is this woman suitable?" I ask coldly. "A *baroness*?"

"Certainly, her birth is humble when compared to your august highness, but she is of noble birth. Very beautiful and caused quite a stir in Paris some years ago. She was obliged to return to Holland, but now she is returned, no longer married and suitably mature—the widow of a merchant."

I grasp the edge of my chair for support and inhale sharply at the monstrosity of what he is suggesting. A *merchant*? A luminous dark shadow, something hooked, something grasping, rises before me.

"She is J-Jewish?" I gasp weakly, almost unable to say the dreaded word.

Aiguillon looks confused. "Madame? Not Jewish?"

"But she was married to a merchant? A merchant . . . Jewish . . ." Oh. To even say that word, and the horrors it conjures up!

Aiguillon stifles what sounds like a snort but must surely have been a sneeze, and dabs his eyes delicately with a handkerchief produced from the pocket of his stiff blue coat. "No, Madame, no, not all merchants are Jewish, certainly not, there are some fine Catholic men who have taken up that calling. Perhaps I should have said a *commercial gentleman.*"

I breathe easier. "But Dutch . . ." I say dubiously. Another thought strikes, almost worse than the first: "Then she is Protestant! What heresy is Choiseul suggesting?"

"No, Madame, indeed not. Albertine—I mean to say Madame Pate—was Protestant but has now seen the inevitable light and is a new Catholic. She is at this moment studying her catechism. Here, in town, in fact, in a house Choiseul has provided for her."

"I see." New Catholics are always a little suspect, but I suppose it is not their fault they were born into the wrong faith.

"But despite being Catholic—or soon to be—and not, ah, Jewish—we are afraid the lady is sadly unsuitable. We were hoping that a word from you to His Majesty, against this lady, will help turn his thoughts away from matrimony."

I bristle with pleasure that my influence with Papa is still considered great; perhaps the estrangement that I fancy is but a function of my imagination. How wonderful! The bond between father and daughter can never be severed, I think in satisfaction.

I purse my lips as I absorb the news. A baroness, widow of a commercial gentleman. A baroness is not a born whore like the harlot, and it could be a morganatic marriage, one that would save Papa from sin but keep precedence and rank intact.

"Well, I have heard worse ideas."

Aiguillon looks frankly astonished, then he remembers his manners and puts his emotions back where they belong.

"But, ah, Madame! I thought you would have disapproved of the match? A commoner, a foreigner?" he says hopefully.

"A baroness is still noble, though I'm not sure Dutch nobility counts for much. I believe she would be suitably humble, and tractable, and willing to be guided in this new world. Father might do worse."

"I had not thought you would be in favor, Madame! We were counting on a word to your father from you, to set him against the match."

"You thought wrong, monsieur," I say coldly. "I consider Choiseul's idea to be perfectly acceptable."

Aiguillon looks confused, then mutters something about lost time, then leaves, exhorting me *not* to talk to Papa.

I sit awhile, alone, a nagging doubt growing in me that I have missed something. Why was Aiguillon appealing to me? Confounded man, I think. So inconstant—one minute wanting my influence with Papa, then the next minute urging me not to talk to him. And Civrac heard that Aiguillon has been corresponding with Choiseul, an unlikely alliance, but the shifting sands of Versailles always bring new surprises.

The dreadful memory of my father's harsh words in the wig chamber has receded safely into the void where it belongs, and though we see him but rarely, I believe his regard for me is still high. Safely married to a pious woman—new Catholics are always the most ardent—who would help him restore this Court to morality?

Yes, I have heard worse ideas.

Chapter Forty

*In which the Comtesse du Barry loses a number of things,
including her temper*

"Traitors, traitors, both of you! Get out, I never want to see you again! Have you no loyalty? I'll have you exiled, fried, I'll get you a letter, you'll be basted in sauce, I'll make the king—"

Aiguillon and the Abbé Terray are frozen in fright in front of me, their hats clutched to their bosoms like shields against my anger.

"I'll fry you in oil, you'll wish you were never born, your *mothers* will wish you were never born, I'll—"

Chon pokes her head around the door. "Jeanne, dearest, are these gentlemen bothering you?" Her eyes dart between me and the men. It was she who brought me the news of the Dutch matter; she even went to visit the lady at her house in town, where every day she holds an open salon.

Chon returned with the following description: beautiful; matronly; soft eyes; the most elegant hands one could imagine, and an air of perfect piety only a new Catholic could pull off. Rumors that the king has visited her twice already. A planned assault, coordinated by Choiseul from Chanteloup, with Terray and Aiguillon as its implementers here at Court. *My* Aiguillon—preposterous man! *My* Terray—traitor!

"You!" I scream, ignoring Chon and pointing a shaking finger at Terray. "I know what you were trying to do with your daughter, pimp her out to the king, did you think me such a fool? And you, you cur," I spit, turning to Aiguillon, who looks as though he might faint. "Your betrayal is the worst. You led that Dutch woman to His Majesty's bed, and *even held the candle*! Don't think I will forget this!"

"Jeanne, Jeanne." Chon is at my side, pulling me away from the two men. "You must calm yourself. Too many people can hear."

I am aware of milling masses in the antechamber, but I don't care. "Get off me! I will *not* calm down!"

"Gentlemen, you may leave," says Chon quickly.

"Traitors," I scream one last time as they dash for the door. In his haste, Terray trips over the edge of the carpet and sprawls in an undignified mess, his wig flying off his head and into the fire grate. He has to be dragged up by a footman before he can scramble away, wigless but safe.

Chon rolls down on the carpet, convulsing with laughter.

"Oh, Jeanne, Jeanne. You should have seen their faces!"

"I did see their faces!" I look at my hands and find them shaking. They thought to replace me with that Dutch bitch; they say *her* hands are the finest in Europe.

"I don't believe they have ever witnessed such a scene, and certainly not one directed at them!"

"Nonsense, I am sure their wives get mad at them often enough," I mutter, thinking of the look on Terray's face when I called him a cursed capon. I pour myself a brandy and remember the fights I used to have with Barry. I take a deep breath and a deep swallow, but my hands still shake.

"Never—can you imagine our dear Duchess Félicité raising her voice to a puppy, let alone her husband? No, my dear, you gave them the shock of their lives—I am sure they had no idea a woman could curse like that. Oh! I am laughing so hard I fear I shall wet myself!"

I giggle, then remember the seriousness of the situation. It will be a long fight to get rid of them, but banish them I will. Traitors. Even if that leaves only Maupeou—though that malevolent bear might also be involved.

"They will pay for this." I sit down and slosh my brandy around in its glass. "They'll see what their little plots bring. And

Aiguillon—I thought he was a friend! I'll exile them so far from Paris they'll think they're in Hungary."

"Don't bother," says Chon, sitting up and hiccuping, as she is wont to do when she has been laughing too hard. "Make what we just saw Terray's only fall. My, that was a scene! And how he looked without his wig—like a pokey-faced turtle! No, just demand the banishment of the Pater woman. It will be quicker and easier; you know if you try to get those ministers dismissed, the king will be in a pother and it could take *months*. I'm sure the king will choose you over Pater, but act fast."

I am surprised at her words, but perhaps they have had punishment enough, I think, remembering Terray's aerial indignity as he tripped over the carpet. Hopefully that story will be all over Court tomorrow, though of course it will be accompanied by a report of my own indiscretions. I did scream rather loudly. I don't care, I think viciously, and I have a sudden desire to flee Versailles and hibernate at Louveciennes. But no—I've got to get rid of that Dutch disease first.

Chon gives one last hiccup and stands up, picking carpet fluff from her hair. "Just . . . do what you do best, you know how to handle the king. I've got to go now—there is a fine pineapple I want to send to Guillaume in Toulouse. Frightful—they found a spider the size of a peach in the same crate from the Caribbean. Let's hope Guillaume is spared that dreadful possibility."

Chon smirks and disappears.

I drink some more brandy and look sadly at Terray's wig, still lying in the hearth and matching the morning ashes. I thought Aiguillon was a friend. Why must people be like this? Always intrigues and plots. And I must bother Louis with them, though his health is troubling him and turning his mood sour these days.

Nothing must happen to him, nothing.

I haven't even told Chon the terror that is buried deep inside me. One cannot fight God, or time. The Court is starting to place their bets on what will happen after my Louis dies. Only one thing is certain: anyone remotely connected with me will be banished. When I look over that dark wall into a future where Louis is no more and that fat pudding and his heinous wife rule supreme . . . dreadful thoughts.

And now this—betrayal by those closest to me.

Richelieu tells me later that Aiguillon felt unappreciated, and thought he might do better with a more refined lady. I also find out the Duc de Duras, with his traitorous little mouth, was another part of the cabal. They stay at Court and continue to share the king's intimacy, and though I sometimes forget myself and joke with them as in old times, I try to remember and be as cold as I can. Chon laughs and says my idea of cold is a sunny spring day.

As expected, the news of Terray's fall spreads far and for weeks he suffers the sharp sting of ridicule. A new dance called the Wigless Wonder makes the rounds and I heard even the dauphine laughed over it.

Glad I could cause her some amusement, I think sourly, for it seems to be the only thing I can give her. My proposed gift of a pair of magnificent diamond earrings, in the shape of chandeliers, went unacknowledged, and she never replies to any of the pretty notes I have taken to writing her. And even when I did her the supreme compliment of copying her hairstyle the day following its debut—a fussy concoction; I prefer simplicity myself—I received nary a compliment in return.

Louis is easier to manage. I storm and scream, tell him I am sick of these marriage plots and I am going to leave him unless he stops it, all of it. He is only sad, not frightened, as he once was—*he* is used to my scenes—and quickly agrees.

"I was intrigued, I must admit," he says glumly. "Her hands and feet were quite magnificent, the finest in two countries, and the doctors were pleased on account of her mature years. But, dearest, nothing is worth losing you."

The Pater woman is banished back to Holland, trailed by a pack of Frenchmen baying at her like hounds after a fox. Chon was right again: women are so much more easily disposed of than men.

Chapter Forty-One

In which the Comtesse du Barry gives the king a present

Chon's biggest triumph is Hélène de Tournon, beautiful and entirely penniless, but most importantly part of the powerful Rohan family, led by the Prince de Soubise. Chon finds her languishing away in Rouen (I know what that's like, she says grimly) and plucks her from obscurity to marry Adolphe.

I was a little disappointed—I had hoped her earlier plan to ally Adolphe with Mademoiselle de Saint-André, one of Louis' bastards by an Irish girl known as Morphise, now the Comtesse de Flaghac—might come to fruition, but a Rohan is an excellent second best.

"Our name is becoming almost as noble as our ambitions," says Chon, quite pink with pride.

Adolphe is delighted, as am I. "My dear, she is beautiful, simply beautiful. Be sure to cherish her."

"Of course, Aunt," says Adolphe. He is as handsome as his father once was, but unfortunately has also inherited his ruinous gambling addiction. Barry—now living a comfortable life of debauchery in Toulouse—wants to be present at his son's wedding but Chon makes the arrangements quickly and after the ceremony dashes off a letter to him, telling him the deed is done but that the couple will visit Toulouse the following month.

A complete lie, but Chon doesn't hesitate.

Shortly after the marriage Hélène is presented at Court as the Vicomtesse du Barry. I had hoped the dauphine would be polite to her, but it was not to be. Other ladies follow her lead and Hélène's time at Court has not been easy.

"Five," reports Chon grimly, summing up the situation a week later. "Only Aiguillon, Mirie, Flavacourt, and Valentinois have talked to her. No one else, except for the Comtesse de Narbonne—a bit surprising, that."

Hélène starts to lose some of her fresh sweetness and takes on a strained mien. She is reputed to be desperately unhappy, and desperately regretting her match.

"Well, you can't raise rabbits in Rouen," says Mirie in her capable way, dismissing the young woman's tears. "Who would choose provincial obscurity over this?"

I am silent; a great many do. We are so few in this gilded world of Versailles, living this extraordinary life, while in the rest of the vast country, others live ordinary, quiet lives. Twenty-five million of them. I hate numbers but I remember that one: the population of France. So many, it makes one's head hurt to think about it. And most of them living in abject poverty, like I used to, but only worse. Mirie once remarked that the vast majority of the French are lazy, and that is what explains their pitiful state. "I mean honestly, how hard can growing a little wheat be?" she remarked, and though I disagreed, I didn't want to argue.

The ladies might be cold to Hélène, but the king is instantly smitten.

"Come and sit on my knee, dearest, you are so young, like a daughter to me. No, wait, not a daughter," he backtracks quickly. "A niece, and such a pretty one. Jeanne, wherever did you find her?"

"Rouen," I say, rather shortly. I don't like the way the king is holding her, and from her expression, Hélène does not like it much either. In truth, I don't particularly care for my new daughter-in-law (as I think of her). She is very quiet, and shy, but underneath her pale hazel eyes, there is a slyness that occasionally leaks out. Sweet Hélène, they call her, and I think of a great bowl of sticky syrup.

The table is strewn with the detritus of a small supper: bones of ham and fish and a great dish almost empty now of figs, jujubes, and candied cherries. The candles are low and another night of games and drink is coming to an end.

"What a delicious perfume," says the king, leaning in and sniffing at Hélène's neck. The girl stiffens and looks up at the ceiling. "What is it?"

"Lilies," she whispers. I take the last jujube from the table and go and sit opposite them. Through half-closed lids I consider the look on the king's face. Pompadour was the great procuress, but I have no need to find a substitute, or any help. The king still needs me, I think in satisfaction, remembering last night. I have not nearly reached the bottom of my bag of tricks of perversion; Barry taught me well.

Ah, Barry, I think fondly, remembering our first lovemaking, the thrill and delights as a new world, hitherto covered in skirts and breeches, opened up to me. If I see him again, I think in my slightly tipsy torpor, I'll give him my favors one more time. Of course the king would never find out and he is far too unaware to ever imagine such a thing.

I lie back on the sofa, feeling very sleepy and full. The other guests have departed and now we three are all that remain. The detritus of the guests, I think with a giggle, we are the ham bones and the last remaining fig.

As I half watch the king wooing Hélène, I think of the Duc de Brissac, who occupies the apartment next to mine. Only a few rooms separate us right now. He was at our dinner, and is a very elegant and cultured man. He recently advised me on my purchase of three new paintings—and even recommended one by little Adélaïde Labille-Guiard, who has now become a well-respected painter.

Brissac is a very handsome man, and in his company I feel a frisson of excitement, such as I used to feel with Barry years ago.

"You are an enchantment," he whispered to me over supper, when the king was engaged with Mirie in a debate about the various breeds of rabbits. "A Botticelli." He put his hand on my forearm, below the table where none could see, and at the pressure of his touch my toes curled in. His Christian name is Hercule, and he is as bold and magnificent as his namesake.

Certainly, I love Louis and would do nothing to jeopardize my position—or his love—but it has been a long time . . . a long time since I felt any pleasure from the services I provide the king. Sometimes I feel like a nurse, albeit one tasked with lovemaking, if such a thing should exist.

"And what was the hunting like in Rouen?" Louis asks Hélène, his hands creeping around her waist, the flashing red of his ruby rings starting to match the girl's face.

The jewelers came today to update me on the progress of my magnificent necklace; they assure me it will be ready next year. I finger my neck and think how wonderful the weight of two million *livres* of diamonds will feel. The pure weight of love. The king sniffs one of Hélène's ringlets and murmurs something about flowers. He gives me so many gifts, I think suddenly; perhaps I should give one to him? And the doctors can't gristle too much—it has been five days.

Is the "gift" unwilling? In the half-light of the remaining candles, Hélène looks like a lovely, frightened nymph. This would help her status at Court, perhaps even restore her to the good graces of the many Rohans who were outraged over her marriage—what a wonder we got the Prince de Soubise's consent.

Keeping it in the family, I think with a giggle. I yawn, loudly, and get up from my sprawl on the sofa.

"Here, Hélène," I say, going over with my glass. "You look like you need some more. Drink."

The girl does my bidding and the king's arms tighten around her waist.

"I'm off to sleep," I announce, pecking him quickly on the cheek. "I'll shut the door and make sure no one disturbs you. You have so much to talk about."

My voice is light and sly, and it holds a meaning the king

cannot mistake. As my women undress me and fluff out my hair, I crane to listen, but there is only silence from the salon.

"Don't make the mistakes of the Pompadour," Chon always warns. "She had so many rivals you could have written a book about them and never run out of chapters."

But did Pompadour really make a mistake? I muse as I settle down to sleep. After all, she stayed by the king's side for almost twenty years, whereas I have been with him for barely four. Twenty years from now—it would be 1793. I try to imagine the world in that time, but can't.

And in twenty years the king would be over eighty.

I roll over and stare at the wall; on the other side is Hercule de Brissac's apartment. His bedchamber? I don't know and I don't want to ask. Chon has taken to glowering whenever I mention his name, as though she knows more than I do the danger he presents. I stare at the wall that separates us, and then from my salon comes a thud—of what I don't know—and then there is silence once more.

Chapter Forty-Two

In which Madame Adélaïde sees the Lady clearly

I wait for the dauphine to be handed hers, then must wait for the two young countesses, the wives of the dauphin's brothers, to receive theirs before it is my turn.

"Your napkin, Madame," says the Duchesse de Beauvilliers in an overly oily voice. She hands me the giant white napkin and takes a respectful step back as I smooth it over my magnificent gold skirt. Behind me the Comtesse de Périgord, as my sisters' *dame d'honneur*, steps forward to proffer the same to Victoire and Sophie. Napkins are unfolded and fastened around the men's necks; we ladies are too delicate for such a thing.

At the table beside us, Papa and his three grandsons are resplendent in their red coats, matching the crimson wall upholstery, all proudly wearing their *cordon bleu* sashes. At our table the dauphine, the Comtesse de Provence, and the newly arrived Comtesse d'Artois sit beside me and my two sisters. Behind us, our attendants are gathered, and a gilt balustrade separates our august royal family from the masses of the Court who mingle around.

All of us together, dining in state to cap a week of festivities marking the marriage of my nephew Artois.

We take off our gloves and hand them to our *dames d'honneur*, who then hand them to our *dames d'atours*, who then place them like pairs of embroidered snakes on a silver platter. We are so many ladies: three of the older generation, and three of the younger. Perfect symmetry, but the large number of us also means

that there is space for only two of our attendants each. Two ladies
to attend a daughter of France! Disgraceful, but such is the cross
we must bear.

In a grand voice, the Comte d'Escars announces that the service shall begin, and all fall silent as the first plates are brought in.

"Oh, horrors!" gasps Victoire beside me. "I think I see eels."

"Snakes," murmurs Sophie.

I hiss that they are not for eating, just for show. Here we are,
a chance for the masses—well, the masses with clean clothes and
swords, at least—to view their royal family. How many times has
Victoire done this? I think in impatience as the plates are passed
down until they reach our attendants. *This* is the finest entertainment that France will see, not like those lowborn jugglers that the
harlot invited last week to entertain the Court.

The eternal minuet of etiquette, the orderly procession, the
calm muteness of our ladies and the male attendants, the whole
glorious show an intricate dance on which lies the very foundation of order. Madame de Tallard, our old governess, told us that
in the days of the previous king—my great-great-grandfather
Louis XIV—His Majesty supped in state almost every night, in an
orgy of ceremony that dazzled all those fortunate enough to witness it. Now we dine thus only occasionally, and mostly on feast
days, and rarely all together like this.

These dinners are not easy—duty never is. Though I know
not why it bedevils my mind, on these occasions I can never shake
the image I have of the zebras behind the bars of their cages in
the Ménagerie.

Eels and plates of striped bass stuffed with sardines are set
grandly on the table and we are all served in perfect order. I
gracefully cut into my eel—my knife does not so much as brush
the gilded porcelain plate—and, though it is beneath my dignity, I am nonetheless an astute observer, and beyond the balustrade I spy an unknown man in a yellow coat and rented sword
whispering to his companion. About my graceful movements,
no doubt.

Delicately I pat my lips and place the fork carefully back on the snowy-white linen. Beside me, Victoire is happily eating away, while the dauphine is staring down at her eel with an empty look.

The Comtesse de Forcalquier, the one they used to call the Marvelous Mathilde, is serving the Comte d'Artois—she is a new member of his wife's household—and if I incline my head so, I can see her from the corner of one eye. She is old now, I think gleefully, just a disgraceful old whore. See how beauty fades!

The world stops as the second course is announced. Four enormous roast pigs, glazed with oranges and stuffed with myrtle, are borne in by the liveried men.

Though these dinners used to gladden my heart, I find these days I am indifferent. To them and to much else. I have taken to eating heartily, in the afternoons, and am especially fond of candied beans. But no matter how much I eat, I still feel empty inside. That plot with the Pater woman . . . as if on cue, the odious Duc d'Aiguillon sweeps through the room, his equerry slapping the man with the yellow coat and his companion out of the path of his august master. I heard . . . my stomach cramps at the memory and I unexpectedly stab my pig, the noise of my knife on the porcelain like a sword on glass.

Aiguillon came to me, wanting me to oppose the marriage to Papa.

Because he knew—everyone knew—that Papa would do the opposite of what I counseled. I take a deep breath, fearful that in my sour mood the Lady of Introspection might appear.

The dance begins again: the third-course plates are brought in with great majesty and even greater aplomb.

Beside me, Victoire fidgets, and I want to reach over and slap her. Just slap her. The dauphine sighs loudly and taps her fork against her glass. Swiftly the Comtesse de Noailles takes her glass away and motions for one of the water bearers to fill it. Confounded chit of a girl! We are now more estranged than ever; she has spun off into her own circle, heedless of the disapproval that surrounds her. And she has even influenced Louis-Auguste against us—I have noticed a new frostiness in our interactions. The dauphin sits with the men, heartily enjoying his meal, occasionally seeking out his wife to smile at her.

A chilled consommé is served as a guard chases a young man wearing trousers through the crowds in front of the balustrade. Heavens—trousers at Versailles! No breeches—*sans culottes*! Such riffraff—how did he get past the guards? But they will catch him and then it will be Bastille for him, no doubt.

I take a measured sip of my consommé and from the corner of my eye see that Antoinette is refusing to touch hers. Louis-Auguste and Antoinette partially consumm— succeeded in their marital mission, and that triumph has given the girl new confidence. At one of the balls last week to celebrate Artois' marriage, I overheard her talking, rather loudly, about her friend (friend! She has not learned that a future queen must not have friends!) Laure's sister, dead at the age of forty and unmarried. Antoinette asked rather loudly who would mourn a woman with no children—a dead end and an affront, she said, with a smirk and an overly loud sneer.

I knew her to be heedless, but I did not think her cruel.

These days Narbonne is constantly urging me to reconcile with the harlot, for through her lies the path to regain the love of my father. But I cannot, simply cannot, and so I watch him as he spins ever further away from us, ever more under the influence of her, and the younger generation.

Yet I can see what I have lost, and what my enmity has cost me.

As though pulled by my thoughts, the Barry harlot appears, laughing loudly in her vulgar way. She is wearing a lovely cream dress, bedecked with a glistening sapphire necklace though it is not yet evening, and accompanied by a buzzing cloud of acolytes. Everyone in the salon turns to watch her, and waves of recognition ripple through the crowd.

I glance at Papa; he is watching her with a look of tenderness and admiration.

I must concentrate on my soup and on my duty. I must eat my soup in the most regal manner, give the spectators a chance to witness the grace and majesty of their rulers. But since that woman entered, no one is looking at us.

"Coo—how lovely!" exclaims a woman in an overly large pink dress.

"Just look at that hair! And those jewels!"

"Like an angel," declares the man in the yellow coat, shaking his head as though in wonder.

The dance starts again, the soup plates whisked smoothly away, the last course grandly borne in through the doors. A quivering mountain of red gelatin is placed before us, and I can hear the dauphine inhale in disgust.

"Quiver . . ." whispers Sophie as though in awe.

Recently I have had a curious shaking feeling that sometimes bedevils me for days on end. I am past forty, the only of my siblings to achieve that age. They say thirty-five is the Rubicon in a woman's life, when she must stop wearing flowers and flounces and put on caps and somber clothes. But we are not in my grandmother's time and I believe the younger fashions look perfectly fine on me, and the new pale colors complement my complexion.

Somehow forty seems more momentous. If I died, who would mourn me?

What use is a childless woman, ever? asks the Lady of Introspection from her perch inside the trembling rhubarb jelly. A lifetime of getting dressed and undressed, endless dinners and endless rituals, a lifetime of waiting for visits, a lifetime of sitting around. A lifetime of doing my duty.

And in return I didn't want much from him—why couldn't he give it to me? My father was the only man for me, ever, yet I was never enough for him.

"This jelly looks *old*," hisses Antoinette as her portion is placed before her with a flourish.

I sense Narbonne and Beauvilliers somewhere above me.

"Sister, dear sister, what is it?" Victoire's voice floats by me and then her face, a well of kindness and worry, comes slowly into focus.

Goodness, what am I doing on the floor? I am helped to my feet by the firm hands of Narbonne, and I am uncomfortably aware that the entire room—my family, the courtiers, those dreadful base people—are all staring at me. Looks of concern on some, amused indulgence on others. Did I fall off my chair?

"Is it the jelly?" whispers Victoire, holding up a spoonful.

"No, no, I—a faint turn, no more. Thank you, Narbonne," I say as she guides me to my feet. My head feels light, as though there is nothing inside it. Nothing inside *me*. "I would return to my apartment."

"Are you sure you're fine, sister? I'll come with you." Victoire's voice is worried, torn between duty and the dessert she is loath to leave.

"No, no, I would—I am fine."

As I am helped away, I glance back at Papa, but he is not even looking at me; he is smiling once again at the harlot. I stumble and catch my equerry's arm.

"Just a slight—indisposition," I say to no one in particular, but no one is listening. No one ever listens. *And no one ever watches you*, a voice, one that sounds too much like Louise's, mocks me.

"What did you say?" I ask Narbonne sharply, but she only looks confused and shakes her head. I am led into my bed, and the curtains are drawn against the outside world and the cold of the November day.

I startle awake—when did I fall asleep? It is dark in my room; from an alcove, candles glitter but the room is empty and silent. I lie inside the bed, not stirring to alert my attendants. I can be alone here, I think, then realize I am always alone, even amidst the crowd of my life.

I start to cry. Everything is sad, and I have a melancholy I cannot shake. Everything I did in my life, I did for him, and now I sense we have become distasteful to him. My fixity of purpose inspired no respect, and he has chosen her—that harlot—over his own daughters.

How dare he?

This time I cannot push my awful thoughts away, and my hollowness is filled with vitriol and bitterness and aching pain. The Lady of Introspection curls into bed alongside me and stretches out to stay the night, and she speaks in the voices of my enemies and taunts me with truths I never wanted.

I hear that mocking girl's voice: *a dead end*. Aiguillon's voice, calm, smooth, treachery underneath, thinking one word from me would send Papa running in the opposite direction. That harlot, looking at me with kindness, even pity. Worst of all, my father's blank eyes.

I stay in my bed, unable to rise, the doctors unable to prescribe anything but bleedings that leave me even weaker still. Was it all a dreadful mistake? Why did my goodness not inspire the love it should have? Why do others have love but never me? I only wanted to be good, and I cry great tears from the deepest river inside me. I am a fool, a joke, a burden. That is what they think I am, and that is what I have become.

Élisabeth, crying in fright, Clothilde wetting herself, even Louis-Auguste impatient with us. My sister Élisabeth, dead now, saying we were like frogs in a well, never knowing the world outside Versailles. But that was not my doing! Why did Papa never have us married? Why did he fail in his duty to us? I hear the taunts mixed with the crowds on the roads to Plombières, where we went to take the waters. So long ago, we were so young then, Henriette with us, Louise with us; now we are so old and ugly and forgotten.

I lie a week or more in the sheltered cavern of my bed, but then one morning I wake up feeling different, and determined. This is not who I am. I must rouse and straighten myself, not hide like a bug in a bed. We all have our duties and our place in this world. The prayer cushions for Saint Agonia's day need to be finished, and I have missed two lessons with our trumpet master—how will I ever learn the piece by Gluck that I was supposed to?

Chapter Forty-Three

In which the Comtesse du Barry hears an awful prophecy

I tap my foot impatiently, and beside me, the Marquise de Flavacourt twitches in disapproval. I cannot believe we are listening to this same damn priest, the same one who railed against the king last year and who caused Louis such sorrow and fear.

I told Louis he must seek new counsel, but he only shook his head dolefully, with that distant, pious look he gets when speaking of things religious (quite often these days) and said the man was just doing his job—tending to souls.

Just doing his job . . . I look down from my box to the king in the center of the chapel below. To think, if the pope had done *his* job and approved the divorce, I could have been sitting down there with the king and his family. But in truth, the view is better from up here. I note in appreciation the Duchesse de Valentinois' hairstyle, piled high and ringed with black roses, rather elaborate and sinful under her black lace lappets.

The priest rails on: "The people of France are in misery while their king resides in sin! The whole of France stinks of want and desperation."

Outside, at least the sun is shining, casting gemlike shards through the dreadful cold of the chapel. I twist one of the ends of my lappets until Flavacourt takes my arm and puts it firmly down again. It has been a grim start to the year: a hailstorm in February, coinciding with Louis' sixty-fourth birthday; a string of sudden deaths that put my Louis in a scared and tremulous mood, and the continuing troubles of a woman after thirty: the specter of caps is starting to haunt me, the need to cover my hair in the name of age and respectability.

And then to crown the series of unfortunate events, the king hurt his arm while hunting. Again. The bone was not broken, thank goodness—last year the Comtesse de Montholon tripped on her train and broke her ankle, then died from the subsequent infection—but still it swelled up and was angry and red for many weeks. Now the horse is forbidden him and it is all he can do to spear some little piglets, specially hobbled by the grooms for the honor of being killed by the king.

Next to the king sit the dauphin and his wife, and I have to admire her hairstyle. She has taken to wearing her hair piled high over pads of horsehair and human hair; these elaborate concoctions, known as *poufs*, are suddenly everywhere. Today, hers is decorated with black bells and silk spring flowers. I pat my own hair in satisfaction—no need for fake hair for me, though many ladies must have recourse to that as styles inch higher.

The priest rants on: "The king is the cause of the people's misery, as sin is the cause of all the misery on earth!" The Abbé de Beauvais is a favorite of Mesdames, the king's daughters; no doubt another one of their ill-advised attempts to meddle in their father's private life.

"Goodness, but he's going too far!" hisses Madame de Flavacourt beside me, frowning in disapproval.

"Don't listen to him," I whisper back, glaring down at the black-frocked priest. Beside the dauphin and his wife are his two younger brothers and their wives; they whisper that the youngest, the Comtesse d'Artois, is pregnant already. How the dauphine must have wept when she heard the news! She remains as cold as ice to me, and amidst my other worries—why are they suddenly so many in number?—is an ever-present little siren that sings: *Forcing her to speak to you was not a good idea.* A Pyrrhic victory, Chon called it, but I didn't even bother to ask what that meant—I don't want to know.

Next to them, in descending order of dullness, are the three daughters of the king, each frumpier than the last. Clumsy, plump old wenches, the Court calls them. How sad it must be to be them: forgotten in a corner of the palace, every year older, every year more insignificant. An old unmarried princess is more useless than a clock without hands, Mirie once whispered to me.

Madame Adélaïde was sick at the end of last year and spent the good part of a week in her bed, the curtains drawn around her, admitting no one. Who would miss her if she died? Perhaps the king: at heart he is a good man, and was once very fond of his daughters.

The priest thunders on: "Jonah warned the city of Nineveh they had forty days until God destroyed them. The people repented and God spared them! Unless the king repents of his sin, this city will be destroyed in forty days!"

Inwardly I groan; Louis is going to be in a pother because of this.

And he is.

"Forty days," he repeats later, with the same solemn intonation. "Then God will destroy the city."

"He said city, not *you*."

"He meant me." Louis sits down heavily, wincing as his arm catches the edge of the chair. "I am convinced of it. His words are clear: if I do not repent, I shall be destroyed."

I trace the back of his neck, then lean over and give him a long wet kiss, to remind him of what he would be missing, were he to repent.

"Nineveh, Your Majesty, was recently discovered by a Dane," informs Chon. After the sermon, Louis had shut himself in his room all day, and even refused to see me. Now it is evening and he has crept out, up to my apartment, but he is a distressed and worried man.

"Mmm. The Danes," says Louis, unimpressed.

"Exactly. He didn't say forty days and *France* would be destroyed. He was talking about Nineveh. Where's Nineveh?" I ask Chon.

"Arabia. Recently discovered by a Danish archaeologist."

"What's an archaeologist?"

Chon sighs and leaves the room.

"It's a parable, silly one," says Louis in irritation. I growl back at him; I hate it when he demeans me, which he does more and more these days. He is increasingly characterized by worry and bad temper, and his dyspepsia is getting worse. Death is all around us: in January the Genoan ambassador fell dead during an audience with the king; the Abbé de la Ville was struck down with apoplexy, and then the Marquis de Chauvelin. Courtiers toppling like cards in front of the king, each sad incident deepening his conviction that he is being punished for his sins.

Even my little attempts with Hélène backfired; after, he railed against me and accused me of inducing him to greater sin.

And now that dratted sermon.

"You're becoming a grumpy old man," I say, thinking ahead to the next ten years, God willing. I kiss him again to remind myself he's only in a bad humor because of his arm and the sermon. It must be terrible to be old and sick, and afraid.

"Priests shouldn't be making predictions," says Chon, coming back into the room with a green-painted box. "They're not fortune-tellers and only God knows what the future holds. Now, I'm a little late, but I was hoping to send my brother Guillaume an Easter gift. This box of nuts—lots of hazelnuts!—will be just the thing, I'm sure he has quite overcome his aversion to them."

I gaze at her in sudden tenderness. Dearest Chon—she refuses to give up, and keeps on trying. But she had best hurry, comes a little voice I can't quell—we're running out of time.

Chapter Forty-Four

In which Madame Adélaïde receives her heart's desire

After our dear Abbé de Beauvais' Maundy Thursday sermon, my father is a changed man—humble, pious, spending more time with us and less with *her*. All the hopes of the previous years rise again like a phoenix from the river. The priest's words hit my father hard and we all sense he is on the verge of repentance.

"Verge," says Sophie softly and hopefully.

His arm is not fully mended and he still cannot hunt. Instead he frequently drops by in the afternoons and takes a kind interest in our little world: he compliments Sophie on the cape she is embroidering for the Comtesse de Montbarrey's greyhound, ensures Victoire has the most delicate sausage from his kitchens, and even spent one delightful afternoon talking with me about trade with our colonies in the West Indies.

My heart aches with both happiness and regret, for this is the father I always wanted, yet so rarely had.

Now he writes Louise daily, and I write to her as well; we scheme between ourselves to continue our father's gradual return to God. I know Papa well, and I fear that once the forty days are done, his heart and mind will go back to her, at least for another year.

Time is of the utmost, but I accept Louise's advice: do not press hard, for his own heart must lead him down the righteous path. She even suggested that Papa should consider keeping the harlot beside him, as a friend, while he returns in soul and spirit to the church. *A soft separation*, she writes. *My sources and the doctors tell me he rarely spends the night anymore; dear sister, you will know what I mean.* I cannot stop some of my old jealousy returning, that Louise in her cloistered world knows more about the intimate life of our father than I do. All I have heard are disgusting rumors about a monkey—a handsome one, Civrac clarified—and dastardly goings-on at that hotbed of sin and vice, otherwise known as Louveciennes.

"But that is very pretty, my dear," Papa says to Sophie, who does not blush as she might have in former times, but only nods her head.

"It is a bluebell," she says in a small but clear voice as our father admires her embroidery.

"My dear," and I start, then realize he is addressing me. He hands the dog cape back to Sophie and gestures to me. "My dear, I would walk with you awhile."

"Of course, Papa." Though his voice and eyes are kind, I cannot stop a small knot of worry binding my stomach.

"Come, let us take a turn in the Salon of Apollo." We walk there in silence, his equerries hurrying ahead to clear a path and keep the intimacy of our walk. He sits down on one of the red velvet benches that line the room and motions for me to sit beside him. I do, my stomach now entirely tied up.

"It has not been easy for you," he says, staring ahead at a giant painting of Icarus and his fall on the opposite wall.

What? What has not been easy? I think in wild apprehension. Have I displeased him? I was so careful to heed Louise's words, I know I have meddled in the past, but—

"Adélaïde, dearest," and here he takes my hand and squeezes it, and through our gloves I can feel the force of his love, and my breathing slows. "This has not been easy for you. I have perhaps not lived my life as behooves a man of family and God. I know the burden you have taken on is great."

"Oh, Papa . . ." Is he really saying these words? Am I really hearing this? "Oh, Papa," I repeat, but I don't know what else to say. Is he apologizing? Repenting? Confessing? Should I get a priest?

"She makes me so happy, Adélaïde," he continues calmly, and I see the best I can do is listen; these words do not come easy for him. "I know I live in sin, but I am not so old, not ready to repent and live my life as a monk. And I know I have you—all of you—praying for my soul, and that cheers me greatly. Thank you, Adélaïde."

"And so we will continue to pray!" I declare fervently. For a few blissful moments we sit in silence, my hand still in his, and I cannot bear to move, for fear of breaking the spell of this wonderful closeness. I sneak a peek and see his face is blank, and tired, and that he is still staring at the painting on the opposite wall.

"It is a very fine painting," I say. I want to stop, but the words keep coming, and then the magic spell is broken. "D'Isle recommended it, and—"

"Ah, my dear, come, let us go back, it is getting late."

I stand up with him and hold my breath in anticipation, but he does not embrace me. Yet I can still feel the touch of his hand, the kindness in his voice, the naked appeal for my understanding. He disappears upstairs with his entourage, and slowly I walk back to my apartment. The king's touch, I think happily, dreamily, the king's touch restores even the basest of lepers. Of course Papa does not touch and cure the beggars anymore—he cannot while in a state of sin—but soon. Soon. Perhaps even this year?

As his lust slackens, his humanity returns, wrote Louise, and though I frowned at the sentiment, now I realize she is right.

She makes me happy, Adélaïde, he said. Was it worth it, ruining my relationship with the only man I have ever loved, over something—someone—who made him happy? Did I cling to my hate because I had nothing else to hold on to?

Strange thoughts, but ones that have been my constant companion since my illness last year. I do not allow myself to dwell on those dark days of despair, but I know they changed me. Others may laugh at me but I only do my duty. I can hold my head high, and know that I have never brought shame or disrepute upon my position or upon the legacy of the Bourbons.

Thank you, Adélaïde.

The door opens and a footman announces Madame Victoire. She comes in with Clothilde on the one hand, Élisabeth on the other.

"Sorry to interrupt, sister, but you just have to hear Clothilde sing this aria! It is so beautiful, and my first thought was that we should come immediately and share it with her dear Tante Adélaïde."

I frown, for seeing Victoire and Clothilde side by side makes me aware just how fat they both are. A certain plumpness is expected in an older woman—even I, despite the strict care in my diet, have noticed a tightness in some of my bodices—but in one as young as Clothilde, only fourteen! And my sister is but forty, with no preg—indispositions to blame. I am about to make a cutting remark to share my displeasure, but then I see the terrified look on Clothilde's face and something in me softens.

She is to be married next year, to the son of the King of Sardinia, a brother of the two new wives of my nephews. Two for one, jokes the Court, in allusion to Clothilde's massive weight. When her future bridegroom heard of her girth, he declared himself in all happiness, for it meant only more to love.

I thought them vulgar words, and had an image of an enormous elephant crushing a dainty mouse, but now I see they were really kind words, to make his young bride less terrified as she prepares to leave all that is familiar. Kind words. And were those not kind words my father said to me? I should share it, I think, instead of keeping this happiness to myself.

"How delight—" My voice is more of a growl than I intend and I check myself. "How delightful," I try again, quieter now, and with kindness. "I should love to hear it."

Victoire smiles happily and pushes her niece forward. Goodness, to see the two of them together, you would think them a circus act, both so fat—but no, they are my family, and I must be kind.

As Papa was to me.

Clothilde clasps her hands and opens her mouth. A tremulous note flies out.

Chapter Forty-Five

In which the Comtesse du Barry visits a meadow

"Two weeks!" I say merrily. "What are two weeks?" The blight of the priest's omen has followed us all month, but now there are but a few days left until we are free of his dratted prophecy about everything being destroyed before forty days are over.

"Ah, my love," says Louis sadly.

"No, really, France, what are two weeks?"

"Are you posing me a question you wish me to answer, sweetheart?"

"Yes."

Louis sighs deeply.

"No sighing!"

"Ah, love, you give me so many rules, and we are not even in the bedchamber. Well, in truth, two weeks is not a long time."

"Exactly! Before you know it, we'll be past the forty days, and all will be well again." I wish we could go and hide in a hut in the woods—as they used to do in times of plagues past—but since we can't do that, we are cloistered at the Grand Trianon on the grounds of Versailles. Close enough for the king to travel back to the main palace when needed, but here we can be happy and free and only admit those we care to see.

His daughters are not among them; he has been spending far too much time with them recently. *His daughters on their knees, or Barry on her back?*

I have to admit the race is getting tighter.

"All will be well again," repeats Louis. He has been complaining for several days of a general feeling of malaise, but I know it is just his mind playing tricks on his body as the final days are counted out.

"Now, come, the carriage is waiting." It is a lovely spring day and we head south from the palace, staying inside the parks, where we are unlikely to pass a funeral that might spin the king's mind back to melancholy.

He has started hunting again—his doctors reluctantly gave permission—but I am nervous every time he does. Another fall—he has already had two—and then where would we be? I keep my fears to myself, for the hunt is too much a part of his life and makes him too happy. But today I insisted we drive out together in my new gilt-and-rose carriage.

"Wait, I know a place," says the king, and directs the driver to a clearing by a stream, a beautiful meadow enameled with wild-flowers of all different colors. We descend from the carriage into the sunlit depths.

"Oh, it's beautiful," I say, twirling around.

"I would make you a garland, Angel. Well, present you with one at least. Forgeron!" he calls, and a young valet comes forward. "A garland of the finest flowers for the lovely countess." As the valet busies himself picking flowers, the king settles down with a wheeze on a folding chair from the carriage.

Dappled sunlight, the breeze brisk but warm, peace in the clearing. A bird trills, answered by its mate. I sit at his feet on the grass, and feel a sudden rush of tenderness for the man he is, for the life he has given me. Some may complain of his faults—nay, all complain of his faults—but who amongst us does not have any? To me, he is the perfect man.

Well, he would be were he younger, and perhaps less crotchety than he has been of late.

I lie back on the grass and the flowers, enjoying the fragrance and the soft sunlight. I pick a bluebell from beside me and toss it up, slowly, floating. My life is a senseless dream of pleasure, I think happily.

"That was lovely, my dear, lovely," Louis says on the ride back. "Worth giving up the hunt for."

I lean over and give him a kiss, one hand holding on to the garland of wild flowers that sits prettily on my head.

"Tonight, Richelieu's coming with his son Fronsac," I say, and then another day will be past. Twelve more, twelve more, then nevermore. We have even abstained from lovemaking, so convinced is Louis that death is coming for him. Irrational and silly. Though I am more nurse than woman these days, I am looking forward to the resumption of our activities.

It is well known that men cannot live without sex, but a woman like me is far more rare, even unnatural, as the priests might thunder. Unbidden, the handsome face of Hercule, the Duc du Brissac, rises in front of me. He is an avid art collector and last week he presented me with a statue of Venus from Pompeii. When he ran his fingers over her marble lines, talking of the perfection of her body and the nakedness of her desire, I almost fainted. He should really be more discreet.

I should be more discreet. Thank goodness he is off duty this year and is mostly in Paris, at Court only once a week on Sundays or so.

I close my eyes, lulled by the rocking of the carriage, and relive the afternoon, the way the sun cast shadows over the clearing, the flowers like gems amid the green of the grass. I open my eyes, startled with an idea.

"I know what I want for May!" I declare to Louis, whose eyes flutter open; I didn't realize he was sleeping.

"Are you getting a present for May, Angel?"

"I am!" I kiss him happily. "A dress, green fabric, embroidered with gems, the sapphires will be bluebells, garnets for roses, pink, I think, not red, and yellow—what stone could be the buttercups? It will be just like wearing a meadow, and then I can remember this afternoon all my life!"

"All your life," repeats the king rather sadly. "Of course, dearest, anything you desire."

✑

"A mincing vixen, when I was finished with her, why she couldn't—"

"Oh, shut up, Rich, you know the king would hate it if he heard you. And I doubt it's true." Louis has always enjoyed Richelieu's smutty stories, but recently they are becoming more painful for him as they remind him of what he no longer is.

"Oh, it's true all right, it's true," the duke insists, mustering a spluttery wheeze of a leer. I regard him under half-lowered lids and remember the first time I met him, with my basket of gloves from Labille's. How I stood in his salon and dreamed about living in luxury. And now look at me. Beside him, his son the Duc de Fronsac, a pale imitation of his father, laughs in his slightly idiotic way.

The king enters, looking a little pale. "A slight headache, nothing more. Too much sun yesterday, no doubt. Or pollen in the meadow."

I brighten, thinking of my dress, then frown, for Louis is looking rather wobbly.

"Are you sure you should be hunting?"

"It is nothing, nothing," he insists, "and Aumont tells me the pickings will be good around Marly this afternoon."

"Take care of him!" I call out as they are helped into the carriage that will bring them to the stables. It is another fine spring day, warm and balmy, only a hint of thunder in the briskly rolling clouds. Louis needs to hunt, to prove he still can, and I must let him.

I rejoin Chon and Mirie in the gardens, and we pass a pleasant afternoon playing with Lucas, a lovely rabbit from Turkey, trained to stand on his hind legs and be fed by hand.

I startle when I hear the men returning. So early, well before dusk.

The king has a fever.

Damn it! I am sure it is a trifle, nothing more—it *was* rather sunny in the meadow yesterday—but I know the effect it will have on him and his overactive imagination. What sheer bad timing, with only twelve days left.

His fever deepens through the next day and I sit beside him, mopping his brow. Richelieu paces back and forth and I know he won't be able to keep the crowds at bay much longer. All day everyone has been riding down from the palace to the Grand Trianon, no longer caring if they have an invitation, all demanding their right to see him.

Mostly he sleeps, but then in the night he takes a turn for the worse and starts to mumble in delirium. Fear grips my heart so hard I fear I might vomit. Get better, France, get better, I whisper through my long night of vigil.

"Two Trianon dairymaids had a case of smallpox last week," whispers Mirie, and I blanch until Richelieu tells me the king had smallpox when he was a young man. I breathe easy. Not the dreaded pox, just a brief fever.

It's nothing, I and my supporters declare, loud enough for the king to hear.

The king is dreadfully sick, hiss back my enemies, and he must be properly attended to.

A king can only be sick at Versailles, insists the doctors who tend him, afraid of being blamed should something happen while not following protocol. They win and we move back to Versailles, where the king is installed in a camp bed next to his magnificent state bed.

I don't let the cruel palace close around my beloved, and every night I disregard etiquette and force my way into the room that is beginning to stink of sin and death. Around me eighteen surgeons, doctors, and apothecaries circle impotently, endlessly checking the king's tongue and pulse.

Light is tiring for my beloved's eyes and the room is kept in darkness. On the third day of his fever one of the doctors brings a lantern close to examine his patient, and sees the dreaded spots on the king's scarlet swollen face.

"Smallpox!" he cries to the antechamber, away where the king can't hear him. The shadows of the room did not allow us to see the spots immediately, but now they are clear, and so is the end.

Of my world, at least.

Chapter Forty-Six

In which Madame Adélaïde has her finest, and saddest, hour

Papa was brought back in high delirium and placed on a small bed. I made sure it was equipped with a decent mattress—no more of that dreadful scene after Damien's assassination attempt, when he was placed on a bed with no mattress.

The cloak of death hangs just by the door, but I know we will save him. When he recovers—he will recover, for the doctors (well, half at least) are adamant—we will be here. Sophie and Victoire and I sit and pray by my father while the doctors, twenty of them at least, endlessly cycle in and out, bleeding him, checking his tongue, bleeding him again, their futile flutterings driving me to distraction.

The doctors have kept the dread news of smallpox from him, and he only believes himself in a fever.

"Madame, you must not," insists Narbonne. "Let me. I cannot be infected again, but you, Madame, you have not had it."

"No," I say firmly, though I am touched by the genuine concern in her eyes. This is my father and I would sacrifice my own life for his. I sit and murmur love to him when he awakens; when he is in delirium I listen patiently and carefully, but he only whispers, "*Bijou, bijou.*" At least he does not call for the harlot.

Five nights and five days in a vigil at his bedside. The rest of our family—the dauphin, his wife and younger brothers, their wives and all their households—is kept safely away, and most courtiers avoid the sick chamber, claiming fear of disease. Even the Comte de Puyrec, whose face is as poxed as a whore's. Papa is more alone in death than he has ever been in life, I think sadly one afternoon as he dozes, a dozen doctors slumped on chairs, the rest of the room empty.

But I am by his side.

His head is now swollen and red, his body blackening, and he senses the end coming swiftly nearer. We cannot keep the truth from him much longer. One morning he holds his hands up, in the faint light allowed in through the shutters.

"Smallpox—but I thought I had it," he declares in amazement, his breath wheezing over the words. When the doctors confirm the truth, he accepts it without demur.

He shall recover. The Comtesse de Chabannes had it last year, and she recovered, as so many do. Like my dearest Narbonne—she lived. He will be amongst the lucky ones. Though God is no merchant and I have nothing to offer, I want to bargain with Him for my father's life. I can't say I will enter a cloister, for God knows what is in our hearts, and that life is not for me. I have nothing else to offer, I think bleakly, staring at the grotesque swollen face of the only man I ever loved. Though he left long ago, I plead with God not to take him from me. Not again.

And now his body is a battleground between those who say he is dying, and must confess, and those who insist he is not. I find myself siding with Richelieu and the harlot—I know that to even mention the last rites would scare the wits, and possibly the life, out of my father.

She comes, every evening when we turn to leave, silent and unassuming, quite ignoring the fact she does not have the entrées to the sick chamber. She just walks in, as though the walls erected by etiquette are completely meaningless. The world doesn't stop turning and nothing breaks, and I see in a moment of sad clarity that if one does not believe in it, etiquette is as meaningless as a crucifix to a pagan. I put that thought aside, for another day.

For now we are united in our fight: I do the vigil of the day, she does the vigil of the night. She may be a harlot, but we love the same man. *And she makes me happy*, my papa said. Can't a king try, like any man, to have some happiness in this life?

She is risking her health and her beauty; they always said she had a kind heart. I never believed them, but I know she must care for Papa to risk all she has. Well, not all; we hear her creature Chon has begun emptying her apartments, taking her jewels and all her treasures to her lair at Louveciennes.

It is almost midnight; no moon tonight and the room is silent. He sleeps, the only sound his tortured wheezing. I gather my prayer book and beads and rise. I do not lean down to kiss him, but I grasp at his hand, and squeeze it, and fancy a tremor passes though.

"Good-bye, Papa," I whisper. "Good night."

"Pomponne?" he whispers back, and the hand that grasps mine is strong and unyielding; in such small things, we take comfort. As I take my leave, I pass her coming in.

Tonight something compels me to stop, and so does she.

"How is he?" she whispers, her face searching mine. I shake my head. A sudden urge to cry comes over me, for I fear I am weak and exhausted. How can God ignore our prayers? Without thinking, I put my hand on her arm, and clench it, as though she can offer me comfort.

"He drank a little bouillon, and the doctors prescribe another bleeding for tomorrow."

The harlot's face is drawn and blank, etched with worry.

"I brought him some chicken," she whispers, holding up a small basket. "Don't tell the doctors—they want him on nothing more than water and thin soup." Then she looks at me in fright, as though she has said the wrong thing, but I can only nod my approval—anything that makes Papa feel better.

As I settle into my own bed, the thought comes to me: But I do have something to offer. If he gets through this, as I know he will, I will be kind to her. I will accept her, even embrace her. I will treat her as a venerated stepmother, and together we will make my beloved father's last years the best years of his life.

Chapter Forty-Seven

In which the Comtesse du Barry says good-bye

"You hear them?"

"Dearest?" I lean in, stifle my senses against his stench. The room is now putrid with the stink of his decaying body and soul.

"Them."

"Who, dearest?"

"The nightingales."

"I can—they sound so beautiful," I whisper back, stroking his cheek but avoiding the oozing pustules. Perhaps he talks of the nightingales at Louveciennes, that used to sing in the summer nights when we held our suppers and parties.

Smallpox is not always fatal; perhaps one of four or three might die, a roulette that gives some hope. Then I think of his old, raddled body, and I am again terrified. I sit with him every night while around us intrigue swirls. Richelieu insists the king would die of fright at the suggestion of last rites, while Choiseul's party is working, from afar, to have me banished regardless of the outcome.

Enough of this intrigue! Just let me be with him.

The doctors, surgeons, and apothecaries that surround him, alongside the puppet ministers, are all walking a delicate tightrope: to predict the death of a king who survives is dangerous, but to allow a king to die without confession? Infinitely more so.

But then his pustules start to close in. All is lost, say his doctors, and even those in our camp cannot fight science. The end is coming—will come—and his confession must happen. And when the last rites come, out the door I must go. We hear the dreadful news and Richelieu tries to bolster me with stories of the Duchesse de Châteauroux at Metz.

"She was banished, but recalled before the year was out. The king couldn't live without her, and he can't live without you."

But now he is so much older, and already teetering on the brink of piety. If I am banished, I doubt I will be recalled.

The doctors tell him the truth of his situation.

"Angel, we must say good-bye. You must leave." He is lucid now; the Archbishop of Paris is summoned, and in the morning he will hear Louis' confession.

"I know, I know." I am crying, great rivers of tears that flow off me and over his raddled face and chemise. I want to encircle him with my arms, wrap him up and fly away with him, far from this sickroom and the grim reality of what is happening.

My Louis is dying.

"My Angel," he whispers again, and a wasted arm stretches out for a last fumble of my breasts.

"My love!" I cannot bear this. It is the greatest grief I have ever known and I don't know what to do with it or where to put it. Give us more, I demand of God. Give us more time, more life, more love! Behind me, the men are massing at the doors, half of them gleeful, the other half knowing that when I go, so go their fortunes.

"Dearest, leave." I know the words cost him greatly, this man who has nothing left. "You must not be here. I am in my last state and now I must give myself to God and my people."

I fly out of the room, as fast as I can run, my face blinded with tears. It was not supposed to happen like this. I hate to leave him to the vultures; the certainty of his impending death has stripped the last vestige of artifice from their faces, and now his courtiers regard him with the contempt they believe he deserves. Wise heads turn to greet the rising sun, Chon remarked sadly.

The clocks chime four and I stumble alone through the great

staterooms, through the grim corridors of darkness, as deserted and as sad as I am now. The same rooms I gleefully ran through with Barry chasing after me, that very first night. Five years ago. I don't want to leave this charmed life and my adoring lover. I want more, more of everything. I want more time! Why did we go to the Trianon? Where did he catch it? Why did we not even consider the new vaccinations? Mirie's two nephews took them, and suffered no ill. Why can't we turn back time and do it all over?

I am crying so hard I don't even see who it is who helps me to my feet and carries me up to my apartment. Only enough time for one last run through my beloved rooms, the scene of all my happiness. They are empty now; all the good things he gave me, all the beautiful things of this life that can mean so much, and do mean so much, are waiting for me at Louveciennes. They are the symbols of our love and the lasting memories of it. But I don't want them there, I want them back here!

"Come now," says Chon patiently, following me as I whirl through the rooms in a maelstrom of grief. The moon is too bright tonight, shining though there is no hope of mercy or redemption. Below, in the courtyard, my carriage is waiting, to take me to Rueil—Aiguillon's house, closer to Versailles than Louveciennes.

"Do you have no heart?" I scream at her, suddenly sick of her capable, cold little face. "I can't leave him! No one cares about him! He can't die alone!"

"It's over," she says firmly, and her voice is sad; there will be no more intrigues and plots to keep her animated. She will mourn this life as surely as I will. "All of it, over. Even if he recovers, he won't recall you. Come, we're not going far, and only God knows the future."

I stumble down into the waiting carriage, the courtyard in darkness, feeling like a criminal. And that is what I will become if the king dies: a criminal.

Over the next few days, we receive visitors at Rueil; each handsome carriage that clatters into the courtyard brings me hope, for some courtiers are still hedging their bets, placing one chip on each side. Two messengers an hour also make the ride, their horses burning the road, but the news continues sober and terrifying.

After I left, his addled brain asked for me, forgetting he had told me to go. My heart cleaves that he might think I abandoned him. Only his daughters remain with him, and only that gives me some comfort; he will not be alone at the end.

But no! This is not how it ends. I will return to Versailles and I will see him again. There is so much more to my life that needs to be written.

It cannot be over. It cannot.

Louis XV of France
February 28, 1710–May 10, 1774

Fulfilling his shameful destiny,

Louis has finished his career.

Cry, scoundrels; cry, strumpets,

You have lost your father.

—*Parisian street song, May 1774*

Part III

Departure

1774–1800

Chapter Forty-Eight

*In which Madame du Barry
is yet again confined to a convent*

I miss . . . so many things. Chocolate in bed with the early sun streaming through the window; mornings with merchants and piles of favorite things; my dogs and my sweet singing birds; my green morning robe trimmed with rabbit fur. Warm baths; my maid Henriette rubbing amber cream all over me, and hundreds of redolent myrtles and roses, gathered in great bouquets around my salon.

And most of all I miss him, and his look of idle, slack appreciation that never lessened in the five years we were together.

The letter came to me at Rueil two days after his death, signed by that pudding himself, now Louis XVI: banishment, by his pleasure, to the Abbey of Pont-aux-Dames, a charnel house four hours from Paris. The night I arrived, I wept, for everything was so cold and my cell reminded me of a crypt. The first months were hell: I was allowed no correspondence, nor even allowed outside of the dripping cell that made my chest suffer—they think to let me die in here, I thought in despair on my darkest days. The only silver lining, yet so faint and gray, was that this bleakness was a fitting place to mourn the man, and the life, I once loved.

I grieved for him, as many did not.

His death was so needless, I often thought, thinking bitterly of all those ancient men we used to remind him of. He should have lived another ten years, twenty, even thirty years—why not? Cardinal Fleury lived to ninety, and Richelieu is almost eighty, still tottering around, though probably not at Court: the new king will give him short shrift.

At first, the nuns showed me no kindness and were afraid to talk to the woman they thought worse than Jezebel. They were either terrified or disdainful, but soon they warmed to me. Even the Mother Superior, at first frosty and curt, became a fast friend. Gradually small luxuries were permitted and winter passed, as it always does.

I was allowed outside and felt the sun on my face for the first time in months. I decided the country was quite charming, and soon I came to think of the abbey not as a charnel house but as a delightful crumbling ruin, romantic in its decay. I enjoyed my daily walks through the countryside, accompanied by two lay sisters who also asked shyly about life at Court. I was happy to entertain them, my stories purified for their benefit, and when I described the life I once had, each telling made it slip further away and into a land as magical as it was improbable.

My grief gave way as sunshine returned, and now I find the slow, indolent life becomes me; routine breeds its own kind of harmony. My cell is furnished with carpets and soft chairs, and I may receive guests and letters, and my chef has been allowed to come from Louveciennes. The nuns are kind and refined, and so pretty in their white habits, and once a week I give bread and soup to the poor alongside them. The abbey has beautiful orchards with apricots larger and even plumper than even those at Louveciennes—the best in seven towns, says Sister Perpetua, the nun in charge of the stillroom.

Through the thick walls of the abbey, news of the outside world trickles in. After Louis' death, they said the "barrel" was leaking, and indeed it was: Barry fled to Switzerland, Adolphe was exiled, Chon and Hélène as well. Terray and Maupeou were curtly dismissed and Aiguillon is no longer welcome at Court. All my friends and supporters sidelined or banished: they called it a purity campaign.

The Comte de Maurepas was recalled by the new king to be

his chief minister. If the king had chosen Choiseul, I would have been here in this abbey for eternity. But Maurepas—banished in 1749, more than twenty-five years ago, by the Marquise de Pompadour—was the chosen one, and so he returned to Versailles, all seventy-nine creaking years of him.

A feeble fool in the hands of feeble fools, writes Richelieu, but Maurepas is a relative by marriage of Aiguillon, and thus a friend. The future holds hope. It must.

"You're a plant, a hardy one, you bloom wherever you are planted," observes Chon, one of my first visitors. She smiles at me and I know she misses me, as I do her. "You look well."

She lives at Louveciennes now, guarding the palace for my return. They haven't taken that, and it appears that all my possessions shall remain mine. All those beautiful things given freely to me by Louis: my jewels, paintings, furniture, and little treasures. Chon oversaw the sale of my Versailles house to the king's brother Artois, and paid off my creditors and now she keeps my servants and staff on hand. Waiting—for the day I will be released.

"Really, it's not so bad here. Very relaxing. Versailles was quite busy," I say, thinking it was so much more than that. It's rather nice to be free of obligation and intrigue. "I am very comfortable here, and the country air is wonderful, and the nuns ever so kind. Mother Superior—she insists I call her Gabrielle—doesn't admonish me at all."

"I'm sure everyone loves you, Jeanne," says Chon, and there is no malice in her voice. She smiles at me again. She is wearing a smart red jacket and looks a little plumper. No intrigue to keep her busy, but perhaps indolence becomes her as much as it does me.

"They danced in the streets," she tells me sadly. "It made me see what a—what is the right word?—a fairyland?—Versailles is. Was. I knew he was not the most admired of kings, but the venom after his death was something else. Sad, really. And disturbing—that people should feel so comfortable showing such a lack of respect for their sovereign, dead or not."

I can't bear to think of Louis lying alone and despised, abandoned; they say even his close servants and gentlemen refused to
attend his putrid body. "And the new king?" I ask, turning the
conversation to a slightly more palatable subject.

"Wildly popular. And the queen. All feel . . ." She pauses,
and shakes her head. "All feel a new era is upon us. A rebirth for
France. Fifty-nine years is a long time for anyone to rule."

"Almost sixty," I say sadly. And it should have been more.

"I suppose you could say he outlived his time. The people
want a king who will listen to them. All this talk of democracy
and revolution from the Americas—it's coming over here too. Everyone hopes the new king will have a new attitude, more in keeping with our times."

"He's still a Bourbon," I say.

Chon embraces me before she leaves. "Soon, soon. Maurepas has your case before the king, and if he can think for himself, without interference from the queen—that is in doubt—we
should be fine. He knows you were kind to his grandfather."

Without interference from the queen.

I can only hope.

~

"Just one more," I say, taking an apricot. I am in the stillroom
with two of the nuns, surrounded by an orgy of apricots—the
harvest has started and the room is thick with the sweet smell of
their juice. I can't resist and take another, though my stomach is
beginning to hurt.

I have been at the abbey now a year and I am starting to feel
as though my life is suspended. Like those pickled cherries, pre-
served in vinegar and time, I think sadly, looking at a shelf lined
with Sister Perpetua's favorite preserves. The months pass, but
still no word of freedom. Though life is pleasant, I know it can be
sweeter still, and I feel my youth slipping away, seeping through
the cold gray stones of the abbey walls.

I am starting to itch for silk on my skin, for the company of
men and their admiration and looks of longing, and for some-

one to hold me. I'm only thirty-one! Out of respect to the nuns, I cover my hair, but secretly I hate my coif.

"What is she like?" asks Sister Catherine, speaking of the queen. She is shy and genteel; the nuns here are of good birth, and Catherine is related to the Marquise de Rambures.

"Well . . . not exactly pretty, but she has a certain elegance and style. I've heard she is starting to dress even more extravagantly, now that she is queen."

"What was her prettiest gown?" chips in Annie, one of the lay sisters, pausing from depitting her pile of apricots, then bobbing a curtsy to excuse her interruption.

"Mmm, it is hard to say." I look at my fruit and remember the pale, luscious colors of life at Versailles. "I think my favorite dress of hers was a green-and-yellow one she wore for Easter two years ago. The bodice was green trimmed with yellow bows, and the skirt yellow trimmed with green bows. It was all rather perfect."

"I hear she wears her hair very high, with ornaments and ducks on it, and everything," says Sister Louise, wistfully running a finger under her wimple. She is one of the newest nuns, only eighteen, and I once asked her why she took the veil. She told me her older sister had been destined for the convent, but then she died, and the dowry had already been paid.

"Yes, she has a very talented hairdresser—he did my hair too."

"How did you wear your hair?"

"Ah, the fashions were very fine," I say, thinking back to the last supper I gave at the Trianon, just before Louis fell sick. "I wore it very high—some ladies were using *poufs*—fake hair—but I didn't have to, and my hairdresser wrapped a long orange ribbon, lace, all through my curls . . . there must have been six yards of it at least. He tied the ends in bows and pinned a diamond brooch at the center of each one." I look down at the half-eaten apricot in my hand—the ribbon was almost that color, and the diamond clusters the size of their pits. Will that ribbon and those diamonds be waiting for me at Louveciennes, if—when—I get out of here?

"Oooh, how fine," breathes Sister Louise, her eyes big with dreams.

"Mmm," I say in agreement, finishing the fruit. Dare I risk another?

A clatter in the courtyard—a coach. Sister Louise rushes to the window and peers out.

"A grand carriage," she calls, and steps aside that I may see. Six matching horses, ducal red velvet, a striped yellow-and-black shield emblazoned on the side.

Oh—I sink down on the window seat.

"It must be for you, Jeanne," says Sister Catherine sadly, hugging me.

"It can only be good news," whispers Sister Louise.

A servant comes to bring me to the Mother Superior's study, and I follow her as though in a dream. No time to change, or do my hair, but I know I look beautiful: lots of sleep and country air have done me well. And I always looked my best slightly *en déshabillé.*

Gabrielle rises to meet me, and hugs me.

"Dearest, we'll miss you," she says, and I follow her out to the courtyard and into the brilliance of the summer sun. A man steps out of the white brightness toward me. His eyes show that he has not forgotten me, and the letter he brings shows that others have not either.

It is the Duc de Brissac.

Hercule, my Hercule, has come to carry me home.

Life can begin again.

Chapter Forty-Nine

In which Madame Adélaïde considers dancing

The Duc de Duras announces the opening of the ball and the dancers take their places. The symphony strikes up and with dignity Madame Clothilde steps forward on the arm of the Sardinian envoy, an odd man with curious black spectacles and no teeth. We watch them as they lurch past us. Both so terribly fat, I think, remembering my brother's deathbed, the wobbling fat, the many chins. But at least Clothilde appears healthy, if rather too rotund. This magnificent ball, held outside in the Court of Honor on this steaming August evening, celebrates her departure for Sardinia, where she is to marry its prince.

"Little Clothilde," says Victoire wistfully, seated beside me under one of the velvet tents. "Going so far away. And how pretty she looks!"

"She's hardly little," I scoff. Clothilde is fifteen, and though there have been copious tears and pretty scenes of regret, she seems resigned to her fate. I think with satisfaction of my triumph over the curse of matrimony, and how I kept my sisters safe. My greatest accomplishment, perhaps, apart from my deep knowledge of Greek.

"Well, I'm going with Civrac to get another plate of cherry tartines," says Victoire, downing the last of her wine. Sophie shuffles over to fill her place, and murmurs something about tarts. I watch Victoire depart, and fan myself against the heat, the dancers continuing their parade before us, the torches and the moon lighting the night.

After dear Papa's death, we were six months quarantined. The three of us survived, though seventeen people perished of small-pox alongside their king; mostly servants but a handful of court-iers as well. When I emerged from quarantine—a suitable time to mourn Papa and his dreadful death—the popularity of our nephew and his wife was a slap in the face to me, and to the memory of my father.

Louis-Aug—he insists on just Louis now—assumed a new dignity in my absence and now he does not seek my input or support as I had once hoped. As his chief counsel he recalled the decrepit old Comte de Maurepas, who arrived at Court blinking like one woken from a deep sleep, with little idea where he was. Well, at least it wasn't Choiseul. So far Maurepas has not fared well—there were riots this spring after a bad harvest—*the flour war*, they call it.

Madame Clothilde and the Sardinian envoy move clumsily past us again, followed by the king and his wife. Louis shuffles along, almost stumbling over his sword—the poor boy is petrified of dancing—but Antoinette floats elegantly beside him. I follow her—and her disgraceful short skirts, showing even her shoes!—with hard eyes, for the Austrian has disappointed in every way.

When I emerged from quarantine, the harlot and all her rem-nants were gone, and I expected to find a Court restored to its for-mer dignity and that the dauphine's flightiness—how I hate that word, with all its connotations of birds and merriment—would be tempered by respect for her new position as queen. Alas, it was not to be.

Freed from anyone to challenge her—our days of influence are long over—she quickly dismissed the poor Comtesse de Noailles and took to her newfound liberty as a robber released from the galleys. She insists on only the joys of queenship but not the du-ties, and regularly disappears for days on end with her louche friends to her little retreat at the Petit Trianon. Last week she was overheard commenting on the breeches of one of her guards, and seen walking arm in arm with her brother-in-law the Comte d'Artois. She has even taken to inviting her hairdresser and her seamstress into her private chambers, in a strict breach of etiquette, and the constant changing of her fashions is causing the ladies of the Court some vexation in their effort to keep up.

Our relationship has grown cold, and Louis is blind where his wife is concerned.

Her only positive influence, I concede, watching her mincing around, her hair completely outrageous and high, overstuffed with ostrich feathers, is that domestic propriety has again returned to its proper place at Court. We are become like the English, Narbonne said last week, and though it is never proper to compare the French to the sniveling British, in this case the comparison was correct: George III is an excellent example of magnificent monogamy.

"If this is a sign of the times, then send me back to my grandfather's day!" spluttered the old Duc de Richelieu, still wobbling around Court, a parody of his former self and his influence entirely gone. There is a rumor that in his Paris house he has a bed attached with bells, and he invites his friends and their strumpets over, then listens as the bells ring merrily with the movements of the bed . . . but why am I thinking such thoughts?

"Madame Adélaïde is not dancing?" inquires Count Mercy, suddenly at my side.

"I prefer to sit," I reply curtly.

"What a glorious spectacle our queen presents," he says smoothly, twirling his cane in his hand. Everyone knows the queen disappoints him dreadfully, but he must of course sing her praises.

"Spectacle," I agree.

A commotion by the entrance; the Comtesse d'Artois is announced. She gave birth three weeks ago and insists on being carried around in a giant gilded chair, weaving around Court like a glorious Gaia, the goddess of fertility.

Unlike her rather placid older sister, this one is quite high-spirited, and is reveling in her position as the mother of the first Bourbon heir of the next generation. Her husband—Charles, the youngest of our nephews—is the only one of his brothers who appears untroubled by delicate masculine issues, and after a few miscarriages, she quickly became pregnant and produced a son.

We heard Antoinette cried buckets. As she should. Five years without being a true wife. The strength of a king is the strength of its nation—even I must admit France is in a poor state and must hope for full consummation.

"Ah, the Comtesse d'Artois," I say to Mercy, smiling. "How radiant she looks! How motherhood becomes her. What a glorious day the birth was for France! And for the house of Savoy! Not so much for Austria, of course."

"Motherhood would become any woman," replies Mercy tightly, "fortunate enough to know its joys." Since the harlot left Court, I have felt a small lack in my life; Mercy helps keep the enmity, and therefore the energy, alive. "Without the blessing of motherhood, a woman risks growing old and gray before her time."

"Yes, the queen's complexion has coarsened lately, unfortunately."

"At least you have an excuse, dear Madame; smallpox can wreak such havoc."

"Oh!" Victoire is hurrying back, her face flushed in distress, Civrac rushing beside her, followed by a footman bearing a giant plate of tartines. "The Comte de Jaucourt seeks the right to dance with Madame Élisabeth!"

"*Jaucourt?* Nonsense," I say crisply. "He's not even a peer! And he should know only Princes of the Blood are allowed to dance with daughters of France. Such effrontery!" Sometimes it seems as if the lax manners of the queen have infected the rest of the Court. In the center of the courtyard, Antoinette executes a delicate pirouette, the gold-stitched roses of her skirts shimmering as she turns.

"I do believe the Duc de Duras will put him to rights, Madame Victoire," says Mercy smoothly, referring to this year's First Gentleman, whose role it is to oversee this ball, and such transgressions.

"Whatever was he thinking? Oh!" says Victoire, squeezing herself back in between Sophie and myself, and taking the plate of tartines from the footman.

"Mesdames," says Mercy with a bow. "If you will excuse me—the Comte de Vergennes requires my urgent attention." He sidles over to talk to the new foreign minister, who has just entered the courtyard surrounded by six young pages. Such a man, I think, narrowing my eyes. He was our ambassador to Turkey, and married a Turkish woman. I feel slightly faint at the thought, and take a steadying sip of my lemon juice. Papa, of course, did not welcome him at Court, but in this new world, he is accepted. Thankfully his wife has the decency not to show herself in public.

Still, another disturbing sign of the times. And in addition to his Turkish wife, this new minister and others have been increasingly vocal about our expenditures. With all the new households for Louis-Aug and his brothers and their wives, and now their children, the Court of France has not been so full for . . . well, perhaps forever. My sisters and I went in the spring to take the waters at Vichy, a quick trip really, but upon our return, Maurepas had the temerity to show me the cost of our expedition: three million *livres* certainly sounded like a lot. He even talked to me of his displeasure about the cost! I am not sure I have quite recovered from that interview.

"Goodness, but it's hot," says Victoire, fanning herself and Sophie.

A new set of dancers arrange themselves as the orchestra takes up the next concerto, by Gluck—the queen's favorite, but far too German for my tastes. I watch Antoinette in the corner, with her new friend, the Comtesse de Polignac, whom she calls Gabrielle and who has become the recipient of an avalanche of inappropriate favors. Antoinette is laughing—a queen should not laugh, especially not at a grand public occasion!—and it appears the woman Gabrielle is mimicking someone, shaking her pretty face and raising her arms as though she were a monkey. Perhaps Vergennes' wife?

The queen's new companion leaves much to be desired. To our despair, the influence of the pious Princesse de Lamballe is waning in favor of this Gabrielle. A woman of decidedly provincial birth, and the niece of none other than the Comtesse d'Andlau, whom I remember from my childhood: the one who tried to corrupt us with that dreadful book, naked pictures, a row of bottoms lined up—

"What?" I say sharply, for it appears Victoire has been speaking.

"These tartines are so delicious," repeats Victoire through a mouthful. "Really. You must try some. Josephine recommended them and I am so glad she did." She talks of the Comtesse de Provence, another of our nephews' wives, with whom she has developed a rather troubling closeness. Bound, I think with narrowed eyes, by their shared love of sweet wines.

Right in front of us one of the new set of dancers—the Comte de Beaurepas—trips over an uneven cobble and in his flight to the floor grabs at the arm of his partner and almost pulls her down with him, crying "Jesu Maria!" as he goes. A giant hush fills the courtyard and the music stops abruptly. Beaurepas recovers his balance and bows, his face scarlet. He apologizes profusely to his partner, but the Duchesse de Chartres looks ready to burst into tears.

"Oh!" says Victoire with a giggle, choking on her pastry. "How exciting! I wonder what they'll call him? It's Beaurepas, isn't it? Beau—*good*. Good-stumble? Good-foot?"

"Don't even try," I snap. Everyone watches Beaurepas as he wobbles unsteadily out of the courtyard, with the look of a man who knows his days are numbered.

"The Comte de Good-bye?"

"The Comte de Good-grief!"

"The Comte de Good-gracious!"

Thus come the whispers, fast and furious, as everyone vies to be the one to bless the unfortunate man with the wittiest sobriquet. We'll know by tomorrow, but it is doubtful the comte will ever show his face here again.

"The Comte de Good-heavens," suggests Narbonne, coming to stand beside me. "Serves him right for aspiring to dance with the Duchesse de Chartres! We must assure the poor duchess she will not share her partner's disgrace."

"That was amusing, but I hope he doesn't kill himself," says Victoire with a worried look, rubbing a speck of cherry jam off her cheek. Last year a Parisian petty noble, who mixed with Court nobles in the Paris salons, thought to attend a Versailles ball. He was given a rude ejection and killed himself in shame the next day. Rightfully.

This modern mixing has its limits and there are some things that Antoinette cannot change, I think in satisfaction, watching as she and Gabrielle disappear behind another tent, accompanied by two gentlemen whose names I don't even know. Such a scandal last year when she watched the sun rise—as though a peasant, needing to get up to tend the fields!—and not in the company of the king.

After that incident, the first of the scurrilous pamphlets about her appeared. The Queen of France, her activities fodder for the scandal sheets, as though she were a . . . mistress.

Look at the Comtesse de Tavannes!" Victoire sighs in contentment, her earlier distress gone. "So pretty, and the color of that gown is charming."

"Puce," whispers Sophie. I shoot her a look—does she know? Has she seen? An awful pamphlet, comparing the queen's new favorite color, an outlandish purple-gray called puce, with *pre-puce*—foreskin.

"Preposterous," I say, watching the countess as she circles, the dance having resumed, cautiously, after the incident with Beaurepas. "And her hairstyle is simply outrageous—you could fit a chair cushion under there."

The Duc de la Trémoille's monkey suddenly comes flying across the courtyard, carrying a squished pastry and screeching above the music. Sophie whimpers in fright as it dashes under the Duchesse de Picquigny's enormous hooped skirts.

"Don't worry," says Victoire kindly, patting Sophie's arm. "I've heard it is most well trained—I am sure it would never be so indecent as to hide under the skirts of a daughter of France."

"And Picquigny has hosted many things under those skirts of hers," adds Narbonne with a flash of malice. Victoire giggles and I frown, feeling I should say something (though it is true, the Duchesse de Picquigny is as loose as a prostitute, or a courtier), but the music and the heat and the commotion—now Picquigny is screeching, alongside the monkey—are quite fuddling my head.

Suddenly the dreaded Lady of Introspection rises demurely from her seat and stands in front of me, dressed, rather alarmingly, in puce. She shows me clearly that all these things, these little changes and breaches, are the signs of a world breaking apart. Queens laughing, feathers in hair, monkeys running amuck, men flouting convention, courtiers tripping, insubordination from ministers . . .

It has only been a year since my father passed, but sometimes I feel I don't recognize my home anymore. And though some may think them small changes, what they don't see is that all these small cracks together are ready to make the whole vase break. What is happening to my world, to my beloved Versailles?

Chapter Fifty

In which Madame du Barry is happy again

My first day back at Louveciennes, I ran through the rooms dotted with furniture covered in ghostly white cloths. I pulled off a few, and twirled in the dust clouds because nothing in my life was ever, ever, as sweet as this moment. I was free and reborn.

I stopped in front of Louis' favorite chair—the one where he always sat when he was here. No one else shall ever sit there again, I decided, and gave it pride of place in the grandest salon.

Life is luscious again and soon I settle into a comfortable routine, eating delicious food, sleeping in a soft bed under cambric sheets, enjoying my beautiful house and gardens. The people in the village are glad to have the château occupied again; many are employed by me, and Chon directs charitable efforts on my behalf.

As the months pass I receive more and more visitors. The courtiers were tentative at first, not sure of their reception back at Court if it became known where they had been. Gradually they became bolder as they realized there would be no consequences.

Just as I rarely think of Versailles, it seems Versailles rarely thinks of me.

Occasionally I will walk down by the river, where the hum of the waterworks reminds me of the fountains at the palace. I sniff the breeze to see if I can smell the peculiar odor of the place, greed and opulence mixed with sweat and orange flowers. I decide I don't miss it, not one bit, for I know something the courtiers can never imagine: there is life, and happiness, all beyond Versailles.

When I am not enjoying the peace of Louveciennes, I am in

Paris. Hercule has a lovely *hôtel* there, with a suite of rooms reserved just for me. The only concession his wife demands is that I never use the staircase that leads to her portion of the vast mansion. A pleasant arrangement—we met several times when I was at Court and she never hid her disdain.

Paris is full and bustling, alive. Those who disapprove of the queen and the state of affairs at Court keep to their Parisian homes and spend only the bare minimum of time at Versailles. And as the decade comes to an end, there is a festive, rambunctious air as never before. Hercule is a progressive man, eagerly interested in reforms and the direction of the country. I'm not—I've always been bored by politics—but these days all anyone can talk about is the American Revolution and their Declaration of Independence. France is supporting them; anything to help them triumph over the English.

"My dearest, I leave you, but not in my heart." Hercule bends down to kiss me and I grab his hand and caress it. He is the hereditary Pantler to the King, in charge of bread and grain supplies, and his duties at Versailles call him back. I am a jealous mistress: jealous of Versailles.

I pout. Hercule gazes down at me with indulgent, savory eyes.

"Back on Tuesday," he promises, but I refuse to let go of his hand. "No more than two days, love." Hercule is the perfect man: kind, gallant, and ever so in love with me. I smile and stretch, release his hand. He leaves and I lie back in the bed and listen to his carriage in the courtyard below. It was here at Louveciennes, in this same bed, that I spent so many happy nights with Louis. Above the mantel, a reminder of my past: a handsome portrait of my king.

"Are you sure, dearest?" whispered Hercule when he saw where I had hung it.

"Louis would approve, I know he would," I whispered back, and I feel it is true. Last month I donned a heavy veil and went to visit his tomb at Saint-Denis. I was sad, but I am sure he is resting well, poor man, and I know he would approve of Hercule. Hercule even reminds me of Louis, though perhaps a more thoughtful, intelligent version. And how refreshing and pleasurable to have a man of my age! Hercule is still virile in his forties, whereas Louis was already fifty-nine when I met him.

Chon bustles in and opens one of the shutters, shattering the warm shadows of the bedroom with strong sun.

"Come on, Jeanne, it's already gone eleven. Your visitor will be here soon, and the chef is still complaining about the rotten oysters delivered yesterday—you need to talk to him."

"Oh, just tell him to order a new batch and throw the bad ones away," I say lazily.

"You know the tradespeople will only take more advantage if you continue being so lax. Money doesn't grow on trees, you know."

It almost does, I think. Hercule is exceedingly rich, and if such a thing is possible, even more generous than Louis was. Rich and generous enough to keep me in all the luxury that I adore, and that Chon declares necessary for my health.

"Oh, get Morin to take care of it, then," I say in irritation, referring to my faithful steward. I turn my thoughts away from oysters and toward my coming visitor. This should be interesting. And I must look my best.

"Call Henriette, if you will," I say, stretching one last time before rolling out of bed, my hands on my enormous nightcap—the elaborate hair fashions make sleeping quite a trial. I attended a ball in Paris two days ago and still keep the style intact: a fresh summer riot of porcelain fruit nestled intricately in my hair, styled as a bowl.

I dress in a beautiful lightweight gown, in a new flowing style that suits me perfectly—*lévites* they are called, wonderfully comfortable—and my maid Henriette carefully pats and refreshes my hair. I dab a tiny amount of rouge on my cheeks and lips—certainly, I am still beautiful. *An ever-blooming rose*, Hercule called me last week; thirty-three is not so old.

"I think," I say, patting a small pineapple above my ear and arching an eyebrow at Chon, "that I am going to charm my visitor."

"If anyone can, you will. Still, I am interested to hear every detail of your conversation. Try and remember *everything*."

"I will. It's a fine day; I will propose we take a walk through the gardens, and I'll show him the pavilion and the fruit beds."

The Comte de Falkenstein arrives a little after three—I was starting to fret he had changed his mind. From the moment he stepped from his modest carriage—only two horses, and not even matching!—and I saw the look of admiration on his face, I knew he would be mine. He is the same age as I am, and not unpleasing to look at, with none of his sister's haughty demeanor or thin, peaked features. He is dressed simply, as a *bourgeois*, in plain brown breeches and jacket.

"But this is delightful, simply delightful," he says as we walk around the gardens. "Strawberries—devilishly hard to prosper in this climate, I'm told."

The Comte de Falkenstein is really the Emperor Joseph of Austria, the elder brother of the queen. He is visiting France incognito, to save on the expense and protocol of a royal journey. His visit, they say, is spurred by his sister's continued virginity: seven long years and the marriage remains unconsummated. I am dying to ask him the details, of course, but keep my prurience well hidden. Besides, there are plenty of pamphlets going around, and while they might not always tell the truth—the ones about me never did—some of them are very amusing. And I have to laugh at the ones that imply the queen is a lesbian: as if she would ever inspire Sapphic passion!

Mirie visits often and keeps me informed of the news from Versailles. "Everyone is disgusted. Five ladies retired last month, including the Marquise de Flavacourt. Queen Marie might have been dull, but at least she was a *queen* and respected the dignity of the Bourbons. This one runs around like a ten-year-old and dresses in nightgowns, albeit draped in diamonds. Such impropriety and extravagance are to be expected of a mistress, but not of a queen. Acting no better than a shopgirl at Labille's." The honeymoon is over, three short years after she ascended the throne.

I have many questions for Falkenstein about his sister, but stick to safer pastures.

"Now, the melon beds, monsieur. We have six different kinds—and I must gift you some preserves before you go—the Comtesse de Montmartre said it was heaven in a jar. Unfortunately, you can see they are not yet ripe, or I would present you with a perfect pair."

"How unfortunate." Falkenstein is a curious man, delighted by and interested in everything; Hercule told me that last week they spent six hours together discussing grain procurement options for the palace. As serious and intelligent as his sister is frivolous, was his opinion. "Madame du Barry, it would be such a pleasure to taste your melons. Madame Victoire has an impressive bed at Bellevue, but when I visited, they were unfortunately not ripe either."

"At Bellevue," I murmur, thinking, as I haven't for years, of Mesdames. They live there now, mostly retired from Court. It was that or a more public exile, Mirie once confided, for the new king is determined to end their meddling. I remember my first dinner party at Bellevue, so many years ago: the yellow sheep, and Choiseul and his sister, isolated by the fountain. Funny to think of Mesdames as mistresses of that fair palace, once cherished by their enemy the Pompadour.

"Yes, indeed, a very interesting trio of ladies," continues Falkenstein.

I stifle a giggle.

"Such a formidable influence on my sister in her formative years, and not always a welcome one," he continues, stooping to pull aside a vine to reveal another immature yellow melon. "Now, Madame Victoire has become quite the horticulturalist—even growing figs! And Madame Adélaïde—how pleasant it was to converse with her in Greek. A woman of culture, indeed."

This time I can't stop myself laughing, thinking of Hercule's words: the man *is* delighted by everything.

"You must try this," I say, offering him a slightly unripe plum. "It's the perfect tartness; another week and it'll be too sweet."

He takes it straight from my fingers, casting a keen and appreciative gaze over me. I smile in satisfaction: it's nice to know I can still get a Holy Roman Emperor to eat out of my hand. Falkenstein smiles back, as though he knows what I am thinking.

After the orchards and vegetable gardens, I show him the formal flowerbeds and we talk about a new style of garden that he is considering for Schönbrunn, his summer residence.

"More natural and free, in the English style. Why strangle a garden with constraint?" he muses. "Flowers and plants, they should be in a state of nature and yet we regiment them, force them to grow with military precision."

"Ah, monsieur, there I agree completely. I must have you talk to my gardener! I was trying to make him understand that I wanted these roses to climb the wall at will. I want my garden to be free."

"Precisely—why must nature be caged?"

"Gardens should stop wearing stays," I say boldly, wondering if he has noticed I am not wearing any.

"As perhaps all women will one day," he says, raising a knowing eyebrow. He offers me his arm as we circle back to the house. "Though I doubt the fair sex would ever put comfort over appearance."

Zamor is sitting on the terrace, frowning at something. Poor thing, I sometimes think: adored and petted as a boy, now grown into a sullen young man. I feel sorry for him, but my pity often vanishes in the face of his rudeness. Hercule says I should dismiss him, or send him back to wherever he came from, but I cannot—he is not a pet to dispose of.

"Look," Zamor says, not even getting up to bow for my visitor. Certainly, he doesn't know it is the Holy Roman Emperor who stands before him, but even were he local gentry, Zamor should still rise. "Look at Saza and Mosa." He motions to two of my white monkeys, recently sent from Siam, engaging in some untoward behavior on the grass below.

"Oh, Zamor, that's not appropriate—showing the count my two monkeys rutting like that! Oh, I am sorry," I say, blushing, but Falkenstein only laughs.

"No, madame, they are all that is natural. And how enthusiastic they are! We cannot curb the instinct, for they are animals, indeed." He shakes his head, and I wonder if he is thinking of his sister and the unnatural instincts of the king.

"It is a sad thing when private matters are of such public concern," I say, and place my hand on his sleeve. He looks down at it, and nods in agreement, and I have the impression he wants to touch me. But he doesn't share any confidences about her, as I so desperately want.

As he takes his leave, he lingers over my hand.

"I shall confess, my dear madame, you were not what I was expecting."

"And what was it that you were expecting, monsieur?"

"From certain letters that my mother thought fit to share with me, letters from my sister, I was expecting a coarse, broad woman. A harlot." He raises his eyebrows slyly, to see if he may continue.

I laugh, and indicate he may.

"A harpy. A filthy trollop, and a vulgar gold harvester, I believe were some of the epithets applied to you."

"A vulgar gold harvester. I haven't heard that one before."

"Madame," he says, his eyes twinkling, and I know he is delighted with me, "it is rare I must disagree with my sainted mother—may God continue His blessings on her—but in this case, I must. You are charming, delightful, and most well mannered."

I nod in happy agreement.

Chapter Fifty-One

In which Madame Adélaïde finds surprising happiness,
and France does too

"Mansart!" I command, and the footman springs forward. "Take up Finfin, we can't have his paws dirty." The footman takes the small dog and rescues him from the muddy vegetable bed where he was frolicking.

"Excellent—you can put him down now."

We are in the gardens at Bellevue, enjoying the warmth of a late spring day. The king our nephew gifted us this house, and with the addition of two new wings, it is a palace now and not the overgrown farmhouse it once was. Louis-Aug suggested we spend our summers and much more here, and at first I was a little apprehensive—to be absent from Court for so long! It felt a bit like exile, and Mercy was reputed to have called Bellevue our home not away from home.

But then . . .

The most surprising thing happened. We like it here! Everything is very pleasant: the gardens, the boat rides, the informal dinners, visitors and cards in the evening. The freedom of our days and nights is rather wonderful, and though I never thought freedom had much sway over my desires, I think I might have been wrong. Strange that the absence of obligation, when one's purpose comes from duty, should be so pleasurable.

I must admit it caused me some philosophical turmoil when I first discovered that inclination, but now I have accepted it and believe progress is not always wrong. I have even—I blame the fresh country air—been lax in my studies. The Lady of Introspection suggested to me one day that sitting inside, in a stuffy room stuffed with servants and reading Greek, was a little . . . futile.

Now we long for the beginning of spring when we may leave Versailles and come to Bellevue—how pleasant it is to have something to look forward to! Here Victoire has positively blossomed, and even Sophie has taken on a new force of personality. She even reads aloud to us, from books that previously I would not have deemed suitable, including *novels*.

I have to confess: looking at Versailles from this delightful vantage point, so much of it seems rather pointless. Those endless ceremonies! The uncomfortable court costume! Here Narbonne wakes me and there is no formal *levée*. I may sip my chocolate in peace, attend a nice breakfast in a robe, then change into a dress that is as comfortable as that robe, and then wear that same dress all day, and sometimes into the evening as well!

Of course we do not take our new freedom too far—Victoire's lady Madame de Ghistelles had a cousin visit last week. That lady had not been presented at Court, and therefore dining with us was out of the question, but all in all it is a relaxed and pleasant life.

Civrac keeps us well supplied with all the gossip we need from Versailles, but I find my disinterest quite genuine. Being in the country makes one more aware and more authentic—I do believe, though it pains me to say it, that Versailles is rather full of flattery and lies and subterfuge.

"*Maman*, a worm!" says one of Civrac's grandchildren, holding up a pale grub.

"Ah, permit me, mademoiselle?" says the Cardinal de Bernis, taking it between two gloved fingers. Bernis is a frequent visitor, and though he was once the fish woman's creature, he has become a firm friend and I appreciate his old-style courtier sensibilities. "*Earth upon worms does depend / Not vile, but our friend,*'" he spouts lightly.

Little Anne frowns. "Your poems don't make any sense! And

that's my worm." Bernis bows and hands the child back her grub, which she tests delicately in her mouth.

I smile at her indulgently. I never saw much use for young children, just little versions of adults and usually screaming about something. But several of our ladies bring their children here to play, and they can be quite delightful. Anne is just the sweetest thing, and for her birthday I presented her with an enormous doll, and we all laughed as she made a bed for it and tucked in the linens. Imagine—the daughter of a noble, granddaughter of a Maréchal of France, making a bed! How we laughed, but such is our new and free life.

Out here we have had many exciting new experiences and I look upon life unflinchingly. Last week there was a dreadful spider on my bed coverlet (country life does have its disadvantages), yet I did not call for one of my women to call for Narbonne to call for the footman to kill it—I killed it myself! After, when I examined the sticky mess, I felt a powerful and almost atavistic surge of triumph—is this what men feel when they hunt?

And just yesterday I had a conversation, without intermediary, with the man in charge of our dovecote. I decided to do the ordering for our table *myself.* He was a peasant—I suppose they have their own hierarchy, but to me he was just a peasant—and though I made my wishes perfectly clear, he seemed not to understand, and the miscomprehension was mutual.

"Is he speaking *dove?*" asked Sophie in amazement, listening to the man.

"No, I don't think so," I replied firmly, but I had my doubts. It was certainly challenging—his dialect was not something I understood well and I had never considered that French was not spoken by all. A most smelly man, and impossible to understand, but I listened, then asked Narbonne to interpret, but she was equally flummoxed, and in the end the man was taken away for my intent to be explained to him.

Now, it makes me angry when I hear of the poor complaining and demanding more bread, as seems to be happening these days with distressing frequency. Do they not understand how idyllic country life is? If I had not been born the daughter of a king and had my destiny thrust upon me, I should have been quite happy living a simple life in the country.

"Now see these," says Victoire happily as we walk along the garden path to inspect her pear seedlings. Our little garden in the corner of the Stag's Court was never enough for her, and out here she can indulge in her love of gardening. Peaches, apricots, pears, figs, and vegetables, including, after some deliberation, marrows.

"They tell me these came from Syria—I'm sure you know where that is, sister, though I don't. And apparently the skin will be brown, rather like the people perhaps? I was thinking if we grafted it with a local French pear, the result might be the perfect one!"

I doubt it, remembering the Comte de Vergennes and his Turkish wife; if they have children, such monstrosities are kept well hidden. But I don't say anything, just allow Victoire to burble on happily about her new pears. Sophie is also with us, carrying a cat and trailed by her dog Finfin. She no longer has a terrible fear of animals, and last week even petted a cow!

"*Pears are ever tasty / Brown outside and on the inside pasty,*'" chirps the Cardinal de Bernis, picking an unripe one and examining it.

"And here my melons are doing ever so well. Richard tells me they will be ready in two weeks, though I think some are ripe today," says Victoire in contentment.

A footman comes down with the message that our visitors have arrived. Ah, excellent—our nephews Provence and Artois often ride over to dine with us. Though neither of his two younger brothers can in any way be compared to my beloved Louis-Aug, even Artois' high spirits do not irritate me as they once did.

"Is His Majesty with them?" I ask cautiously.

The footman bows. "He is, Madame."

"How wonderful!" exclaims Victoire. "It's been so long since he has visited. I wonder why—I must ask him."

"No need to do that, Victoire," I say, a little more sharply than intended. I know the reason for the king's absence. Last year his marriage was finally consummated, and he rode over to Bellevue to tell us. I still blush at his words; he said it was a pleasure he regretted long being unaware of, and now when I see him, I am anxious, in case another inappropriate conversation should ensue.

But far worse, far worse . . . I determined to lecture Louis-Aug once and for all about the abominable behavior of the queen that only gets worse with every passing year: inappropriate favorites, flouting of court conventions, disgraceful fashions, allowing lax talk of her husband, her extravagance at cards. His wife is making a mockery of the institution of queendom, if such a thing could be imagined.

I prepared well my lecture—starting with the myth of Sisyphus, then proceeding on to a homily about the virtues of thrift. Though in matters of statecraft Louis-Aug has moved beyond my influence, I am still the only mother he has, and must fulfill my maternal duties and guide him as concerns his personal affairs.

Well . . . my nephew did not take kindly to my advice, and his tone was frosty as he replied that I should leave such matters to him, and that I should not hesitate to absent myself for longer periods of time at Bellevue. His words were not as cold and awful as Papa's were, during that dreadful scene so many years ago, but even a pale imitation was enough to make me tremble.

"Oh, goody," continues Victoire. "And I am positive these melons are ripe. Mansart, tell Civrac to tell the kitchens that we need five of them, sliced, for after dinner!"

We head back to the terrace—in these times, we may go straight from the gardens to the dinner table, and without even a change of jacket! "But make sure Chastellux is well hidden," I hiss to Narbonne, who nods back in perfect understanding: Civrac's daughter the Comtesse de Chastellux, infected by

Rousseau, has taken to breast-feeding her own babies. At any time and any place.

Back on the terrace—under the watchful marble eyes of Philotes, the goddess of friendship—we greet Provence and Artois, then ah—my dear Louis-Aug!

"It's been a while since we have enjoyed the pleasure of your company here, dear nephew," says Sophie, coming to the front and speaking quite clearly.

"My dear aunts," says the king, beaming and looking—if a man can—positively radiant.

"I am bursting to tell you some good news," he announces, and his brothers nod in agreement. "The best of news for my kingdom!"

"Has Necker been dismissed?" I say, without thinking. *Stop it*, says a little voice inside, and I half snort, attempting a light laugh. "A joke, of course." Though were Necker—the chief finance minister—to be dismissed, it would definitely be good news. The man is a Protestant!

"No, no news of the political sort. I'm famished—let's get started and I will tell all over dinner." We seat ourselves in the dining room, at a round table—a new invention that does away with the fiddling necessity of finding the correct place for everyone. Victoire advocated its installation, and though I resisted—certainly, these are modern times, but rank remains eternal—now I see its use.

We seat ourselves around it—I discreetly order Bernis away when he wishes to sit next to His Majesty—and the footmen serve the doves we so bravely ordered yesterday. One per guest, served in a simple style, each adorned with feathers of lettuce and small currants as eyes, a delightful country custom—we are even eating like the peasants! Louis-Aug munches down two then settles back with a flourish.

"Tantes, I wanted to be the first to tell you. I am"—he looks around, his tight blue hunting jacket straining valiantly against a sextet of gold buttons, holding the fort together—"to be a father!

France will have its dauphin at last! My wife, the Queen of France, is with child."

His eyes well with tears.

"Oh!" squeals Victoire in delight.

"But that's wonderful!" says Sophie.

"A real pleasure, for all of us," says Provence, rather grimly.

"What wonderful news, nephew!" I exclaim, and it is. Unexpected, certainly—one had simply assumed the queen was barren, after all that horse riding and disavowal of stays, but this is good news. Perhaps motherhood will tame her?

"Finally, a new generation for France," says Louis. "How proud I am to be able to fulfill all of France's hopes and wishes."

"Indeed," mutters Artois—he has two children already, and they will most definitely be displaced by this new child, if it's a son.

Bernis raises his glass: "*For France's greatest glory, a dauphin / Might I be permitted to say: enfin!*"

Chapter Fifty-Two

*In which Madame du Barry and her guests talk of
liberty, equality, and fried nettles*

"It is true: men are born free, but everywhere they are in chains," declares Lenoir passionately.

"I did not know our late friend Rousseau was an admirer of the Marquis de Sade," says Richelieu with a wicked smile. He's ninety but still going strong, and his new wife, Catherine, sits adoringly beside him. "So we must thank our enlightened *philosophe* for this sudden craze for bondage."

"Oh, la, don't be so smutty," I say lightly as my assembled guests titter.

"You make light," says young Lenoir boldly, "but it is true." The young Chevalier de Lenoir, a nephew of Hercule's, is recently returned from America, and though I find his boldness pleasing, it sits ill with the older guests. He is young and unwigged, his hair wild and sticking out at odd corners. One thing about wigs, I think, patting my own loose hair—thankfully those dreadful high styles and heavy *poufs* are things of the past—was that it kept hair calm, even in the face of turmoil.

"Well, I have heard the Americans are very dull, in the bedchamber, all that British blood," I add, continuing Richelieu's wit, but Lenoir will not be stopped.

The young man loops enthusiastically back to his earlier ideas: "In America, one feels free, and only when coming back here do we see that indeed, we are in chains."

"Do tell us more," says Pauline, eyeing the young man in languid appreciation. Pauline is the wife of the Comte de Lauraguais, who played the trick with the "Countess of the Barrel" so many years ago; she is entirely antipathetic toward her husband and we have become fast friends.

"It is hard to explain," says Lenoir, looking eagerly around at the assembled guests, "but there, there is freedom in the air! There are no constraints or shackles, as though those chains do not exist."

"We're hardly in shackles here," says Hercule stiffly, "and slavery is illegal in our country, though it is the bedrock of that supposed free America that you so admire."

Lenoir shakes his head—he does not hesitate to openly contradict the older man. "No, I am not talking of physical shackles, but of unseen and invisible ones that our etiquette and all our trite conventions impose upon us. Over there! How different!"

"I would hardly call politeness *trite*. Etiquette is the foundation of our order and society."

"And besides, that's Versailles not Paris!"

"But what sort of foundation is it," says Lenoir passionately, "built upon old usages and old distinctions? Over there, you can walk into a coffeehouse and converse with the other patrons, without knowing who they are, or who their parents were! Education, inquiry, curiosity—those are the only virtues that matter."

"Sounds positively horrible," murmurs Pauline.

"Why would I want to talk to someone I had not been introduced to?" I query.

"A country where it is possible for anyone to rise sounds like a very irregular society, and I would not countenance it," harrumphs Richelieu, a drip of drool sliding down his jaw. Catherine reaches over and wipes his chin. I once asked Richelieu why, if he wanted to marry again, he had not considered Chon, but he replied that an intelligent mind in a woman was a pleasure outside the bedchamber, but an abhorrence within.

"But you must agree that many of these old conventions are out of place in our modern world!" cries young Lenoir, looking around at the amused faces of the other dinner guests. "The current system needs to be changed!"

"Certainly, most will agree France is a rotten tree, and it will only take a mere wind to fell the branches," observes Breteuil, an important minister and Pauline's lover. We all murmur our agreement.

"Look at us all—we are all in favor of change!" cries Lenoir. "If even the class allied with the monarchy can find much to criticize, then can we not say we are in trouble?"

"An excellent point, monsieur," says Hercule sadly. He is a staunch supporter of the king, but even he does not hesitate to deplore the state of France. "We all criticize the monarchy, and especially the queen, but can we not see that bringing her down will bring the nobility down alongside her? Are we not participating in our own destruction?"

There is a puzzled silence.

"Monarchy!" spits Lenoir, his face growing red. He's had too much champagne, I think, as I motion to the steward to clear away the first-course dishes. "What do we need with a king? Americans have taken charge of their destiny and cast off the oppression of their rulers!"

Once such words would have caused vehement protestations, but now we all nod, excepting Hercule, who alone defends the monarchy.

"The Americans cast off the oppression of their *English* king," warns Hercule.

"But, Uncle, I think we can all admit that despite their faults, the English kings are less oppressive than our kings! Surely if there was a rule that needed to be cast off, it would be that of the French crown!"

"The boy is right—our monarchy is positively antediluvian compared to the British. We need less ruling, and more governance, with the input of the people," adds Pauline; these days even women talk of politics.

"And the Academy of Notables will do just that, madame,"

says Breteuil, pointing his fork at Lenoir. He speaks of a group that will convene to try to push through tax reform, and sort out the finances of France as the country careens toward bankruptcy.

"Pah," spits Lenoir, motioning to a footman to pour him more champagne. "You think a group of nobles and clergy will vote against their own self-interest? Never! For real reform we need the participation of everyone, including the *bourgeoisie*."

"La, you're beginning to sound like that red-haired radical Lafayette!" I declare, growing tired of this talk. Politics still bores me, but I like the effect it has on my guests: they are enlivened, as indeed the whole of France is enlivened, by this talk of reform. Words like *constitution*, *upper house*, and *Magna Carta* are bandied about, and there is a mania for all things British—though our traditional enemies, their political system has become widely admired.

"An honor to be compared to Lafayette," insists Lenoir; he fought with the great general in America. "Only men like him can bring true freedom to France!"

"Now what have we here?" says Richelieu in greedy appreciation as the next service is brought in. A magnificent silver tureen piled high with a steaming mass of green is placed grandly in the center of the table.

I smile wickedly. "Something new and *radical*, to match the times. Guess!"

"An Indian vegetable," says Pauline inconsequentially.

"Some of your sublime shallots from the gardens," declares Hercule gallantly.

"Perhaps something outlandish from America?" inquires Richelieu.

"No, no, and no. Lenoir—what do you think?"

Lenoir looks at the dish in irritation; he wants to return to his passion for politics, but he needs curbing before he takes things too far. He waves an annoyed hand at the dish. "Grass?"

"Indeed, my young chevalier, you are very close. These are fried *nettles*."

"Fried nettles! Isn't this taking the pastoral theme a tad too far, Jeanne?" Pauline affects an overly shocked manner.

"Well, with all this talk of equality, and to honor our young guest's enthusiasm, I thought to prepare some country food. Come, let us try them."

The general consensus is that they are passable, but certainly enhanced by the truffle-and-whiskey sauce.

"Delicious—in their perfect rusticity, one finds the echo of this new freedom we all crave," says Breteuil gallantly.

"Well, I for one hardly think that more freedom would bring anything positive," says Pauline, shaking her head and echoing a common complaint of the times. "You must have heard Sidonie de Sabran—the peasants complained when her husband rode through their cornfields, even though it was the season of the hunt! They would never have dared, before these new ideas infected them."

"As bad as the smallpox," agrees Richelieu, and Pauline involuntarily touches her scars; though I adore her and her candid humor, her beauty was marred in youth.

"But why should he have the right to ruin the peasant's crops?" demands Lenoir, and inwardly I sigh. Though Lenoir is French, obviously his time in America has robbed him of that essential tact, so necessary for good living: knowing when to stop. Perhaps it was a mistake to include him. Young bucks such as he are perhaps best left to the salons and coffeehouses where these new ideas percolate, and often boil over.

Hercule laughs dryly. "That it is Sabran's land is not in dispute, and if he owns the land, can he not do what he wants with it? I agree one should make all attempts not to ruin crops, but if he chooses, it is his right."

"And last week, no one bowed their heads when I entered church! Such a thing has never been seen before!" adds Catherine, cutting up her husband's nettles and patting his arm.

It is true the world is changing, and at a fast clip. Talk of reform is everywhere, and everyone is now a philosopher, ready with radical notions about the future. At Louveciennes, I even heard my maid Henriette, whom I had assumed illiterate, discussing Rousseau with Zamor, and was it just my imagination or is she taking a trifle longer than usual to answer the bell?

"Pauline, my dear, tell us the gossip of Court," I say as the remains of the nettles are removed and a service of *entremets* is placed on the table. "No, my dears, do not be scared, I shan't serve you gruel, not yet at least. Rabbits from Limoges, dressed in sorrel sauce, are coming. I do promise." I love nights such as these, reminding me as they do of our little suppers at Versailles, but here the atmosphere is even more relaxed, and the food even better.

"Yes, let's hear about Versailles," agrees Catherine eagerly. Richelieu is rarely at Court these days and so neither is she; she was living on charity in the Tuileries, in rooms reserved for impoverished nobles, before she met and married the horned old goat.

"Well, of course, all anyone can talk about is the Affair of the Cardinal," says Pauline knowingly. As Breteuil's mistress, she generally passes a few days a week at Versailles.

We all nod in agreement. The queen always seems to be careening from one impropriety to another, but this scandal is the biggest to ever hit the monarchy. The Cardinal de Rohan purchased a magnificent diamond necklace, believing he was buying it on the queen's wishes. When the cardinal went to present the necklace to the queen and receive his payment and gratitude, she claimed she knew nothing about it. It appears the cardinal was duped by a pair of dishonest upstarts, and that the queen never desired it. The king was outraged and insisted the cardinal be tried, in public, for attempting to defraud the monarchy.

What a titillating fiasco!

The necklace was the one intended for me, that magnificent diamond collar worth two million *livres*. I remember the design well, six enormous pear-shaped diamonds surrounded by hundreds of smaller ones. My Louis died before it was complete, and though I was excited about it, in truth it seems vulgar and tawdry to me now. The world has become simpler in recent years, and even in the high salons of Paris, there is not the ostentation of just a decade ago. Besides, I have enough jewels, I think in satisfaction: for my birthday last month, Hercule gifted me a bracelet studded with emeralds, each one engraved with a myrtle flower.

The queen insists that she was offered the necklace by the jewelers when it was complete, but that she refused. Though flaunting and extravagant in her youth, she has become more restrained now, and even if the necklace had not been intended for me, I doubt she would have wanted it. Yet no one believes her.

"Well, I think anyone who knows Rohan and the queen knows the whole thing is false, but really, it doesn't seem to matter," says Breteuil, shrugging.

"Public opinion has already condemned her," observes Hercule sadly. "She is a symbol of the excesses of the monarchy."

"Well, it's her own fault," concludes Pauline harshly. "She has gone too far; a queen who acted no better than a hoyden cannot turn around and expect people to believe her, when her conduct in the past was so disgraceful." The queen is the mother of three children now, including two sons, but her reputation is in tatters and was perfectly shredded even before this scandalous episode.

Pauline says that these days, unless a courtier is part of the magic inner circle of the queen, there is not much for anyone to do at Versailles. The Polignacs reign supreme, and the queen spends far too much time closeted away at the Petit Trianon or at her Hermitage, while the nobility circle impotently back at Versailles. Now the oldest families only make the bare minimum of appearances at the palace, annoyed to be put second behind the queen's upstart friends. Never has court life been so dull, and never has a queen been so unpopular.

Poor woman, I sometimes think, though she scarcely enters into my thoughts these days. If anything, I pity her for the hate that surrounds her.

Everything that ails France is put on her shoulders. They call her Madame Deficit, but though extravagant, she is hardly responsible for the giant debts of the Seven Years' War that caused my Louis such grief, nor for the costly war with the Americans against the British. Nor is she responsible for France's flawed governance (Hercule's words, not mine). Regardless, she has become a center for all the hate and turmoil of the times. Traditionally, it was the role of the royal mistress to absorb the public ire, but now . . . in these new times . . . poor lady.

I hope those rumors about her and the Comte de Fersen are true; she should have some happiness in her life.

"What I don't understand . . ." says Hercule, taking my hand and leaning back in satisfaction—I know he likes these evenings with friends, family, and spirited conversation—". . . is why the people's respect is needed? This public opinion of which we speak—a curious thing, whose influence grows every year. All these new journals and newspapers, all these people reading—is it advisable?"

And then Lenoir is off and running, rabbiting on—*mmm*, excellent, I think as the rabbit in sorrel sauce is brought in—about the common man and the need for universal literacy.

Chapter Fifty-Three

In which Adélaïde witnesses a procession of . . . of what exactly?

"I think they're coming through the gates!" squeals An- gélique in excitement. Victoire's beloved Civrac died three years ago, after marriage plans for her son with Gabrielle de Polignac's daughter were thwarted. The Duc de Guiche, of the powerful Gramont family, pipped that prize, and Civrac's ensuing rage and attack of apoplexy did away with her. Now her daughter Angélique, the Comtesse de Chastellux, has taken her mother's place as Victoire's confi- dante. Victoire calls her by her Christian name, and reluc- tantly I follow suit.

We are standing in a gallery overlooking the Court of Honor and the main gates to the palace. In vain, the guards in the court- yard below attempt to push the scrum out of the way to clear a path for the coming procession. There is even a scrum inside the palace, and there is a certain lack of dignity in the way the mem- bers of our household are pushing against us in their efforts to see out the window. I am positive I can feel Angélique's pregnant belly pressing against my back.

I feel the knot of a headache coming on, and curse again this dratted procedure that has caused us to delay our departure for Bellevue.

"There they are!" A hush falls through the room as the proces- sion emerges into view, led by the king and queen. As he passes through the gates the crowds in the courtyard cheer for him and cries of *Vive le roi! Long live the king!* are heard.

"Thank goodness," remarks Narbonne. "Wasn't sure which way the crowd would go."

I'd like to reprimand her but I don't think I can—we all shared the same fears.

The king looks highly dignified and resplendent in his red jacket, his *cordon bleu* sash draped magnificently over his vast belly. There is no sign of the sadness or depression that has haunted him in recent months, as the country, and his family, spiral out of his control.

"No one's cheering for *her*," observes Narbonne. The queen, walking alongside her husband at the head of the procession, is greeted with stony silence. Well, better that than shouts of—no, I cannot repeat the dreadful things they call her. She rarely goes to Paris anymore, and if she does, she is hissed at the Opéra.

She has mellowed and matured, and is in all ways a wonderful mother, yet even as her dignity grows, she is accused of more heinous crimes. Now they say she has cuckolded the king and the children are not his, and distressing rumors of a Sapphic nature still float around. I even feel a little sorry for her, then quickly flick away my sympathy—we reap what we sow, and she must pay for her childish foolishness and for her behavior that never behooved a queen.

Today she looks regal but strained, her face washed with melancholy. Their eldest son, little Louis-Charles, lies dying at Meudon. He is only seven, and a most agreeable child. I know Antoinette wishes she could be there with him, and not here, attending this . . . But what is this? I think for the hundredth time. This spectacle—but of what?

The country is bankrupt and every attempt to raise taxes and reduce the deficit has been made, but Parlement, in its self-interested manner, has refused to ratify any reforms. An Assembly of Notables was called; the nobles and the clergy assembled, looked notable, and then also refused to reform the tax code. A graver move was planned: a calling of the Estates General, with the goal of finding a solution to the taxation crisis that paralyzes the nation. And now here they are, arriving at Versailles, all three Estates together.

The Second Estate, the king and nobility, lead the procession, which started in town with a blessing at Notre Dame Cathedral. Behind them will come the First Estate—the clergy—and then representatives of the Third Estate: everyone in France who is not a noble or a churchman.

"Ah, she's wearing a necklace—look at that," murmurs someone behind me.

"As well she should," agrees the Comtesse de Lostanges. Since the Affair of the Cardinal, the queen has been careful not to wear much jewelry, but today she is showing her dignity by dressing as magnificently as her position dictates.

"Artois certainly doesn't look happy," observes Narbonne. The king's brother, walking behind the king, is violently opposed to compromise and has been complaining bitterly about this move, which he says will be the undoing of the monarchy. Nonsense— despite his fixity of purpose, he has a penchant for overdramatic, inflammatory pronunciations.

Fixity of purpose—that true backbone that kept my father strong. Louis-Aug has a troubling penchant for compromise and these days he suffers from a curious apathy, as though the burden of kingship weighs too heavily on his shoulders, and soul.

"Turtle," said Narbonne once, and I did not rebuke her, for it is true: he is as a turtle withdrawing into his shell, looking unhappy and depressed at the unexpected events forming around him. He takes refuge in the hunt, and drink. They say he even fell asleep in a council session and snored!

But others are more optimistic about the calling of the Estates General. A historic day for France, say many, a new beginning.

"This will avert revolution!" declared Louis, Narbonne's son. "This is the century of reason and light and the time of greatest change! We will reform by the power of the pen, and not the blood of revolutions."

I thought his words foolish; of course there won't be a revolution. We are not those American barbarians!

Louis de Narbonne is of the right age to be inflamed and optimistic, but of late I feel too old for this new world. Already it is 1789, and all around us seem eager to throw off the strained ties of the old century and usher in the new. Will I live to see 1800? I wonder, as I often do these days. I am already fifty-seven, approaching my sixtieth year. Victoire is growing old too, and beside me, I can feel her shifting uncomfortably in the summer heat.

And Sophie. Her ghost is not here with us. Neither of them: not the ghost she was for most of her life, nor the ghost she might be now in death. And then Louise died two years ago—suffice to say, we are now two.

"There's Lafayette!" someone points out in the parade of nobles, speaking of the hero of the American Revolution.

"No wig," observes Victoire in distaste.

"Red-haired radical," I snort.

"I don't see Orléans," says Narbonne ominously.

I frown; not even the fine spectacle of almost three hundred French nobles, marching so proudly, can shake the irritation and unease that has plagued me all morning. I find it quite annoying that whenever I return to Versailles, the good humor that surrounds me at Bellevue almost completely disappears. I shift and surreptitiously push at my waist, where my rigid pearl stomacher is quite cutting into my side. And my dratted train, bearing down on my back like a beast and causing my shoulders to ache. I wish I could determine what causes me to be in such a bad mood at Versailles; suffice to say, I am eager for this spectacle to be over and done with, that we might journey back to Bellevue for the summer.

Now the clergy is starting to pass beneath us, a colorful sea of red and purple. Later, the whole procession will end at the Cathedral of St. Louis in town, where the king will give God thanks for . . . for what? I see our beloved Bernis, proud and regal in his flowing cardinal robes, wobbling slightly—gout has attacked his knees, but his vanity and pride are such that he cannot give up his beloved high-heeled shoes—as well as the Cardinal de Lévis, and our dear confessor, the Abbé Beauvais. Their magnificence is overshadowed by the enormous sea of black that is starting to take shape behind them.

"After the peacocks come the crows," mutters someone as the Third Estate, made up of provincial rabble—*bourgeoisie*, lawyers, petty estate people—begin to pass through the palace gates.

"Goodness, what a grim lot. In black—all of them! Do they not have colors in the provinces?"

"I heard there are bakers, amongst the lawyers and the government officials."

"That one looks like a peasant. What a dreadful hat!"

The Third Estate, "the people," as they are calling themselves, move into the courtyard like a murder of black crows, inching closer and closer. I suddenly feel faint.

"Give me some space," I demand of Angélique, glaring at her. She moves over and she and Lostanges put their arms around each other, as though to comfort. They are hugging and standing close—my eyes narrow, and I decide they are not wearing panniers. And this a grand state occasion! I shake my head—the small cracks, I think, running along the vase . . .

"I do hope they don't smell," says Victoire in worry. "You remember how that dovecote man smelled? And there are so many of them—"

"Almost six hundred," I supply. Almost outnumbering both the First and Second Estates combined, as someone observed. Not that that should matter; they aren't voting or anything.

"Well, I think they are revolting," says Narbonne. "Look at that one's coat—so shiny it's probably a hundred years old, cotton pretending to be satin."

"Yes, peasants are always revolting," someone else agrees.

"They're hardly peasants. They are educated men, and representatives of the people," says Angélique rather stiffly.

"La, I hadn't thought you for a freethinker!" exclaims Victoire.

Six hundred black crows breaching the walls of our palace. Who are these men? Nothing, their blood denuded of that essence that marks the noble races. The nobles have defended France, the clergy has prayed for France, but what have these men done? Probably they do some tasks that are important, but they are menial ones, and why should they have any glory or power for that?

Suddenly I feel old, and tired. I wish we were at Bellevue, but the uneasiness of life has percolated out into the countryside and it is no longer the haven it once was. Everywhere are pamphlets for liberty and against the clergy and the nobility.

And last year—an incident. When we traveled back to Versailles last autumn, our carriage was pelted on the road and someone even shouted: *À bas les vieilles coquines. Down with the old hussies.* And they were talking of us! Apparently our experience was not uncommon—ladies in carriages are starting to be insulted as if they were whores. Ridiculous—whores don't ride in carriages.

My thoughts wander over to the harlot and I wonder if *she* is in town, watching, as seemingly all the people of France are. But she was like the queen, never interested in politics. As I grow older, somehow the harlot and the Austrian are mixed in together in the stew of my memories, both responsible for this sad state of France.

"Oh, he's done it," whispers Narbonne in amazement. We fall silent as the Duc d'Orléans comes into view, in the middle of the black crowd. "There he is. He's really done it."

The cries for him are frenzied and hysterical, and my stomach tightens. Traitor. Though a close cousin of the king, and one of the foremost nobles in the country, Orléans claims himself to be for the people, whatever that means, and has allied himself with the Third Estate against the king.

Disgraceful.

"Just a symbol," replies the Duchesse de Laval curtly; she is related to Orléans' wife. He's dressed in a black suit, and isn't even wearing his *cordon bleu*!

"What is the Third Estate? Everything. What has it been until now, in the political order? Nothing. What does it want to be? Something." That cryptic statement has been making the rounds, and I think of it now as the black crows start to enter the palace. Inside the palace—here with us. They are something, certainly—but what exactly?

Nothing into something, something into nothing, I think as the last of the men pass through the portals of the palace, followed by the guards.

"I just can't see why those plebeian men have to be involved for it to be considered real reform," I huff to Narbonne, shaking my head and leaving the window. I sink down in a chair and Victoire slumps beside me, looking tired and lost. Last night I dreamed of a large black bird that swept in and stole everyone's eyes.

There will be a grand banquet tonight, with speeches and toasts. My head is pounding but it is my duty and obligation to attend; the freedom of life at Bellevue cannot follow us here. I must never, especially in these distressing times, forget that I am a daughter of France.

Chapter Fifty-Four

*In which the Comtesse du Barry gets her portrait painted,
and a few other things happen*

"They are saying it is a revolution," says Élisabeth, shaking her head. The painter Élisabeth Vigée Le Brun is remarkably pretty and remarkably talented, and has become a good friend. "For those men to simply declare themselves a National Assembly—in the old king's time, they would have all been clapped in the Bastille, and nothing doing about it."

Since the convening of the Estates General at Versailles, there is a sense that the world is on the brink of great changes. Life is alive with talk of reform and the future. I close my eyes. Politics, politics, politics. All around—it has become the new religion and suddenly everyone has an opinion about the best way to reform France.

When I was at Versailles, no one bothered much with those details; it was more about intrigue, more about the person who was actually the minister than about his actual policies—who cared about that? Now everyone cares, and even servants read political pamphlets and don't hesitate to share their views.

"Turn your head slightly, there, thanks," says Élisabeth, chewing on the nib of her brush. We are on the terraces at Louveciennes and she is painting my portrait. I am wearing a plain red dress, my hair partially undone. I do like the new simple styles, and some of my friends have even taken to wearing aprons. Not all approve: apparently Hercule's wife refused to see her daughter, declaring that she looked like a milkmaid.

I'll give this painting to Hercule, I decide, thinking of him fondly. Last night I dreamed of my mother, who passed away last year, but she wasn't unhappy. I close my eyes and enjoy the lazy late-afternoon sun. Life is sweet these days; Hercule remains as devoted as ever, and I love my lazy, carefree and luxurious life.

Chon is also with us, enjoying the conversation. "What is most surprising is how fast they expanded their initial mandate. First it was about taxes, and now it is about *everything*," she remarks, petting one of the cats that has wandered onto the hot terrace.

"That's a good thing," says Élisabeth, frowning and touching her finger to her nose. "Jeanne, a little to the left, I think. This light is *perfect*."

The Estates General, convened for the purposes of reforming the tax system, quickly became something else. Reform failed, but the Third Estate refused to go home. They spun off from the main group, and now these men, who call themselves the National Assembly, are demanding a constitution—like the Americans!

"And it's exactly what everyone was afraid of," continues Élisabeth. "Give the Third Estate a small say, and look what happens—they want the world!"

Hercule supports the need for reform and was sad not to be called as a representative of the Second Estate, sad not to be a part of the new world he has so many hopes for. Too old, he sighed, and it was all I could do to comfort him. And now he does not like the way this group of base *bourgeois*, and worse, have taken over the reforms and presume to speak for everyone.

"Well, you presumed to speak for them before," I reminded him, but for once his pleasant demeanor deserted him, and he snapped that though reforms were certainly needed, low men did not have the vision nor the education to lead a country.

"Well, I for one think it's a good thing. If the country had sat around waiting for the king and his ministers to implement real reform, we'd all be dead before anything happened," Chon says. Chon is pleasantly radical and she reads Rousseau and Locke, and is happy to digest them for me and share the salient points. She and Hercule like to argue, and occasionally I even join in. "At least, they speak for the people."

"No, they don't—they're just speaking for the *bourgeoisie*. It's not like they would want to include someone like my father, who was just a peasant, and give him a voice," I chip in.

"Not unreasonable to expect a man to read before he can have a say in the affairs of a nation," retorts Chon.

"Though sometimes I wonder why *we* are concerned with this," adds Élisabeth, frowning at her palette. She is still searching for the perfect red-orange to match my dress. "Being female, we are not included in any of their plans, or any of their proposed votes. A real suffrage"—here she uses a word commonly heard these days, and which I now understand—"would include women."

I giggle at the pleasantly silly idea, and Chon snorts that that will happen only when chickens grow teeth.

"We laugh," says Élisabeth, "but look at me—I work and I earn money. I pay taxes, so why should I not have a voice?"

"Well, your husband speaks for you. After all, he takes your money," observes Chon, and the two women laugh grimly. There is an American radical who is very *à la mode* in Paris these days— Jefferson is his name—and he declared that the tender breasts of ladies were not made for political convulsions, and I think I agree with him.

"Well, I for one would not want to vote," I say. "I don't think anyone should be voting! Let the king decide, but have him be governed by reasonable men." I am parroting Hercule's words, but they seem fair enough to me. If one must have an opinion—and it seems that these days one must—then his shall be mine.

I steer the conversation to more interesting matters. "How's Adélaïde?" I ask. Little Adélaïde Labille, from all those years ago at Madame Labille's—how does time pass so quickly?—is also a painter, and she and Élisabeth know each other.

"Doing well, certainly," says Élisabeth. "Her paintings of the king's aunts are still garnering acclaim and winning her commissions."

I shudder gently, thinking of the hideous portraits of Mesdames Adélaïde and Victoire, exhibited at the Paris Salon two years ago. "Why would a painter choose an ugly subject? Isn't the purpose of art to capture beauty?"

"Sometimes," says Élisabeth, "beauty can be found in ugliness."

Not in that case, I think, remembering Madame Adélaïde's frizzled gray hair and heavy features.

"And the queen—how does she suffer?" I ask lightly, though I bear her no real malice.

"Ah, the poor lady," sighs Élisabeth. A few years ago, she painted a very controversial portrait of the queen in a simple white gown. We always did share similar tastes in fashion, I think, remembering her penchant for light colors and—

Boom! An enormous sound, louder than a thunderclap, louder than all the hate in the world, cuts through the peace of the late afternoon.

And so it begins, I think, then shake my head—what begins?

Chon jumps up. "What on earth was that?"

Élisabeth drops her brush. "Oh, bother, it's in the gravel." She too turns to look into the distance. "Sounds like a cannon. It must have been—nothing else is that loud."

"It's coming from Paris," observes Chon, and without a word we head down to the river, to the pavilion at the top of the embankment. And indeed it is Paris; over the city, a thin black curl of smoke rises, and then another. A sudden uneasy feeling coils inside me. Hercule is the governor of Paris and is there right now. "Be careful," I whispered as I said good-bye to him after a brief visit two days ago. There have been riots all week—the finance minister, Necker, who apparently was very popular, has been dismissed and the people are calling for his reinstatement.

"There has been unrest all week," says Élisabeth, echoing my thoughts, "but nothing too serious. What on earth was that? Where is there gunpowder in Paris?"

"At the Bastille?" says Chon. "Has there been an invasion? Or perhaps our new National Assembly has decided to take Paris, as well as Versailles?"

"I should go," says Élisabeth as we walk back to the château, the heat of the July afternoon adding to the mysterious unease in the air. "This could be serious. I'll come back and finish the portrait—next month, shall we say?"

A footman carries the half-finished portrait inside and places it against a wall in one of the smaller chambers. By nightfall, a messenger comes from Hercule with the news: the Bastille prison, that hated symbol of all the arbitrary repression of the monarchy (Chon's words, not mine), has fallen, its governor massacred, its prisoners freed. And the cannons that we heard mark the beginning of a summer that will end with a new and terrifying France.

Chapter Fifty-Five

In which Madame Adélaïde . . . In which . . .

We never made it to Bellevue, and now it is autumn. Apparently Sophie's dog Finfin had puppies, and Victoire's melons were sweet beyond compare. All we can hope for now are some jars of preserves, which should be with us by Christmas.

Though we missed our time at Bellevue, in truth I am glad that this summer is over. What a few months it has been! Hopefully as the heat lessens, so too will this new madness. All my fears of those black-garbed men came to pass. Order within the Estates General quickly broke down, and the Third Estate, quite without permission of the king, installed themselves in the covered tennis court just beside the stables. There they made an oath to stick together, and quickly things devolved from there, events sliding down a slippery slope greased with lard and enthusiasm.

They—who are they? I ask you—decided that France needed more than just taxation reform, it needed a *constitution*.

Like the Americans.

It was open rebellion, and then came the storming of the Bastille, kicked down like a sand castle. A summer of siege, shots and stones abounding. Artois and his wife fled the country, along with many of our friends.

"I'm thinking of it as a little vacation," chirped the Comtesse de Chabannes before she set off. "I've always wanted to see Switzerland, and besides, when Marie told me last week about the waters at Givenchy, I thought it better to leave, until things are back to normal."

"Sister?" asked Victoire, looking to me for guidance. But I refused to even reply; our place is beside our nephew the king, and always will be.

Then, in August, a dreadful night: all feudal privileges abolished by that usurping group of *bourgeois* who now call themselves the National Constituent Assembly. Taking away the king's God-given right to rule and deciding on laws themselves! Yet Louis-Aug ratified their demands, saying he was scared of what would happen if he didn't. A king—scared. And by what? An enemy that cannot be counted, cannot be named—carried on the wind and in the people's hearts.

"At least the Austrians bled like the rest of us," muttered the old Maréchal d'Estrées.

"It's just a piece of paper, they can hardly make us all disappear, now, can they," said Narbonne sourly, but it came out as more of a question than she intended.

Throughout August we heard troubling stories from the countryside, of peasants turning on their masters, châteaux burned, families killed, or worse. Even the royal guards declared themselves in favor of the National Assembly, and their loyalty to the king is in doubt. Everything is in doubt.

A new guard regiment comes to replace the old one and their arrival is an excuse for a magnificent banquet, such as the Court has not witnessed all summer.

"Like the old times," says the Duc de Brissac, looking around in satisfaction at the assembled guests. The entire royal family— minus of course, Artois, who is now in Turin—is wearing court finery. "If you close your eyes, you can almost imagine yourself back at one of the splendid court dinners that used to inspire with their magnificence."

I glare at Brissac; he is the harlot's paramour. "I think your words inappropriate, monsieur," I say coldly, "implying as they do that the old times are gone forever." I am convinced that in a few months this will all die down and those dratted *bourgeois* will go back to the provinces where they belong—surely they have fields to till or shops to attend to? Isn't autumn harvest time?

"I agree, Madame," says the Comte d'Osmond, coming to stand beside me. His face is as grim as mine, and as the festivities of the banquet grow more raucous, it grows darker.

"Oh, smile, Louis!" snaps his wife.

"No, madame, I cannot," he retorts sadly. "This festive air is misplaced. One does not celebrate a funeral."

The next day was blustery and cold and the first signs of winter crept in. Last year there was snow beyond all that France had ever seen—how difficult it made even the simplest of journeys!

Word came in the afternoon that fishwives from Paris were marching on Versailles, and by evening a most ragged bunch had descended on the town. The Marquise de Pracomtal canceled the musical concert we were to attend, and left immediately for her country house. We were left with nothing to do but pace around in our apartments and listen to the cries outside as the mob grew closer.

Apparently they are complaining about the lack of bread, even though the king had ordered the release of more grain last week.

"They're still rabbiting on about that aristocratic plot to starve and weaken the people," tuts Narbonne; she had planned to go to visit her grandchild in town tonight, but is now forced to stay here.

"Not a bad idea to starve the people," I remark tightly. "They seem to be at the root of all our recent troubles."

Victoire intently sips her cordial; the sound of the rabble from the courtyards is making her increasingly nervous. "I remember when I was younger, I thought they should eat pastry crusts if they had no bread. But now I know that to make both bread and pastry, you need flour and water. Do you remember the scones we made in the kitchen last year at Bellevue? With those delicious raisins from Turkey? But perhaps pastry crusts use less flour? Lighter than bread?"

"I don't think it is only bread they want," says Narbonne.

"What more could they want? Really, their demands are never-ending."

"My son says they want more—more power, more influence," she replies. "They want the world, it seems."

I snort. "They should just be content with their bread. I feel as though I am a prisoner in these rooms!"

Louis de Narbonne comes in to say the mood in town is turning ugly, and the men—for it seems there are a lot of men amongst the fishwives—are demanding to see the queen. They are also demanding that the king cooperate with the National Assembly, and move to Paris as a sign of good faith in addressing the widespread discontent and to show his support for the reforms.

"Maybe now he'll see that his optimism is ill-founded," declares his mother grimly after her son has left. "Youth. Though I was never quite so silly in my younger days. We knew then to focus on what was important, not on this political fingle-fangle."

I fling down the sampler I have been aimlessly clutching all afternoon and go to stand by the windows overlooking the terraces and the Orangerie. The vast expanse is deserted save for three dirty women aimlessly milling around.

"Fishwives in the parterres!" I say in disgust. How did they get past the guards? Certainly, the gardens are open to all, but it is understood that *all* includes only those who are suitably dressed.

Narbonne comes to stand beside me. "Can you imagine . . . if we were taking a stroll, and then came upon them?"

"I can't," I say shortly. At Bellevue, certainly, we occasionally come upon laborers, and the interactions are mostly pleasant—or at least they were—but to find one of *them* inside the gardens? Worse than the Beast of Gévaudan, I think, remembering that afternoon so long ago. Or perhaps he has already arrived?

"Look." Narbonne points at one of the women, who is holding up her skirt—less of a skirt than a rag—and bobbing down awkwardly, the other two women laughing. "Is she trying to curtsy?"

Victoire starts crying, about the fish women coming to tear Louis-Auguste to bits.

"Oh, don't be silly," I say, but not harshly, for I see she is genuinely upset. I send one of the women—who protests, saying she doesn't want to go out alone, for now there are rumors that some of the motley crowd is inside the palace—to the kitchens to bring more bottles for Victoire; anything to help ease her through the coming night.

We sleep, then wake to the end of our world. In the first pale light of morning, the sound of rough voices and anarchy, and then a shattering of glass.

"But surely they won't come through the windows?" wails Victoire. "That wouldn't be proper, would it?"

We gather in my library as all around us we hear the sound of mobs breaking into the palace. We close the shutters to make morning night and wait in fearful darkness, all of us huddled around one solitary candle.

"What do they want?" whimpers Victoire. "Where are the guards?"

"So few guards," says Angélique.

I pat my sister's arm; in her fright, she reminds me of Sophie. Little mercies, as they say, that Sophie did not live to see this day, for it would have killed her.

Now the barbarians are beyond the gates and even beyond the walls, inside our sanctuary and the very heart of France. Someone yells in the rooms above us and we hear a great pounding of feet running, chasing, falling—what is happening?

Two royal guards race through our rooms, not even stopping to bow, and cry at us to bolt the outer doors and secure the shutters. We do what we can, but this is Versailles and few of the doors of our private apartments have locks. We can hear the mobs outside our rooms now, the untamed beast coming rapidly closer.

"We shall show them we have no fear," I say loudly, going to stand in front of the door. "We shall teach them how to die!"

"Be quiet, Adélaïde!" hisses Narbonne. I turn to her in amazement, but before she can apologize, the doors burst open and a man with a flaming torch flies in. I shriek and shrink behind Narbonne's comforting bulk.

SALLY CHRISTIE

"We're looking for the Austrian," cries the man. He has a dirty, bearded face and a ragged shirt, his stench making me gasp.

Victoire wails, but the man is unmoved; it seems he does not know whom he addresses.

"We want the Austrian," he repeats, and then is distracted by his reflection in a magnificent mirror to his left, the flames of his torch leaping around his image. His hand strays to a dirty kerchief at his neck, as though to adjust it.

"The queen is not with us," Narbonne declares in a strong voice at the front of our little group. I think I perhaps should be there, but I would not want to address such a man. Is that an apron he wears?

"Not Antoinette," sobs Victoire, and the man looks at her in irritation, then back again at our little group.

"À la revolution!" he cries, taking one last look at himself in the mirror before dashing out, calling to others to never mind, there are just old ladies in there.

I sit down heavily, my heart beating, still clutching at Narbonne.

"You were very brave," I say.

"For you, Madame," says Narbonne, and we hug tightly, something I have never done before, but in her capable arms I feel such comfort. A hug—who would have thought?

A royal guard staggers through our still-open door, which Angélique rushes to close behind him. Narbonne leads him to a sofa and we see he is bleeding from a great gash on his leg.

"It's Jérôme," whispers Victoire, shaking her head, looking dazed. "Dauriac's son—what are they doing? Why?" She starts to cry again and I put my arms around her—no better time for another hug—and we hold each other through the remains of that awful day. Around us the sounds of the massacre of our life continue—gunshots, screams, mirrors shattering, statues falling, cries of revolution and revenge, all mixing with the groans of Jérôme on the sofa as the lifeblood drains out of him.

Versailles, it is no more, I think dully, still hugging my sister.

What are they doing to it? What are they doing to *us*? Will we die in here? Perhaps better to die now rather than see what this future that I no longer understand holds for us?

Louis de Narbonne rushes in, breathing heavily, and assures us that all is well, that they were looking for the queen but that now she is safe, as is the rest of our family. "Stay here," he says, and disappears out again into the madness. At some point Angélique's children are hustled in through a back staircase and they huddle with us in the darkness, and we eat bonbons for strength and courage—thank goodness for Victoire's little stores in the cupboard.

Louis de Narbonne bursts back in, now with a cut on his face, his beautiful blue coat stained a dark red. "Lafayette is with the king, and the crowds are under control." He grabs a handful of jellied candies and downs them with a swig of Victoire's cordial. "Come, let us ascend to the king."

We make our way out of our dark sanctuary into a changed world, up the marble staircase now littered with shards of glass, the top steps slippery with blood. A smashed vase, mirrors cracked, the gilt and the gold burnished with blood. Toppled girandoles, smashed chandeliers, the sad sound of water from a broken barrel, dripping down the stairs. The body of a guard draped over a stool, mercifully facing the floor.

We embrace our nephew and his children with more hugs—such wonderful things, I have time to think amidst the sorrow. Antoinette is as white as a sheet and later we learn that she had to run for her life from her bedroom to the king's.

Outside we can hear a great mass teeming in the Marble Court. The Marquis de Lafayette is circling the room, biting his lip—he is indecisive at the best of times, as inconstant as a weather vane. What is he doing here, and do we even trust him?

From outside we hear calls of "The king to Paris! The king to Paris!"

"Should we go, Lafayette?" asks the king, his face racked with indecision. Lafayette looks back at him, their doubts mingling and growing.

"Sire, we must placate . . ." says Lafayette at last, staring at a point over the king's shoulders and looking as though he would like to take a nap.

The king sighs and rubs his belly. "I will ask them what to do," he says, and motions to one of the guards to open the windows to the balcony. I close my eyes—it is the end, they will tear him to bits, they will—

"*Vive le roi!*" The crowd, so bloodthirsty and terrifying, explodes in cheers as Louis appears on the balcony. *Long live the king!*

Lafayette nods vigorously, suddenly alert and awake. "Yes, yes, indeed, the people need to see their king!"

Then the cheers for the king die down and another one rises.

"They are calling for you, madame," says Lafayette, turning to Antoinette, now clutching her eldest daughter. And it is true—they are calling for *the Austrian*. The queen's face is clenched in rage, her anger trumping the fear she must surely be feeling.

"They would call me to come to them," she hisses, her hands gripping the thin, trembling shoulders of her daughter.

"*Maman*, you are hurting me," pleads little Thérèse, and her mother releases her and hugs her with a sob.

"Madame," says Lafayette tentatively. "We must placate . . ."

"Well, they can have me," says Antoinette, loudly and clearly, and then she too is out on the balcony and at the mercy of the masses. Through the open windows we can see her rigid back, her cap slightly askew, her breath even and measured. She sweeps down in a graceful curtsy, and Victoire, huddled beside me, gasps in horror. "But they are of no rank! How could the queen curtsy before them?"

There is silence as the mob regards the figure of all their hate and hopes. Silence broken only by the ragged thump of my heart. Then a thin voice rises through the October air: "*Vive la reine! Long live the queen!*" Others take up the chant and then suddenly the rabble erupts in rapturous acclamation, which for Antoinette is but a memory long lost.

"Oh my goodness!" says Lafayette, breathing again.

I exhale and bury my face in my hands. They want us in their power, but why? Where does this anger come from? They would bring us low, kill us even. I think of the body draped over the stool, then of Jérôme streaming blood over the fabric of the sofa—it will never be clean. His mother, such a kind woman—her grief will be immense. She came to visit us at Bellevue last year, a most pleasant time, she brought a little music box for Angelique's daughter, that played a melody by—

"Tante, Tante." It is Louis-Aug, shaking my shoulder. No, not Louis-Aug—I must remember he is the king, though sometimes I think I would prefer it were he still a little boy, when all was right with the world. He was so charming when he was younger, and I regret my sternness with him—why did I not hug him? Why did I not hug anyone? I don't think I ever—

"Come, Tante, we are leaving."

"Leaving?"

"We are going to the Tuileries," announces the king. His voice is firm now, but his eyes, focused on his cuffs, hold the depth of his shame. "We must do everything we can to avoid more bloodshed."

"Best to wear these," says Lafayette, sprightly now that the danger has passed and a course of action has been decided upon. I watch the detested man as he goes around the room, handing out tricolor cockades to each of our group. After the fall of the Bastille, these red, white, and blue cockades made their first appearance, and Angélique was obliged to get rid of a new summer dress that was sadly in the same detested colors.

"Now, no!" says the king, and I wonder that he acquiesced to the mob's demands, yet resists this little symbol. He even accepted one after the fall of the Bastille, but he was never decisive, poor boy, never able to understand the right time and place to take a firm stance.

Antoinette takes one from Lafayette and pins it on her breast herself, and I note with amazement that her fingers are not shaking. "Come, dear, we must all do what we can in these dreadful circumstances."

Louis-Aug puffs and grows red. "Have they not taken enough? Will they take our dignity too?"

"Dignity can never be taken," says Antoinette quietly. She takes another cockade from Lafayette and pins it on her husband's chest. "We must wear these."

We want the Austrian, the man who plundered our rooms said: *the Austrian*. Funny, I don't even think of her as the Austrian these days—she is a Bourbon, the mother of our future king, and my queen, and she rather seems to be handling this whole dreadful mess better than anyone.

Lafayette bows in front of me. "Madame, if you permit."

With trembling hands, I take the detested ribbon and pin it to the front of my gown. Silent and mute, for there are no words to describe this humiliation, we head to the courtyard and are bundled into waiting carriages: myself, Victoire, Narbonne and Angélique, a few of her young children, all together in one. The king and queen and their children in another.

"The hearses of the monarchy!" someone cries, and the mob surrounds our carriages, screaming and singing. Narbonne closes the curtains but Lafayette, riding alongside us, orders them open again.

"Oh, they are horrible, horrible," sobs Victoire, and one of Angélique's babies starts crying lustily. Flames from torches light the night and the scene around us, the faces of the mob twisted in hate and triumph, a head on one pike, a strung ginger cat on another.

"We have the baker, wife, and boy! We no longer need bread!" they chant in terrible glee.

"What baker do they have? Have they taken the cooks as well?" wails Victoire, and one of Angélique's children pipes up in a very calm and assured voice—children can sometimes see the truth through the strangeness: "They mean the king, Madame. He is the baker of whom they sing."

On the road to Paris we stop and a decision is made. Lafayette allows us to peel off and head for Bellevue, leaving the king and the rest of the royal family to go to Paris.

"They are like prisoners," wails Victoire, and I tell her she is being silly—they are not prisoners. Or perhaps they are: captives of a wild time.

And Bellevue—will we be safe there?

Chapter Fifty-Six

In which Citizen Jeanne loses everything

I stretch, open my eyes to the goddess painted on the wall, Hercule's touch still a memory on my body. I am in a bedroom at his Paris house; last night he gave a feast to celebrate the Epiphany and the New Year: 1790. A whole new decade, the start of a new world. It was a lovely night: the guests pleasing, the food superb, the conversation as sparkling as the diamond earrings he gave me as a New Year's gift. I wore them to bed and now I finger them idly.

So many have fled the unrest, which never seems to end, but still there is a pleasant, gay society in Paris, and all—most—are enthused by the change in the air. Last night we drank toasts to the coming constitution, and I prepared beautiful cockades, made with dyed feathers and tied with a small ruby, for the guests to pin to their breasts; only the archconservative Comte de Montmorin refused and sat on his instead.

I reach for the cup of warm chocolate on the tray beside me and delight in finding a small portion of fresh biscuits, still warm, in a porcelain basket. Lovely. I stretch and play out the memories of the night some more. Upstairs I can hear something heavy being moved, a table being dragged over the floors, no doubt.

Hercule was up early and has already left, and I'll go back to Louveciennes later today or tomorrow. I yawn and sip my chocolate, frown at the slight heaviness in my head. Too much champagne last night; I can no longer enjoy it as much as when I was young. Hercule is busy these days, but it is not Versailles that keeps him, for the royal family are now lodged at the Tuileries.

After that dreadful day at Versailles when the family was forced to go to Paris, like cattle being herded to the slaughter, two of the wounded palace guards found their way to Louveciennes and I gladly offered them shelter. Chon and I cared for them and treated their wounds.

Afterward I received a letter from the queen. A simple letter, thanking me for my support. My emotions, when I read it, overwhelmed me; I had thought that Versailles and that ugly contest of wills between us had ceased to be important to me. But her heartfelt words brought it all back: that silly struggle; her humiliation; my triumph. What did it all matter, and why did it have to be that way?

When we were young we were more alike than either of us cared to admit: carefree, informal, wanting only a life of luxury and pleasure. And why not? She has matured now, become sober and responsible, but I . . . well, I still enjoy the good life. *A sensuous sybarite*, Chon always calls me, and I tease her that she should follow my lead. In one respect she has: she now has a lover.

I happily replied to the queen and assured her of my endless devotion. Hercule told me she received my letter, but there was no reply. No matter; I am happy now that she knows of my loyalty and that she and the king can count on my support should they, in their sadly reduced circumstances, need it.

In Paris, the royal family, and even the queen, are more popular than they have been in years, and when they ride out they are acclaimed. The people are convinced that having the king in their midst will lead to great changes. Having the royal couple in Paris, Hercule says, has removed some of the majesty and mystique that grew too thick around the crown, but it has also restored some of the humanity.

"Was Versailles a mistake?" Hercule mused one night. "To remove the King of France so far from his capital? Should he have been in Paris from the beginning? In London, they have

St. James, and even in Austria, the Hofburg Palace is in the heart of Vienna."

Versailles—a mistake? It hardly seems possible. "Versailles is not so far from Paris," I said doubtfully. "I wonder if they will ever return there?" When I am at Louveciennes, I often think to ride over and have a look, but never find the time. Perhaps I don't want to see it; they say the rooms are desecrated, and a pack of wild dogs has completely overtaken the chapel.

The furious, dizzying pace of change is enough to make one's head spin. Feudal rights abolished, the king seemingly at the mercy of the people, and now religious orders are under attack. The monk Guimard could marry now; how sad Ma is not around for him.

A little of Hercule's earlier optimism is replaced with concern at the pace of change, the hatred for the Church, and the radicalism of some of the factions of the National Assembly. Still, he is confident that a compromise, and a new constitution, will be achieved before the year is over.

"It doesn't seem they are too interested in compromise. Not everyone is as rational as you, my dear."

"Nonsense." Hercule traveled to his estates in Brittany last year, and there his people still acclaimed him. "And they may abolish titles, but they can't abolish blood. I am still a noble at heart, yet can proudly wear the title of *citoyen*—citizen. Who is to say one is better than another?"

"Fairly much everyone." I am now the Citoyenne Barry, which really doesn't have the same ring to it as the Comtesse du Barry, but does sound rather modern and exciting. Sometimes I fear I am too old for these new times—I am nearing fifty—but then in many ways I still feel as youthful and spry as twenty years ago.

Nonetheless, it is true what Hercule says: they may abolish titles, but really, not much has changed, apart from some rudeness where before one expected deference. My friend Pauline complained at dinner last night that her coachman had to physically strike a wretch to clear him off the street, whereas before they would have leaped out of the way, and bowed, before the whip could fall.

From above, I can hear Hercule's wife's loud, imperious voice, ordering chairs to be moved. She is here more often, now that the royal family is at the Tuileries, and last night we had a stiff encounter in the courtyard. Then footsteps running higher and higher up the stairs. A sudden sense of foreboding and I put my chocolate down with shaking hands. Henriette, my maid who traveled with me, bursts in with Dénis Morin, my steward from Louveciennes.

"Oh, madame, madame," he says, falling on his knees before the bed. "Gone, all gone."

"Morin, what are you doing here? What's wrong? Who is gone?" I pull my robe around me, worried by his frantic look. Behind my two servants I can see some of Brissac's people crowding in, their eyes hungry for more of whatever this is.

"They are gone. The jewels, all of them. Your treasures. Thieves, last night."

With a shaking heart I piece the whole story together. Thieves—they stole everything. Well, not everything, but most of my jewel collection that Louis gave me, all my memories and all my treasures. I race back to Louveciennes in mounting distress and throw myself in Chon's arms. She is leaving; she is going back to Toulouse and is busy packing for her departure. She says Paris is a beast she wants to get far, far away from, but I think she is over-reacting. At least she's not going to Switzerland, but still, Toulouse is quite the ends of the earth.

We hug and she tells me the whole sordid story: a ladder discovered outside my bedroom, thieves that came through the open window, my rooms ransacked. All gone. I sit down and feel as though I will never get up. Who would do this? Not someone from the village, surely. They love me and I give so much to charity; just last year, I paid for the new church roof. Who would do such a thing?

The constabulary arrives and assures me that my remarkable jewelry will be very difficult to dispose of, and that I should not worry: they will recover all of the pieces. He recommends publishing the detailed inventory he has taken, but Chon counsels prudence.

"This is not the time to be flaunting your wealth," she warns, and says the list will only stimulate envy and greed. I am having none of it.

"You don't understand! They are not just jewels, they are everything to me."

"Private riches are an abomination against the natural order of men," says a grim voice from the corner.

"Oh, shut up!" I cry to Zamor, passionately sick of his sly, black face. "Get out of here. You and your radical mewlings—just get out."

"Jewels are just jewels; you should just be glad you've still got your life," Chon says. There has been more unrest in the countryside, more châteaux looted and burned. But minor incidents, and in places where the nobles were not loved.

"Of course I have my life! The people of Louveciennes love me." They do, and besides, I'm not a hated aristocrat.

"You're living inside a cloud, Jeanne! This gathering storm will not be good for the aristocrats, or for those that live like them. All the charity in the world won't stop them hating you."

"Nonsense; I'm a woman of the people. They'll never hate me."

"Perhaps not yet. But listing all your jewels isn't going to help anything."

"Of course it will! It will help me find the *jewels*! Which is the most important thing right now!" What is wrong with everyone this morning? Chon and I glare at each other. I wish she wasn't going, though her lack of sympathy is making her departure easier.

"Well, you make your own decisions now," says Chon finally, shaking her head. "I've delayed the coach until tomorrow, but I've got to finish packing. Good luck, Jeanne, and do write."

Only Hercule sees reason and agrees I must do whatever I can to recover the items that mean so much to me. The list makes me sad, each one associated with a memory and a treasured time that will never come again:

A pair of bracelets, each with 6 rows of pearls, clasped by an emerald mounted on a bed of diamonds. To celebrate our first year together.

A pair of diamond buckles with 84 gems. New Year's, 1773

A studded hair clip with 3 large emeralds, with smaller gems on both sides. Our first fight.

A set of sleeve buttons, one emerald, one sapphire, one ruby and one yellow diamond. Winter, 1773

A necklace with 24 diamonds. "Because I love you," he whispered.

A ring with a heart-shaped sapphire, encircled with diamonds. When I was upset over Madame Pater.

A ring with a portrait of Louis XV in onyx, his hair worked in sardonyx. On his sixty-third birthday.

And so much, much more.

Chapter Fifty-Seven

In which Madame Adélaïde undertakes a journey

When I was younger, my sisters and I visited the spas at Plombières and we traveled there in the style befitting our rank as daughters of France. I was accompanied by a gentleman-in-waiting, a lady-in-waiting, a lady of the chamber, three lady companions, a first woman of the bedchamber, three other female attendants, two women of the wardrobe, and one woman for the bed linens. Three gentlemen ushers, one footman, a porter, one equerry, two grooms, two pages, one doctor, a surgeon, an apothecary, and a confessor. Three guards and a lance corporal. Then the same again for each of my sisters, all of us in twenty-two carriages with sixty-six horses alongside. We were all together then: me, Victoire, Sophie, Louise, even Henriette, and what a sweet time it was, and how joyous the acclaim!

Now . . . we flee in the night like criminals, with only our ladies and a handful of servants, in carriages without proper heaters, only dear Louis de Narbonne and Angélique's husband, the Comte de Chastellux, riding beside us as escort.

The country I grew up in is no more, and I am not who I was. I am no longer Madame but a simple *citoyenne*. Not even the Comtesse de Provence is Madame now—that dignified title, that spoke of glory in its simplicity, is gone. France has turned against its rulers; all that was once sunny and dear is now dark and wrong, midnight in morning.

After that dreadful day in October, the trickle of *émigrés* (as they are now so hatefully called) became a flood. We resolved to stay, but life became intolerable. Daily wondering if we would be safer in the Tuileries, daily waiting to see what new humiliation would come our way. At Bellevue, we were prisoners of fear and nerves: the reply of a servant—was her pause a second too long? The disemboweled chicken found on the terrace—a fearful omen or just a fox?

The dissolution of monastic orders and the subordination of the clergy in February 1790 decided us—I want no part of this country that turns not only against its rulers, but also against God. A France where we can no longer worship in peace? Never. And by leaving, I decide, we will lessen the burden on our nephew.

A burden—something we have been all our lives, but I had never properly realized it before. A burden, I think as the freezing carriage rolls over the winter roads, my head resting on a cushion. The dreaded Lady of Introspection accompanies me on this worst of carriage rides, but now I look at her squarely, and see that she is me. Perhaps I was always a burden, but I think everyone is, in their own way. And it is not my fault; I was born a Princess of France, and that role defined a life that was perhaps not of my choosing.

Before we left, we visited the Tuileries to say our good-byes and get our passports—we used those hateful "rights of man" that everyone talks of these days, and stated it was our right to travel freely. Emigration was still not illegal, though pressure was on the king to make it so; he acquiesced only eight days after we left.

As we said our tender and tearful good-byes, I could not help but contrast it with the traditional leave-taking due to a sovereign on the eve of departure: the informal clothes allowed in the presence of the king, the priests to bless the journey, the pretty curtsies and bows. Did Versailles even exist? How could October have happened, how could any of this have happened? It all seems so long ago; sometimes when I try I can't even remember the color of the wallpaper in my study, or whether my sheets were blue or green, or whether the windows opened in or out.

Up to the last minute, I was afraid the king would change his

mind—in the face of difficult decisions, he is frighteningly irreso-
lute. He does not understand what is happening; this is not what
he was born to nor is it the world he deserves. Instead, it is Antoinette who has become my hope. She is fast by her husband's
side and all the dreadful events have turned her into a woman of
strength. I am glad to leave her to Louis.

"Dearest Tante," she murmured to me; her hair is now almost
completely white but her dignity is solid and she exudes fortitude.
"Godspeed, and thank you for everything."

"God willing we will all be together again soon," I replied, and
we embraced. When I held her in my arms, a clear vision came to
me: we were back in the gardens at our beloved Versailles and she
was just a young girl, so recently arrived, and yes, lost and unsure
of herself, caught in intrigues beyond her ken. I felt a flash of regret, for I could see that I had not been overly sympathetic to her.
But perhaps adversity is what makes us, and she has had plenty,
and she has survived.

I embraced each of her children in turn, and then my niece
Élisabeth, now a woman of twenty-nine. I wanted to bring her
with us, but she refused to leave her brother. Her piety and fixity
of purpose are strong, but where once I might have been envious,
now there is only admiration, and a heart-wrenching sadness.

Finally I said good-bye to Louis-Aug, and that was the hardest.
Victoire could not stop the tears, and even I felt my eyes well up.
My darling nephew, so good and sincere, yet so poor in judgment
and decision, and what a terrible place that flaw has led him to.

We returned to Bellevue with our passports and started packing, but then a rumor came that the fish women were coming to
drag us back to Paris. And so we fled in the night, leaving everything behind, including the memories of our only happy days.

As dawn starts to filter into the carriage, Narbonne shifts under
the weight of two of Angélique's children and opens the curtains.
But what do I want to see of this frozen landscape, of this land
that has turned against us?

"Are we there yet? At Plombières?" asks Victoire in a small

voice, waking up and looking around her in confusion. My sister has not the strength that I do, and this has all been so hard on her. How she wept over her melons that froze last winter, when we were unable to procure the burlap to cover them.

I reach over to take her hands, and hold them tightly. "Soon. Soon we will be at Plombières."

"Oh, wonderful," she says sleepily. "Do you remember how warm the waters were? What a relief it shall be—it's so cold in this carriage."

"Do you remember the little girls, with the flowers, and how prettily they sang in greeting?" asks Narbonne, leaning over to pull Victoire's bonnet back around her ears.

"Oh yes! But why aren't they cheering for us now? It's so quiet outside."

"It's early as yet, Madame. The crowds will come out soon enough."

"And the reception at Chaumont, I don't know why but I always remember that well," says Victoire dreamily, opening her eyes. "Will we pass through there again? Do you remember that, Angélique?"

"Now, I wasn't with you then, Madame, but I am with you now, and look forward to it all the more," says Angélique kindly.

"Ah, good. And I hope your mother will be there. Dear Civrac," says Victoire, and closes her eyes again.

"My sister is not yet fully awake," I whisper across to Angélique, but I think she understands. Has always understood.

"Of course, Madame, of course."

Narbonne puts her arm around me and I can't stop myself and soon I am sobbing openly. Tears from such an old woman may be foolish, but I don't care anymore. There is love in this carriage, I think in the midst of my misery, there is love. They can't take everything.

☙

A journey of cold and humiliation, sullen peasants refusing to get out of the way of our carriage, ugly cries in the villages we pass through.

"There go the royal bitches!"

"The old carps from Bellevue are fleeing!"

"How ugly they are!"

At Ancy, two days from the border, we are detained, the people declaring our passports not in order. We are forced from our carriage and into a hovel that Narbonne claims is an inn. The innkeeper is a fat, older man who has a hard job of balancing his disdain with his awe; he keeps bowing then stopping himself, alternating between "Madame la Princesse" (as though I were a mere Princess of the Blood! I do not correct him—it hardly seems to matter now) and "Citoyenne."

His wife is another matter. My age, I would say, though it is always hard to tell with these people; they age so much quicker than we do. As fast as dogs, Bernis once said, and now I see the wisdom of his words.

To eat, we are seated at a table that is really just a rough plank of wood, and I can feel splinters through my skirts from the bench. When she brings us our meal, the innkeeper's wife fair throws the plates down and then to my horror sits herself opposite me. She starts to eat, without my permission, and I realize I am at the same table—plank of wood—as a *peasant*. I start trembling—is she mad?

The woman looks at me defiantly, a grim smile playing around her lips, her eyes glittering. Victoire moans and slumps over the plank of wood.

Narbonne instantly understands. "Madame, you are not well? Perhaps you would care to retire and eat later, in solitude?"

"No, no," I say, my voice catching. "No, I shall eat right now." I am strong, I think, taking a spoonful of the soup, raising it with a steady hand to my mouth. This new world will not defeat me. I take a mouthful and will myself not to splutter out the foul swill that tastes more of worm than the chicken we were promised. "But get my sister a glass of brandy—she is not as strong as I am."

Narbonne turns to the innkeeper. "Some brandy," she barks.

The woman turns her defiance to Narbonne. "It's in the cellars. You'll find the way."

Oh my goodness. I close my eyes, then incline my head, indicating to Narbonne that she may go. I can do this. Then I am alone, at the table—plank—with the woman. I remember the labyrinth at Versailles and how terrified I was. Now, sitting with an unwashed grub, and a rude and surly one at that, with only two feet and one plank separating us.

"You enjoying the soup?" asks the woman with a smirk, addressing me not with the respectful *vous* but with the familiar *tu*. A form of language I had heard about, but never expected to experience.

"No," I say. I shall speak directly to this woman who speaks directly to me. "It's disgusting." I glare at her, but the force of her hate is so much stronger, and it pushes back against me. There are so many of them. How did they grow so powerful, and where did all this hate come from? For one ludicrous moment I want to ask her why she hates me, but then I decide I don't want to know the answer.

I force down the rest of the vile soup, and when Narbonne returns with the brandy I take my share. The woman and I stare at each other a good while longer, but then she rises abruptly and leaves; she has duties to attend to, more important than tormenting a princess, more important than showing the world that she is worth something, even though we both know she is not.

After eleven long days, we are free to go, and we continue west. A crowd gathers at Beauvoisin, where we will cross the border to Italy. As we roll across the bridge, there are derisive cries from behind us, and an armed guard to salute us and welcome us. In the carriage we are all crying as we leave our country behind.

We are just four citizens and two little children in this carriage, sharing all the burdens and the humiliations of a world gone wrong. It is not only France we are leaving, but all our memories of all those who didn't make the journey with us:

Papa; my mother; my brother; his wife, Josepha; all my lost sisters.

After Turin and a tearful reunion with Clothilde—how I regret that we arrived without her sister Élisabeth—we travel south toward Rome, and when we are in sight of the holy city a great calm comes over me. We made the right choice, and all will be well. God oversees all, and Louis-Aug and his family will be fine. A constitution, which those wretches want, will be agreed upon and then life will return to peace. We could be like England, perhaps, where the king is heavily bound by his parliament, but at least they still live in their palaces. Of course, their king is mad; no one blames their constitution for it, but I have my suspicions.

A whirl of dust as a carriage approaches. It pulls up alongside us and Narbonne opens our window. A small, elaborate carriage, the two prancing horses decked in scarlet robes. A corpulent man greets us with the face of a friend: the Cardinal de Bernis.

"Welcome, Mesdames, to Rome. *'In times of sorrow and sadness / We welcome you with joy and gladness.'*"

Chapter Fifty-Eight

In which the revolution finally comes for Citizen Jeanne

"My mother was at the fish woman's presentation," says Julie de Clermont in her little high voice. "Sorry, Comtesse, those were her words, not mine. I remember her saying the world was turned upside down, but really, she had no idea. I wonder what she would say to see her daughter thus?" She looks sadly down at her lap. "I'm a seamstress! And I told Madame Smith I would have this cover done by tomorrow, and so can't join Victor's charade party tonight. And look at this finger—my dear husband demanded to know what horned crud trailed across his back last night? I was so ashamed!"

She puts out a thin, white finger, and to oblige I feel the tip and the beginning of a faint callus.

I cluck. "Poor duck! You shall have all of my aloe cream. I will send Henriette over with the entirety of it."

Julie smiles sadly. Her mother rents two rooms on the top of this house in London, and I make a point of visiting as often as I can. London—two months after the theft, my jewels were found here, and I was obliged to travel to England to push the slow, and complicated, wheels of the judicial system forward.

I was quite excited—I had never traveled far from Paris—but I have been quite disappointed by London so far. It's cold and rather dirty, and everything seems plain and poor. Even the finest of their houses are drab in comparison to ours, and often the walls are covered in just plain paint, with not a single panel of beautiful scenery to be found! There are many *émigrés* here; it is

1791, almost two years since the first of them arrived, and their early optimism about a quick resolution to the troubles, and a quick return to France, has been replaced by worry and increasing penury.

"*Dames aux tabourets* becoming milliners, countesses becoming courtesans," sniffs the old Duchesse de Bouillon, sitting erect, though we are only amongst women. She is wearing a dreadfully old-fashioned jacket—pink, a color one hardly sees these days—that looks as though it hasn't been cleaned for years. "I used to sit on a stool, and now I find myself making covers for one. And not for pleasure, or charity."

Julie laughs sadly. "Countesses to courtesans is right! I didn't tell you, Comtesse," she says, turning to me, "when my cousin Stéphanie first arrived, she was accused of being a trollop, and simply because she thought to be polite and wear some rouge!" She runs her callused finger over her cheek. The English hardly wear any rouge, but even if it were the fashion, none of these ladies could afford it. I still keep some and wear a small amount; I'm almost fifty and though my complexion is fair, it does need help.

There are many sad pockets such as these ladies amongst the *émigré* groups in London, the women passing their days using their needlework skills to make money, or giving music lessons, the men hiding in shame and drinking their idleness away. They receive me—anyone from home, with money, is very welcome— but I find the sadness too trying for me and keep my visits as short as possible.

"Dear ladies, I must be going," I say, getting up and pressing a shilling coin into the palm of Julie's little girl, who earlier sang us a beautiful aria. "Mr. Forth says he has some news for me, though it'll probably just be another ring around."

I leave the small room and the muted hopes of the *émigrés*, who can only dream of their homes so fair and far away. Hercule writes that a constitution is just around the corner—though he's been saying that for years now—and is confident it will have a clause for the return of these impoverished aristocrats.

I have been many weeks in London, but so far, the investigation into the theft has proven frustrating. It has been determined that indeed, my jewels are somewhere here in this city (stolen and smuggled over by a group of Jews), and though that knowledge gives me great comfort, the wheels of bureaucracy are hardly even spinning and everything is achingly slow.

I want to go back to France and Louveciennes, and away from the cramped cold of London and the aching sadness of the *émigrés*.

One more meeting, then another, and another, and I am still no closer to my jewels. Finally I decide nothing is going to be resolved, and I depart with Pauline and the few servants who accompanied me.

At Calais, they are looking for *émigrés* departing, not returning.

"They caught the Comte de Puysieux last week," says Pauline sadly. "Wanted for crimes against the National Assembly, whatever that means. I hear they put him in La Pélagie."

I shake my head; I don't want to know about my imprisoned friends. Imprisoned for what? And what are they planning on doing with them?

I present my papers to the controller and he raises his eyebrows. "Forty-two? Madame?"

"Yes," I say defiantly. I will keep my small vanities, even as the world crumbles around me. Beside me, Pauline stifles a snort and I pinch her arm and suddenly feel like laughing. It's good to be home.

"Oh, my dearest, how happy I am you are back, but how I fear for you—should you have returned?" Hercule takes me in his arms and slowly we walk through the rooms at Louveciennes. Nothing has changed, except I notice the three west salons have not been properly dusted.

"I had to come back. For you."

"I missed you dreadfully. But I fear France is becoming quite unsafe."

"La! I'm not going to be the one washed away in this rising

tide of discontent, I'm not a dreaded noble like you were. My mother was a chicken roaster and I'm just Citoyenne Jeanne. It's *you* we must be worried about." Hercule is now the Commander of the King's Constitutional Guard, placing him worryingly close to the monarchy and the royalist cause. In London, Pauline's husband the Comte de Lauraguais—we embrace now as friends, the rivalries of old times forgotten—declared one night at supper that our king was doomed. Of course not, but still, I wish Hercule had not accepted the command that places him so close to the royal family.

Hercule shakes his head. "Ah, blood does not mean what it once did, nor does birth; all these changes are troubling for everyone."

"Nonsense." He has aged, I think sadly, pushing a gray lock of hair back and adjusting his spectacles. Few men wear wigs now; I miss the smell of powder and the deep odors of life that used to get trapped in them.

In September 1791 a constitution is finally accepted by the king, and Hercule has faith that the hostilities will soon be over. He even prepares a copy of that vaunted document for me to read:

> *The National Assembly, deciding to establish a French Constitution based on the principles which we believe in, abolishes irrevocably any institution which harms liberty and equality: There is no more nobility, nor peerage, nor hereditary distinctions, nor . . .*

I decide it is a silly document, and suddenly I am tired of everything. I want my old life back, not the one at Versailles— that one is gone forever—but the pleasant sweetness of my life at Louveciennes before all this madness started.

And Paris is looking far too much like London: too many somber-clad men and even the women wearing dark colors. I miss a world where men wore pink and everything was soft and easy;

now all is hard and dark, everyone a drab *citoyen*. Where have the gorgeous dresses gone?

Hercule advises me and I start hiding my remaining jewels, my plate and porcelain. My paintings, my knickknacks and gewgaws. Slowly the rooms empty and now my treasures lie in sacks beneath the chicken coops, the greenhouses, the outhouses. Morin and a few faithful men are my foot soldiers, and we sneak around like thieves in the night, for I am not sure who I can trust in my household—Zamor is still spouting his revolutionary nonsense, and I have noticed a new truculence amongst some of the staff.

I make another trip to London but the wheels of justice are moving far too slowly. I hate London, and leave back for France again, despite the entreaties of my friends. I miss Hercule more than I thought possible, and I think I am being spied on; in April, France declared war on Austria, and international tensions are rising.

I return to an evil, ugly country, and though I hide myself at Louveciennes, even my charmed pleasure palace cannot keep the outside world away entirely.

Then Hercule is imprisoned, accused of conspiring to free the king. Last June the royal family attempted an escape. They didn't even tell Hercule of their plans, despite his years of devoted service. He thinks it is because of his association with me that he is still not fully trusted by the people he serves so faithfully. The plan failed and they were caught and brought back to Paris and kept under guard; since then they have been real prisoners in the Tuileries.

I visit Hercule at his prison in Orléans, three strings of pearls hidden neatly in a pot of apricot preserves, but he refuses to bribe the guards and make his escape.

"What would be my life?" he says sadly. I also brought him fresh linen and a new jacket; his wife helped me pick it out and praised my strength and courage for making this journey. "To flee this country and live as a fugitive? I have done no wrong and all know me to be a man loyal to France. My place is here with the king, as my ancestors have always been."

I stare at him in distress. "Please? Please? I would be lost without you." We have been together for almost twenty years; he is not a part of my life, he *is* my life.

"You will not be without me. Do not fear, my angel, I shall be with you at Louveciennes before the month is out. But for now, my proper place is next to the king."

"But you aren't next to the king! And he doesn't deserve your loyalty."

Hercule raises a hand to counsel prudence, but then we both stop and start laughing. In this new world, insulting the king is not the crime it once was; indeed, it might even help our cause. I grip the pot of apricot jam tightly, for it holds the future. I need words to convince him that he must escape. He sometimes accuses me of being blind, but he is the one who cannot see the reality of this new hatred. He cannot see past the blinkers of his blood and birth and what he thinks his honor means.

"Please! Please!" is all I can say. I need Chon, someone who can muster the words to convince him that France no longer wants him. As I struggle to find them, I see too late that words do have power, perhaps even more than beauty or love. "Please. Come with me. Today."

Yes, he is a good man, and has done no wrong and only followed orders, but these animals don't know reason. They have a new killing machine; I saw it on one of my rare visits to Paris—we went to watch a few common criminals beheaded, then had a picnic on the grounds of the Palais Royal—and it made me shudder. Though we may be modern and live the best of lives the world has ever known, at heart we are still beasts. If this new machine makes killing easier, will there also be more deaths?

But Hercule will not bend and finally I leave, sobbing openly, clinging to him as the guard comes to see me out. I leave the jam with him, but I know he won't use what is inside.

August 1792 is a terrible month: the king, a prisoner of the Legislative Assembly, is stripped of all his royal prerogatives and he and his family are moved like the prisoners they are to the grim

Temple. When I hear the news I sit in my Louis' chair, and feel such sadness—how distressed he would be to see his grandson so reduced! I must hide his portrait, I think, staring up at him in sadness. I don't want him to see any more of this world that has turned ugly and dark with hatred everywhere.

I feel as though the world has started to move too fast and I am caught up in something I don't understand, and won't until it is too late.

Now it is September but summer still lingers in the heavy heat. In Paris, mobs attack the prisons and there are horrible massacres of monks and others, including the Princess de Lamballe. Torn apart by barbarians: I almost fainted when I heard the news.

Hercules will be transported to Versailles today, then on to Paris, where he will stand trial. Morin told me the cages at the Menagerie on the grounds of the palace are going to house him and his fellow prisoners—like animals. As the day passes and no word comes, my unease mounts. I prepare a package to bring him in Paris, a new set of sheets and a few books, another pot of jam, filled with more hope.

Pauline is with me at Louveciennes, escaping the heat and the turmoil of Paris. I would prefer to be alone with my worry and my prayers, but at least she keeps me occupied. I miss Chon, I think suddenly. She writes me copious letters from Toulouse, and I try to return the favor, but I wish she were here beside me. I need her.

"Ah—wonderful. It's been a week since I've had a coffee. All these shortages!" The supper is over, and now it is only Pauline and I at a small table in the dining room. Due to the revolts in Saint-Domingue—it seems the whole world is in a fever—the coffee situation is critical.

"Ah, I have my connections," I say lightly. Hercules procured some for me before he was imprisoned and I dole it out carefully. . . . Despite all the changes and reforms, and despite the constitution, life is still hard for the common people, and is even becoming hard for me.

Pauline takes a long, luxurious sip. "And this stuff is fine. Do you think taste serves as memory? When I drink this, it seems as though I drink another life." She sighs deeply.

I look down at my cup. She's right; the steaming richness does bring back the aroma of a better life.

"Is that singing?" asks Pauline suddenly, putting down her cup and cocking her head.

"Yes, I think so. Probably some festivity down in the village," I say, then realize it's not.

"Sounds like one of those new revolutionary songs."

"It does." The singing is coming closer and I realize I am holding my breath. Wordlessly we stand up and I am aware of the rest of the household creeping into the room, moving silently and tentatively, all of us listening to the approaching song.

I have no guards, and suddenly the house, the entire vast, stupid house, seems dreadfully unprotected. The gates and fences that goodwill and harmony built—was I a fool to rely on them? We hear the songs coming closer to us through the stillness of the summer night.

Morin holds up a hand for silence. He approaches the open windows, and peers out into the blackness. There is no moon tonight.

"Torches," he whispers. "Not a lot, just a few. Coming up the path from the village."

"Who are they? What do they want?" I whisper as fear curls inside me.

"They sound happy?" says Pauline dubiously, but they don't.

"Why are they coming here?" I whimper as Henriette blows out the candles. Soon the dining room is as dark as the night outside and through the windows we can see the bobbing torches of the approaching men. Some laughter, the song dying off, then silence and footsteps on the terrace outside, but only a pair, quick and light.

And then Hercule's bloody head, and the revolution, are thrown through the open doors of my dining room.

Chapter Fifty-Nine

In which Madame Adélaïde receives the worst news

It seems all news is bad news these days. I am like a frightened hare whenever the messengers arrive, as nervous as dear Sophie used to be. What we learn with each letter only makes us dread the next one more.

The contents of Versailles, auctioned off: seventeen thousand lots, all my furniture and belongings amongst them. And my books—where did they go?

The abolition of the monarchy—how could they?

Antoinette and her children, imprisoned in the Temple, reputed to be without any of the comforts of life—why must they make them suffer?

My cousin the Princesse de Lamballe massacred like a calf, torn apart by the mob—who are these people?

And then, the trial of the king.

It is Narbonne who brings me the worst of news at the end of January 1793, two years after our arrival in Rome. Italy is not as cold as France, but still the chill here is sharp. I know from the look on her face that the tidings are bad, but nothing could prepare me. How could one ever be prepared for a country to kill its own king?

They beheaded my beloved nephew, that darling boy who only did what he thought was good, who had not a malicious bone in his poor, awkward body. A good man who loved his wife and his family dearly, but who loved his country even more.

They killed him.

Chapter Sixty

In which Citoyenne Jeanne saves herself

W hat am I doing here? This cell is cold and damp and stinks of the sewer underneath. They have taken my shoes and winter approaches; I wrap my feet in bands of dirty linen the serving girl brings.

"This is the cell where she was kept," whispers the girl in sympathy, talking of our slaughtered queen. I shiver on the bed and remember my convent days at Saint-Maur—back to where I started, I think, then try to imagine the palace at Schönbrunn where Marie Antoinette grew up. She could never have been prepared for this, poor woman. She did nothing to deserve the fate that was thrust on her.

I am held in the Conciergerie, that dreaded prison that they call the antechamber of death. But not for me. This is all a mistake, a dreadful, stupid, horrible mistake. I ran away to London again after Hercule's death; to get my jewels back, but also to flee a country that had become distasteful to me. In London, I spent too much time reliving the past, just like the pathetic *émigrés*, wishing for a world that would never come again. How could it? You can't smash a vase into a thousand pieces then expect to glue it back together.

I mourned the king's death in London; unbelievable and barbaric. What did they hope to obtain by murdering that poor man? They said the queen was next, but surely not. Exile or a convent, there are plenty of places to put an inconvenient woman, I thought, remembering when I was sent to the Abbey of Pont-aux-Dames.

The revolution continued to grow like a beast no longer tamed, determined to ravage the land until all decency and virtue are swept away.

Then Morin sent news that Louveciennes had been sequestered in the name of the revolution. My Louveciennes confiscated by hateful, base men. Pauline begged me not to return—she herself stayed in London—but she could not know what Louveciennes meant to me. On the boat back over the grim sea, I played stupid games—if I had to lose one, for it seems everyone is losing something these days, which would I prefer never to see again: my jewels or my house?

I *must* keep my house.

I got the seals removed from the gates of Louveciennes—I still have some friends, and charms—but gradually I became aware I was back in a hostile country, without powerful protectors.

I was alone.

And I had an enemy. A man called Grieve, an Englishman. All this new radicalism has brought out adventurers, poseurs and philosophers who flock to Paris to take part in this bloody farce they are now calling the revolution. By chance this man Grieve met a disgruntled Zamor and my butler, Salanave, whom I had dismissed for insolence, and who were both nursing their grievances down in the village of Louveciennes. This man Grieve, a radical zealot, fixed upon me as both a fallen woman and a symbol of the excesses of the previous regime, and thought to make a name for himself by championing my downfall.

He worked with my disgruntled former employees and openly accused me of helping *émigrés* and harboring enemies of the revolution. He tried to have me arrested, and failed, but too late I realized he was an enemy like I had never had before, and that we were locked in a battle I did not understand. This was not a battle over precedence or respect, but a battle for my life.

Grieve didn't give up and I felt a net closing around me. He applied again for my arrest and this time he was successful. I could have saved myself, because hidden under his hatred for me there was also lust. But no, I could not—he had the eyes of a serpent and they reminded me of that man in Frederica's bedroom.

At first I was not worried; the whole world was being arrested. In the prison at La Pélagie, I saw so many friends and foes from my past: the Comte de Montmorency; the Marquis de Pons; Beatrice de Gramont; the old Comtesse de Forcalquier, the one they used to call the Marvelous Mathilde. We laid carpets over the slimy floors and played games and drank too much wine.

Beatrice was angry, not fearful, and we laughed in a cherry-wine haze about our old enmity and all the things we used to think so important. Her brother Choiseul died in 1788, a year before it all went wrong. And Richelieu died the same year: his timing as impeccable as always.

"Has anyone, ever, witnessed such a change in circumstances?" Beatrice asked one night. "We are the true adventurers and travelers, journeying from one extreme of existence to the other."

"Did we ever think a few years ago this is where we might be? How awful it all is," says the Comtesse de Forcalquier. Once the most beautiful woman at Court, now her hair is gray, and not from powder, and her eyes deep with terror and sadness as she struggles to remember where she is.

"I'm on a return journey," I remarked, and we all laughed. We were actors, playing our roles in a ridiculous, never-ending, terrifying charade. Grim reality only intruded when a long, curled finger beckoned its next victim out the door.

A riddle: What is it that you can feed, and feed, but that always stays hungry? The guillotine, of course.

They even executed the queen, on a grey day in October, and I remembered Hercule's words—she was a symbol. Not just an inconvenient woman, but a symbol.

And too late I realize I am too.

I saw I was a fool to come back to France. When I am released I shall leave, even if it means forfeiting all I have. The answer to the question I asked myself on the boat was not my jewels or my house; it was me. My life is worth everything.

Then they took me here to the Conciergerie to await my trial. Finally! I can tell the men I am nothing more than a simple woman who loves France and did nothing wrong. They will listen to me, for I cannot believe they are past all reason, and then they will put an end to this madness. And I have something they can't take away from me, something the other prisoners don't have: my birth.

"Madame, come, you must put this on." The girl holds out a greasy, bloodstained garment and something in me recoils and cracks, just a bit.

"Whose blood?" I whimper.

"Madame," whispers the girl sadly. "Citoyenne—please do not think of it."

Wearing that disgusting shroud, I am led to the tribunal. How can I charm them when my hair is unwashed and I am wearing this disgraceful chemise? When I greet them I see no appreciation in their eyes, no interest, but I do see what I am to them: a hated reminder of the excesses of the *ancien régime*, a woman once loved by a man they consider an ogre.

I answer their questions calmly, refute their stupid accusations of spying and helping the royalist cause, and though they seem to listen, they do not.

They pass their judgment: death.

When I revive I am back in my cell. Death. At first I give way to despair and scream and howl, but as the night passes my strength returns and I determine what I must do. I summon my courage, chew my lips to redden them, smooth back my greasy, graceless hair. There is no man with me to help me now, but I can do this. Only the ghost of my Louis is beside me—he brought me here, and he will guide me through and see me to safety.

"Messieurs," I say warmly, greeting the two men who enter my cell. "Please sit down. Thank you for coming. I must protest the decision of the tribunal! There is no need, I have much I can give to France." My voice is kind and inviting.

"All you have already belongs to France." The men look bored, and contemptuous, and my stomach clenches. I'm fighting for my life, I think in utter bewilderment.

"Of course, messieurs, but I can give you so much more. I have much more treasure." I smile at the men, but neither of them lights to the possibility in my eyes. I remember a time when I was the greatest treasure on earth, but now these men are looking at me as though I am sexless, more concerned with their stupid revolution than with the charms of life. "Much treasure—buried and hidden. Let me tell you where, I will show you I am a good *citoyenne*, that I support the revolution!"

Finally the men look at me with some interest. There is hope, and there is always a way.

And so I begin. "Hidden in the icehouse, a chest with diamonds and a pair of golden candlesticks, heavy. Beneath the hawthorn bushes, a bag with loose gems, some beautiful sapphires amongst them."

The men scribble, but their eyes are still cold. I must think of more. "Six pairs of silver plate buried under the vegetable gardens." I go on and on. Outside, I am aware of the rising sun, the faint chirp of a bird, my senses heightened and my life suddenly and painfully in sharp relief. Is it enough? Will it ever be enough? It must be. I continue my list and the men continue scribbling.

"What else, *citoyenne*?"

"A box with five thousand *livres d'or*, buried under the myrtles, to the west of the music pavilion."

There is only one thing I keep from them that shall stay hidden forever—my portrait of Louis. *That* they shall not have. The bells outside chime ten, then eleven, then noon, and still I keep listing my treasures.

Outside, someone screams. The men start to look bored, expectant. I am reaching the end of these words that must be my savior. The last drip of sweet wine into a handsome gold goblet.

"What else, *citoyenne*?"

"Candlesticks and silver plate under the dovecote. A collection of jeweled snuffboxes, in a bag."

"What else, *citoyenne*?"

"Is that not enough?" I say in a small, hopeful voice. This is a game to them, I think—but what is it they are playing? "I . . . that is all . . . you see my devotion to the Revolution . . ."

"That is all," repeats the man, and I smile but my lips tremble as his words become real. He gets up and calls to the guard and then the man is upon me, grabbing my hair. Not my hair! He cuts it off roughly as I start to shriek. The kind girl comes in and gathers it, but she can't look at me, as though . . . as though I am condemned.

"I gave you everything," I plead with the men who are now rolling up their scrolls, looking at me with amused contempt. "You must save me!"

They exit with a laugh.

No! No, this cannot be! I whirl around in fright, but the guard hits me in the stomach and binds my arms behind me and my head is light because my hair is gone and they are bundling me into a cart, but no! No! This cannot be!

No, no, I continue to scream to the darkening afternoon as the tumbril rolls through the streets. There are crowds of people—waiting to see me? They want to see me, because I am one of them, there is still hope. There must be!

"Oh, please, you people, pity! I have done nothing! Mercy!" I shriek with all the strength of my beloved, precious life. "Help me! I don't want to die!" The cart rumbles along the rue Saint-Honoré, and on the second floor, above a shop, a group of girls stare down at me, and I see myself in a flash in their eyes, but why have they no pity?

Why will no one help me?

"Help me," I scream, and the others in the cart urge me to start my prayers, but there is no time for that. Prayers will not save me, only man can. Someone must help me!

The gray shadow of the guillotine rises before us, flanked by an enormous crowd. A beast to be fed, but surely not with *me*! No, not with me. It cannot be. I hear a great shrieking, like a crow caught in a net, then I realize the sound is from me. I fall down and one of the guards catches me and I see he has tears in his eyes. Hope.

"Please, please, monsieur! No! Why? Why are you doing this?" I shriek, and a great mass of birds rises up against the dark December sky, crying out with angry caws. "I don't want to die, mercy, please, what are you doing?

"Monsieur, monsieur." I fling myself toward the executioner, then back away as I remember who he is, but he catches me. "Don't hurt me, don't hurt me. Please, monsieur, more time— mercy! No!"

I am forced down on a plank of hard wood and I can't believe— please—no—not me! More time! Just one more minute! I continue to implore, beseech, plead to the silent crowd, and then all is lost in a great, white silence. For a quick second, so precious because it was all I was ever going to have, I blink one last time, and from the straw on the floor I see a man in the crowd, and he does pity me.

Then, nothing.

Epilogue, 1800

In which Madame Adélaïde remembers

Our last years were a pitiful peregrination as we traveled from one place to another, escaping cold hospitality or the ravages of war and the madman Napoléon. Our latest flight was from Naples by boat to Manfredonia—one month on board a cramped and freezing vessel, our only protection Angélique's husband, the Comte de Castellux.

That escape through the snow and over chilly waters was the end for my dear Victoire, and when we arrived at Trieste she died in my arms, the priest alongside us. She had been suffering for a while, of a cancer in the breast. When she died a part of me did too. How lucky I was, I thought as I cradled her in her last dying agony, how lucky I was to have you. I said it, but too late—she could no longer hear me.

These days I try not to think too much, for my thoughts lead nowhere but to sorrow and regret. Instead, I stay busy with sewing and charity work, some reading—nothing of these new philosophers and the madness that has overtaken the world—but other times I am too tired to resist the force of memory that comes upon me.

I am glad all my sisters died before me. To wish Élisabeth, and Henriette, and even little forgotten Félicité an early death is cruel, and though Victoire, Sophie, and Louise lived long enough lives, I am glad they are dead. Is it not better to die young and know only sweetness and no sorrow than to grow old to witness a world of disenchantment?

And I did grow old, I think, as the bells outside in the square peal for evening prayers, and even lived to see the nineteenth century. It is now February 1800—how strange that sounds, especially to one born in 1732. A lifetime and another world ago. My home now is in Trieste, in two humble but warm rooms; I have ceased to regret the luxuries of my old life. I live like Louise, I sometimes think in contentment.

I wish I had died—when? I pick through my memories, enjoying this moment of self-indulgence. I have a glass of sweet sherry in my hand and Narbonne sits beside me, writing a letter. It is Papa's birthday today. February 21. He was born in 1710, to a world so much sweeter and finer than this one. I am glad he never saw any of this—he would never have understood. The king's birthday used to be celebrated throughout the Court and the country with fireworks and festivities, an orgy of thanksgiving to celebrate the birth of a divine monarch. He would have been ninety today. Not impossible.

October 1789, I decide. That is when I should have died. Before I saw my beloved Versailles, and all that it stood for, desecrated. Before my nephew and his wife were executed, before I saw the truth of man and what he was capable of. Seventeen eighty-nine: I would have been almost sixty, and would have outlived both my parents and all my sisters save for Victoire.

But I could never have left her alone.

"Who are you writing to, Françoise?" I ask Narbonne, using her Christian name. She calls me Adélaïde sometimes, and when she does it is like music to my ears. I never knew a word could be so sweet. Perhaps it was the title I wanted all my life—just Adélaïde. I take another sip, the sherry making me sleepy and peaceful. I should not have been so harsh with Victoire when she found comfort from her empty life in her cherished cordial.

Narbonne smiles at me, the wrinkles on her skin hiding some of her pockmarks. No rouge, not these days, though I heard that even people in right society eschew it as well.

"I'm writing to Addie," she says, referring to her son's wife.

Louis de Narbonne is in Germany now, seeking to return to France. We hear *émigrés* are trickling back, but I will never return to that country that turned on us so viciously.

"Please pass her my love," I say. "And inquire after Louise and little Charlotte."

Narbonne still has a family, but mine is sadly depleted. Little Madame Royale survives, Antoinette's eldest daughter; she married Artois' son last year. If only they had all succeeded in escaping in 1791—perhaps they would never have regained France, but they would still be alive. They could have made a modest Court somewhere, perhaps someplace like Bellevue was for us, and they would all still be alive.

They even killed that harlot du Barry, and apparently she shrieked like a fiend at the end of her life. When I heard the news, all I could think was that she knew how precious life was. We all want to stay longer, somehow, and even those with the purest of faith resist their Maker. I sometimes think with sadness of all the energy I wasted on her, on all the petty trivialities of life. But such is the way of youth, or of the world.

"Thank you," I say to Narbonne, watching her in the fading light of the afternoon. She hasn't lit the solitary candle on her desk yet. We count candles these days, as we count everything—abundance is gone forever.

"Madame?" she says.

"Just thank you." I look away, suddenly embarrassed. "For everything."

"Of course."

"It is my father's birthday today. He would have been ninety." Above the mantel in our small, mean room hangs a portrait of him, a cheap copy that has become my most treasured possession. Bernis acquired it for us. The cardinal is dead, some six years now, but what a comfort he was in our early days in Rome.

Narbonne shakes her head and pauses at her desk. "He was a great king," she says, even though we both know he wasn't. "And a good man."

"He was."

Sometimes I wonder if Papa had aught to do with the state of the world. If he had lived? If he had stayed with God? If she had never come—both the Austrian and the harlot? Could it have been different, could this bloodbath have been avoided?

Perhaps; perhaps not.

Why could it not have been like the American Revolution— some battles, yes, but overall restrained? What is it about the French, about our tortured history, or perhaps—here I face the truth head-on—about our family that made the violence so inescapable?

But the time for questions, and answers, is over. I am so very, very tired.

I smile at the cracked portrait over the fire and raise my glass in a toast to a man long dead.

"To Papa," I say, and close my eyes. My memory takes me back to a day in my youth when I was young and pretty and Papa loved me. We had been out riding, galloping through the crisp autumn of a beech forest, the orange leaves carpeting the ground. We stopped by a stream and I remember his face, flushed and hearty, happy with the hunt and with his life. It was a perfect day when all our sorrows lay ahead of us, as did the knowledge that the best was past.

"To King Louis," echoes Narbonne.

To him.

Author's Afterword

Adélaïde died on the twenty-seventh of February 1800, ninety years and six days after her father was born. She was almost sixty-eight and was buried in Trieste alongside her sister Victoire. After the revolution, their nephew Louis XVIII (the Comte de Provence in this book) brought their bodies back to France. At the Basilica of St. Denis you can still see, through the dim light in the crypts, their two coffins, side by side.

The bones of the rest of the Bourbon family, including Louis XV and Adélaïde and Victoire's sisters, are held in a communal crypt where they were gathered after being exhumed and desecrated during the revolution. On one placard (there are two) that lists the bones held within, Sophie is erroneously identified as *Sophie de Bourbon, sixième fille de Louis XVI*—Sophie de Bourbon, sixth daughter of Louis XVI, not Louis XV. A sadly appropriate epithet for a princess as overlooked in death as she was in life.

Jeanne du Barry was guillotined in December 1793 at the age of fifty. She kept her spirit to the end, and they say her death traumatized those who saw it: the stiff dignity of the aristocrats as they faced death only increased the people's disdain, but Jeanne's wild pleas for mercy touched everyone who bore witness. As the people wearied of bloodshed, the worst of the guillotining stopped the following year. Let's give Jeanne the legacy that in her own small way, dying as she did, she helped to save others.

After her death, her body was taken to the cemetery of La Madeleine and thrown into a mass grave. Today her bones are among the thousands that line the Paris Catacombs.

૮⁄ઝ

The Mistresses of Versailles trilogy examines the personal life of a controversial monarch through the lives of his many mistresses, with a focus on those intimate and personal moments that make history, just as surely as wars and great men do.

The history books have not been kind to Louis XV and certainly this trilogy has not been either. But from our vantage point of history and our current understanding of psychology, we must remember that he had a strange and lonely upbringing, orphaned at an early age and surrounded by sycophants his entire life. He sought out, as all humans do, the pleasures that comforted him.

More than any other French king, Louis XV was defined by the women who loved him and led him, and each book in the trilogy represents a discrete chapter in his life: his beginnings with the Mailly Nesle sisters in *The Sisters of Versailles*, showing his transformation from timid, faithful husband to unfaithful lover; the middle part of his reign in *The Rivals of Versailles* with his most influential mistress, the Marquise de Pompadour, in which he went further down the path of debauchery, aided and abetted by her; and finally his last years in *The Enemies of Versailles* with the Comtesse du Barry, and then forward to the revolution.

Louis XV was also "on trend" with his preferences in women that coincided neatly with the emerging egalitarianism of the Enlightenment: after the Nesle sisters (from the high nobility) he was the first king to have a *bourgeois* mistress (Madame de Pompadour) and then followed up that scandal by becoming the first king to install at Versailles an official mistress from the lower classes (the Comtesse du Barry).

The world in 1730—when the first novel in the trilogy opens—was a very different place from the world in 1800, when this book closes. While it is impossible to wind all the skeins that led to the French Revolution around the foot of one man, there is unanimous agreement that Louis XV certainly contributed to what came later.

Thank you for reading! For more information on the main characters in this trilogy, as well as secondary characters and places, and for more of my research and writing process, please visit my website at www.sallychristieauthor.com.

Acknowledgments

Bringing a book from draft to publication is definitely a team effort. Lots of thanks and gratitude must go to my editors Sarah Branham at Sarah Branham Editorial and Sarah Cantin at Atria, and to my agent Dan Lazar at Writers House. Thanks to my readers Sylvia, John, and Vivienne for their early feedback.

Thanks again to Odile Caffin-Carcy in France for answering my questions, no matter how small or silly, and to Deborah Anthony at French Travel Boutique for arranging a backstage tour of Versailles that was invaluable in giving me much of the sensory detail that informs these pages. Thanks to the marketing and publicity team at Simon & Schuster US and Simon & Schuster Canada, and to the many helping hands behind the scenes that I never get to meet or talk with, responsible for all the editing and great design work, both on the cover and inside the book.

And finally, thanks to all the eighteenth-century witnesses who left behind their impressions and their stories that brought to life their amazing, tawdry, foreign, and fantastical world, and which informed so much of the fun I had in writing this trilogy as I immersed myself in their world.